Cameron Daniel Murphy.

Sarah's heart pounded. Her mouth went dry and her knees went weak and she thought she might hyperventilate.

Cam Murphy.

He looked . . . *Wow* . . . *Oh, wow* . . . He looked like he'd come straight off the cover of a paperback romance. The boy she'd known two decades ago had disappeared beneath mature muscle and suntanned skin. He was still lean, his stomach still flat, but his shoulders had broadened and he'd added definition to his abs. He wore his hair a little longer and his beard lost-my-razor-three-days-ago scruffy. The words *beach bum* and *surfer dude* and *pirate* sprang to mind.

But his eyes—those mesmerizing eyes—hadn't changed. He stared at her with eyes of shades of green. Mountain eyes. Just like Lori's.

Lori.

Sarah gasped and twisted around to look at her daughter. *His daughter. Our daughter.* Lori stared back at her with a question in her eyes. His eyes.

Oh, Lori. The potential consequences of this chance meeting hit Sarah like a brick.

Also by Emily March

Angel's Rest
Hummingbird Lake
Heartache Falls

Lover's Leap

An
Eternity Springs
Novel

EMILY MARCH

BALLANTINE BOOKS • NEW YORK

Lover's Leap is a work of fiction. Names, characters, places, and incidents are the products of the author's imagination or are used fictitiously. Any resemblance to actual events, locales, or persons, living or dead, is entirely coincidental.

A Ballantine Books Mass Market Original

Published in the United States by Ballantine Books, an imprint of The Random House Publishing Group, a division of Random House, Inc., New York.

BALLANTINE and colophon are registered trademarks of Random House, Inc.

This book contains an excerpt from the forthcoming book *Nightingale Way* by Emily March. This excerpt has been set for this edition only and may not reflect the content of the forthcoming edition.

ISBN: 978-0-345-52877-3
eBook ISBN: 978-0-345-53212-1

Cover design: Lynn Andreozzi
Cover illustration: Roberte Steele

Printed in the United States of America

www.ballantinebooks.com

9 8 7 6 5 4 3 2 1

Ballantine mass market edition: January 2012

For Nic Burnham.

Thanks for everything.
I am blessed to have
you as a friend.

First love is dangerous only
when it is also the last.

—Branislav Nusic

Lover's Leap

ONE

March
Near Cairns, Australia

"Mom! Hurry up," Lori Reese urged, sounding more like a six-year-old than a young woman in her sophomore year of college. "We don't want to be late!"

At the sound of her daughter's voice, Sarah Reese rolled over in bed, buried her face in the thick, downy pillow, and contemplated taking up bank robbery in order to afford a return trip to this resort. She and Lori were nearing the end of their two-week all-expenses-paid Australian vacation, and the experience had given her a tantalizing taste of traveling in the lap of luxury.

"Ten more minutes." This bed was heaven.

"It's already six-fifteen."

Their ride to the marina was scheduled to arrive at seven o'clock, and getting ready would take fifteen minutes, tops. She didn't need to hurry. "Five more minutes."

Indulgent frustration laced Lori's voice. "When exactly did we switch roles? I think it must have been the first day of the trip, when you spent half of that interminable plane ride flirting with the man across the aisle."

Sarah grinned into her pillow, then lazily rolled her head and looked at her daughter. Her heart melted with a potent combination of love and pride. Lori was a sophomore majoring in biomedical science at Texas A&M University and making excellent progress toward her goal of earning admission to A&M's College of Veterinary Medicine. She'd worked hard to work ahead and cleared an extra ten days of spring break with her professors. At twenty, she was taller than her mother by seven inches—a fact she loved to tease five-foot-nothing Sarah about at every opportunity. She had Sarah's high cheekbones and dark hair, and her grandmother Ellen's sweet smile. Her eyes were a beautiful blend of shades of green. Sarah's late father had called them mountain eyes, because her eyes were a mountainside of aspen and fir and piñon and cottonwood.

Sarah didn't see the mountains when she looked at Lori's eyes. She saw Cam Murphy. Her daughter had her father's eyes. She had Cam's height and Cam's eyes—two distinctive characteristics that provided Sarah an unwelcome reminder of the man she'd just as soon forget.

"I wasn't flirting with the guy across the aisle. I was just being friendly. He was the one doing all the flirting."

"Yeah, right." Lori's eyes gleamed with amusement as they made an exaggerated roll. "Okay, here's the deal. I'm going to wander over to the lobby and get two cups of coffee. If you're not out of bed by the time I come back, I'll drink both of them."

Sarah scowled and grumbled, "Obviously I didn't spank you enough when you were little."

Lori laughed, and a moment later, Sarah heard the door to their suite softly close. She gave a wistful sigh, rolled onto her back, and sat up. Her reluctance to rise had more to do with the fact that today was the last day of their dream-of-a-lifetime vacation than with fatigue.

They'd had an absolutely, positively wonderful trip, seeing enough of the country to make them feel like they'd gotten a taste of Australia but not so much that they felt rushed. The past three nights they'd spent here at a magnificent resort on the Coral Sea, and today they'd ice their vacation cake with a catamaran trip out to the Great Barrier Reef.

Sarah stretched as she gazed out through glass-pane French doors, past the veranda, with its private spa tub, and across the golden-sand beach toward the turquoise sea. She crossed to the doors and pushed them open, then took time to count her blessings. This trip had been the grand prize in a contest sponsored by Angel's Rest, the healing center and spa owned by her friend Celeste Blessing in the little Rocky Mountain town where they lived. Back home in Eternity Springs, snow covered the ground, and the day they'd left, the thermometer flirted with zero degrees. As the seaside breeze softly stirred, Sarah murmured, "I still can't believe I'm here."

She'd dreamed of visiting Australia since childhood. Back in high school, she and Cam had stretched out on a quilt up at their favorite make-out spot, Lover's Leap, and planned how they'd backpack across Europe, explore the pyramids of Egypt, and dive the Great Barrier Reef. When life took a pair of unexpected turns their junior year, youthful dreams had faded in the face of stark, cold reality.

She wished one of those realities would hurry back with the coffee.

Sarah turned away from the breathtaking view and headed into the bathroom. When she emerged showered and dressed ten minutes later, she spied Lori seated outside on the veranda. Two cups of coffee and two huge cinnamon rolls waited on the small table between the chairs.

"You are both wonderful and wicked, my child," Sarah told her daughter as she took her seat. "I'll gain two pounds just looking at that roll."

"Nah, we have a strenuous day ahead of us. We need the calories. Besides, you need to check out the competition. You might want to tweak your recipe for the cinnamon rolls you make for the Mocha Moose."

Sarah sipped her coffee and raised her brows in disdain. "My cinnamon roll recipe doesn't need to be tweaked, thank you very much."

Lori tilted her head, considering, then said, "Okay, you're right. It's impossible to improve on perfection."

Sarah operated Eternity Springs's only grocery store, the Trading Post, established by her great-grandfather and run by family members ever since, but she supplemented her income by baking breads and desserts for a number of the businesses in town. She knew her way around a cake of yeast. She dipped her head in regal acceptance of her daughter's compliment, then tore off a piece of roll and popped it into her mouth. Sweet flavor exploded on her tongue. "Yum, this is good. Could use a tiny bit more vanilla, though, I think."

The two women shared a grin, then polished off their breakfast. Moments later, tote bags stuffed with necessities of a day on the water in hand, they exited their suite. Seeing that the tour company van had yet to arrive, Sarah lamented, "I could have had my ten minutes, after all."

"Oh, stop it. I'm too excited to listen to you whine. Aren't you excited?"

"Yes, I'm excited." Sarah threaded her arm through Lori's and squeezed. She *was* excited. The tour's itinerary sounded divine. First, the catamaran would sail to a cay famous for its protected sandy lagoon, gorgeous beach, and migratory bird population. Then while Sarah snorkeled—she'd never learned to dive—Lori, who'd earned her certification while away at college, would join other tour members in a drift dive along the reef. Following a gourmet lunch and some beach time, they'd sail to the Outer Barrier Reef for more snorkeling for Sarah and a wall dive for Lori.

Diving the Great Barrier Reef. Wow. As a passenger van sporting the Adventures in Paradise Tours logo pulled into the resort's circular drive, Sarah couldn't help but think of Cam. She seldom allowed her mind to go there, but today, as their daughter was about to fulfill one of those Lover's Leap dreams, she couldn't hold back the memories.

Cameron Daniel Murphy. In so many ways, he'd been born a troubled soul. His mother had been a Cavanaugh, the darling daughter of the town's leading family until she'd rebelled against her parents by marrying the town scoundrel, Brian Murphy. They'd disowned her, disinherited her, moved away from Eternity Springs, and died in a plane crash shortly before Cassie gave birth to Cam.

Cassie and Brian Murphy had struggled to make ends meet, and when Cassie showed up a time or two with bruises on her face, it set tongues wagging, but no one stepped in to help. Cassie died when Cam was eight years old, and Brian Murphy surrendered to alcoholism like his father had before him. It surprised no one. After all, he *was* a Murphy.

Cam had never stood a chance in Eternity Springs. For as long as Sarah could remember, Eternity Springs had waited with bated breath for the Murphy curse to show itself in Cam. They didn't have to wait very long. Cam first ran afoul of the law when he spray-painted threats on the courthouse wall when he was nine, and for the next few years, he was in trouble more often than he was out of it.

But my, oh, my, he'd done it for her—long before she even knew what "it" was. As a young man he'd been as wild and beautiful as the cougars that prowled the surrounding forests. In the end, he'd proved to be much more dangerous.

Their relationship had begun innocently enough when Cam had come to her rescue up on Murphy Mountain.

On a Saturday in the spring of their freshman year, while on a camping trip with kids from church, a mix-up in car assignments and an afternoon nap in the sunshine had left Sarah stranded. While she hiked down the mountain, Cam drove past on his motorcycle. When he stopped and offered to help, she hesitated. He was too young to have his driver's license, and she knew her parents would kill her if she rode with him—especially on a motorcycle. But her feet hurt and the forbidden thrill beckoned. They'd taken the long way home.

Cam Murphy had charmed her that afternoon, and the relationship that developed between the two teenagers over the next year had remained a secret pleasure. To this day, most people in Eternity Springs believed the lie about Lori's paternity that she'd told to protect her precious child's shoulders from bearing the weight of "Murphy bad blood."

Yet Sarah had loved Cam Murphy with every fiber of her foolish, teenaged soul. She'd had to grow up in order to put her love for him behind her. His rejection and the reality of a dependent child had made it easier to accomplish.

The van braked to a stop in front of them, shaking Sarah from her reverie. The driver's door opened, and a young man with sun-streaked hair, suntanned skin, and a bruised and swollen black eye exited the shuttle with a spring in his step. "G'day, ladies," he said in that wonderful Aussie drawl. "Reese, party of two, for Adventures in Paradise Tours?"

"That's us," Lori confirmed. Her eyes widened and she winced when she got a good look at his injury. "Wow. I bet that hurts."

The boy flashed a grin. "Not much. I've had worse. M'name's Devin, and I'm your transportation to the marina and the *Bliss*. Hop on in, and I'll introduce you to our other guests."

The two physicians and their wives were from Minnesota, the men in their mid-forties, the women a decade younger, nearer to her age, she'd guess. The doctors claimed to be experienced scuba divers. One of the wives planned to snorkel, but the other confessed to a fear of sharks that kept her out of the ocean.

"I'm perfectly happy to sunbathe," she told Sarah. "Some friends of ours took this tour a year ago and said the scenery of the cay alone is worth the price of the ticket."

The other wife leaned toward Sarah and lowered her voice. "She also said the captain and crew weren't half bad to look at, either."

Lori must have overheard that exchange, because she glanced at Sarah and mouthed "No flirting."

Sarah smothered a smile, then listened in as her daughter peppered the young driver with questions about the tour.

"No, I wish I went out on the boat every day," Devin was saying. "I'm suspended from school this week, and I have some fines I have to pay off, so I'm working with my dad on the tours."

"Oh. Well, um . . . what does your dad do on the tours?" Lori replied, obviously floundering on how to respond to the boy's revelations.

Devin shrugged. "He does a little bit of everything, but he's a water rat at heart. He'd rather be diving the reef than just about anything."

"Will he be diving with us today?"

"Maybe. Don't know. He had a party that ran pretty late last night, but don't worry. Our regular crew are great mates. We're still small—we run only two boats—but we're the best tour operator in Queensland. You're gonna have a bonza time today."

If the boy's father had been up late partying, then Sarah hoped he wasn't part of this trip. She admitted to being somewhat nervous about her baby diving today—she'd seen the movie *Jaws* way too many times over the years—and she didn't want the lead diver suffering from a hangover.

"I'm so excited," Lori said to Devin. "This is going to be the highlight of our trip."

"That's our goal at Adventures in Paradise. Customer service is king." He flashed a grin and added, "I sound like a used-car salesman, don't I?"

Lori laughed, and Sarah's attention was pulled away when the sunbather doctor's wife asked her where she was from. It came as no surprise that the obviously wealthy Minnesotans had been to Telluride, Vail, and Aspen but had never heard of Eternity Springs. "Next time you plan to visit Colorado, you should consider a stay at Angel's Rest, our new healing center and spa. It's a heavenly place. You'd love it."

"We'll keep that in mind," one of the doctors said.

"I adore spa vacations," his wife added.

"Is there golf?" the other doctor asked.

"No, I'm afraid not. But we do have some of the best trout fishing in the world nearby at the Taylor River."

"Taylor River rainbows," he responded. "I've heard of them. We'll have to put your Angel's Rest on our bucket list."

Satisfied that she'd done her part as an Eternity Springs ambassador, Sarah sat back and tuned in to Lori's conversation once again.

". . . when I finish school," the boy said. "University isn't for me. School already interferes too much with my days on the boat."

"So what's your average day like?" Lori asked.

While the young man spoke of sun and surf and the deep blue sea, Sarah considered her daughter. Lori had never been a shy child, but the time away at college had elevated her natural curiosity to new heights. The girl never stopped asking questions, never stopped wanting to learn. *I'm so proud of her.*

For the second time that day, Sarah thought of Lori's father. This time bitterness overpowered any sweet. *You blew it, Murphy. You made a huge mistake when you turned your back on us. Our little girl is special. She could have brought such joy into your world.*

She could have been your redemption.

Cam Murphy was dragging. The party aboard the *Bliss* during last night's private charter had been going so strong that the host offered him double the money to stay out two hours extra. As a businessman with a payroll to meet, he couldn't turn down the extra work, but the late night combined with another lousy night's sleep had made this morning's run more challenging than usual.

Cam had been running on the beach every morning at daybreak for more than a decade. He ran for exercise. He ran on the beach in order to enjoy the beauty of the sand and the sea before the hordes of tourists descended. He used the time to organize his thoughts and make his plans for the day.

Lately, his morning run had helped chase away the what-ifs and if-onlys that plagued him while he lay awake in the middle of the night.

A recurring dream had disturbed his sleep at least three times a week for the past three months. Today, as his feet pounded the damp sand, he worked to shake off the effects of yet another nocturnal blast from the past, another night spent in Eternity effing Springs.

Considering that he'd reviewed today's bookings before bed last night, he should have expected it. "Reese, party of two" had topped the list. It wasn't an uncommon surname. Tourists named Reese went out on his boats at least two or three times a year. Inevitably, each time the name showed up on his manifest, he dreamed about Sarah or Eternity Springs or both. While it wasn't exactly the recipe for peaceful sleep, he could deal with Colorado dreams two or three times a year.

He didn't know why he was having these dreams now. He'd lived half of his life since leaving Colorado. An occasional dream about Eternity Springs he could understand, but this repetitive nonsense he'd endured since Christmas? It made no sense, and it was wearing him down.

Dreams of Sarah at nighttime meant thoughts of Sarah by daylight, along with the woulda-shoulda-couldas that invariably followed. Sharp as shark's teeth, they nipped at him for hours on end. It would have been different if. He should have made another choice but. He could have changed everything if only.

Cam rubbed his eyes. He had his share of regrets in life, and some of them were huge. Most of them involved the holier-than-thou citizens of Eternity Springs, Colorado, and their precious, darling queen of the Good Girls, Sarah Reese.

Sarah Reese. High school sweetheart. Mother of his child. Destroyer of his heart.

Cam summoned a burst of speed, then dashed the final hundred yards to his beachfront home. An hour later, showered and dressed in his favorite shorts and an Adventures in Paradise T-shirt, he unlocked the door of the tour office and went to work.

He had hours of paperwork ahead of him today. Not for the first time, he wished for the days when his sole job was to introduce divers to the wonder of the reef. Life certainly had been simpler then. No payroll to make, no bankers to keep happy, no unexpected repair bills or skyrocketing insurance costs or increasing rents to fret over. Of course, he'd had no family to support then, either. At least, no family who wanted his support.

The ghosts of his youth flitted into his mind once again. Sarah, her head thrown back in infectious laughter. His father, belt in hand and meanness in his eyes.

His mother, lying in a pool of blood on the bathroom floor.

Cam shuddered and gave his head a hard shake, trying to flutter those images right back out again.

Today he needed to keep his thoughts centered on Devin. The boy would be the death of him yet. He landed in one scrape after another these days, and reminded Cam of himself at sixteen too much for comfort. Cam wanted better for Devin, so yesterday, when his son walked into the tour office sporting a black eye and brandishing a school suspension slip for fighting, he had just about lost it. Where had this self-destructive streak come from? What had changed for the boy in the past six months?

Cam suspected the source might be the new group of friends Devin had taken up with last summer. They were polite young men from good families, the kind of youngsters most parents wanted their children to befriend. Not Cam. Something about the group of boys bothered him. They were almost too polite, their handshakes too firm. They definitely had too much money to throw around.

Most telling of all, they rarely looked him in the eyes when they spoke to him. That made Cam's trouble-coming antenna quiver.

He glanced up at the clock on the wall. Devin would arrive at the marina in thirty to forty-five minutes. Maybe he should put the paperwork on hold and go out on the boat with his boy today. Better yet, he could call in a sub for Devin, and they could both play hooky from work, leave the tourists to the rest of the crew, and take the *Freedom* out, just the two of them. Maybe a little father/son time would help Dev remember to make good choices next time the opportunity for stupidity reared its head.

Cam liked the idea. He was overdue for a day off. This paperwork could wait. He picked up the phone and made the arrangements. Ten minutes later, he boarded the *Bliss* to grab his personal diving gear. He'd just hauled it topside when he saw the owner of the *Wanderer,* the cruiser that occupied the slip next to Cam's, standing at the stern, scowling fiercely down into the water. "G'day, Martin. Got a problem?"

"Yes, I'm afraid so. Looks like there's a line tangled in my propeller shaft. I have a banker on board and a tight schedule. Wasn't planning to get wet, but . . ." He started shrugging out of his suit coat.

Cam set down his gear on the deck of the *Bliss.* "Hold what you've got. I'll check it out for you."

Martin sighed with relief. "Thanks, man. I'll owe you."

Cam tugged off his T-shirt and toed out of his deck shoes. He pulled on his mask, then grabbed his diving knife and a flashlight and slipped over the side of the *Bliss* into the water. The harbor water was murky. He switched on his flashlight and swam to the cruiser's stern. He spied the problem immediately. Unfortunately, a simple slice with his knife wouldn't get the job done.

He surfaced and called up to his friend. "'Fraid it's a little more complicated than a snagged line. You're dragging trash, but I can handle it. I'll need a bolt cutter."

Cam grabbed hold of a dock line and treaded water while Martin went to get the tool he required. Above him, on the nearby bridge, he spied the Adventures in Paradise Tours van arriving. *Good.* When Martin handed down the tool he'd requested a minute later, Cam said, "Our van is pulling up. Would you please tell Devin I want to talk to him?"

"Sure."

Cam clamped his diving knife between his teeth, then, with the bolt cutters in hand, submerged himself again. He went to work on the tangle around the prop shaft. The wire cable the cruiser had picked up somewhere dragged on the assembly, but he couldn't see that the junk had caused any real damage to the unit. It took him a couple of breaths, but Cam managed to cut the trash away and free the cruiser's prop.

He surfaced and swam to the *Bliss*'s swim deck. He hauled his tools aboard, then levered himself onto the deck. A *Bliss* crew member tossed him a towel. Cam dried his legs and then his chest before flipping the towel over his head to pull it back and forth across his back.

Aboard the *Wanderer,* Martin called, "Many thanks! I wish you fair winds and following seas, Cameron Daniel Murphy."

Cam opened his mouth to reply when movement on the *Bliss*'s gangway caught his attention. He froze, his fists clamping the towel in a white-knuckled grip.

Twenty years might have passed, but he'd know her anywhere. No bigger than a minute and curved in all the right places. Dark hair cut short and sassy in a way that suited the angles of her face. And those eyes. Those gorgeous, long-lashed, Elizabeth Taylor violet eyes.

Sarah Reese.

Cameron Daniel Murphy.

Sarah's heart pounded. Her mouth went dry and her knees went weak and she thought she might hyperventilate.

Cam Murphy.

He looked . . . *Wow* . . . *Oh, wow* . . . He looked like he'd come straight off the cover of a paperback romance. The boy she'd known two decades ago had disappeared beneath mature muscle and suntanned skin.

He was still lean, his stomach still flat, but his shoulders had broadened and he'd added definition to his abs. He wore his hair a little longer and his beard lost-my-razor-three-days-ago scruffy. The words *beach bum* and *surfer dude* and *pirate* sprang to mind.

But his eyes—those mesmerizing eyes—hadn't changed. He stared at her with eyes of shades of green. Mountain eyes. Just like Lori's.

Lori.

Sarah gasped and twisted around to look at her daughter. *His daughter. Our daughter.* Lori stared back at her with a question in her eyes. His eyes.

Oh, Lori. The potential consequences of this chance meeting hit Sarah like a brick.

Lori had wanted to contact her father ever since Sarah confessed the truth about his identity to her when Lori turned sixteen. In the months that followed, Lori had spent hours tracking the name Cameron D. Murphy on the Internet. Although she'd come up with what she considered to be half a dozen likely suspects, as far as Sarah knew she'd never taken the search for her father beyond that. At one point, when money was especially tight around the Reese house, Lori had asked her to hire a private investigator to find Cam to demand child support.

Now this beautiful, confident young woman watched Sarah with wary mountain eyes. "Mom? It's not an uncommon name, right?"

Sarah tried to force words through her throat, but the sound that emerged was a strangled gurgle.

At her mother's reaction, Lori's expression slackened with shock, then she jerked her stare back toward Cam. "That *is* him?"

Feeling a little bit sick, Sarah braved another look, too. His gaze remained locked on Sarah, heated and intense.

Her stomach took another turn. She swayed slightly, feeling dizzy. Then abruptly, he shifted his stare toward Lori, and for a long moment, Sarah held her breath. He looked stunned.

"That's *him*?" Lori repeated. "He's your Cam?"

Cam mouthed a word, and Sarah was pretty sure that word was *mine*. He took one step forward just as the boy from this morning—Devin, the van driver—approached him, saying, "Hey, Dad. I didn't think you were coming down here this morning. Martin said you wanted to see me?"

Dad.

Dad?

Dad!

Fury stormed through Sarah like a hurricane. That boy was only a few years younger than Lori!

Lori reached out and caught hold of Sarah's arm, steadying herself. Her voice broke on the words, "He has a family."

Oh, baby. No. Not like this.

"Mom, let's get out of here," Lori said, an anguished look in her eyes. "Now."

Cam's gaze upon them was tangible. Sarah felt frozen in place. "But, honey—"

"Please, Mom?"

Her daughter had gone white as the sails on the cruiser next to the catamaran, and seeing it, Sarah's mama-bear instincts roared to life. "Sure, honey. We'll go."

"I'm sorry. I just can't." Lori had tears in those big green eyes of hers. "I'm not ready for this."

"You know what? Neither am I." Sarah gave Cam Murphy one last look—he hadn't moved one of those outdoorsman muscles—then tucked her arm through Lori's and turned her back on the man she'd once loved.

Once off the gangway, mother and daughter walked

briskly. When they turned a corner, no longer in sight of the deck of the *Bliss,* Lori urged Sarah into a run.

It took some time, effort, and creativity, but the two Reese women ran all the way home. Back home to Colorado. Back to the caring, comforting shelter of Eternity Springs.

TWO

Eternity Springs, Colorado

The thermometer read a balmy twenty degrees as Lori loaded her suitcase into her car to begin the trip back to Texas and the second half of her spring semester at college. Smiling bravely against both her sorrow and the bitter cold, Sarah gave her daughter one last hug, then opened the driver's-side door. "Drive safely. Call when you make a pit stop."

"I will." Lori took her seat behind the wheel and buckled her seat belt. "Love you, Mom."

"Love you, too, Sunshine," Sarah replied, proud that her voice didn't crack. "Be safe."

She stood out in the cold, her shoulders hunched and her hands in her coat pockets as the car backed out of the drive. As was her habit, Lori hit the car horn in two short bursts, then headed south on Aspen. Sarah watched and waved until the car was out of sight, then told herself that the tears in her eyes resulted from the cold wind.

Yeah, right. Sending Lori back to college at the end of a break was still as hard as it had been her freshman year. Harder, in fact, considering recent events.

Of all the boats in all the world, why had Cam Murphy been drying himself off on that one?

She reentered the house through the front door and was met by Daisy and Duke, her golden retrievers. Her dogs sensed her mood and nuzzled at her legs, begging to be petted. She glanced at the clock, noting that she still had forty minutes before her friends showed up for the planning meeting for next summer's quilt festival. The Patchwork Angels meetings usually took place at Angel's Rest, but Sarah had asked them to come here this morning, since she hadn't been sure of Lori's departure time. With time to spare, she hung her coat on the rack in the entry hall and sank down onto the floor, where she took a few moments to bask in the dogs' comforting company.

As Duke licked her face, she heard her mother call, "Frank?"

Frank Reese, Sarah's father, had passed away when Lori was in middle school. Sighing, Sarah rose and walked toward the living room and her mother's line of sight. "It's Sarah, Mom."

From her usual seat in her recliner, Ellen Reese looked up. "Where's Daddy?"

Sarah drew a breath, silently cursed Alzheimer's disease, then gently said, "He's gone, Mama."

Ellen nodded. "I thought so. I just had to ask."

"I know, Mama."

Ellen's expression turned quizzical. "What am I supposed to do?"

Sarah smiled tenderly. "Why don't you read the newspaper now, Mom? There's a new edition of the *Eternity Times* on the table beside you."

Ellen spied it and said, "All right. Thank you, dear."

"You're welcome." Sarah waited to make sure that her mother was situated, then continued on to the kitchen. She poured another cup of coffee and contemplated the baked goods lining her counter that her restaurant customers would pick up later today. Ordinarily, she didn't sample her own creations. This was no ordinary morning. Sometimes a girl simply needed a little high-caloric comfort.

She chose a lemon bar to go with her coffee, and she'd just sat down at her kitchen table to indulge when a rap sounded on the window glass of the mudroom door. She leaned over to look and saw Nic Callahan waving red-gloved fingers. Sarah gestured for her to come inside. Nic was Eternity Springs's veterinarian, the mother of precious two-and-a-half-year-old twin girls, and she'd been Sarah's best friend from childhood. A gust of frigid air blew in with her. "You're early."

"I know. I wanted to see Lori before she left." Nic pulled off her gloves. "Did I miss her?"

"By about five minutes."

"Well, darn." Nic removed her stocking hat and scarf and stuck them into her coat pocket, then gave her long blond hair a shake. "She got off sooner than I'd figured."

"She woke up early. Our body clocks haven't quite adjusted to the time change yet. Her plane doesn't leave Colorado Springs until mid-afternoon, but this way she won't have to hurry."

"She's leaving her car at her friend's place again?" Nic asked as she hung her coat on a rack in the mudroom.

"Yes." Sarah rose and poured Nic a cup of coffee. "Her car already has one hundred twenty thousand miles on it, so the fewer trips back and forth to Texas, the better. We need it to last until she's out of college."

Lori didn't need her car at school, and she had a friend whose family owned a storage unit and allowed her to keep her car there for a minimal charge. Flying out of Colorado Springs was much cheaper than flying from Gunnison-Crested Butte, and this way, Sarah didn't have to make the drive to the airport in order to pick her up or send her off.

Nic took a seat across the kitchen table from Sarah, cradled her coffee mug in both hands, and asked, "So, how are you doing?"

"Fine. Grab a cookie if you want. I tried a new recipe

for oatmeal-raisin cookies and they're wonderful, if I say so myself."

"Thanks, but I'm trying to resist the temptation, and you are attempting to change the subject. You are not fine, Sarah. Something is wrong. What is it?"

Nic knew her too well, but Sarah tried to fend her questions off. "It's always tough to see Lori leave."

Nic tilted her head to one side, and her blue eyes studied Sarah. "Yes, but it's more than that, isn't it? I think you need to talk about it."

"Talk about what?"

"Whatever happened on your trip."

"We had a wonderful trip. We told you that."

"Yes, you did. You two put on a good act. You might be able to hide it from everybody else, but I know you, and I know Lori. Something happened while you were away. Something not-so-wonderful."

Daisy padded over to Nic and rubbed against her, silently demanding to be petted. Nic obliged before continuing, "I suspect it involved the tour to the Great Barrier Reef. We heard all about the rain forest but hardly anything about coral. So spill, girlfriend."

Sarah took a bite of lemon bar and considered her response. She wasn't really surprised that Nic had picked up on the undercurrents humming between her and Lori since they arrived home from Australia three days ago. From the moment she had spied Cam Murphy standing aboard that boat, Sarah's emotions had swung all over the map. Lori, bless her heart, had all but curled into a fetal position and tuned out the world.

Sighing, she explained, "Lori didn't want me talking about it while she was still home."

"Oh, no." Nic reached out and touched Sarah's arm. "Was she hurt? Were you hurt?"

"No. No. It wasn't like that." Sarah grimaced. "Actually, I guess in a way it *was* like that. We saw Cam."

At first, it didn't click. Then Nic's jaw dropped. "Cam? *Your* Cam? Cam Murphy?"

"He's not *my* Cam," Sarah snapped back. The resentment that had simmered inside her all the way across the Pacific flared, and she tossed her half-eaten lemon bar onto her plate. "He never was *my* Cam. The man has a son who is not that much younger than Lori. He must have married the first girl he saw when they let him out of juvie jail."

"No." Nic set down her coffee mug hard.

Sarah folded her arms, sat back in her chair, and nodded. "Yes."

"Wow. Okay, tell me everything."

Sarah took a moment to organize her thoughts, then gave her best friend in the world a blow-by-blow account of the events that had taken place at the marina in Cairns, Australia.

"Wait a minute," Nic said. "You're telling me that *Lori* wanted to run away from him? The same Lori who wanted you to hire an investigator to track down her father?"

"The very same. And she didn't just *want* to run away from him. She *did* run away from him. I couldn't believe it." Sarah sighed and reached for her lemon bar once again. "I wasn't all that steady myself, but Lori's reaction floored me. She just wilted right in front of me."

"Was it because of the boy?"

"You mean her *brother*?"

"Ow." Nic winced.

"Yeah. Ow." Sarah polished off her lemon bar, then said, "I'm sure that was part of it. You wouldn't have recognized her, Nic. She was devastated. I've never seen her look like that. Not even when my dad died."

"Poor Lori." Nic winced on behalf of her friends. "So you left the marina and then what? Did he chase you down? Show up at your hotel?"

"I expected him to follow us. I know he recognized me. I was ready for him, too, I'll have you know. But the sorry coward didn't show. He had plenty of time, because it took us almost an hour to pack, check out, and get a cab to the airport. In hindsight, I should have known he'd keep his distance. He's had years of practice, after all."

"I don't believe that."

"It's true. Lori and I talked our way onto an early flight, then we ignored the tears in each other's eyes all the way across the Pacific."

Sarah recalled how Lori had taken one last look around the airport terminal before they passed through security. Her daughter hadn't missed the fact that despite having time to do so, Cam had chosen not to follow them. Once again, he had blown off his own child. Thinking about it now, fresh anger stirred inside Sarah.

"So that's the real reason you didn't get to see the Great Barrier Reef," Nic said. "Not because you were sick."

"Oh, I was sick, all right."

Nic nodded and sipped her coffee, letting a long moment pass before she asked, "How did he look?"

Sarah scowled. "Disgustingly gorgeous. Sun, sea, and sand scruffy. Built, with a capital *B*. One thing about beach bums, they use their muscles."

Nic gave in to temptation and reached for an oatmeal-raisin cookie and a paper napkin. "Lori got his height."

"And his eyes." Sarah closed her own eyes and relived that moment when Cam's gaze locked onto hers. "It's a good thing he ended up on the other side of the world. Anyone who saw them together would recognize the family resemblance."

Nic started to say something, then obviously thought better of it and took a bite of cookie. "Yum. You're right. These are spectacular."

"And now you're the one holding back." Sarah chastised her friend with a frown. "What did you start to say?"

Nic set down her cookie, picked up her coffee, and looked at Sarah over the top of the mug. "If people found out, it wouldn't be the disaster you think it would be, you know."

Sarah bristled. "You've got to be kidding. Of course it would be a disaster. I *lied,* Nicole. I lied about who fathered my baby to everyone. Even to my own mother! Do you know how guilty I feel about that?"

"Look, you were sixteen and you had a good reason for doing it."

"And the reason hasn't changed, I might point out. People in town still hate Cam Murphy."

"But we love you," Nic fired back. "More important, everyone loves Lori. That wouldn't change."

A lump of emotion formed in Sarah's throat at that. She truly did have the best of friends. "Maybe not, but I'd just as soon not test the theory. Lori feels the same way. We talked about it. She really has made a one-hundred-eighty-degree turnaround where Cam is concerned."

"That's more surprising than anything," Nic mused. "Finding her father was the focus of half of her conversations back when she worked as my vet assistant."

"Really? You never told me that."

"Remember, that was right after you told her the truth about who her father really was. She was confused and angry with you. She vented to me."

"I think she needs someone to vent to now. I asked her to make an appointment with a counselor at school, and she said she would."

"Good thinking. But don't forget, Lori is a levelheaded, goal-oriented girl. She's done well with her grades. She's shown a great deal of maturity when it comes to relationships. How many girls would have handled the situation with Chase as well as Lori did?"

Sarah thought of Nic's reference to Lori's relationship with their friend Ali Timberlake's son, Chase. Chase and Lori had been summer sweethearts when Lori was in high school. Despite the fact that they liked each other a lot, the pair had recognized and acknowledged that they weren't ready for something more serious and had chosen to remain friends.

"I don't think you need to have any regrets," Nic continued. "You've done a fine job with Lori. I hope that I can do half as well with my girls."

Sarah smiled at her friend's compliment and asked, "And how are Meg and Cari?"

"They're two and terrible, and they make us so happy."

"Are they with their dad this morning?"

Nic nodded. "Gabe's brothers came in last night, so we had lots of helping hands around the kitchen this morning. They're closing on the new family cabin that they're buying out at Hummingbird Lake today."

"That's exciting."

"Yes. I've missed having family in town since Mom and Aunt Janice moved to Florida. It'll be nice to have the Callahans around more."

"Family." Sarah's lips twisted in an unhappy frown as she brooded over the word. Mothers and daughters. Fathers and daughters. Fathers and *sons.* "I'm so angry at Cam, Nic. I don't think I've ever been this angry in my life. He tells me he can't be a father to our baby, then he turns around and has a child with someone else as quick as he can. The dog. I deserved better. Lori and I deserved better."

"Yes, you did. But honey, maybe it's a good thing this happened."

"Why? So that our vacation ended on a sour note? Because I didn't really need to mark the Great Barrier Reef off my bucket list?"

"No," Nic responded, her voice patient. "Because personally, I think the anger is a good thing. I think that all these years you've needed closure on your relationship with Cam. Maybe now you'll be able to finally let him go and open your heart to someone new."

Sarah rolled her eyes. "Not that old argument again."

"Just saying." Nic held up her hands, palms out. To Sarah's relief, she changed the subject and asked, "How is your mom doing?"

"Okay. She's content to sit in the living room and watch sports on TV. All I can say is thank God for cable TV and especially ESPN Classic. I do see progression of the disease, but I believe the new medication has slowed its pace."

"Good. Let's hope that trend continues."

"Amen to that."

"Now that you're back from your trip, will the church group resume helping you with caretaking?"

"Yes." Sarah didn't know what she'd do without the St. Stephen's Women's Group, because as her mother's health had deteriorated, they had stepped up. Someone visited Ellen twice a day, which substantially reduced the need for paid caregivers and made it economically feasible for Sarah to continue to care for her mother at home. "Someone will check on her at mid-morning and mid-afternoon. We can get by okay with that for now. Hopefully by the time the busy season hits, I'll have something else arranged."

"What are you thinking? Live-in help? That worked well while you were gone on your trip."

"Yes, but it would consume my monthly budget."

Nic opened her mouth to speak but apparently changed her mind, because she shut it abruptly. It didn't matter. Sarah knew what she'd been about to say, because Sarah knew Nic as well as Nic knew Sarah, and they'd had this discussion dozens of times in the past.

"I know a memory-care facility is in our future, but neither Mom nor I are ready for it yet."

Sarah nibbled on her lower lip and silently debated spilling the beans about her new plans. For some reason, telling Nic would make it more real than signing papers at the bank. Yet she was glad she'd have the distraction in the weeks to come. Nothing would get Cam Murphy out of her head faster than flinging herself into something new. That as much as anything had helped her decide to green-light the change. "I have something else in mind. I'm selling the Trading Post, Nic."

Nic's brows arched, her eyes bugged, and her mouth gaped. She worked her jaw, but no sound came out. Sarah found the fact that she'd shocked her friend speechless twice in one day immensely satisfying.

A note of panic in her voice, Nic asked, "Are you moving away?"

"No." Sarah straightened her spine, squared her shoulders, and declared, "I'm going after my dream, Nic. I have Lori's college expenses taken care of now, and after three successful summer tourist seasons, I've been able to set aside enough for start-up expenses. I'm going to remodel this house to suit Mom's needs and mine, and open my dream business right here."

Nic sat back heavily against her chair. "Your bakery. You're going to open your bakery!"

"I am."

Beaming, Nic jumped up and threw her arms around Sarah in a fierce hug. "How exciting! That's wonderful news. I know this is something you've wanted for a long time. Tell me everything. When did you get serious about the idea?"

"I met with Bob Carson at the bank the first time back in October. Someone tangentially connected to Lorraine Perry had contacted him looking to buy an established business in town, so he asked me about the store."

Nic winced. "Not another Lorraine Perry!"

Lorraine was a reality TV show chef who had brought Hollywood to town by leasing the Bristlecone Café, turning it into a restaurant more suitable for Aspen than Eternity Springs, and using it to launch her newest TV series. Unfortunately—or, fortunately, depending on one's viewpoint—the series had aired only twice before being canceled in February. Lorraine hadn't been back to town since. Sarah and her friends viewed that as a blessing.

"No. The buyer is a man with a family who wants to raise his kids in a good environment."

"Oh. Good." Nic carried her empty mug to the coffeemaker and refilled it. "Well, the Trading Post is as established as it gets, since your family has owned it for over a hundred years."

"That didn't make this decision any easier." Sarah glanced at the clock, then rose and set out mugs for the others along with the coffee cake she'd made for the morning meeting. "It took me a couple of months to work my way through the whole severing-the-family-tie part of the decision. But Lori doesn't want the store, and not long before he died, Dad told me not to consider myself chained to it, so I don't feel like I'm abandoning a legacy or anything like that."

"Good." Nic clucked her tongue as she took plates from the cupboard and set them beside the coffee cake. "Wow. Times have sure changed in Eternity Springs."

"Thanks to Celeste and Angel's Rest." Sarah exhaled heavily and added, "Bob Carson says the buyer is anxious. He has papers all ready to sign."

"This is so exciting, Sarah."

"Scary, too. The butterflies in my stomach have butterflies."

"How soon before you'll begin your remodel?"

Sarah swallowed hard. "If I sign the papers today, then tomorrow."

"Tomorrow! How in the world did you manage that?"

"It's a cash sale. I'm going to use Jarrell Construction, and they had a cancelation in their schedule. Joe told me he can have the bakery ready to open in six weeks."

"No!"

"Yes. I'll believe it when I see it, though."

"Whoa. That's great, Sarah. It's just wonderful. I'm so happy for you."

"Thank you. It'll make things easier with Mom, I think, especially as time goes on. Change is hard on Alzheimer's patients, and with the remodel we'll be able to keep her space like it is, only I'll be within earshot just steps away instead of across the street at the store. I'll be able to keep her home longer."

"In that case, I think it's just what you need. You've spent all these years taking care of Lori, putting her needs first. Now she's well on her way to being settled, and it's your turn. You can have a brand-new start doing something you've always wanted to do."

"That's the way I'm looking at it." Or at least the way she was *trying* to look at it.

"You know what I think? I think seeing Cam in Australia was fated."

"Or arranged," Sarah muttered.

"Arranged!"

"Think about it. How did it happen that we took the trip?"

"You won a contest."

"Sponsored by Celeste. Who made all the travel arrangements, including booking the tour with Adventures in Paradise? Who is one of the handful of people in the entire world who knows that Cam Murphy is my daughter's father?"

"Celeste." Nic considered the charge for a moment, then slowly nodded. "You have an argument there. She's lovable, but she does like to dabble in people's lives."

"Dabble?" Sarah scoffed.

"Have you asked her about it?"

"Why bother? She'd never admit it. She'd make one of her philosophical statements and change the subject."

"True." Nic grinned. "Nevertheless, whether the hands of fate made it happen or Celeste Blessing poked her pixie nose into your business, seeing Cam was a good thing. You needed to say goodbye to the old to make way for the new. You'll have a fresh start—a new home, a new business, who knows, maybe a new man."

Sarah wrinkled her nose. "I didn't exactly say goodbye."

"Didn't you?" Nic waited until Sarah looked at her to explain. "Maybe not face-to-face, but turning away and going away says it pretty clearly."

The knock at her door saved Sarah from responding to that. "Speak of the devil," she murmured.

"Cam is here?" Nic asked innocently.

Sarah laughed and started for the door, saying, "Celeste."

Ali Timberlake, the owner of the Yellow Kitchen restaurant, had arrived with Celeste. Sage Rafferty pulled her car into the driveway as Sarah opened the door to let the other women inside. Sarah watched as Sage, an artist and the owner of the local gallery, Vistas, removed a large tote bag from her backseat and hurried toward the house. A few minutes later, her best friends in the world were seated at her kitchen table, moaning with pleasure over the taste of cinnamon and sugar and coffee cake that melted in their mouths.

Well, except for Sage. She'd refused the high-caloric treat and opted for an apple instead. Sarah knew why, and judging by the gleam in Sage's green eyes, she suspected that the others were about to learn, too. "You look especially beautiful this morning."

"She does, doesn't she?" Ali Timberlake agreed. "You've done something different with your hair. It's gorgeous."

"Thank you." Sage lifted her long auburn tresses. "I cut three inches off and had it layered while Colt and I were in Denver yesterday."

"I saw that Vistas was closed yesterday," Nic said. "I didn't know you went to Denver. Was the trip for work or fun?"

"Actually . . ."

Sage glanced briefly at Sarah as she paused significantly, and Sarah knew her suspicions were correct. A smile played about her lips as she saw Sage reach for her tote bag. "Mostly fun. I had a doctor's appointment, and then Colt and I went shopping. We're redecorating one of our bedrooms, and I want your opinion. Help me decide which theme to use." She pulled two canvases from the back and held them up. "Bunnies or ducks?"

It took a moment for the revelation to take. Then Ali sat up straight and grinned. Nic's mouth gaped in shock for the third time that day, and Celeste folded her hands and beamed. Sarah allowed herself a smug smile.

Nic cleared her throat. "Sage, correct me if I'm wrong, but those look suspiciously like nursery designs."

"You're not wrong," the artist said, her eyes bright.

"You're pregnant?" Ali and Nic said simultaneously.

"I'm into my fourth month and scared to death and happier than I ever would have imagined."

With a chorus of cheers and delighted squeals, Sage's friends jumped to their feet and wrapped her in hugs. Sarah had known about the pregnancy since before Christmas, when she'd stopped by Vistas and caught Sage in the throes of morning sickness. Sage had asked her to keep her secret, and while it had tested Sarah's self-discipline, she'd done so.

Now, as she witnessed Sage's joy, Sarah didn't even try to hold back the tears. Presenting her news to her friends with such obvious pleasure showed just how far Sage had traveled in her journey to healing. Not long ago, due to trauma she'd suffered while working with Doctors Without Borders, Sage couldn't have held a baby, much less looked forward to giving birth to one.

The happy mood continued throughout their planning meeting and grew even more boisterous once Sarah shared her own news with her friends. By the time Sarah crossed the street to open the Trading Post at nine-thirty, the comradery had chased away her lingering sadness at Lori's departure.

The store enjoyed a steady stream of business, and Sarah stayed busy until lunchtime. After fixing a sandwich for her mom, she phoned the bank and made an appointment with Bob Carson. By two o'clock, the deed was done. She'd agreed to operate the Trading Post for two more weeks. After that, the Reese family business would be some other family's responsibility. Joe Jarrell confirmed that the remodel on the Reese family home would begin bright and early tomorrow morning.

It was a new beginning, a fresh start. "Maybe that's what I should name my bakery," she murmured as she swept the floor at the Trading Post after closing the store for the night. "The Fresh Start. Or just Fresh. That's hip, edgy."

She liked it. She liked the entire thing. Nic had been right. Sarah did need a new start. By summer, she'd have a new business, and essentially a new home. And yes, maybe she would see about finding herself a new man, too.

Why not? The time had come to say goodbye to the old and hello to something new. Something exciting. Something wonderful.

Her work done for the day, Sarah headed home. As she crossed the street, she looked up toward the postcard-worthy view of a snowcapped Murphy Mountain standing against a brilliant blue sky and said, "Something new. Something exciting. Something wonderful."

She was ready. Finally, she was ready.

She lifted a hand and made a symbolic wave toward the mountain. "Just in case you didn't hear me before, I'll say it loud and clear now. I'm over you, Cam Murphy. I'm done with you. Once and for all. Goodbye and good riddance."

THREE

June

"Hello, and welcome to Eternity Springs." From the front passenger seat of a rental Jeep Cherokee, Devin Murphy read the sign aloud. " 'A little piece of heaven in the Colorado Rockies.' How hokey is that?"

"Hokey enough," Cam replied, sparing the roadside sign a negligible glance as they passed it. One corner of his mouth lifted in a lazy smirk that belied the nervousness churning in his gut. He made an effort to relax the tension in his grip on the steering wheel. Had anyone told him six months ago that he'd be back in Eternity Springs by summer, he'd have called him crazy to his face.

The Jeep approached the Hummingbird Lake scenic overlook, and on a whim, Cam pulled in next to a motorcycle and parked. Devin questioned him with a look but didn't speak as Cam opened his door and climbed out into the crisp mountain air. He shoved his hands into the back pockets of his jeans and gazed down at the lake and the little mountain town beyond.

From this perspective, little appeared to have changed in Eternity Springs in the decades he'd been away. Four avenues ran north and south. Eight streets tracked east and west. He did note some new construction on the grounds of the old Cavanaugh family estate, and he briefly wondered who owned the property now. His mother had grown up there, but someone else owned it by the time he'd been born.

"Eternity Springs isn't very big, is it?" Devin asked, coming to stand beside Cam. "Lots of cars around, though."

"Tourist season. Also, it looks like something's going on today. They have Aspen blocked to traffic."

"Cool. I like a good street festival." Devin shot Cam a sidelong glance as he added, "Or maybe they heard that you were coming home and decided to throw a party in your honor?"

Cam snorted. "You're such a comedian, son."

Devin knew what to expect from the people of Eternity Springs, because Cam had told him the whole ugly story after Devin's first less-than-positive reaction to the news of their pending trip. Self-centered in the way that came naturally to teenaged boys, Devin had assumed that Cam had planned the trip in order to separate Devin from his friends. He'd pitched a fit and pouted like a two-year-old until Cam clued him in on the real reason for the trip.

Cam hadn't denied that removing his son from the influence of his friends had played a part in his decision to travel to Colorado. However, he'd made sure that Devin understood that Cam's primary purpose for the trip was to make peace with his past, particularly that part of his past named Lori.

The explanation had proven to be a game changer where Devin was concerned. He'd even quit whining about the independent-study projects his teachers had assigned to substitute for days in the classroom. Armed with new knowledge, he'd been both insulted on Cam's behalf and intrigued, since he finally understood his dad's weird reaction to the way the Reese party of two had bolted that day in March. At first Devin had wanted to go into Eternity Springs with proverbial guns blazing, but after reflection, he'd agreed that some reconnaissance was in order prior to going into battle. The plan for today was to check in to the rental cabin they'd booked under the tour company name, then nose around town a little bit, incognito.

Cam didn't expect to be recognized by people in town, so this tension humming through his blood was premature, though not unexpected. Returning to Eternity Springs was the most difficult thing he'd done in years.

He set his jaw, then turned around and strode toward the Jeep. "Let's do this."

More than twenty years after leaving Eternity Springs in handcuffs and locked in the back of a sheriff's sedan, Cam Murphy returned to the scene of his crimes.

He drove slowly up Spruce, the main thoroughfare in town, noting changes and those things that looked the same as he remembered. The tourist center was new, as was a restaurant named—translating from Italian—the Yellow Kitchen. The library and bank hadn't changed one bit. At the intersection of Spruce and Fourth, he did a double take upon seeing an art gallery named Vistas. An art gallery? In Eternity Springs?

He turned right onto Fourth and spotted the sign for the Elkhorn Lodge on the next block. The Elkhorn was a grouping of ten 1950s-era freestanding cabins built in a U shape around the perimeter of the large lot. Years ago, the two-story structure in the center had served as both office and home for the manager. That didn't appear to have changed, but the swimming pool in the center of the U was new.

Cam didn't recall ever seeing the interiors of the cabins, but he wasn't looking for anything fancy. He had chosen to stay at the Elkhorn because the website had advertised cabins equipped with kitchenettes and the best mattresses on the western slope. Considering that he'd brought an Aussie eating machine with him, the kitchen would come in handy, and while Cam could sleep anywhere, his no-longer-young muscles thanked him each morning he climbed from a decent bed.

He pulled the Jeep into a parking space in front of the office. "I'll get us registered."

"Want me to do it?" Devin asked, his gaze focused on the office door. "I see a rack of brochures inside. I'd like to check them out for market research."

For the past year or so, Devin had designed the marketing collateral for Adventures in Paradise, so the claim wasn't too big of a stretch. Cam didn't believe him. Devin's protective antennae were extended and quivering. "They'll want me to sign a credit card receipt, but you can come in with me if you'd like."

Bells sounded as he opened the door to the office and stepped inside. A man about Cam's own age entered from a back room. Cam tried to place him as the man said, "Welcome to the Elkhorn. How can I help you?"

The voice helped Cam put a name to the face. Brad Lawson. He'd been a year behind Cam in school. His father had owned the barber shop. "G'day. I have a reservation for two under Adventures in Paradise Tours."

Lawson's wince put Cam on guard. "Hmm. Paradise Tours. Yes. We had cabin number seven reserved for you."

"Had?"

"Don't worry. We found a place for you. I'm afraid we had a bit of a bear problem in number seven yesterday, and we're gonna need to do some work before it's habitable again."

"Bear problem?" Devin repeated.

"I don't have another unit to put you in—we're full up, due to the quilt festival—but I called around and found a place for you. A great place." He beamed with pride. "Instead of two bedrooms, you get an entire house—at the original rate, of course. It's a rental unit that Angel's Rest recently purchased and remodeled. The owner just made it available for rental yesterday, which is why we could get you into it."

Lawson opened a wooden box and removed a set of keys. Checking the round tag on the end, he nodded, then handed them to Cam. "Here you go. The address is 354 Seventh Street, and you can reach it by—"

"What?" Startled, Cam dropped the keys. They hit the wooden floor with a clunk. "Where? What's the address again?"

"It's 354 Seventh Street."

"You are kidding me."

Lawson blinked. "Is there a problem?"

Yeah, there was a problem. Cam's lips flattened into a grim line as he bent to retrieve the keys. He'd grown up in the house at 354 Seventh. Remodel or not, it would be full of ghosts. "Is anything else available?"

The innkeeper shook his head. "No, sir. Eternity Springs is hosting a quilt festival this week, and we're busting at the seams. I don't believe there's a room to be had within a hundred miles. These ladies are serious about their craft."

"A quilt festival?" Devin repeated. "That's the reason for the tents lining part of that one street?"

"The tents are mostly from vendors who have followed the crowd. The quilts on display are in the school, including a special traveling exhibit from the Alzheimer's Art Quilt Initiative. That's a great cause. Proceeds from that go toward Alzheimer's research. Hope you'll consider buying tickets."

When Cam still hesitated, Lawson added, "You know, I recall taking your reservation—just about three weeks ago, right? The call right before yours was a cancellation, which is why we had a spot for you at all. Honestly, man. You're lucky to have a place to stay."

Cam shook off his hesitation and stuck the key ring into his pocket. He'd come to Eternity Springs to face old ghosts, had he not? Might as well get started. "The house will be fine."

"Good. Now, if you'll just sign here." The innkeeper handed over a registration slip, then took a tourist map from the top of a stack. He marked an *X* at the spot of the Elkhorn Lodge and said, "You're here now, and the rental is—"

"The old Murphy place," Cam said, then deliberately added, "I know it."

Taking unusual care to make his handwriting legible, Cam signed the slip, then passed it to Brad Lawson. "Thanks, Brad."

"I'm sorry. Have we met?" Lawson's gaze dropped to the registration slip, and he audibly gasped. His head jerked up, and he stared at Cam with eyes rounded in shock. "Murphy? Cam Murphy?"

The reaction was expected, but it still annoyed, so Cam showed him what Devin called his great-white-shark smile. "You can be the first to welcome me home, Brad."

The innkeeper's mouth opened and his jaw worked, but he didn't make a sound. With an amused chuckle, Cam turned away and looked at his son. "You ready?"

"Sure. Except . . ." Devin glanced at Brad Lawson. "Mister, I've had a sudden craving for popcorn. Know where I can get some? I always like to munch on a tub of popcorn when I'm watching a show."

"Smart aleck." Cam smirked as he turned and left the office without bothering to listen for a reply.

He expected Devin to pepper him with questions as they made the short drive to the house on Seventh, and the teenager did not disappoint. "So which team did ol' Brad belong to? Friends or enemies?"

"Neither. *Acquaintance* is a better word for it. In a town this small, everyone knows everyone."

"And this place we're staying? You called it the Murphy place. So it's your house?"

"It's where I grew up, but it's not my house. After my old man died, I couldn't pay the taxes on it. Didn't want to, to be honest. The place doesn't hold many happy memories for me."

"That sucks. Sure you want to stay there? I have Jack's number in my phone. We could call."

Devin's "Jack" was Jack Davenport, a distant cousin of Cam's, whom he'd met when Jack rented the *Bliss* for a private day cruise seven or eight years ago. Idle conversation had revealed the family connection, along with the fact that Jack had built a house on inherited land outside of Eternity Springs.

That had been the first of a half-dozen visits Jack had made to Cairns, and he and Cam had become friends. When Cam decided to make this trip, he'd debated taking Jack up on his standing offer of Colorado lodging but eventually decided against it. This was a trip, an effort, he needed to make on his own—even if it meant sleeping with ghosts.

"It's just a house, Devin," Cam replied, meaning it. Now that he'd taken action and outed himself, the nervousness that had churned in his gut on the way into town had dissipated. Unfortunately, however, the weight of the old familiar chip had slipped right back onto his shoulder with ease.

Childish of him, Cam admitted, but he wouldn't beat himself up over it. His anger at this town and these people had simmered inside him for most of his life. No sense trying to pretend otherwise.

He pulled his Jeep to a stop at the curb in front of 354 Seventh and took time to study the little two-bedroom house. The place looked good. It sported a fresh coat of appropriate Victorian-era blue paint and white shutters and gingerbread trim. Baskets of red geraniums adorned the porch, and hummingbird feeders swung from the eaves. The grass was trimmed, the rosebushes tended, the flower beds tidy. The house had never looked this good when Cam and his father lived there.

"This is it?" Devin asked. "Home not-so-sweet home?"

"This is it."

"Looks girly. Like a dollhouse. I can't imagine you living here."

"Not exactly my style," Cam agreed.

Their home in Australia had the smooth, sleek lines of modern architecture. It occurred to Cam that whenever he had a choice to make, if one option reminded him of Eternity Springs in any way, he always chose the other.

Cam tensed as he unlocked the door. He couldn't help it. Drawing a deep, bracing breath, he stepped inside.

The scent of fresh paint and varnish swirled in the air. Wood floors gleamed; the light fixtures, window curtains, and furnishings were all new. The walls sported photographs of scenic views of the mountains around Eternity Springs and framed and matted inspirational quotations. Taking a closer look, he saw that the quotation theme extended to pillows on the sofa, doo-dads on the tables, and even the throw rugs on the floor. The interior looked nothing like how Cam remembered it, and he relaxed. No ghosts here, after all.

"Which room do I get?" Devin asked. "Both bedrooms have queen-size beds."

"Take your pick." Devin chose the room that once upon a time had been Cam's. Cam carried his suitcase into his parents' old room. A skylight and new windows had transformed it. He could be comfortable here. Tossing his suitcase on the bed, he began to unpack. His gaze fell on the two black velvet jewelry boxes tucked in with his socks. He debated for a moment, then picked up the smaller box containing the white-gold earrings shaped like boomerangs that he'd purchased to give to Lori. He stuck the box in his pocket, then, when he turned to leave the room, he caught a glimpse of his reflection in a mirror. Hmm. Maybe he should run a comb through his hair before he went looking for his daughter. He'd already given her a bad first impression. He wanted to improve this time around.

Cam took another look in the mirror, then said, "Devin, I think I'll take a quick shower."

He wasn't putting off one of the biggest moments in his life. He was practicing good grooming.

Yeah, right.

The truth was that he was nervous about how Lori might react to seeing him. He hadn't chased after her that day at the marina because at the time, he'd thought it the best for everyone. What if he'd been wrong? What if today turned into a disaster? Judging by his daughter's reaction that day, Sarah hadn't been singing his praises all this time. What if Lori hated him? What if she told him to take a flying leap off Murphy Mountain?

If that's what happens, you'll deal. You'll be persistent and win her over. You can do this.

With his thoughts on his daughter, Cam stepped into the bathroom, where everything was new, from the ceiling light fixture to the bathtub, sink, and commode, to the twelve-inch tile on the floor. Just why Cam looked at the tile and saw beige linoleum, he didn't know, but that's what happened. Suddenly, he was eight years old once again.

Fear leached into his bones as his eyes flew open. He lay in his bed, staring into darkness, not knowing what had awakened him but sure that he didn't like it. His heart pounded. He gripped his sheet with trembling hands and yanked it over his head. He lay hiding, cowering, trying not to listen, but listening hard.

Finally, he heard it. A cry. A sob. His name?

Mama.

His mother had called for him. He needed to go see

what she needed. But he was afraid. So afraid. Something was wrong. He tried, but he couldn't make himself move.

"Cameron," came his mother's thready voice. "Help me."

Cam bit his lip and willed himself to move his feet. Daddy wasn't home. Daddy was never home anymore. Go. Go. Go. Go. *Tears rolled across his temples.*

He held his breath and listened hard. He couldn't hear her. He couldn't hear anything. Finally, panting like a tired dog, he slipped out of bed. The hardwood floor was cold against his bare feet. Cautiously, he opened his bedroom door. He didn't see anyone or anything. Biting his lip, he stepped into the hallway.

Something smelled bad, and it made his stomach churn. "Mom?"

No *answer. Light shone from the bathroom, so he moved toward its open door. One step. Two. Three.*

He saw the blood first. A stream, a river of it, against the beige linoleum. Then his mother's dark blood-soaked hair, her pale white face. Her eyes were closed. "Mama?" he asked in a little voice.

Her lashes fluttered. Opened. Her voice was little more than a whisper. "Hurry. Get help."

Where before he couldn't move at all, now he couldn't move fast enough. He whirled around and dashed for the phone in the kitchen. He punched 911 and lifted the receiver to his ear, and then he remembered. No *dial tone. They hadn't paid the bill. He dropped the phone and dashed out the door just as the clock chimed two a.m. Where was his dad? His dad should be here!*

Cam ran to the house next door and pounded on the door, shouting, yelling, "Help me. Help me. Please. Help!"

He knocked on the door for what seemed like a long time, but no one answered. The Roosevelts didn't like the Murphys. "Help! Please. Help!"

He saw a light come on, but nobody answered the door. Sobbing, he gave up and ran across the street. The Barlows didn't hate his dad. Maybe they'd answer the door.

Pain sliced into Cam's foot. He tripped, cried out, and fell. His foot slammed against the ground, knocking the lid from the tin can free. Getting up, he ran and did his best to ignore the pain. He knocked and knocked and knocked, but the Barlows didn't answer, either. Finally, at the third house, a woman answered the door. "My mama. She's bleeding bad. Please, please, help us."

Knock. Knock. Knock. Devin's voice jerked Cam back to the present. "Dad? You okay?"

Cam blew out a harsh breath. Holy hell. His hands were shaking, and his knees were weak. Guess he couldn't avoid those ghosts, after all. Clearing his throat, he said, "Yeah. I'm fine."

"You sure?"

"Yeah." He reached over and switched on the hot water. "Everything's fine. I'll be out in a few minutes."

Half an hour later, he emerged from his bedroom showered, shaved, combed, and dressed in his newest pair of jeans and a freshly pressed long-sleeved green sport shirt.

Seeing him, Devin's eyes widened in surprise. As a rule, Cam seldom bothered to iron. In a demonstration of good instincts, Devin held back any smart-aleck remarks surely fluttering through his mind and simply asked, "So where is our first stop?"

"I think it'd be better if I did this by myself."

"I think it'd be better if I had your back." When Cam continued to hesitate, he added, "Am I a member of this family or not?"

Dev's question came right from the heart of old insecurities. Recognizing that fact, Cam surrendered. "Good point. All right, first stop is the Reese house. It's just a few blocks away. We'll walk. We can check out the street vendors on our way. It's possible we'll run across them there."

"You want to approach Lori in public? I don't think I'd like that if it were me."

"No, but there's no reason we can't walk up and quietly request that we all retire to a place with privacy."

They exited the house and headed west on Seventh until it intersected Aspen, where white tents lined both sides of the street, offering a wide variety of merchandise for sale. The street was crowded with people, more people than Cam had ever seen in Eternity Springs. The first person he recognized and made eye contact with was his third-grade teacher, Mrs. Auld.

He'd always liked Mrs. Auld. She was a good teacher who nursed his interest in reading and instilled the love for books that he'd enjoyed ever since. She'd been kind to him. After his mother died, when he'd missed school for a week because of the raging infection caused by the neglected cut on his foot, she even came by his house with a stack of books for him to borrow.

Of course, that had been before the incident with Andrew Cook. Today, when she spied him, Mrs. Auld's eyes went round with shock, and she brought both hands up to cover her mouth.

Guess she'd recognized him, too. Cam was insulted and, frankly, hurt in a third-grade sort of way.

He gave her his shark's smile, then glided away.

Two booths up Aspen he spied the banker, Mr. Carson, and received a similar reaction. After the third such response, by the owner of the gas station—what was his name? Barker? Parker? Something like that—Cam kept his smile pasted permanently on his face. He began to hum the theme from *Jaws* below his breath.

By the time he'd crossed Sixth Street, the weight of the chip on his shoulder had doubled. *It's been twenty years. Can't these people realize that things have changed? I've changed? But no, Eternity Springs is a Colorado version of Brigadoon. Time passes, but nobody knows it.*

Cam knew it. He'd grown up and somewhere along the way realized that while he might have been a full-blown delinquent at fourteen, he'd started out as a scared little motherless kid who desperately needed someone to have his back. None of these fine, upstanding citizens had bothered.

An oil painting on display in one of the tents caught his attention and distracted him from his dark thoughts. It depicted a springtime view of his favorite place in Colorado, the high mountain plateau called Lover's Leap. A blanket of goldenrods covered the ground and led straight to the edge of the mountain and the ocean of blue beyond.

Noting his interest, a lovely red-haired, obviously pregnant woman approached. "That's called Lover's Leap. It's a spot about ten miles from here."

"I know it," Cam said. His daughter had been conceived there. The painting stirred a storm of emotion inside of Cam. Love, despair, anger, joy. Infinite sadness. A part of him wanted to own the artwork. Another part of him never wanted to look at it again.

"I'm happy to answer any questions you might have," the redhead continued. "That's my work."

"You're the artist?" Cam tore his stare from the painting and looked at her. Studied her. He didn't know her. "Are you from Eternity Springs?"

"I moved here a few years ago." Her smile was friendly, but he thought he saw a new note of curiosity in her eyes. "You recognized Lover's Leap. Are you from around here?"

"No."

He didn't elaborate, so she tried again. Extending her hand, she said, "I'm Sage Rafferty, though professionally, I've kept my maiden name, Sage Anderson."

Cam took her hand but ignored the hint. "It's a pleasure to meet you and to view your art. You have a gift."

"Thank you, Mr. . . . ?"

"Is this for sale? The Lover's Leap painting?"

"In a manner of speaking, yes. This painting is my contribution to the auction we'll be having later today to raise money for the Alzheimer's Art Quilt Initiative. It's a charity our local quilt group contributes to. You're welcome to bid on the painting, um . . . I'm sorry, I didn't get your name."

"I didn't give it," Cam replied, impressed by her persistence.

Devin walked up and said, "Dad. I'm in luck. Someone is selling popcorn. You want a bag?"

"No thanks."

"That accent." Sage Rafferty's gaze shifted from Cam to Devin, then back to Cam. "You're from Australia, aren't you?"

She knows Sarah. "Yes, we are."

"You're Cameron Murphy."

"Yes, I am."

Now her eyes flashed, but not with fear, like the other Eternity Springs residents. Sage Rafferty's eyes snapped with frustration. "Well, it's about time you showed up."

Okay, that reaction surprised him.

She put her hands on her hips and stepped toward Cam. "Does she know you are here?"

He spared a glance around. One person out of three appeared to be watching him with wide-eyed interest. "If she doesn't know yet, it won't be long. Is she at home?"

Now the woman folded her arms, thought for a minute, then shook her head. "She's at the Fresh tent. It's on the northwest corner of Second and Aspen."

Cam turned to leave, and Sage called out a warning: "You take care with her, Murphy. She has friends in this town."

The unspoken "And you don't" swam after him and attached itself to his back like a remora, but it didn't bother him in the least. Sage Rafferty hadn't grown up in this town with him and Sarah. She wouldn't know that for as long as he could remember, Sarah Reese had been the quintessential Eternity Springs princess beloved by all. He had been the gutter rat the townspeople barely tolerated and didn't like one bit.

Except for Sarah. She had liked him. For a short, bittersweet, teenage-angst-ridden few months, she had claimed to love him. And he, fool that he'd been, had believed her.

Cam continued down Aspen, only now he didn't spare a glance at any of the vendors' tents. He ignored the buzz of conversation that followed him and turned a blind eye toward shocked, vaguely familiar faces. He was a man on a mission. A hunter tracking his prey.

A great white shark at the end of his swim from Australia's Great Barrier Reef to the middle of Nowhere, Colorado.

Then the crowd before him parted and he saw Sarah standing with a pair of tourists. He caught his breath as his body tensed. He gave her a quick once-over.

In high school, Sarah had been the wholesome, fresh-faced pixie-next-door. Now all grown up, she was a sexy, sparkling sprite, still tiny but deliciously curved. She wore a hot-pink T-shirt tucked into form-fitting jeans, and pink canvas shoes. When she threw back her head in carefree laughter, a hollow ache spread through his chest.

He had loved Sarah Reese. Deeply. Completely. *If only . . .*

She turned her head and saw him. Those big, beautiful eyes went round with alarm, and her face drained of color. She mouthed the words *No, oh, no. Not you.*

Not me.

A volatile mixture of anger and grief rushed in to fill the hollow place inside him.

Not me. Yeah, well, so what else is new in Eternity effing Springs?

Emotion took control and propelled Cam forward. He turned his head first left, then right, scanning the area for Lori. He didn't see her. His gaze locked on Sarah's. In the gorgeous eyes that had haunted his dreams for years, for decades . . . in the same violet eyes that had once shone with love for him . . . he now saw fear.

Fear. Of him? Really? After all he'd done to protect her?

Well, fine. Just fine. Maybe it's time I earn it.

Sporting the great white shark's cold, dead eyes in addition to its smile, Cameron Murphy strode up to Sarah Reese in front of dozens of people on a public street in Eternity Springs, Colorado, and said, "Hello, Sarah."

"Cam." She swallowed, hard. "You're here. Why?"

"I want to speak with our daughter, Lori. Where is she?"

FOUR

Sarah thought she might just have a heart attack and die right here in the middle of Aspen Street. Surely that would be better than watching the shock and surprise and scandal on the faces of her friends and neighbors as they realized who had walked up and said what.

Cam was here. Here, in Eternity Springs. Looking fierce and ferocious.

And talking. Talking about Lori. *Our daughter.*

Oh, shoot. Oh, shoot, oh, shoot, oh, shoot.

Sarah's stomach took a nauseated roll. Heat flushed her body. She was horrified and embarrassed and afraid. He'd outed her. The man had outed her! Here, in front of the whole world, he'd revealed her deepest, darkest secret—that he was Lori's father.

Why? she silently screamed. Why had he come here? What did he want?

Lori. He wanted to speak with Lori.

Over my dead body.

Thank goodness Sarah's daughter was safe and sound and away in Virginia, working a summer internship at a horse farm. He'd be hard-pressed to track her down there. The last thing Lori needed was to have Cam Murphy show up without warning to turn her world upside down.

Like he's just done to me.

Okay. It had happened. That milk had been spilled.

The water was already under that bridge. The horse had already bolted from the barn. So now what?

I've used up all my clichés, that's what!

Damage control. She needed to do damage control. Quickly.

Sarah cleared her throat and managed to squeak out a shaky "Hello, Cam. If you'll give me a moment to secure my booth, I'll be happy to go somewhere with you and discuss . . . things."

"Just tell me where to find Lori," he repeated, his expression hard, his eyes twin green glaciers.

Sarah glanced frantically around in search of a friend. Where was Nic? Where was Sage or Ali? Where in heaven's name was Celeste? *I need help!*

But instead of a friend, she spied Pauline Roosevelt watching with avid fascination from the tent directly across from hers. Sarah softly groaned. Pauline had lived next door to the Murphys when Cam was little. She'd inherited the title of Eternity Springs's biggest gossip after Glenda Hawkins moved to Florida, so of course she'd be the one to witness this disaster. The other woman's eyes gleamed with scandal and disapproval.

Sarah wanted to melt into the earth and disappear. She turned a pleading gaze back to Cam. "This isn't the place for this discussion. I'll be with you in just a minute."

She didn't wait for a response but turned away and reached for her cash box. She'd no sooner picked it up to leave when a pair of tourists approached, asking to purchase more of the poppy-seed muffins they'd had for breakfast. A quick glance at Cam's impatient expression had Sarah ready to tell the tourists to help themselves for free, but then an Aussie-accented voice offered, "I'll be glad to man your booth for you."

Sarah turned her head and spied the teenager who'd driven the tour van the day of their ill-fated reef trip. The one who'd called Cam "Dad." While her stomach took a little flip at that particular memory, he flashed her a grin and added, "You can pay me in some of those chocolate-chip cookies. I'm starved."

"Oh." This was the child Cam had wanted. Sarah knew she shouldn't hold his father's betrayal against him. It wasn't his fault that his father was a sorry rat bastard. She should be sensitive to that fact. Wasn't the whole "sins of the father" nonsense at the heart of this trouble? She would be above that. Besides, she needed the help. "Okay. Thank you, um, Donnie?"

"Devin." He stepped up and smoothly slipped the cash box from her hand. "You have a price list somewhere?"

"Yes." She tugged a tri-fold brochure sporting the Fresh logo from a plastic display box and gave it to him. "Thanks."

"Happy to help." Devin turned to the tourists and flashed a smile. "G'day, ladies. Would you two lovelies care for a drink with your muffins? Looks like we have lemonade, iced tea, or bottled water."

For just a moment, Sarah stood, watching the teenager from Australia flirt with the middle-aged women from Georgia. Devin appeared to be completely comfortable with the situation, and she had no more reason to delay. Besides, Cam looked like he was about to blow.

She moved out from behind her sales booth and took off walking up Second Street, away from the crowd, away from Pauline the Nosy. Cam Murphy strode along beside her.

Cam Murphy at her side! Sarah swallowed hard against a nervous giggle. *Holy Moses*. This was certainly a first. She and Cam had never walked together in public when they were teenagers. Had she ever dared, her parents would have heard the news before she'd ever made it home. Her dad would have met her at the door with his arms crossed and his brow furrowed in a disapproving frown. Her mom would have wrung her hands with worry, tears pooling in her eyes. It would have been just like the afternoon that they confronted her about her obviously pregnant belly.

What a difference twenty years made. Dad wasn't alive to frown, and Mom didn't know how to worry anymore. *Am I lucky or what?*

A strangled laugh escaped her. *You're hysterical, that's what you are.*

Sarah fought for control by focusing on her surroundings. It was a beautiful afternoon in Eternity Springs. The sky above was clear and a crisp, brilliant blue. Sunshine warmed the easy breeze fanning through the mountain valley. On any other day, she would have taken delight in the sight of a red-tailed hawk making lazy circles around the spire of Sacred Heart Church. Ordinarily, she would have appreciated the riot of pinks, reds, yellows, and purples blooming in flowerpots and baskets at every residence and business along the street. Today she barely noticed the beauty surrounding her.

The beast at her side overwhelmed all her senses.

Anger emanated from him in waves. The farther they walked, the faster he walked. Since she took two strides to every one of his, Sarah soon jogged to keep up even as she wondered why she bothered. Then, just as they approached Cottonwood Avenue and Angel Creek beyond, a thought occurred to Sarah that brought her to an abrupt halt. *Whoa, did I dodge a bullet.*

Lori had considered coming home this weekend for a visit, but a last-minute camping invitation from a college friend had changed her mind. Sarah had been disappointed, but since she knew she'd be busy due to the quilt festival, she hadn't protested. Now she realized that the camping opportunity had been a blessing for them both.

Cam's voice broke into her thoughts. "Do you really want to do this here? Beside a trash dumpster?"

"What? Oh. That's not . . . No, I thought we'd go there." She gestured toward Angel Creek and the grounds of Angel's Rest. But before she could explain further, a familiar voice interrupted her.

"Sarah, my dear," Reverend Hart called out from the porch of Alton and Wendy Davis's home. "I'm surprised to see you away from the Fresh tent. Don't tell me you've sold out already. I've been planning to blow my diet on one of your brownies."

The Methodist minister wore a welcoming smile as his gaze shifted expectantly toward Cam. *Oh, no.* Sarah had no intention of introducing Cam to the local clergy.

"Just taking a break, Reverend. You'll still find plenty of sweets to tempt you at my booth." She started walking away before she'd finished speaking. When Cam fell in beside her, she said, "We can talk at Angel's Rest. There's a gazebo across the footbridge and behind that stand of cottonwoods. We'll have some privacy there."

He smirked. "Some things never change, do they? Still afraid to be seen with me."

The unfairness of the comment stung her. *He* had been the one to insist they keep their relationship a secret, not her. At one point she'd been more than willing to tell her parents about him and to go public with her love for Cameron Murphy, but oh, no. He wouldn't have it. He'd wanted to protect her reputation.

At least, he'd wanted that until the fight with Andrew Cook that sent him to juvenile detention. After that, he didn't care about anything or anyone but himself.

Rather than respond, she gave him a withering look and continued toward the footbridge, her temper sizzling, aware that he followed half a step behind. How dare he say that *she* didn't want to be seen with *him*. He's the one who rejected her. Rejected their child. Now he shows up here out of the blue, outs her, and wants to be Lori's father? After he'd spent most of Lori's life being daddy to somebody else? The nerve of the man!

She flexed her fingers against the itch to whirl around and slap him. No, to make a fist and punch him, over and over again, while she railed at him, telling him exactly what she thought of him. That wouldn't do. If she got started, she wouldn't stop, and a public street was not the place for what she needed to say.

Not that privacy was possible now. Not after he'd said what he'd said within earshot of Pauline Roosevelt. Why in heaven's name had he approached her in public? Had he intentionally wanted to blow up her world?

With each step and every new realization of ways in which his action would affect her, her temper soared. By the time they crossed the creek and approached the gazebo, she was about to explode. She stepped into the shelter and rounded on him, spitting out her words like machine-gun fire. "How dare you!"

"Where is she?" he shot back.

"How dare you waltz into town after all this time and try to ruin our lives!"

"What poison did you feed to her about me?"

"Do you have any clue what you've done?"

"Why did she run away that morning?"

"Why did she run away?" Sarah repeated, blinking back furious tears that made her all the angrier. Be damned if she'd let him make her cry. Not again. The ocean of tears she cried two decades ago was enough. "I'll tell you why she ran away. Because you're a loser, Cam Murphy! She doesn't need you in her life. She doesn't want you in her life. You aren't worth having in her life!"

He clamped his jaw shut. A muscle ticked at his temple, and at his sides, his hands fisted. In the tiny part of her brain that remained rational, Sarah waited to feel fear that he'd use those fists against her—like father, like son. That fear never came, because deep down inside, Sarah had never believed that Cam was anything like Brian Murphy.

With that reminder of his reality, she felt a pang of shame for the cruelty of her words, but she ruthlessly buried it, saying, "And now you've gone and spouted off in front of half the town that Lori has Murphy blood."

He took a step toward her. "I won't let you keep her from me anymore."

"What? Keep her from you! You blew her off. Remember that afternoon when I visited you in juvie jail? When I told you I was pregnant? You replied in no uncertain terms that you wanted nothing to do with . . . and I quote . . . *the mistake.* I haven't kept her from you. You. Did. Not. Want. Her!"

A muscle worked his jaw. "Well, I want her now. She's my daughter!"

Sarah put the frost of February in her voice. "No, she's not. Lori is *my* daughter, Cam Murphy. Mine and mine alone. You can't have her. It's too late."

Cam froze, standing with his fists clenched at his sides, all expression wiped from his face. He could have been carved from the granite on Murphy Mountain.

Sarah held her breath. For years she'd dreamed of this moment, of looking this man in the eyes and telling him that he was a sorry SOB. Well, she'd done it. He'd heard her loud and clear. He hadn't liked it one bit, either. *Good.*

Sarah lifted her chin, daring him to challenge her. Instead, Cam closed his eyes and slowly lowered his chin to his chest.

Seconds ticked by like hours as she waited for his next move. The fragrance of roses from the memorial rose garden drifted on the air, and in the distance, she heard St. Stephen's church bells ring the quarter-hour. She couldn't have moved to save her life.

Finally, Cam lifted his head and looked her straight in the eyes. "Sarah, turning my back on you is the most shameful thing I have ever done. It's the biggest regret of my life."

Oh. Sarah blinked as shock overcame her anger. He'd blindsided her with that. Emotion clogged her throat. She would have thought that the assault on Andrew Cook that put the seventeen-year-old into the hospital and sixteen-year-old Cam Murphy in jail was his biggest regret.

She waited expectantly, but he remained stubbornly silent. Anger returned. Wasn't he going to offer up an "I'm sorry"? Regrets were well and good, but she deserved an apology. She and her daughter both deserved a great big fat apology for what he'd done and said twenty years ago *and* for what he'd done and said today!

She folded her arms and waited.

Cam raked his fingers through his hair, sighed heavily, then showed that he wasn't a total idiot by saying, "I'm sorry."

Then he took a seat on the bench ringing the gazebo's six sides. In a voice sounding tired and defeated, he said, "Maybe we should start this over. Hello, Sarah."

The flicker of hope in his eyes caused the sting of unwelcome tears once again in hers. Furiously, she blinked them away. She wasn't sixteen and stupid. He wasn't going to make up for this. He couldn't. "I wish it were that simple. Unless you can figure out a way to unsay the words you said on Aspen Street, I have a huge mess on my hands. You see, until you opened your mouth in front of my festival booth, Eternity Springs didn't know that you were Lori's father."

The look he shot her was sharp but showed no sign of surprise.

"You said you didn't want us, so I lied to everyone—even my parents," she explained further. "I said I had

had too much to drink at a party over in Crested Butte and slept with a tourist. For a while there, I was the biggest scandal to hit Eternity Springs since, well, you."

"Better to have been with a stranger instead of me?" he drawled bitterly.

"In Eternity Springs, months after you went to juvie jail for harming one of the town's favorite sons? Yes. Besides, I was angry at you for rejecting us. I also thought it would make life easier for Lori if she didn't have Murphy baggage to tote around."

"Made your life easier, too, didn't it?" he shot back. "Am I even listed on her birth certificate?"

Sarah shrugged her answer and tried to ignore the twinge of shame. "I'm not going to apologize for it. You called my baby a mistake."

Cam looked away. "I never imagined you would lie about her paternity. You never lied."

"Well, I did about that." She lifted her chin, silently telling him to stuff his complaints.

"Wait a minute." Cam sat up straight and frowned at Sarah. "In March, Lori went pale as a ship's sail at the sound of my name. Who does *she* think I am?"

"She knows. I told her the truth when she turned sixteen. A handful of my closest friends know, too, but up until you opened your mouth, everybody else in town believed that the guy who got me pregnant was a transient tourist from Texas who gave me a fake name, plied me with alcohol, and took advantage of my poor naïve teenaged self."

"So when I asked where my daughter was—"

"You outed me." Suddenly exhausted, Sarah took a seat on the bench opposite Cam.

He scowled. "I guess I could have handled this better."

"Ya think?"

"I didn't set out to cause a scene."

"I hate to think of what might have happened had you

tried. Pauline Roosevelt was about to wet her pants, she was so excited at her front-row seat."

His mouth quirked in a sheepish grin that made Sarah do a double take. She remembered that grin. Once upon a time, it had made her melt.

Shoot, it still made her melt.

Now that her temper had waned and her panic subsided, she was able to see past the haze of emotion to view him clearly. She almost wished she was still in a lather. The man was too darn sexy by half. It wasn't fair. He should have lost his hair or found a beer gut or had his nose broken or his teeth knocked out in a fight. When he shoved his fingers through his hair once again, she recalled how much she'd enjoyed running her fingers through his hair while they cuddled after making love up at Lover's Leap. *Get a grip, Reese.*

"Damn." He winced, shaking his head. "I walk back into this town and first thing I do is let my temper get the better of me. That's something I don't do anymore. But today . . . the way people looked at me and the way I reacted, the last twenty years might never have happened. I'm still the punk troublemaker."

"Well, you've certainly caused trouble for me," she grumbled. "Why have you come here, Cam?"

He rested his elbows on his knees and leaned forward. "I want to meet Lori and get to know her."

"Why now?"

He hesitated before saying, "Because I'm haunted by my past. Seeing you in March made me face it. It made me want answers to some questions I have." His tone rueful, he added, "Although now that I've had a taste of the answers, I'm not sure I want them."

Sensing that he referred to her "worthless" remark, Sarah regretted the choice of words. She searched for a way to explain something she wasn't at all sure of herself. "Seeing you was such a shock. We weren't ready. Lori wasn't ready."

"Why not?" His jaw hardened, but he kept his voice neutral. "What have you told her about me?"

Sarah straightened her spine. "I didn't bad-mouth you, if that's what you're thinking."

"When she heard my name, she looked at me as if I'd killed her dog."

"I can't help what other people said about you, Cam. Lori's always been a curious girl with an interest in Eternity Springs's history. When she started asking about you, people around town didn't think twice about it, or hesitate to give her their views. You still have quite a reputation in town."

"I figured that out myself five minutes after I hit town. I take it you didn't defend me to her?"

Sarah let silence speak for her.

"I guess I can't blame you." He studied her for a long moment, then rolled to his feet and moved to the center of the gazebo. There, he waited for her to meet his gaze before saying, "I *am* sorry, Sarah. I'm sorry I pushed you away after I put Andrew Cook into the hospital. I'm sorry I turned my back on you and our child when you came to me, looking for help."

Again, pesky tears stung her eyes. She was glad to hear a sincere apology, but at the same time, it stirred the coals of her anger. Apparently "I'm sorry" couldn't wipe away years of heartache.

He put his hands into his pants pockets and rocked on his heels. "Is Lori her first name or her middle name?"

"First. She's Lori Elizabeth. Lori Elizabeth *Reese*."

His smile was sad. "That's a beautiful name. She's a beautiful young woman. I'm anxious to meet her."

"Well, that isn't going to happen anytime soon. Lori isn't here." Sarah folded her arms. "She has an internship this summer, so she didn't come home."

His hard look suggested he didn't believe her, but once Sarah met his gaze with the righteousness of truth, he sighed. "Maybe it's best it occurs away from Eternity Springs. Where is she?"

Sarah opened her mouth, then hesitated. "I don't know yet if I'm going to tell you. This is a mess. I have to figure out what is best for her. Plus, she's an adult. It's her choice if she wants to see you or not. I can't force her to do it. I won't try."

Now it was Cam's turn to open his mouth, then hesitate. Rather than speaking, he stepped forward and took a seat beside her. Not *too* close. No danger of touching. But she could smell the scent of soap on his skin. Irish Spring, of course. Some things never change. "I quit carrying that soap in the store because of you."

"Pardon me?"

"Never mind." Closing her eyes, she rubbed her temples. "For crying out loud, Cam. Why did you have to take the bull-in-a-china-closet approach here? For all that Eternity Springs has changed, in some ways it's still the same. Hummingbird Lake will always be cold. The hot springs on Angel Creek will always stink. Murphys will always have 'bad blood.' Now Lori will be a bad-blooded Murphy whether she wants it or not. You took away her choice."

"That's ridiculous." He kicked at a pinecone lying beneath his feet.

Yes, it was. But it was also reality, a patch of dirty, threadbare cloth in the quilt of Eternity Springs's history. "Maybe so, but that's the reputation your family has had around this town for over a hundred years. Just because no Murphys have been living here doesn't mean that people here have forgotten them—or their evil genes."

"That's just small-town, small-minded idiotic." His mouth thinned and his eyes went hard as he shoved to his feet and began pacing the confines of the gazebo. "I didn't have bad blood. I had a father who beat me and nobody—*nobody*—stepped in to help."

Sarah winced at the charge. That was true. Shameful, and true.

"That's why I acted like an ass growing up. I was an angry kid who didn't know any better than to act out. I'll tell you something else, too. If these people start treating Lori like dirt just because of who I am, then she's better off living elsewhere."

She couldn't argue that point, either. And yet . . . "This is our home."

"Only because you've never tried anything different," he snapped back. He flung out his arm, pointing west. "It's a big world out there, Sarah, and there are plenty of great places to live. Places a whole lot better than Eternity Springs."

A ribbon of nerves fluttered through her. What he said, how he said it, sounded like a veiled threat. What was he thinking?

Would he try to take Lori away from here? Away from me? Sarah's stomach sank. Until that moment on the wharf in Cairns, Lori had loved Australia.

No, don't be silly. He couldn't do that. Her daughter wasn't going anywhere. She and Lori were tight, and besides, Lori didn't want to have anything to do with this man.

And yet what did Sarah really know about him? She knew he had a son, lived in Australia, did some sort of work for a tour company, and could model for *GQ*. But what about the boy's mother? Sarah hadn't missed the fact that Cam's ring finger was bare, but that didn't mean he wasn't married. Why had he really traveled halfway around the world at this point in time?

He could be the world's biggest liar and she wouldn't know. She hadn't spoken to him in more than twenty years. For all she knew, he was sick and needed a kidney and that's why he'd come looking for Lori!

"Are you on dialysis?"

"What?"

"Never mind." *You're losing it, Reese.*

Maybe so, but she would do anything to protect her daughter. Did Cam Murphy pose a legitimate threat to Lori? To make that determination, she needed more information—whether she wanted it or not.

She'd spent years trying not to think about Cam, telling herself to resist the urge to track him down. For more than two decades, she'd assured herself that she didn't *want* to know what had happened to him after his release from juvenile detention. For the most part, she'd meant it. Now, for her daughter's sake, she couldn't afford that approach any longer.

She bent over, let out a frustrated groan, then gathered herself, stood up, and faced him. "All right, here's the deal. Lori and I will weather this storm. The people who matter won't give us grief, and those who don't matter, don't matter. My only priority is to do what is best for Lori. But in order to decide what that is, I need to know more about you."

He braced his hands on his hips and appeared vaguely insulted. "I'm happy to answer any question you have, Sarah. I have no intention of hurting our daughter. However, you need to know that I do intend to meet her. One way or another."

"Did you mean to make that sound like a threat?" Sarah folded her arms. "Because if you did, I'll tell you right now that I'm the gatekeeper. Only my dearest friends know where she's working, and they won't tell if I ask them to keep quiet."

Unexpectedly, he grinned. "You're a lioness, aren't you?"

"Darn right."

"Then I won't mention that I have an open-ended return ticket to Australia. I can hang around and wait indefinitely for her to come home."

Indefinitely? She narrowed her eyes. He had to be kidding. He had a school-age son. Surely he was kidding.

"It's good you're not going to mention it." She returned to her seat on the bench, crossed her legs, and folded her hands. "So, Cam, tell me about yourself."

"What do you want to know?"

"The basics. Work. Family. How you came to live in Australia. Normal stuff."

He leaned a shoulder against one of the gazebo's posts, folded his arms, and casually crossed his ankles. "I'm the owner/operator of the tour company you ditched, Adventures in Paradise Tours."

He was the owner? Not just a deckhand? *Well. Okay.* "Hey, thanks for refunding our reservation fees."

"That was an exception in policy," he commented drily, then continued. "As far as family goes, it's just me and Devin. We lost our twelve-year-old Weimaraner, King, in March."

"Oh, I'm sorry." It was a sincere expression of regret—for more reasons than one. By sharing the death of the family pet, he'd made it awkward for her to ask about Devin's mother. It hadn't escaped her notice that he'd neglected to mention either a wife or an ex-wife or a deceased wife. Or a girlfriend.

"The story of how I got to Australia hasn't changed from what I outlined in the first letter," he continued. "Have you forgotten? Or did you not bother to read it?"

First letter? She uncrossed her legs and sat forward. "What are you talking about?"

"Ten years is a long time, but I'm still surprised that you'd forget." Hurt flashed briefly over his face. "As I recall, that part of the story filled up the front and back of three pages."

"Wait a minute," Sarah said, holding up her hand, palm out. "I don't know what you're talking about."

"You don't remember that letter?" His eyebrows arched above accusing green eyes. "That's almost humiliating. Guess you must have been sidetracked by the check."

Check? Sarah's brows rose. *What check?*

"I admit they were late in coming. The first ten years I didn't have two quarters to rub together, but once I got on my feet, I did try. I made a couple of phone calls, found out that you still worked at the Trading Post, so I sent the letters there."

Sarah's heart began to beat double time. *Letters. Checks.* She cleared her throat, then stated, "You sent me a letter."

Cam stared at her hard, his gaze measuring. "I sent you *six* letters."

She shook her head. This was crazy. Why would he lie like this? "You never sent anything to me. What trick are you trying to pull here?"

His brows dipped in a mean scowl. "You're the one who's playing tricks. I sent letters and checks, two a year for three straight years. When you never cashed the checks, I figured that was your way of giving me the finger."

"I didn't . . . I never saw them, Cam. This is the first I've heard about letters or checks." *Six letters? Six checks?* And she never received one of them? How could that be?

He snorted derisively. "I could possibly buy that you never saw the first one. I sent it regular mail, although it did have a return address. The rest of them I sent by registered mail to the Trading Post. You signed for them."

"What?" Sarah's jaw gaped. She couldn't believe what she was hearing. She'd never signed for any registered letters from Australia. That's not something a girl forgot. But if he sent them and someone signed for them, that meant someone had intercepted her mail.

"After three years of trying, I threw in the towel, but

I did leave the bank account open. I continued to add to it. The money is still sitting there, collecting interest."

He spoke with such sincerity that she had to believe him. Besides, it would be easy enough to check. Letters. Checks. What had happened to them? Who had intercepted them? Mail tampering was a federal offense!

Even as she asked herself the questions, movement beyond the gazebo caught her attention. Nic Callahan approached at a run, her face wreathed with worry. Sarah's stomach sank. She called out, "Nic?"

"Sarah. Thank goodness I found you. We've been looking everywhere. April called. Your mom fell. She's at the clinic."

"Oh, no. How bad is it?" she asked, stepping toward the gazebo's exit.

"I don't know."

Nic's gaze slid past Sarah's to Cam. Sarah glanced over her shoulder. "I have to go. This conversation isn't over."

"I hope she's all right, Sarah," Cam solemnly replied.

Me, too. Dear Lord in heaven, me, too.

Sarah took off running, leaving all thought of missing letters and Cameron Daniel Murphy behind.

FIVE

After Cam watched Sarah dash away without a word to him, he turned a wary look toward Nic Sullivan. Blond, blue-eyed, and still beautiful, he thought. Once upon a time, she had been one of his few friends in town. However, she'd been Sarah's *best* friend, and based on the disapproving frown she turned his way now, he knew she rooted for the home team still today.

"Well, look what the mountain cat dragged in." She wrinkled her freckle-dusted nose. "You always did know how to get people's attention."

"Hello, Nicole."

"I don't know whether to hug you or give you a roundhouse to the chin."

"I take it you heard the news I spilled today?"

"Sarah clued me in a few years ago when she was trying to figure out what to tell Lori."

"Then I'm surprised that a hug is even a possibility."

"It's a slim one. Very slim."

His gaze trailing after Sarah, Cam wore a troubled frown. "Is her mother seriously injured?"

"Rose—our doctor—didn't think Ellen broke anything, but she's ordered X rays to make sure. This is the last thing Sarah needs on her plate right now, especially after you dumped a load of . . . liverwurst . . . on it."

Cam chose to ignore the food reference. "Where's Sarah's father?"

A shadow passed over Nic's face. "He died when Lori was in middle school. Sarah has taken care of the whole family since then—all by herself. It hasn't been easy. Her mother has Alzheimer's."

"That's too bad." Ellen Reese had been nice to him. Not so nice that she would have wanted her daughter to date him, but kind. She'd had a gentle soul, and people in town had really liked her. "How bad is it?"

"It's not end-stage, but I suspect that's not too far away. Sarah's doing everything she can to keep her mom home as long as possible." Nic explained how Sarah's bakery came to be, adding, "It's definitely bought them more time together."

Cam lifted his hand and rubbed the back of his neck. "I sent money to her, Nic. Half a dozen times, years ago. She says she never got it."

Nic's eyes widened with surprise. "What?"

"We had just started talking about it when you ran up. She didn't know about it, did she?"

"No, she didn't," Nic replied, sincerity gleaming in her blue eyes. "I'm sure about that."

Cam thought it through, his anger flaring once again. He paced the gazebo. Someone had done this. To him. To Sarah. To their child. Dammit, he'd tried to do the right thing and someone had purposefully interfered. "Someone intercepted my letters."

"Wow." Nic tucked a stray strand of long blond hair behind her ear. "Who would have done that?"

"Her parents, I guess. Who else would it have been? Unless . . ." He gave her the dates he'd sent the letters. "Was there someone else around at the Trading Post during that time? A new boyfriend, perhaps?"

"I don't think so, but I wasn't living in Eternity Springs at the time."

"I need to find out who the postman was then.

Someone forged Sarah's name, signing for the letters. The postman would have known."

"Mr. Fain. He was still our mailman. He retired five or six years ago. He would have let her mom or her dad sign for them."

Nic considered the question some more. "It probably was her parents. Why would they do that? She never told them about you."

"If they read the letters I sent, she didn't have to tell them. They learned everything."

"But why would they have read the first letter to begin with? Sarah was an adult by that time."

"Who knows? Maybe the first offense was an accident. Maybe they opened all of her mail." Cam shrugged. "With her father dead and her mother ill, we may never get that answer."

"Oh, man. I can't believe this." Nic looked in the direction where Sarah had disappeared and shook her head. "Okay, I now have the answer to another question."

"What's that?"

"I'm definitely not going to punch you." Nic crossed the gazebo and gave him a hug. "It's wonderful to see you again, Cam. I missed you."

With that, a tension deep inside of Cam eased. He returned her embrace and said, "Thank you, Nicole. It's good to see you again. You look great."

"Thank you. I'm a happy woman. I have an outstanding husband, spectacular twin daughters who are almost through the terrible twos, and a career I love."

"I'm glad for you," he replied, meaning it. "I recall that you wanted to be a veterinarian. So is it Dr. Nic?"

"It is."

"Congratulations."

She tilted her head and studied him. "You know, Murphy, contrary to what I was hearing in the streets, you don't look like the devil incarnate."

He didn't know how to respond to that, so he shrugged and remained silent. Amusement brightened Nic's face, then she glanced at her watch. "I have to get home, but I have a bazillion questions for you. Want to tag along?"

"Sure." Cam had plenty of questions of his own, and he suspected he'd have better luck getting answers out of Nic than Sarah. First, though, he needed to check on Devin. The boy claimed that he could hold his own against the slings and arrows of Eternity Springs, but under the circumstances, Cam couldn't help but be a little nervous. Tugging his phone from his pocket, he said, "I need to text my son and let him know where I'll be."

"He probably won't see it right away. When I left Aspen Street, my friend Celeste had taken charge of Nic's booth so that Devin could head to the school's baseball diamond for batting practice with another friend, Colt Rafferty. Colt is coaching a summer league, and apparently Devin told him he could hit. Colt will keep him busy for at least another hour."

Cam thought it sounded like Devin had dealt with any arrows just fine. "The kid does swing a mean bat."

"You gonna be around awhile? Colt would be thrilled to have another bat for the team."

"That's still up in the air."

While they walked, Nic caught Cam up on the details of her life, including her first marriage and divorce, then her return to Eternity Springs and subsequent second marriage to Gabe Callahan, a landscape architect originally from Texas. They lived in her aunt and uncle's old house with their daughters and dog. Her aunt, a widow, had retired to Florida along with Nic's mother a few years back. Cam noted that she took the long route home, avoiding the crowd on Aspen. She also kept the conversation comfortably away from Sarah and Lori. Guess she preferred privacy when she administered the third degree.

As they approached her house, Nic groaned and muttered, "I swear I'm going to kill that man."

She picked up her pace. Spying what had raised her ire, Cam grinned just as she called out, "Gabe Callahan, I can't believe you put the girls in a dog crate!"

The tall man, dressed in jeans and a Texas Rangers T-shirt, wore a leather tool belt around his hips. He took off his sunglasses and shot Nic an offended glare. "Hey, I took off their leg chains first."

He strode over to the wire crate and flipped open the latch. The door swung open. Identical twins crawled out. Barking.

"Oh, for goodness' sakes," Nic said.

Gabe folded his arms, arched a brow, and drawled, "They ate half a box of dog treats. Meg likes the red ones the best."

Nic gave an exaggerated sigh, then picked up one toddler and propped her on a hip. "They really ate dog biscuits?"

"Yep." Gabe Callahan scooped up the other girl, carrying her like a football. She giggled and kicked her legs while he extended his free hand. "I'm Gabe Callahan. Welcome to the animal-out-of-control facility."

Cam laughed and shook Gabe's hand. "Cam Murphy. Nice to meet you."

"Cam Murphy," Gabe repeated, his gaze shifting briefly to Nic. "I've heard a lot about you."

"I just bet you have."

"Cam arrived in town today," Nic explained. "He and Sarah went off to talk, but I had to chase them down and interrupt things. Ellen fell this afternoon."

"Oh, no."

Nic relayed what little she knew about Ellen Reese's injuries, then added, "I invited Cam to tag along with me. I want to grill him."

Gabe swung his daughter upright and asked Cam, "Charcoal or gas?"

Nic sniffed. "Real women use charcoal."

The afternoon played out differently than Cam had expected. For all her talk about bazillions of questions, Nic asked surprisingly few of them. Instead, while he entertained her daughters, she caught him up on local events, gossip, and answers to his queries, which usually began, *Whatever happened to . . .* The only grilling that took place was to a quartet of rib eyes after Devin called him to ask if he could grab a pizza with some of the Grizzlies—the baseball team—and in anticipation of another dinner guest, a friend of the Callahans' named Celeste Blessing.

She arrived on a Honda Gold Wing motorcycle, wearing white leathers trimmed in gold and a helmet decorated with angels' wings. She had silver hair, happy blue eyes, and just enough wrinkles on her face to suggest wisdom but not old age. She approached carrying two colorful gift bags.

"You have to stop giving gifts to the girls," Gabe chided when she drew near. "Between my father, Nic's mom, and you, they are beginning to think Christmas comes once a week instead of once a year."

"Wouldn't that be lovely!" Celeste said, turning a beaming face toward Cam. She extended her hand. "Hello. You must be Cameron. You have certainly set the town abuzz today. I'm Celeste Blessing. Welcome home."

Welcome home. She was the first person who'd said that to him, and it made him feel a bit strange. Then, as he took her hand for the handshake, the sensation he got was downright disturbing. Warmth. Reassurance. Familiarity. *I've met this woman before.* "Um, thank you. Have we met before, Ms. Blessing?"

"Call me Celeste, dear." She patted his hand and smiled into his eyes, into his heart. Into his soul. "People ask me that all the time. I must have one of those faces. Now, where are my girls? And don't give me more grief about presents, Gabe Callahan. Today I'm giving them the gift of Serenity."

She reached into one of the bags and pulled out a little stuffed animal, a fluffy white poodleish dog.

Nic brightened. "Your order finally arrived. It's taken forever." Celeste handed the animal to Nic, who added, "Oh, Celeste. They're so cute."

"Serenity is part of our Angel's Rest branding," Celeste explained to Cam. "She's our mascot. Your Sarah won the contest to name her, the prize of which was the trip to Australia."

Cam was so distracted by her use of the words "your Sarah" that he almost missed the import of the rest of her sentence. So he owed this chance to connect with his daughter to a stuffed animal. "Can I buy one? I'd like to have it sent to Lori. Could you do that for me?"

Celeste positively beamed. "Absolutely. She'll be thrilled."

Nic's mouth twisted. "Maybe not, Cam. Sarah probably won't be thrilled."

"She will come around." Celeste patted Cam's arm. "You'll see."

Dinner was enjoyable, served on the Callahans' patio while the twins played on a plastic jungle gym under their parents' watchful eyes. The adults talked a little politics, some Major League Baseball, and quite a bit about good fishing spots around Eternity Springs. Celeste drew Cam out about life as a tour operator, and he and Gabe discussed different dives they'd each made in various spots around the globe. Between the good steak, nice wine, and pleasant company, Cam relaxed, so Nic caught him a bit off guard when she served up a pointed comment along with ice cream for dessert. "So what's the deal with Devin's mother? Are you married? Divorced? What?"

No one would have missed the accusation in her voice.

Before he could frame his response, she added, "You must have hooked up with her the minute you got out of juvie jail, or else Devin looks awfully old for his age. That one's hard to forgive."

"Wait a minute."

She didn't wait. She was on a roll. "It's probably the biggest reason Lori wigged out the way she did that day on the wharf, and why she hasn't come to terms with you being you yet. It's definitely the biggest hurdle you'll have to overcome when dealing with Sarah. Think about it, Cam. You rejected her and her baby, then first chance you get, you knock up someone else. Only this time, you keep the kid and raise him!"

Cam jerked back in his chair. He set down his spoon, blinking hard. *Whoa. Is that what they . . . Yeah. Of course they did.* He grimaced and shook his head. What an idiot he'd been. He'd never gone down that path in his thoughts, but he damn well should have. "They're girls," he murmured.

"What?" Nic demanded. "Girls? You have more?"

"No. I said 'girls' because Sarah and Lori are girls. Devin and I are guys, and our brains didn't go in that direction. Nic, I adopted Devin. He came to live with me when he was six years old after his mother died."

"He's not your son?" she said.

"He damn sure is my son," Cam snapped back.

"No, I'm sorry." Nic shook her head. "I didn't mean it the way it sounded. Of course he's your son. What I was processing was that you didn't get another girl pregnant the minute you got out of juvie."

Placated, he explained further. "It wasn't like that with me and his mom. We were friends, never lovers, certainly not married. Elise managed the office for the tour company I worked for before I started my own business. She was a single mom, and the owner allowed her to keep Devin on the premises. He was a cute little kid. He and

I got to be buddies. In fact, being around Devin and his mom brought home to me how much wrong I'd done Sarah by bailing on her like I did. They're why I sent that first letter. When Elise got breast cancer, she asked me to be Devin's guardian."

"What happened to his father?" Gabe asked.

"He was never in the picture, not even named on Dev's birth certificate."

"So you stepped up," Nic said. "That was a big commitment, Cam."

Cam shrugged. "I love the kid."

Nic gave him a measuring look. "Was there no wife or significant other around to object?"

"Fishing, Nic?"

She flashed a grin. "We do that here in Colorado."

He sighed, and with a rueful twist to his mouth provided the answer he knew she sought. "No wife. I've never been married. No significant other. Not when I took in Devin, and not now, Nicole."

Then, because the moment seemed right for it, he added one more piece of information. "The truth is, I never got over Sarah."

The alarm sounded way too early for Sarah the following morning. Ordinarily, she loved getting up before dawn, and the early-to-bed, early-to-rise lifestyle of running a bakery suited her. As she reached into the darkness to bang at the button atop her alarm clock, she absolutely, positively didn't want to get out of bed. All day.

Cam Murphy was back in town.

She groaned and buried her head in her pillow. She'd been up twice with her mother during the night, and she hadn't slept well at all. Thankfully, Ellen hadn't broken any bones in the fall, her injuries limited to a bad cut on her forehead that required stitches, scrapes on her arms, bruises, and aching muscles. Dr. Rose Anderson had warned Sarah that her mom's equilibrium might be off until she healed, thus elevating Ellen's risk of suffering a second fall. As a result, Sarah awoke each time her house creaked. Her eighty-year-old house creaked a lot. Once awake, she'd invariably started to think.

Thinking is what had caused her fitful sleep, not her mom, not her house. Thinking about Cam. Cameron Daniel Murphy. The man from her past who had exploded into her present and promised to change her future by insisting to be part of Lori's life.

Funny how quickly things could change. One minute she stood discussing bread recipes with ladies from Georgia and the next thing she knew her world had irrevocably tilted on its axis.

Turns out Cam Murphy wasn't really a deadbeat dad. He'd tried to help. Late, it was true, but late truly was better than never. He'd sent money, money that she and Lori had desperately needed a time or two over the years. He'd sent money that her parents—one of them or both of them—had kept from her.

Actually, they'd stolen that money from Lori. Her parents! How could they have done that? It had to have been them. No one else could have intercepted her mail. They'd committed a felony. Felonies. Six of them.

Why? Why had they done it? Sarah had been an adult. They had no right or acceptable reason for making the choice they had to keep the letters from her.

Letters. In her heart of hearts, she acknowledged that the loss of the letters was emotionally devastating. What had he written ten years ago? He hadn't shared that information yesterday. What if he'd begged her for forgiveness and asked for another chance? What if he'd wanted to be a father to Lori then? What if she'd had help parenting through those tumultuous teenage years? The what-ifs all but drove her crazy.

And she couldn't do a darn thing about it. Her father

was dead, and as much as she would like to confront her mother about it, she couldn't do it. Ellen Reese might or might not become upset if Sarah mentioned letters from Australia. She might or might not remember them. She might or might not say whatever she thought Sarah would like to hear. Whatever she did say Sarah couldn't trust, so what sense was there in asking?

Besides, except for satisfying her curiosity, answers wouldn't change a thing. Sarah couldn't reset the clock to ten years ago. That water wasn't simply under the bridge, it had reached the Gulf of Mexico. The only thing that mattered was going forward.

Going forward meant dealing with the reality that her ex was in town and her daughter needed to be informed. It was too early to call now, and she wouldn't have time once she began her baking day. She'd call Lori tonight. She'd send a quick email this morning, asking Lori to be at her computer for an online call at nine tonight. She wanted to be able to see her daughter's face when she broke this bit of news.

That done, she finally dragged herself out of bed and began the morning's tasks. When she closed the bakery at the end of her workday after lunch, she wanted nothing more than to roll back into bed and take a nap. Instead, she had to trek over to Angel's Rest. Celeste had called an emergency meeting of the Patchwork Angels—something to do with the festival that had just ended, she guessed—and skipping it wasn't an option. Not only would Celeste give her grief if she tried, but Sarah didn't want to miss out on any scoop her fellow Angels might have to spill on the biggest gossip topic of the year—Cam Murphy.

After a bit of internal debate, she decided she wasn't up to a stroll through town. She checked on her mom, confirmed plans with Ellen's regular afternoon caretaker, April Simpson, then took the car to Angel's Rest.

She pulled into the parking lot right behind Ali

Timberlake. Ali and her husband, Mac, were building a home a short distance from town up at Heartache Falls, and Mac, a former federal judge, was doing a lot of the work himself. He claimed that the activity would help him figure out what he wanted to do when he grew up.

"Hi, Sarah," Ali called when they both exited their cars. "How's your mom?"

"She's a mess. She has six stitches across her forehead, ugly scrapes on her arms, and a badly pulled muscle in her leg."

"Bless her heart. Do you have enough help for her? I have some time tomorrow morning. I could take a shift."

"Thanks, but I talked to April and she's willing to work extra hours for a while."

"Okay, but you let me know if I can help."

"I will. Thanks." Needing something different to think about, she said, "Did you know you have a handprint on your butt?"

"What? No!" Ali twisted around, trying to see. "I swear I'm going to kill that man!"

Sarah chewed the inside of her mouth. The Alison Timberlake Sarah first met had worn cashmere twin sets atop neat wool slacks, carried designer handbags, and sported a stylish bob that screamed high-dollar haircut. Paint-stained jeans and a Vanderbilt University sweatshirt were a new look for her. "Is that the color you chose for the dining room? I like it."

"Aargh." Ali pulled off her sweatshirt, revealing a Yellow Kitchen restaurant T-shirt beneath. She tied the sweatshirt around her waist as they walked up the gravel path toward Cavanaugh House, the converted Victorian mansion that was the heart of Angel's Rest Healing Center and Spa.

The quilt group met weekly during the off-season. As the official hosts of the quilt festival, the Patchwork Angels had logged numerous extra hours leading up to the event. The plan had been to adjourn until after tourist season. Sarah wondered what had changed.

"Do you know what this emergency is all about?" she asked Ali as they climbed the staircase to the attic workroom.

"Haven't a clue. I figure it has to be something to do with the festival."

"I hope nothing happened to the exhibit quilts. Shipping them always scares me. What if they get lost or something being shipped with them breaks and ruins them?"

"That's why we carry insurance." On the second-floor landing, Ali slipped her arm through Sarah's and lowered her voice. "Are you doing okay, honey?"

Sarah knew what she meant, and she attempted to deflect the question. "It's difficult to see Mom all black and blue."

Ali gave her a chiding look. "I'm sure it is, but I'm not talking about your mother's injuries. I'm talking about your heart."

"My heart isn't the one at risk here, Ali. Lori's heart is the one I'm worried about."

"Did you call her with the news?"

"No." As they made a turn at the third-floor landing, Sarah spied Sage coming up behind them, and she waved. "With Mom's accident, I haven't had time. I'll call her later tonight. I don't want her learning about it from anyone else. I'm afraid to think about how she'll react."

Ali gave her arm a squeeze. "One thing the last year or so has taught me is that we're stronger than we think we are. All of us. You'll deal with this, Sarah. So will Lori. Personally, I think it's a good thing that Cam Murphy made the trip to Eternity Springs. Ignoring problems doesn't make them go away. I'm an expert on that. Sometimes the very act of facing those problems and dealing with them opens up new and wonderful possibilities in life."

"Like blue handprints on your butt?"

Ali laughed. "Absolutely."

They had dawdled, so Sage caught up with them, her baby belly leading the way. "Hey, guys. Do you know the reason for this afternoon's summons? Was there a problem with the festival that I don't know about?"

"I don't know," Sarah said. "I'm afraid that's the case, though."

"It's nothing legal," Ali added. "Mac would have known. He's as in the dark as I am."

"Aha. That's the reason for the handprint? It was dark and he thought he was reaching for a paint rag instead of your rear?"

Sage asked, "What handprint?"

"Ali has a paint stain on her butt. Shaped like a hand."

"A big hand," Ali added, apparently deciding to make the best of an embarrassing situation. "He knew exactly what he grabbed."

Then she licked her finger, touched her butt, and made a sizzling sound.

The three women laughed and entered the workroom. Sarah glanced around and froze. Instead of a ten-to-fifteen Patchwork Angels contingent, she saw only three other people: Celeste, Nic, and Cam.

Uh-oh. Something told her she wasn't going to like this.

Bracing herself, Sarah flatly asked, "What is this?"

When no one immediately spoke up, she met Cam's sheepish look and narrowed her eyes. "If you try to claim that you've taken up quilting, I'm calling BS."

"Hey, this wasn't my idea. I'm just here because *she*"—he hooked a thumb toward Celeste—"issued a command invitation. And I do mean command. I couldn't turn her down. She wouldn't let me."

Sarah folded her arms. "Celeste?"

The older woman straightened her spine, squared her shoulders, and lifted her chin to a regal pose. "Come in, all of you, and sit down. We have much to discuss, and it's silly to waste any time on histrionics."

"Histrionics! I asked a simple, calmly stated question. That wasn't histrionics."

"You are correct. My intention was to put an end to them before they start. Sarah, please sit here beside me."

Celeste patted the red brocade slipper chair that was Sarah's favorite in the attic workroom. Ordinarily it sat near the dormer window. The furniture had been rearranged for this meeting. Or was it really to be an inquisition? Or . . . She recalled prior events with this group of women. "Is this gonna be another intervention?"

Sage sniffed. "If it is, you can't complain. It's certainly your turn to be on that side of the conversation."

"Yeah," Nic agreed.

Sarah wrinkled her nose, but she couldn't argue the point. These interventions had become a pattern for their group of friends when one of them needed . . . encouragement. Nevertheless, she hooked her thumb toward Cam. "Why does *he* have to be here? When we held Sage's intervention, we brought breakfast, not boys."

Nic rolled her eyes. "How old are you? Mid-teens instead of mid-thirties?"

"Bite me," Sarah replied as she sank into the comfy chair.

"Now, Sarah, Nic," Celeste chided. "You two behave or I'll get my teacher's ruler out and bust some knuckles. We've serious business to attend to today. Now that we are all here, Cameron, would you please shut the door?"

As he strode across the room, Sarah couldn't stop herself from looking at the way his jeans hugged his very nice butt. Since she was there, she surrendered to the urge and imagined a handprint on his jeans. A small, feminine handprint. In red paint.

The door snicked shut, and Celeste said, "Thank you all for coming today on such short notice. Under the circumstances, I thought this get-together couldn't wait. Cam, tell Sarah what you told Nic and me last night about your son."

He leaned a shoulder against the door and folded his arms. "Devin is my son, but I am not his birth father. He was six when I adopted him after his mother died. Lori is my only natural child."

"He's never been married, either," Nic added.

Sarah sank slowly against the back of her chair as the breath whooshed from her lungs. It was too much to process. "We thought . . ."

"So Nic told me," Cam drawled, a hint of Australia in his tone.

Celeste patted Sarah's knee. "Lori is his child, and that's why I have gathered you all together. We have a project before us now that will take a dedication of effort similar to what was required to create our contest quilt."

Ali frowned. "I've been a project person all my life, but the contest quilt almost made me swear off needles. That was hard!"

"This one will be hard, too," Nic said. "One good thing about it is that it doesn't require needles."

Celeste folded her hands. She met the gazes of each person in the room in turn, then focused on Sarah as she said, "We found the quilt project satisfying. This one will be gratifying. Fulfilling. This project will change lives, in particular, the life of someone near and dear to us all. My friends, on behalf of our own dear Lori, today we undertake the redemption of Cameron Murphy in the eyes of our fellow citizens of Eternity Springs."

Sarah's gaze flew to Cam. He straightened away from

the wall and frowned at Celeste, who continued, "I have made a list of a few places we can start, but I want us to brainstorm more items. First, I think we should ask Emily Hall to set up an interview with Cam for the *Eternity Times*."

"About Lori?" Sarah squeaked.

"No. Cameron needs to talk about the accident."

Cam crossed the room and stared out the window, keeping quiet while Celeste elaborated. "I've read the newspaper accounts of what happened that night. They interviewed the sheriff, the Cook family, and Andrew himself. I only saw one quote attributed to you, Cameron, and it was damaging. Do you remember what you said?"

Simultaneously, Cam and Sarah and Nic recited, "He was asking for it."

Cam softly banged his head against the window glass.

"You need to explain that comment, dear."

He hesitated before turning around. "I don't talk about that night. I was responsible for what happened to Andrew Cook. I don't try to defend myself."

"I didn't say defend, Cameron." Celeste's expression was kind and tender. "I said explain."

"I don't know, Celeste," Nic said. "What good will it do to drag up old ugliness? Isn't that like poking a sharp stick at a wound?"

"When the wound has festered for a long time, it's important to let the poison out."

"It's not a good idea," Cam declared. "Dredging up the past won't make anything better. Everyone knows what happened. I put Andrew Cook in the hospital and went to jail because of it. End of story."

"It's not the end of the story." Celeste held Cam's gaze. "*People* should know why you hit him."

Meaning me, Sarah thought.

Cam shook his head. "It would only cause *people* pain. I won't do it. Frankly, my motive doesn't matter. It's best left in the past. All I care about is the future, and the future is Lori. I want to do the right thing for Lori."

"He's right," Sarah said. "I've been thinking about the whole situation myself. We can't change what happened in the past. The only thing that matters is doing what is best for Lori going forward. Primary to that is taking her wishes into account with every decision we make. She's an adult. She has a right to be treated as an adult in this situation, a right to be part of the process. It would be wrong of us—me and Cam and all of you—to make potentially life-changing decisions without her input."

Recent developments made Sarah resolute in this respect.

Celeste responded to both Cam and Sarah with another one of her special smiles. "You are quite correct, Sarah. Lori's well-being is paramount. That said, what Lori wants isn't always what is best for her. As a parent, you know that."

Is that what her parents had thought when letters from Australia arrived? Sarah cleared the sudden lump from her throat, then repeated, "She's an adult."

"Yes, she is. And so are you, and so is Cameron. It's good that you both consider your daughter's feelings as you go forward, but I caution you not to shortchange yourselves. You see, sometimes the best thing we can do for our children is to see to our own happiness."

Sarah stole a glance at Cam and found him stealing one right back at her.

Nic asked, "Have you spoken to Lori yet?"

"No time. We have an online date tonight."

"Excellent." Celeste clapped her hands. "We'll develop our strategy here now, and you can share it with her tonight."

Sarah knew Celeste well enough to know she'd be

wasting her breath to argue any more, so she didn't. After a moment of awkward silence, Ali cleared her throat. "As the mother of a daughter the same age as Lori; as your friend, Sarah; and as, like Cam, a descendent of Eternity Springs's founder Harry Cavanaugh, I want to say that I think this project to rehabilitate the Murphy name is a wonderful idea. I also agree that a newspaper interview of some type would be beneficial, and I don't see why you couldn't set some ground rules about what topics you will and will not address, but I have to ask. Emily Hall grew up here, too, didn't she? What sort of prejudice might she bring to the interview? I have some friends at *The Denver Post* who owe me a favor."

Nic glanced at Sarah. "Ali has a point. I don't think Emily has ever forgiven you for getting the lead in the senior play. I could see the high school girl coming out in an interview with Cam."

Sarah shrugged. "I don't know. She had a crush on Cam our sophomore year, and she's single again. She might write an article that makes him sound like a saint."

"That would be just fine," Celeste said. "What other ideas can you suggest? Ali, can we count on you to prevail upon Mac to befriend Cam?" To Cam, she added, "Mac retired from the federal bench in Denver before moving to Eternity Springs."

Cam muttered a curse, then turned away from the window to face them. "Look, Celeste, I appreciate the idea and your effort to enlist your friends on my behalf, but this just isn't how I work. I'll be damned if I'm going to parade around Eternity Springs like a suck-up."

"You're thinking about it wrong," Sage said, absently rubbing her tummy. "Getting along with people isn't sucking up. Think of it like a campaign. What's wrong with kissing a few babies if it'll help achieve the goal?"

"Just because I have a criminal record doesn't mean I'm slimy like a politician."

Sage laughed and looked at Sarah. "I like this guy."

Sarah didn't know what to make of Cam. Yesterday, the world as she knew it had tilted on its axis. Maybe he didn't deserve all of the scorn, but he still wasn't blameless, and changing two decades of attitude didn't happen overnight.

"How long do you plan to be here, Cam?" Ali asked.

Cam darted a glance toward Sarah before saying, "We're not on a set schedule. People are covering for me at the tour office, and Devin's teachers have given him independent-study projects to make up for missed class time."

"I have a thought," Sage said. "Community service is always appreciated. Colt could use an assistant coach for his baseball team. Devin says you taught him how to swing a bat. You should consider helping Colt with the Grizzlies, Cam. I know he'd be happy to have your help."

Nic pointed toward Cam. "That's a great idea. You need to do that. Still, there is one thing I want to point out. The ultimate success of this project is as much up to us as it is to Cam. You all know that most of the talk about Cam will take place behind his back. We need to be out there, speaking up every time anyone says something negative. You especially, Sarah."

"I don't know that I'll have the chance," she replied. "I expected to be bombarded with questions this morning, but believe it or not, nobody said a word. I had a lot of curious looks, and business from the locals this morning was at an all-time high, but people didn't mention Cam. Everyone asked about Mom's accident, though."

"Pauline Roosevelt didn't say anything?" Ali asked, aghast.

"She didn't come in."

Celeste said, "She left town after the festival closed yesterday. She's meeting friends in Denver."

"I bet the timing of that killed her," Sage observed.

"At least she had a front-row seat for yesterday's thrill," Nic added.

Cam muttered, "This is humiliating."

"It's for Lori," Sarah said, speaking to him directly for the first time. "They're right. If we can pull this off, it will make her life at home easier. She'll see that. She's not stupid. And this is really a separate issue from what sort of relationship she'll want to have with you. That'll be between you and Lori."

A muscle ticked in his jaw. "Could I talk with you? Privately?"

She swallowed a sigh. She guessed it was time they finished the conversation they'd had yesterday. Might as well just get everything out on the table. "Sure."

She glanced at Celeste, who made a little go-along sweeping motion with her hands. Both Ali and Sage gave her smiles of encouragement as she walked past. Nic winked at her.

In the hallway, she looked at Cam and asked, "Here?"

He shook his head. "No. Outside. I'm done with walls."

They didn't speak as they made their way downstairs and out into the sunshine. There, Cam took the lead, walking in the opposite direction of the gazebo where they'd had their aborted discussion the day before. He took an old path that led away from the hot springs into the stand of aspen that hugged the base of the mountain rising behind the estate. It was the most isolated section of the Angel's Rest property, one she rarely visited. No one would look for her here. They wouldn't be interrupted today.

Okay. That's good. They needed to come to an understanding about Lori. Celeste's idea to rehabilitate his name was a good one, and for Lori's sake, she appreciated the effort. But that was a separate issue from any relationship Cam might forge with her daughter. Sarah needed to finish yesterday's interrupted conversation with him. She needed to know what his intentions were toward Lori. She wouldn't keep secrets from her daughter, but neither would she keep her opinions to herself. She darn well wanted ammunition for her arguments. Just how big of a fight did she have on her hands?

Abruptly, Cam halted. He turned and faced her. Sunlight beaming through the leaves on the aspens cast dappled shadows across his face. He looked rugged and rough and almost pained. Sexy and oh, so serious. Her mouth went dry. *What now?*

His chest expanded, and he drew a deep breath before exhaling in a rush and saying, "Sarah, maybe you and I should get married."

SIX

Cam watched her mouth fall open and a look of alarm spread across her face. "What did you say?"

Insulted, Cam braced his hands on his hips and widened his stance. "I said maybe we should get married."

Her mouth worked, but no sound emerged. Finally, she squeaked out, "Why in heaven's name would you say that?"

Cam scowled. She didn't have to act like he'd just asked her to help him drown puppies. "I don't know. I just thought . . . Look. I can't change what happened that night behind the Bear Cave Bar, but I can right the wrong of making you an unwed mother and our daughter illegitimate."

Sarah sighed heavily. "Unwed mother? Illegitimate? That's awfully old-fashioned of you, Cameron. This is the age of the baby mama, after all."

"Even in Eternity Springs?"

She responded with only a shrug. He resumed walking, frustration riding his blood until he spied an overgrown path a few minutes later. He remembered this path. "Is that old mine shaft entrance still up on the hill?"

"The county blocked off all the old holes for safety's sake years ago, but they didn't haul off any of the old wooden structures. I don't know what's left of this mine. I haven't been up there in years."

He eyed her jeans and hiking boots. "Are you up for a little climb?"

Her expression declared no, but aloud, she said, "Sure."

He needed the physical exertion of the climb. By the time they reached the big flat-topped boulder near the entrance to the abandoned silver mine that had been his goal, twenty minutes had passed and he'd burned off much of his frustration.

Joining him, Sarah eyed the boulder with a frown. He recalled that due to her petite stature, she'd never managed to climb atop it without help. Well, she hadn't grown any taller since he'd been gone. Without asking her permission, he put his hands on her waist and lifted her up onto the rock.

Touching her proved to be a distraction. He experienced a momentary flashback to the days long ago when he'd put his hands on her, all over her. He'd loved her so much. The what-ifs and if-onlys all but brought him to his knees.

He released her the second she was settled, and stepped away. Feeling the need to put even more distance between them, he said, "So I take it the answer to my question is no?"

"What question? That was more a suggestion than a question, and while I appreciate the gesture, I don't think our getting married would really solve anything."

"Would it make Lori happy?"

She drummed her heels against the rock. "Is that what is behind this?"

Cam stared down at the rooftops of Eternity Springs. How long had he hated this place? All of his life or only most of it? "I screwed up yesterday, going public like I did."

"So this was a damage-control marriage proposal. How flattering."

"That's not . . . Oh, hell. Until the day I die I will

remember the look on Lori's face when she realized who I was. She was horrified. I need to fix that." He glanced over his shoulder at Sarah. "I know you probably won't believe this, but I love her. I always have."

Her eyes flashed like jewels, and her chin came up. "You're right. I don't believe it. You don't know her. How can you possibly claim to love her?"

Cam turned around and faced her, capturing her gaze with his own. "Because I loved her mother when Lori was conceived."

Sarah shut her eyes and swayed backward as if warding off a blow.

Determined to make his point, Cam stepped toward the boulder. "I knew you'd had a girl. I asked the social worker assigned to me in juvie. As time passed, I imagined what she looked like, what her laugh sounded like. I wondered what her favorite food was, what her favorite color was, what her first word was."

"Dog," Sarah said without opening her eyes. "Her first word was *dog*. It broke my heart at the time. I wanted her to say Mama."

Cam imagined a dark-haired toddler pointing at a puppy and saying "dog." He'd missed so much. It was his own fault. He had no one to blame but himself. Well, himself and his father.

Now, though, the situation had changed. He was no longer a boy afraid of his own fists. Cam was a man who in life had been pushed to his limits a time or two. He knew what he was capable of doing and what he wouldn't do in a million years. Oh, he had demons. What person went through life without collecting a few? But his demons weren't those of his father's. Cam didn't drink. He didn't do drugs.

He didn't hit kids.

He wasn't a danger to Lori. He knew that with certainty, something he hadn't known twenty years ago when he sent Sarah away, then ran away himself. Shoot, even ten years ago he'd had his doubts that he'd had anything positive to offer Lori other than money. That had changed. He was a good father to Devin, and he could be good for Lori. He yearned to have her in his life. But would she want him in return?

"You told me yesterday that you didn't bad-mouth me to her. What *does* she know? What does she think of me?"

"She knows the Murphy family history. She read every local history book in the library, and she asked around town under the guise of doing research for a history paper for school. I'd say she has a good grasp on the public version of who you are. The private one, less so. I told her we were high school sweethearts who let our hormones get carried away. I told her about Andrew's accident and your sentence. I told her that we were too young to deal with two crises at once and manage to stay together."

"So she must hate me."

Sarah thought about it, then said, "I think you were a fantasy for her. I think she concocted various story lines for why you never contacted her. She reads romances with secret-agent and witness-protection-plan plots. I think she liked to project those possibilities onto you. Once she saw you and discovered you had a son, well . . . I think you went from being hero to villain."

"And once she learns my side of the story?"

"I honestly don't know, Cam. I'll know better after I talk to her tonight, but I suspect you'll meet some resistance. Lori's a sensitive young woman, and her emotions run deep. Despite my best efforts, the whole fatherhood issue has left her wounded."

"Then I need to focus my efforts on helping her heal, wouldn't you say? This Angel's Rest bills itself as a healing center. They must have mental-health people on staff. Maybe they offer some programs we could look into. I'll go to counseling with you two, or just with Lori, if that's what's best."

"You're serious, aren't you?"

"Totally serious." He levered himself up onto the rock to sit beside her. "When I saw her and she ran away, she tore a scab off my own heart. Lori is my daughter, and I want to have a relationship with her. I want to fight for her. Will you help me, Sarah?"

A long moment dragged by as Sarah traced the rough edge of the rock with her index finger but didn't respond. Cam tried again. "Please?"

She cleared her throat. "There's part of me that wants to refuse. I've resented you for a long time, Cam."

He didn't know how to respond to that, so he chose to say nothing. Eventually, Sarah continued. "Due to what I've learned in the past two days, I guess the paradigm has shifted. Apparently you're not the total jerk I believed you to be."

His mouth twisted ruefully. "Just a partial jerk?"

"Don't expect miracles, Murphy." She lifted her face toward the sky, where puffy white clouds drifted against a cerulean blue. She'd been pretty as a teenager, Cam thought. Now she took his breath away.

A little voice whispered in his mind, *You didn't come back just for Lori. You came for Sarah, too.*

Startled by the thought, Cam jerked and almost slipped off the rock.

"I'm so angry at my parents," she said. "They had to be responsible for keeping your letters from me. It just can't be anyone else. I don't know why they did it, and I'll never be able to ask them. It's totally frustrating."

"Yes, that was a big piece of interference they pulled. They must have really hated me."

"I hate to agree, because it sounds awful, but I think you must be right. They hated you and wanted to control me." Sarah tucked a flyaway strand of her short dark hair back behind her ears. "Or maybe they truly believed they were doing what was best for me. Maybe they didn't trust my judgment. That makes me a little crazy, too. I'm so angry at them. I have too much I'd like to say and nobody to say it to."

"Say it to me if that would help, Sarah. I understand about this better than anybody, I would think."

A long minute passed before she responded. "Their decision hurt me. Some of it is obvious, but other aspects less so. It's things like my book club. When Lori was little, I joined an online book club. I had almost no social life at the time, and I became friends with these women. They planned a group cruise the summer Lori turned eleven. I wanted to go so badly. I saved every possible penny, worked every hour I could work. Then Lori broke her arm and the doctor bills wiped out my savings. I missed the cruise. Not that big of a deal, right? Except I was the only person in the book club who didn't go. When they came home, they'd bonded in a new way, and I was never able to break through and be a real part of the group again. I hated that."

"If you'd had the money I sent, you could have gone on the cruise."

She lifted her shoulders. "I sound like a pouty child, don't I?"

The offer to take her on a cruise now hung on the tip of his tongue, but he bit it back. Instead, he said, "Not at all. What they did was wrong, Sarah. You have a right to your anger. You should have been able to go on that cruise."

He almost apologized for his part in making it impossible. For being careless with birth control in the beginning to quitting too easily when she didn't cash the checks and respond to his letters. But he kept his mouth shut. She'd probably take any condom remark as a wish that Lori had never been born, and that wasn't how he felt at all. He truly believed that Lori was one of the greatest gifts he'd ever been given. He just had to figure out how to cut the ribbon and open the box.

Sarah dropped her chin to her chest. Cam sensed that she was working toward saying something difficult, and he tensed. When she lifted her head and looked him in the eyes, he held his breath.

"I'll help you with Lori," she said. "I think it's in her best interest to make her peace with you. It's only fair that she knows the whole truth. What happened, how it happened, and where the responsibilities lie. You, me. My parents. I need to lay it all out for her and let her process it."

Cam exhaled in relief.

Sarah narrowed her eyes and continued, "But be on notice, Murphy. I'll be watching closely. If I determine that this is in any way harmful to Lori, I'll put a stop to it quick as a minute. And if she eventually decides she wants nothing to do with you, I'll support her decision. Fair enough?"

"Fair enough."

"So what's your plan?"

"My plan is to ask you to help me come up with a plan."

Amusement lit her expression. "That's not a bad plan, Murphy. I'll have to think about it, though."

"That's fine. I want our plan to be the best it can be. In the meantime, will you tell me about our daughter?"

"What do you want to know?"

"I want to know about the little girl she was and the young woman she's becoming. Tell me everything, the little things, the big things. Help me know her, Sarah."

Sarah stretched out her legs and crossed them at the ankles. "She has always loved animals. Growing up, her favorite television show was *Jack Hanna's Animal Adventures,* and she started begging me for a pet almost as soon as she could talk. I had quite a time convincing her that it simply wasn't possible for her to have a koala bear for a pet."

"A koala bear, huh?" He liked the sound of that. "She's stubborn?"

"Beyond stubborn."

"That probably doesn't help my case."

"Doesn't make it any easier."

Cam couldn't help but grin. "I guess she comes by it honestly."

Sarah challenged him with an uplifted brow, and Cam's smile widened. "So what pet did she talk you into getting her?"

"It might be easier to tell you what pets she didn't have." Ticking them off on her fingers, she added, "We had turtles and chickens and hamsters. Fish. Cats. Snakes—"

"Snakes?"

"My father's doing. We also had a guinea pig, hermit crabs, parakeets, and, of course, we had Honey. We lost her right after she turned eleven. Lori was devastated. Nic really did get me our next dog."

Honey was the golden retriever pup he'd given Sarah for her sixteenth birthday, the gift Sarah had told her parents came from Nic. "Another golden?"

"What can I say? I love them. I have two at home now. Daisy and Duke."

Cam laughed. "Fans of *The Dukes of Hazzard*? That doesn't seem like you."

She gave an exaggerated roll of her eyes. "That I can blame on the man I was seeing at the time."

That comment distracted him from thoughts about his daughter, and he casually asked, "Have there been a lot of them?"

"Dogs?"

"Men."

"That's really none of your business, now, is it?"

Her smile turned secretive, and Cam was compelled to ask, "What about now? Are you seeing anyone now? I mean, I don't want my being around to cause you any problems on the personal front."

That smile went from secretive to amused—at his expense, he thought. "What's so funny about that?"

"I was thinking about the man I dated recently. If Jack and I were still seeing each other, something tells me he would make sure you weren't around enough to cause me personal problems. Jack can be . . . intense."

Honey, you don't have a clue at how intense I can be. "Just who is this Jack, so I'll know to watch out for him?"

"You'll probably never see Jack Davenport. He owns a home here, but he seldom visits."

At the name, Cam whipped his head around and stared at her. "Davenport! You dated Davenport?"

"You know Jack?"

Uh, yeah, he damn sure did know Jack. After seeing Sarah and Lori in Australia, he'd called Jack and asked him what he knew about the pair. Jack's information had been sketchy. He'd said he knew Sarah from shopping at the Trading Post during his trips to Eternity Springs. He hadn't known Lori.

Cam hadn't requested a personal investigation, and he damn sure hadn't asked him to date Sarah! "Jack Davenport is my cousin. Sort of."

"I know that from Eternity Springs history. You have the same great-grandfather. I didn't figure you knew him, since you didn't have contact with any Davenports when you lived here." Her lips lifted in a smile. "After I told Lori about you, she wanted me to ask Jack how to find you. She was certain he would know."

"She'd have been right. Jack and I met seven or eight years ago. We stay in touch."

"He never told me that." Surprise shone in her eyes, then she scowled. "Does he know that you are Lori's father?"

"I told him in March."

She folded her arms. "I dated him in April. That dirty dog. He never said a word about knowing you. You know, Sage told me I was an idiot not to go out with him again, but I knew something just wasn't right. Just because a man is drop-dead gorgeous, wealthy as sin, and a superb kisser doesn't mean he's necessarily a good catch. He asked a lot of questions, but I never met someone so guarded when it comes to sharing information about himself. The man makes a mime look like a blabbermouth."

A superb kisser? I'm going to kill him. "How long did you see him?"

She narrowed her eyes. "Are you asking if I slept with him?"

"No." He'd ask Jack. Right before he decked him.

"We had two dates. Like I said, he's not here very often."

And she wouldn't be so open about Jack if she'd gone to bed with him. Mollified somewhat but wanting a distraction nonetheless, he said, "Back to Lori. Does she still like animals?"

"Loves them. She's a biomedical science major. She wants to be a vet."

"Oh, yeah? So she's smart?"

"Very. She loves school, and getting this internship was a thrill for her."

Quiet pride filled Cam. Over the next half-hour, he asked dozens of questions, and for the most part, Sarah answered them all. He learned that Lori liked tropical colors, shrimp scampi, Texas country music, and college football. When Sarah added that their daughter enjoyed all kinds of water sports, he said, "She's a certified diver. She didn't learn that in Eternity Springs."

"No, she took classes at school and dived off Cozumel when her roommate's family invited her along on their vacation." Sarah licked her lips and added, "She was looking forward to the dive in Australia."

"You never learned to dive?"

She shook her head. "No, that's one dream I didn't achieve."

"It's not too late."

She laughed. "Right. I'll just run down to the local dive shop and sign up for classes."

"I could teach you. Jack has a swimming pool at Eagle's Way. Knowing him, he has equipment, or we could rent some."

"Oh, I couldn't."

Cam didn't miss the yearning on her face, and he made a mental note to look into making it happen.

Sarah checked her watch, then said, "I have to be getting home. I still have a lot to do today."

"So you're all set to talk to Lori tonight? Will you let me know how it goes?" When she nodded, he slid down off the rock and reached into his pocket for his phone. "What's your number? I'll call you now so that you'll have my number to give to Lori. Just in case she wants to call. If she doesn't, then you can call me with a report. Okay?"

"Okay." Sarah repeated her number, then, as he punched it in, added, "I wouldn't hold your breath, Cam."

"Hey, I'm all about the power of positive thinking." Her ringtone was a Frank Sinatra tune, and hearing it, Cam smiled. "It's nice to know that some things don't change. Want some help down?"

After a moment's hesitation, she nodded. "Thanks. I still hate being short."

"Diminutive," he replied, the response automatic as

he grasped her waist. In that moment, as the old, often repeated exchange hung between them and his hands found the familiar spot around her waist, the line between past and present went hazy.

Cam looked into Sarah's eyes and did the most natural thing in the world.

He kissed her.

Oh, Sarah thought, as Cam's lips captured hers. *Oh. Oh. Oh.* She settled her hands on his shoulders, so firm, so broad. *Cam. My Cam.* And then she quit thinking.

His mouth was warm and firm against hers. He tasted faintly of coffee and memories. Sarah responded, just as she'd always done. She was sixteen and lovestruck; thirty-six and needy. She opened her mouth, and their tongues touched and mingled, sliding sensuously against each other. Electric shivers raced along her skin as he moved forward until her back fit against the boulder, her feet dangled two feet off the ground, and her front pressed against the long, hard length of him.

I've missed this. I've missed him.

Her heart pounded as she melted into him. She was lost in a sea of sensation, hot and achy and hungry. He was strong, broader now than he'd been as a teenager, his frame filled out with lean ropes of muscles that told the tale of a physically active life. She felt tiny in his arms. Feminine.

Frightened.

What in heaven's name am I doing?

The hands that had been caressing his shoulders slid down to his chest and pushed. She tore her mouth away and gasped out, "Cam, stop!"

It took a beat for the message to get through. When it did, he stepped back and released her suddenly. Too suddenly. She bumped her head against the boulder on her way to the ground. "Ow!"

She glared up at him as she rubbed the back of her head. He looked mortified. "Sarah. I'm sorry. I don't know . . . I didn't mean . . . Oh, hell. Are you okay? Are you bleeding?"

On the inside, maybe.

"Let me look."

She whipped up her free hand, palm out. "Stay back. I'm fine."

She was starting to shake. *I have to get out of here. Now.*

Sarah stepped carefully around him and started down the mountain path, going just a little too fast. Her boot slipped on loose rock. He said, "Wait. Let me help."

Suddenly, unaccountably, furious, she whipped her head around. "I don't need your help, Cam Murphy. I've been climbing these mountains by myself for years. Keep your distance from me, do you hear?"

Wisely, he didn't reply. He followed her down the trail, and about halfway down, she heard him start to whistle. Whistle! The "Do Wah Diddy Diddy Dum Diddy Do" tune. Sarah huffed aloud, and it wasn't because she was breathless from the descent. She was furious. With him. With herself.

At least that's what she tried to tell herself. That she was furious. Not excited. Not aroused.

Oh, dear.

At the bottom of the hill, she picked up her pace, aware that he kept up with her step by step. As she broke from the trees onto the manicured grounds of Angel's Rest, Cam spoke up. "Hey, Sarah? That apology I made? Just so you're clear . . . that was for bumping your head. Not for the kiss. I'm glad the kiss happened, and not because I wanted to wipe my cousin's kiss from your memory. Well, maybe that's a small part of it."

It worked.

"Mainly, though, I'm glad we kissed because I've been dreaming about kissing you for the past twenty years, so this was a dream come true for me."

Sarah threw a scathing look over her shoulder at him, then continued on her way.

Smiling.

SEVEN

Sarah quietly shut her mother's bedroom door, then walked to her family room, poured herself a glass of wine, and sat down at her computer desk. She contemplated the task before her and decided that additional liquid courage might be called for. She rose, retrieved the bottle of wine, and brought it back to her desk. It was time to call Lori.

She booted up her computer, sipped her wine, then clicked the icon to make the call. Noise squawked from her speakers, which were turned up too loud. She lurched for the knob to turn the volume down before the sound bothered her mom. Mom couldn't remember much anymore, but there was nothing wrong with her hearing. The video window appeared on her computer screen, and as always, pleasure filled her at the sight of her daughter's face.

"Hey, Mama."

"Hey, Sunshine. How is your world today?"

"Oh, I had the best day." Lori then launched into a lengthy description of helping the vet treat an ill racehorse, and the signs of recovery the filly made afterward. "It was so cool, Mom. These animals are beautiful. The rhythms of the farm are both soothing and exciting."

"You sound happy."

"I am happy."

I so don't want to spoil that. Sarah studied her daughter, searching for signs of Cam beyond the obvious height and similar eyes that she'd noted before. Maybe something in her smile? She took a sip of wine, bracing herself to broach the subject when Lori did it for her.

"So, Mom, what's up? Did you have something in particular you wanted to discuss?"

"Yes," she blurted out in response. Lori waited, an expectant look on her beautiful, suntanned face. Sarah nibbled at her bottom lip, then said, "I have some news. It's not really bad news. It could have been bad, and at first I thought it was, but it turns out I was wrong. It'll be okay. It's a change, certainly, but a good change if you'll only look at it that way. I hope you'll do that, Lori."

Lori frowned. "Mom, what are you rambling about? You're scaring me."

"Don't be scared. It'll be okay. I really think it will be okay. Eventually."

"Mom, to quote Granddad, say something when you talk."

"It's Cam. Cam Murphy. He's here. In Eternity Springs."

Lori went unnaturally still. "What did you say?"

"Your father has come looking for you, Lori."

Abruptly, Lori rose and moved beyond sight of the webcam.

Sarah instinctively moved forward, wishing she could reach out and touch her daughter. "Honey? It's okay. Really. Come, sit back down where I can see you."

She heard the sound of water running. "Lori? Sweetheart? Let me see you."

A full minute ticked by before Lori returned within sight of the webcam. The damp strands of dark hair around her face told Sarah that she'd splashed her face with water, though the wetness swimming in her eyes was all internal. The big green pools of pain and trepidation made Sarah's heart hurt. She summoned her sternest mom's voice to say, "Sit down and listen to me, Lori Elizabeth. There are some important things you need to know."

Once her daughter did her bidding, Sarah shared her news, focusing on the pertinent details that would matter to Lori the most: the missing letters and checks, and the circumstances under which she'd come to have a brother.

Lori didn't say a word throughout the entire tale, and what Sarah had to say didn't appear to make her happy.

Sarah had hoped her daughter would take the news better, but she couldn't say she was surprised. Like she'd told Cam, the girl was stubborn. Once she took a position, getting her to change her mind proved almost impossible. "So that's the story. He gave me his phone number in case you'd like to call him."

Lori didn't hesitate. "No. I'm not going to call him. You didn't tell him where I am, did you, Mom?"

"No. I told him you got to make that decision."

"Good. The last thing I need is him showing up here out of the blue." Lori flopped back into her desk chair and folded her arms, a mutinous look on her face. "When will it be safe to come home again?"

Sarah chose her words carefully. "I know you probably need some time to process what I've told you. I'm not going to try to push you, honey, but you should recognize that the man has made a real effort."

"Twenty years too late," Lori grumbled.

"Is it? Is it really?" When all her daughter did was shrug, Sarah felt a wave of maternal frustration. "The situation isn't as black-and-white as we previously believed. You need to think long and hard about this."

"You sound like you're on his side."

Sarah wanted to roll her eyes but, mindful that her daughter could see her, thought better of it. "This isn't about sides. It's about doing what's right."

"What does that mean?"

"I think the fact that he's made the effort—ten years ago, and again now—means that you owe him a conversation. Not necessarily a relationship but a conversation."

"I don't want to talk to him."

Experience told Sarah not to push any further now. She had planted the proverbial seed, and it needed time to take root. This time, she was the one to shrug. "I can't make you, and I won't try."

"Good."

Not right now, anyway. Sarah cleared her throat. "In other news, your poor grandmother had a fall yesterday."

"Oh, no! Is she okay?"

They spent a few minutes discussing the issues with her mother, and after that, Sarah gave her daughter a rundown of the quilt festival. "With Celeste's matching gift, we raised twenty-five thousand dollars for the Art Quilt Initiative."

"That's awesome."

"We had some beautiful pieces on display. Sage offered representation to three new textile artists in the gallery."

"That's cool. How is she doing? Getting ready to be a mommy? It won't be long now, will it?"

"Another couple of months. She's doing great, but I have to say I hate her. She hardly looks pregnant at all. No fat face, no fat ankles—she's just carrying a basketball in front. When I was at seven months I was as big as a house."

"That's because you're a shortie, Mom. I'm lucky I'm tall like Sage."

"Yes, you definitely got your father's height."

After a moment of silence, Lori abruptly changed the subject. "Speaking of artists, how were your sales of the new caramel cookies?"

"Wonderful, thank you very much. They sold out first thing. Of course, Colt Rafferty bought twelve dozen."

"For himself?"

"No, for his baseball team," Sarah said. She briefly considered mentioning the fact that Colt had recruited Devin Murphy to play, but better sense prevailed.

As the conversation drew to a close, Sarah ventured once more into territory Lori obviously preferred to avoid. "What should I tell him, honey?"

"To go jump in the nearest billabong." When Sarah's only response was a chastising look, Lori scowled. "Mom, I don't know. I just don't know."

Progress, Sarah thought. Cam might not realize it, but from their daughter, that was significant progress.

The women said good night, then ended the call. Sarah checked on her mother and found her sitting up in bed with a book open in her lap—the history of Eternity Springs that Sarah's father had compiled and self-published. "Hey, Mom. How are you feeling?"

Ellen Reese glanced up at Sarah, her eyes a shade more alert than they'd been of late. "Did I fall or get run over by a truck?"

Was that a joke or a real question? Sarah couldn't be sure, but she suspected her mom was somewhat "here" at the moment, so she teased, "You have to stop doing cartwheels in the living room, Mom."

"Yes, your father won't like it." A shadow crossed her face, then she asked, "Is Daddy dead?"

"Yes, Mama."

Ellen nodded. "I thought so. I was with him when he died, wasn't I? I held his hand?"

"You did."

"Good. I'm glad. He was a good man. He loved his family."

"I know he did." Sarah focused on the book in her

mother's lap. Her father had been a real local-history buff—and he'd held the Murphy family in disdainful regard. "He didn't like Lori's father, did he?"

Ellen Reese's lips pursed, then she said that line Sarah had heard repeated her whole life: "Murphys are no good."

Okay, then. Wow. That proved it. She did know that Cam was Lori's father. That pretty much confirmed that her parents were the ones who'd intercepted the letters.

"Your daddy wants to keep that boy away from our precious baby."

"What baby, Mom? Me or Lori? Daddy called us both his precious babies."

Ellen frowned up at her and asked, "When do I get my hair done?"

It was her third most frequently asked question, and upon hearing it, Sarah knew communication was over. "Two days from now, Mom."

For the first time in a long time, a ribbon of resentment fluttered through Sarah as she looked at her mother. It didn't really matter whether they'd wanted to keep Cam away from her or from Lori. They'd made a choice and, in doing so, had robbed her of hers.

Her gaze drifted to the wall where the twenty-fifth wedding anniversary picture of her parents hung, and resentment flared into real anger. It's true that she had lied to them about her baby's father as a frightened, pregnant teen, but their lie to her ten years later was worse, far worse. They'd had no right. None. They'd taken away her independence. They'd denied her freedom. They'd used their own version of a leghold trap to keep her here in Eternity Springs.

I can't play the dutiful daughter or even the caring, concerned mother anymore, not tonight. I'm done.

She turned without another word and walked to her

kitchen. She picked up the receiver of the wall phone and dialed the first name on the list pinned to the bulletin board beside the phone for sitters who could take up the slack after April left for the day. It took four calls, but she finally found a teenager who could be there in five minutes, willing to sit with her mother. "Great. Thanks, Liz. I'm leaving now, but I'll leave the front door unlocked for you."

This was, after all, Eternity Springs.

She grabbed her purse and her keys and headed out the door. Her heart was pounding, her blood racing. She felt furious and hurt and manipulated. Trapped. By the people who were supposed to love her the most.

Briefly, she considered going to Cam, since he'd be wondering about her conversation with Lori. But she decided she didn't have it in her to be the sympathetic former lover, either. He'd just have to wait. She didn't have room right now for anyone's anguish but her own.

Climbing into the car, she backed out of her drive and started down the street, waving at the teen who arrived to stay with Ellen. Sarah headed out of town with no real destination in mind.

Cam paced the tiny living room that didn't look a thing like he remembered but managed to make him recall events he'd crossed an ocean to forget. That lovely flashback in the bathroom had opened the gates for ghosts, and he'd begun to see his father and his belt in every corner.

He didn't care about the dead right now. He was worried about the living. Staring at his cellphone where it lay on a small table beside the front door next to a framed quote about patience, he willed it to ring. It remained stubbornly silent. Lori wasn't going to call.

Had Sarah even bothered to ask her to phone him?

Maybe he had screwed that up with the kiss. He'd reacted instinctively, and he couldn't claim to regret it. Kissing Sarah Reese gave him as big a thrill as spotting a whale shark while diving in Thailand. Still, his timing probably could have been better. He'd always had lousy timing where Sarah Reese was concerned.

The front door opened, and Devin stepped inside. Cam took one look at his son and forgot about the phone. "What happened to you?"

Devin's left eye was swollen almost shut. His nose was bloody, his lip busted, and his shirt ragged and torn. Despite the damage, he appeared defiant and still angry. "It was nothing."

Dammit. Frustration boiled through Cam. Not again. This kid and his hotheaded temper—he was a magnet for trouble. Cam had blamed it on his running buddies and hoped they'd left this sort of crap behind in Cairns. Apparently not. "We had this discussion before we ever left home. You promised, Devin. You gave me your word."

"Sorry."

Devin tried to push past Cam to go to his room, but Cam grabbed his arm. "Hold it right there. Sorry doesn't cut it. And 'nothing' doesn't begin to answer the question I asked you. Talk to me."

Sullen, the boy said, "Fine. I got in a fight. It ended. I came back here."

"Dammit, Dev. Don't do this to me. Is it drugs? Alcohol? I thought we had a deal."

Devin's head whipped up. His eyes flashed, and he yanked his arm away from Cam. "I didn't break the deal. I gave you my word."

Something in the young man's eyes gave Cam pause, and then he realized he was looking at righteous indignation. *Okay. Well, good. No drugs. No booze. But still, a fight.* His son in a fight in Eternity effing Springs. *I really don't need this.*

"Who did you fight?"

"I dunno. Just some big dumb bully."

"What was his name?"

"I don't know. Honestly. His buddies called him Moose."

Moose. The visual on that didn't help Cam's blood pressure one bit. Dev getting into fights was bad enough. Fighting kids twice his size was downright stupid. Cam sighed and rubbed his temples. Fretting about Lori, and now worrying about Devin, had given him a headache. Couldn't he have issues with only one kid at a time? How did parents manage when they had three or four or more? Made him shudder to think about it.

"Devin, here's the deal. I'm tied up in knots already as things stand, and I just don't have patience tonight for teeth pulling. This is Eternity Springs, and there's a back-story here you don't know. Tell me the details—who, what, when, where, why—and don't leave anything out."

"Tomorrow," Devin said, turning toward his room. "I don't have patience for this, either, right now. My nose is killing me."

"That's not all that will be killing you if you don't stop right where you are and start talking. I mean it, Dev. Consider this . . ." Cam lifted both arms chest-high, fisted both hands, and crossed them at the wrists.

This was the diving signal for danger. He'd taught Devin the importance of it before he ever took him into the pool for his first diving lesson. The kid knew not to ignore the signal. Ever. Cam used it on such rare occasions, Devin understood he had no choice but to spill the story. He exhaled a hard, frustrated sigh, then said, "Fine. Ryan—he's the third baseman for the Grizzlies—he got a call from his ex-girlfriend tonight. She'd gone to some roadhouse with a guy."

Cam got a sudden bad feeling. "What roadhouse?"

"A dive called the Bear Cave Bar."

Cam shut his eyes, and his stomach took a nauseated turn. Devin knew what had transpired to land Cam in jail all those years ago, but he didn't know the details. Bear Cave was one of the details. Bad things happen at the Bear Cave Bar.

"He was drunk, so she was begging a ride home," Devin continued. "I went with Ryan to get her. The thug was hassling her, and I distracted him so that Ryan could get his girl into the car."

"You threw the first punch?"

Dev hesitated just a second before saying, "Yes."

The evasion in Dev's eyes caused Cam to keep pushing. "You threw a punch to distract a guy? I don't think so. You're smarter than that, Dev. You can talk your way out of almost anything. What really happened?"

Devin scowled, then winced as the movement made his face hurt. "All right. Look, the goon said something that wasn't called for, and I let it get to me. It was dumb of me. I know. I lost my temper. What is it with the people in this town, Dad? Some of them are great. The nicest people ever. But others . . ." He tested a tooth with his tongue and muttered, "Assholes."

Now Cam had a sense of what had transpired. This was about him. "What did he say about me?"

Fury flashed across his son's face, proving that Cam's instincts had been spot-on. "I'm not going to repeat that trash."

"Do you know the names of any of the kids he was with?"

Cam recognized two of the surnames his son mentioned, and he wasn't surprised. He also had a pretty good clue of what "trash" they were talking. "They were kids, not men my age?"

"They were young. Well, except for this one guy. They

called him Hoss. He looked older than you. He acted like he owned the bar, but he was the one doling out the beer, and when the law did show up, he disappeared."

Now Cam's stomach rolled. "The sheriff showed up? An old guy? Sheriff Norris?"

"Nah, this guy's about your age. Zach Turner. He's okay. He made sure nobody was too tore up, told us not to be stupid anymore, and sent us home."

"What about the drunk who was hassling the girl?"

Devin smirked. "He was arrested. Minor in possession and public intoxication. It was great."

As Cam released a heavy sigh, Devin continued, "That's all that happened. Really, Dad. I'm sorry I lost my cool. I won't let it happen again."

Cam rubbed the back of his neck. "Dev, I told you to expect some grief from people around here."

"That wasn't grief. It was bullshit, Dad."

"Nevertheless, we knew we'd get some of it. I appreciate that you'd want to defend me, but fists aren't the way to do it. You know how I feel about fighting. You know why." His mouth twisted in a sad, troubled grin. "I cannot believe you managed to get into a fistfight at the Bear Cave. 'Of all the gin joints in all the world.'"

"Huh?"

"That's where the accident happened, Dev. In the parking lot behind the Bear Cave Bar."

His son's eyes went wide. "You're kidding."

"Nope."

"Oh, man. Whoa. That sucks. I'm sorry, Dad. Really sorry." He thought for a moment, then added, "That explains a thing or two about some of the things he said."

"Remember what I've preached to you for months. You can't talk with your fists or think with your fists, son. You gotta use your head. Always."

"Yeah, yeah. I know."

When Cam narrowed his eyes and stared hard, Devin quickly added, "That wasn't a smart-ass answer. At least I didn't mean it to sound that way. I said I know because I *do* know you're right. It was a stupid thing to do. I guess my head just checked out. When we first came here I was ready for anything, but when everybody was so nice and welcoming, I relaxed. The nimrod at the bar caught me off guard."

Cam reached out and put a hand on Devin's shoulder. "If being in Eternity Springs gets to be too hard, you tell me, and we'll figure something else out. That was part of the deal, too."

"I like it here. It'll be okay, Dad. It will."

"You'll stay away from the Bear Cave?"

"Sure." He hesitated, then flashed a wicked grin. "Rick says the Mountaineer Club is a much better place for kids our age to go drinking."

"Brat." Cam lifted his foot and gave the boy a gentle kick in the rear. "Go take a shower. Wash off that blood."

Devin grinned and headed for the bathroom. Moments later, the shower switched on.

Cam stood in the center of the small house, his hands on his hips, thinking about Devin and Lori and past sins and future hopes. The walls began to close in around him.

And the phone still didn't ring.

"Enough of this," he muttered, then strode toward the bathroom door. He rapped on it with his knuckles. "Dev, I'm going out for a little while. Consider yourself confined to the house. Got it?"

"Yes, sir."

The devil rode Cam's shoulder as he climbed into his rental and pulled away from the curb. He debated stopping by Sarah's, but he knew it'd be a waste of time.

If Lori's reaction had been positive, either she or Sarah would have called. The silent telephone told it all.

Cam turned onto Spruce Street and, without admitting his destination to himself, took the highway south, toward the Bear Cave Bar. Toward his biggest nightmare.

EIGHT

The highway sign hadn't changed—red neon letters against a white background and a poorly designed logo of a bear poking his head out of a cave. The building was long, narrow, and windowless; the parking lot, gravel. Cam had never entered the place—all of the action had taken place behind the Bear Cave Bar.

Eternity Springs teens had worked hard to get alcohol back in Cam's day. The Trading Post had stocked beer and wine, but Sarah's parents had kept an eagle eye on who bought how much. The liquor store's owner hadn't sold to minors, and he'd followed the Reeses' example when it came to selling to young adults. If Old Man Wilson suspected a guy of buying for someone else, he'd cut him off. Of course, kids always found a way, and in Eternity Springs, the Larabie brothers had a nice little import business going. They'd taken orders, made a beer and booze run to a supplier in Gunnison, then sold it out of their trunk.

The other source in the county for beer had been Lana Freeman, the weekend waitress at the Bear Cave. She'd sell beer out of the back of the bar when her boss wasn't looking.

Having a drunk for a father had given Cam almost unlimited access to alcohol—the one positive thing he credited to being Brian Murphy's son. He hadn't needed to buy from the Larabies or to go out to the Bear Cave to drink. He'd gone to the Bear Cave to hang out, because that's what high school guys did after taking their dates home.

Now twenty years out of high school, Cam counted two cars and four trucks parked in front of the Bear Cave as he pulled into the parking lot. The old ghosts controlling his steering wheel guided him around to the back lot. There, he shifted into park, stared into the shadows, and traveled back into his past.

"I gotta go," sixteen-year-old Sarah said, pulling out of his arms. They were hidden in the shadows beneath the sprawling cottonwood tree in the empty lot two doors down from her house. "If I'm late for curfew again, Daddy's gonna kill me."

Cam groaned and reached for her. "Just one more kiss."

Sarah laughed and swatted at his hands. "That's what you said three kisses ago."

"I can't get enough of you," he said as she buttoned up her shirt. "You are so beautiful, Sarah. Friday can't get here fast enough."

Friday night they had plans to go back up to Lover's Leap, the picturesque bluff high above Hummingbird Lake where they'd made love for the first time four months ago. With winter closing in, their opportunities for blanket time were dwindling. In anticipation of that, Cam had been working around the dump where he lived with his dad, trying to fix it up to the point where he wouldn't be embarrassed to bring Sarah into his room when it was too cold for them to be together outdoors.

"I can't wait for Friday, either," she told him, reaching up to cup his cheek in her hand.

Her shy smile reached all the way into his heart. "I love you, Sarah Reese."

"I love you, too, Cameron Murphy."

She went up onto her tiptoes, pressed one last quick kiss against his mouth, then raced home to beat the clock, leaving Cam itchy with arousal and looking for a distraction. He thought about going for a run on the trail that ringed Hummingbird Lake, but he decided that he didn't want to be alone. He'd drive out to the Bear Cave and see what was happening out there.

Fifteen minutes later, he spotted his father's truck parked in front of the roadhouse and almost turned around but didn't. Chances were slim that he'd run into his old man outside the building. Cam pulled his rattletrap Jeep around to the back lot of the Bear Cave and pulled in beside the shiny red Firebird—the high school graduation present of one of the rich kids in town.

The back lot was feebly lit by a single light atop a pole and the headlamps of two pickup trucks, one belonging to Cam's friend Les Ayers. The crowd this weekday night was small. Les and another friend, Rob Knautz, sat on the lowered tailgate of Rob's pickup. The Firebird driver and two of his friends milled around two girls Cam didn't recognize. Tourists, probably. He pegged the blue Ford sedan parked on the other side of the Firebird as theirs, likely a rental.

Cam climbed out of his Jeep and approached Les and Rob. Rob handed him a flask, and two quick swigs of whiskey preceded two beers that he bought from the waitress at the Bear Cave's back door, then downed in less than ten minutes. He figured the quicker he got drunk, the faster he'd be rid of his blue balls.

"Whatcha been doing tonight?" Les asked.

"Watching baseball. St. Louis scored four in the bottom of the ninth to beat the Mets four to three." He knew this because he'd heard it on the radio on his way out of Eternity Springs.

He and his friends talked baseball for a bit, and Cam was considering buying his third beer when he saw Andrew Cook grab for one of the girls. She pulled away from him, giggling nervously, and when Cook kept after her, Cam frowned.

"That guy is such a prick," Les Ayers said of Cook as he took a swig from his bottle of beer.

The second girl snapped something at the boys, then flounced away toward the car, calling for her friend to join her. The first girl stepped toward the car, but Cook latched onto her arm and pulled her back toward him. Cam tensed and took a step toward the pair, prepared to help, when the girl wrenched herself away from Cook and dashed toward the car. Tires scrunched against the gravel as the girls drove off.

"Bitches," Cook's companion called after them.

It was only the first in a long list of ugly slurs that flowed from the others' mouths. Cam got tired of listening to it.

The soon-to-be frat boys reloaded on beers and expanded their discussion about cock-teasing females, both in breadth and in volume. Cam attempted to bring his own conversation back to baseball, but when Cook started spouting off about local girls, Cam couldn't help but tune in.

They were talking about the females in their class. This girl put out. That girl liked girls. Another one would die a virgin. When they brought up a girl in the junior class, Cam tensed. Something needed to distract them before one of them up and said something about Sarah.

Cam thought he'd get his wish when the back door of the Bear Cave banged open and a man stumbled out, unzipped his fly, and began taking a piss off the back stoop. Cam identified the drunk at the same time Cook called out, "Hey, Murphy. Isn't that your old man? Talk about a worthless piece of crap. How does it feel to be related to the town drunk?"

"Maybe you should ask your sister," Cam returned.

Cook's alcohol-glazed eyes flashed. "Very funny coming from the son of a killer."

Cam didn't want to defend his father in any way, shape, or form, but he couldn't let that particular rumor go unchallenged. "My dad didn't kill anybody."

"That's not how I heard it." He hollered toward the stoop. "Hey, old man. Didn't you kill your wife? Didn't you knock her up then leave her to bleed away her baby and die on the bathroom floor?"

Brian Murphy lifted his hand to shield his eyes from the headlights pointing his way. Slurring his words, he asked, "Who's there?"

"Your guilty conscience," Cook's friend called back.

"Go away." Brian lurched around, then stumbled back inside.

Cook's group laughed and continued to make catcalls. Cam turned away from them, pretending not to see the pity on his friends' faces.

Officially, Brian Murphy wasn't responsible for his wife's death. He hadn't done anything directly to bring on her miscarriage and subsequent hemorrhage, but he had been out drinking instead of home where he belonged when the tragedy happened. Eight-year-old Cam had been the one who found his mother and summoned help that had arrived too late.

The paramedic's words at the time were etched in his mind. It's not your fault, Cam. It's not anyone's fault. Sometimes, these things just happen. It's Mother Nature.

"Who wants another beer?" he asked Les and Rob as another car pulled into the back lot. "I'm buying."

A few minutes later, he headed back toward Les's truck carrying three cans of beer. Two older guys had joined Cook's crowd, and the group had drifted closer to Cam's, which meant Cam walked within arm's reach of Cook. He halfway expected words, but he didn't anticipate that

Cook would make a grab for the beers and steal one, saying, "I'll take this. Don't want you ending up a drunk like your dear old dad."

Cam hesitated, denting the two remaining cans as his hands clenched them hard. It was all he could do not to throw the remaining beers at the bully's head. "Do it," Cook sneered. "I dare you."

It was just what Cam needed to walk on by. Be damned if he'd give Cook that level of control. "Keep it, Cookie," Cam drawled. "I suspect you've already used up all the allowance your mommy gave you."

Cook muttered something beneath his breath. At the truck, Cam handed a beer to Les, but Rob refused his. "You drink it. I gotta get going. I have to be at work early."

"Do you still like working at the Double R?" Cam asked. "Maybe I'll look into a job there next summer." He took a long drag on the can. He wasn't sloppy drunk, but he wasn't feeling any pain.

"Yeah, I do. The tourists are usually pretty happy to be taking a trail ride up to the high meadows. It's fun."

"You loser," Cook said, having drifted closer to the truck and eavesdropped on the conversation. "You ride horses with tourists. Me, I prefer riding tourists."

In the next minute, a number of things happened almost simultaneously. Les told Rob that he needed to get a movie out of his truck before Rob left, and Cam's two friends crossed the lot to the cab of Rob's truck, taking them out of earshot about the same time one of Cook's buddies said, "I thought you were riding Nic Sullivan."

Then the back door of the Bear Cave banged open and Brian Murphy stormed outside just as Cook replied, "Not yet. Though she's on my radar. She is one sweet piece. Her and her little friend, Sarah Reese. A sweet piece and a tasty morsel. I know. I have proof. A picture I snapped in the locker room showers. A naked piece and morsel. Wanna see?"

Locker room pictures? *Cam's spine snapped straight.*

Brian Murphy called out drunkenly, "I didn't kill my wife! I loved her. Damn you to hell for saying I hurt my Cassie. Cam. Tell him. Tell him I didn't hurt your mother."

While Brian was talking, Les started back toward his truck with a rental video in his hand, and Rob turned the key of his truck and started the engine. Cam started toward Cook, who was pulling a wallet from the back pocket of his jeans, saying, "They never saw me. Best dare I ever took. Earned me fifty dollars and I got this." He smirked and added, "Excuse the stains."

Sarah. *Cam went red with rage. He launched himself at Cook, reaching for the wallet, determined to get that photograph and destroy it.*

"Tell him, son," his father cried. "Tell him I didn't do it."

Cam grabbed the wallet with his left hand and drew back his right. "You bastard. You sorry bastard."

His fist flew. Knuckles connected with jaw. Pain radiated up Cam's arm from his fist.

Cook staggered back a step, then regrouped and came at Cam, landing a puffball of a punch. Cam went after Cook hard with punches to his gut followed by another one to his jaw, just as Rob's truck turned in the parking lot. The beam of the headlights tracked across the log lying to the right of the fight as Cook's head snapped back. He staggered again, but this time couldn't maintain his balance. Cam yanked the photograph from the bastard's wallet as Cook went down, his head hitting the log with a terrible thunk.

Cam shoved the photo in his pocket.

Cook rolled to the ground and lay still.

Dead still.

Two decades later, Cam once again experienced that rush of horror, wash of panic, and wave of shame. That moment and the twenty-four hours following it remained etched in his memory. Cook's stillness. The frantic calls for help. The arrival of the sheriff and, following an interminable time, the ambulance. Being arrested, the verbal attack of Andrew Cook's father. Sheriff Norris's reaction when he referred to the contents of Cam's pockets.

Cam tried to explain that Cook had taken the photograph, not him, but the sheriff refused to listen to it. After all, Cam was a no-good Murphy. Case closed.

Cam had tried to tell the truth one more time to his public defender, who did appear to believe him, though it didn't do him any good. His lawyer pointed out that while protecting the modesty of two Eternity Springs teens was a laudable action, it didn't offset the fact that Cam had beaten a prominent Eternity Springs citizen into a coma.

Besides, presenting the motive would mean presenting the photograph. Did Cam want to do that? Did he honestly believe it would be enough to overcome a jury's prejudice against him?

The answer had been clear. Cam kept his mouth shut.

In the end, his case hadn't gone before a jury. Andrew Cook awoke from his coma and recovered from his injuries, and Cam's public defender wrangled a plea deal and convinced Cam it was in his best interest to accept it rather than risk a trial, since Andrew's father was promising vengeance. After Andrew awoke from his coma but before he'd recovered from his injuries enough to be released from the hospital, Cam had been whisked off to juvie jail.

A knock on the driver's-side window startled Cam. He twisted his head to see the end of a flashlight and a uniformed man bent over and peering into his car. A sheriff.

Oh, great. Cam thumbed the button and the window slid down.

"Good evening, sir. May I see your license and registration, please?"

Cam fished the items from his wallet and handed them over. "Is there a problem, sheriff?"

"Wondering what your business is here, sir. This spot tends to be a trouble magnet for the young people in the area."

"I'm not meeting anyone. Just visiting with some old demons."

"Demons? Oh." The sheriff looked up from Cam's driver's license. "You're Cam Murphy."

"My reputation precedes me."

"More than you know."

Cam waited for him to instruct Cam to get out of the car so he could be frisked and cuffed, just like the old days. Instead, the sheriff returned his pen to his pocket and the identification to Cam, and extended his hand. "I'm Zach Turner. Welcome home. I'm a good friend of Sarah and Lori Reese."

"Oh." Shocked, it took Cam a moment to accept the handshake.

Sheriff Turner said, "I've been curious to meet you for quite some time."

"You have?" Cam hesitated, then qualified, "Even before I showed up here?"

"Lori told me about you a few years ago, back when Sarah and I were dating."

Dating? Cam gave the sheriff a disgruntled look. *Dating.* Sarah and the sheriff. Was there a man in this town she hadn't dated?

"I looked at your file," Zach Turner continued, causing Cam to stiffen. "I'm also friends of Gabe and Nic Callahan."

The significance of the comment wasn't lost on Cam.

"Just thought you'd want to know that my predecessor kept a particular item in your file buried."

"Oh." Cam drummed his fingers against the steering wheel. "I had hoped that had disappeared."

"It was buried deep. I doubt it saw the light of day since Sheriff Norris put it away."

"Good. I'd hope it never sees the light of day again."

"Rest assured on that, Murphy, unless circumstances lead you to choose otherwise."

"Me?"

Zach Turner glanced toward the Bear Cave's back door. "What happened here that night was a bad break for lots of people, but I have to tell you, I'd have gone for Andrew Cook's throat, too. Nic and Sarah didn't deserve what he did to them."

What a difference decades and a new sheriff make, Cam thought. "Did anybody ever tell them?"

"About the photograph?" When Cam nodded, Zach Turner replied, "No. I don't believe so. Not that I've ever heard, anyway. I'm sure Sheriff Norris didn't say anything. He had your file locked up tight."

"I'm surprised he didn't destroy the evidence. He was a friend of Sarah's father."

"He did everything but destroy it." Zach straightened and stepped away from the car. "I need to be going. Nice to meet you, Murphy. And as one friend of Sarah and Nic's to another . . . thanks."

He was halfway back to his cruiser when Cam called after him, "Do you know what happened to him? To Andrew Cook? Someone told me his parents are in Pagosa Springs, but they didn't know where Andrew ended up."

"Actually, I was curious myself, so I looked into the question. He's a real estate broker in Phoenix. He's married and has two kids." Displaying insight, the sheriff added, "He made a complete recovery from his injuries, Murphy. You can let that worry go."

After the sheriff's car pulled away, Cam sat, lost in thought, for a few more minutes, brooding about Andrew Cook, Sarah Reese, and bad breaks. Finally, he put his car into gear and pulled around to the front of the Bear Cave. Instead of following the sheriff's car back toward town, he turned the opposite direction. Tonight was apparently the night to face old ghosts, to bury old demons.

Two miles later, Cam took the turnoff that led up to Lover's Leap.

Sarah sat atop the painted wood picnic table at the scenic overlook officially marked on maps as "scenic overlook" but known to area residents as Lover's Leap since the 1940s, when a grieving widow jumped to her death following official notification that her young husband, a Marine, had fallen at Iwo Jima. High up a tall mountain, this piece of public land was in an isolated corner of an isolated county, far enough away from town so that teens on the hunt for a parking spot usually stopped before getting here. Not Sarah and Cam. Due to the clandestine nature of their relationship, they'd made Lover's Leap "their" place.

Sarah had loved the big sky above Lover's Leap. She'd loved the vast panoramic beauty of the Rockies visible from this spot. She'd loved the special sense of joy that filled her whenever she visited. She'd known from the first time she came here as a child that Lover's Leap would be meaningful in her life. Unfortunately, "meaningful" didn't always happen in a good way.

This was only the third time Sarah had returned to Lover's Leap since the night Cam Murphy was arrested. Her first visit had occurred after her visit to the juvenile detention center, when she'd told him about the baby and he'd sent her away. She'd gathered up all her mementos of him, and all the gifts he'd given her, and brought them up here. She'd thrown them off the cliff.

She'd made her second visit after her father died, looking for somewhere she could mourn in private and in peace while she adjusted to her new reality as caretaker to both her daughter and ultimately her mom.

She had always experienced big, intense emotions here at Lover's Leap. Under this huge sky, surrounded by infinite beauty, she had grieved to the depths of her soul. Here, she had loved freely and completely with every fiber of her being. On this little piece of the planet, she had embraced her inner turmoil, suffered through her unbounded grief, and surrendered to soul-shattering heartache.

What drew her back to Lover's Leap tonight, she didn't know for sure. Big confusion, maybe. She was in a weird mood.

What a roller coaster she'd ridden of late. It was enough to make her head spin. The one thing she knew for certain was that now, tonight, she didn't want to worry about anybody else. Tonight, for just a little while, she'd indulge in being selfish, self-pitying Sarah.

"I'm lonely," she said to the closest fir tree. "I'm lonely and alone, and I don't like it."

For so long, Lori had kept Sarah's life full, but now Lori was filling up her own life away from home and Eternity Springs. Sarah's mother was still there, and while Sarah would be loath to admit it, having Ellen's body around but her mind off on another plane only intensified Sarah's loneliness.

The recent changes in her friends' lives played a part in her lonesomeness, too. Nic and Sage were giddily married, and Ali acted like a newlywed. Sarah was happy for her friends—truly, she was—and they all went out of their way to ensure she never felt like a third wheel. But their kindness didn't change the fact that she often was the odd man out.

It was too bad that she and Zach Turner had never fallen in love. That would have made life neat and tidy. She wouldn't go through life making numbers uneven, and she certainly wouldn't have kissed Cam Murphy today if she'd been in love with Zach Turner.

And wasn't that kiss at the heart of the confusion plaguing her tonight? She could understand why she hadn't resisted him. Curiosity and all that. What she couldn't wrap her head around was her reaction.

With one touch of his lips against hers, the years had melted away. She'd forgotten the heartache, forgotten the struggles and resentments, forgotten the other men who'd passed through her life. Cam had come home and kissed her, and she'd forgotten everything she'd held against him for two whole challenging decades.

Well, wasn't that just peachy.

Sarah stretched out her legs, leaned back on her elbows, and raised her face toward the sky, searching for peace. Light from the almost full moon muted the stars, but the beauty of the silver sphere against the black velvet sky was a worthy trade-off. The world up here was a delight for the senses, even at night. The world was moonlight and shadows, perfumed with evergreen and serenaded by the faint rush of a waterfall and a gentle breeze whispering through the trees. Such beauty. She'd been a fool to deny herself the pleasure of this place all these years. It . . . healed . . . her.

When she heard the hum of a car engine climbing the hill, she slowly straightened. She wasn't afraid, and maybe that was stupid of her, since she was a woman alone in an isolated spot. She did take the precaution of turning around to face the road.

When the vehicle stopped, the door opened, and the dome light flickered on, she wasn't even surprised.

"Sarah, is that you?" Cam asked.

"You didn't follow me up here, did you?"

"No. I was out driving. Took this turn." He waited for a moment, then asked, "Care if I join you?"

"Be my guest." She turned back around, scooting over to one side of the picnic table as she did so. When he sat beside her, she noted that he'd changed from the jeans and T-shirt into khakis and a sport shirt. She could smell that darned Irish Spring soap again. He'd taken a shower since their trip up the mountain. Pride made her hope it had been a cold one.

"You spoke to Lori?"

Sarah took a moment to choose her words carefully. "She's going to need some time to get used to the idea of your being here."

"That good, huh?"

Her mouth twisted. "She's young."

He sighed. "That's okay. I have time."

Sarah decided it was time to change the subject. "Just how is that, Cam? How can you afford so much time away from your business?"

"Good people working for me, primarily. We've worked together for so long that everybody knows his own job and everyone else's, too. Plus, I made extensive preparations. That's why it took me more than two months to follow you here. I admit that on one hand it tweaked my ego a bit to learn how little I'm actually needed, but on the other hand, it's a blessing. I can manage most everything that needs my attention with a few hours every day online while I wait for Lori."

"What about the diving? Devin has told me that you usually join the tours a couple of times a week. Do you miss it?"

She sensed, rather than saw, his mouth twist. "Honestly, not as much as I expected."

He turned his head and looked at her. "Speaking of diving, are you going to let me teach you?"

Sarah considered it. Saying yes probably wasn't smart, but tonight, the mood she was in . . . the *place* she was in . . . old dreams and desires prodded her response. "Yes. Yes, I am."

"Good." His smile flashed in the moonlight.

They sat without speaking for a few minutes, and Sarah found the silence surprisingly comfortable. She was almost sorry when he spoke again. "Do you come here often?"

"Hardly ever."

"It's still beautiful. That was a long time ago, wasn't it? Last time we were up here together."

"More than half our lifetimes."

"Ouch. That makes me feel old."

Cam rested his elbows on his knees and leaned forward. "I went by the Bear Cave earlier."

Sarah glanced at him in surprise. He told her about the fight Devin had gotten into and how that had precipitated tonight's old-times'-sake tour. "I met a friend of yours there."

"At the Bear Cave?" she asked, shocked.

"Actually, behind the Bear Cave. Fellow knocked on my window with his flashlight. I thought he was going to arrest me at first."

"Oh. Zach."

"Yep. Zach Turner. He said the two of you dated?"

Sarah silently debated her response. Her inner hussy urged her to talk up her relationship with Zach, but she didn't want to lie to Cam. She simply said, "Yes."

He wasn't willing to leave it to simple. "Was it serious?"

"No. Unfortunately."

"Why unfortunately?"

"I think Zach and I both would have liked it to become serious, but we figured out pretty fast that we were meant to be friends, not lovers. He is a good friend." She grinned and added, "I'm surprised he didn't arrest you."

"Me, too," Cam replied. "So anyone else I should be worried about running into? Someone who you were serious about, perhaps?"

"Are you asking me about my relationships, Murphy? Again?"

"Yeah, I guess I am. I should know about the guys in your life, because that might factor into my situation with Lori." After she chastised him with a look, he added, "Okay, I'm curious."

"Me, too. You first."

He pushed off the picnic table and walked toward the knee-high stone wall that divided the overlook area from the edge of the bluff. He stood staring out into space for a long minute. "I tried to fall in love. I came close twice, but I never could take those last few steps. Could never make the leap."

"Why not?" Sarah asked.

"I think . . . I didn't realize it before . . ." He turned around. "I never got over you, Sarah."

Okay, call her foolish, but that made her feel darn good. Especially since she felt compelled to be just as honest when she replied, "I tried, too, Cam, but halfheartedly, I think. At first, I pretty much waited for you to change your mind and send for us. Then when I knew you had been released after serving your time, I waited for you to show up."

"And I didn't."

"No, you didn't." She extended her legs and circled her ankles, stretching away the kinks. "For the longest time I had this fantasy that you'd gone somewhere to make your fortune. I told myself that any day you'd come roaring back into town—probably on a motorcycle—and you'd sweep me and Lori up and cart us away to a three-bedroom, two-bath house in the suburbs somewhere."

"Excuse me. I'll just jump off the cliff now."

"It's okay, Cam. I was able to righteously nurse my grudge against you for years. I think that being able to blame you for everything from Lori's diaper rash to the termites in the attic has made it easier for me to weather some of life's more challenging times."

He folded his arms and studied her. "So I was your scapegoat?"

"And my shield. When I did start dating, I carted you along with me."

"A threesome, hmm?"

She rolled her eyes and snorted. "Actually, I tried very hard not to invite you into another man's bed. I'd say we were part of a love triangle. It took time and a patient man to overcome that."

"So this was a serious relationship? Someone other than the sheriff? Other than my cousin?"

"Yes, someone else." Part of her wondered why she shared this information with Cam. Another part of her wanted him to know that her life had not stopped when he left. Not completely, anyway. "You don't know him. He doesn't live here anymore."

"Is that why you're not together?"

"That's part of it. He worked for the National Park Service and was offered a promotion that meant a transfer. Maybe if we'd had more time together before he moved it could have worked, but my father had just died, and I couldn't leave Mom and Eternity Springs. The long-distance relationship proved too difficult to overcome."

His hands went back into his pockets. "I wish I'd come back."

Sarah shook her head. "To what? A town where you couldn't get a job? Where people were ready to lynch you because of the accident? And if we'd left town, how would we have supported ourselves? Child care was horribly expensive, even back then. And diapers?" She shuddered. "We got them wholesale through the Trading Post, and that was bad enough."

Cam folded his arms and scowled. "I'd have come home to the girl I loved and our daughter."

"Emphasis on *girl*. Let's be honest. Cam, we were kids. Chances are good that if you'd come home and married me, we'd have been divorced by now."

"We can't know that," he snapped.

"True, but I do know that I wouldn't be who I am today if I'd married you at sixteen. And guess what? I *like* me. I'm proud of my independence and what I've accomplished. I own my own business. I am a good daughter and an excellent mother. I'm a fantastic friend. And what about you? You've done well for yourself. Shoot, Cam, you are living one of our dreams."

He kicked at a stick on the ground. "But I gave up a lot for it."

"You made choices. Life is all about choices. You made choices that changed your life. So did I. My parents made a choice that changed all our lives. But once those choices have been made, they're made. We don't get to go back for a do-over. You and me and Lori cannot magically become the family we might have been. The choice you made brought Devin into your life. Would you change that?"

"No," he quickly replied. "Although there are times I'd happily sell him to the circus. He *is* a sixteen-year-old boy, after all."

Sarah grinned at that. Cam bent and scooped a handful of gravel from the ground. He drew back his arm and began to toss the pebbles one by one out into the void beyond. Sarah couldn't help recall how many times she'd watched him do this before.

He went through a whole handful of rocks before he spoke again. "When did you get to be so smart, Sarah?"

When she'd looked at the stars above Lover's Leap, she decided. When she'd let the anger at parents and the past go and invited the peace of this place to soothe her troubled soul. Instead of trying to explain, she kept it light. "I've always been smart. I just hid it well in my youth."

"You let your heart rule your head back in those days."

"My heart and my hormones."

"God bless teenage hormones." Cam glanced toward the trees where they'd once traveled hand in hand toward "their" hidden spot. "You know, I've been a lot of places in this world, but this place is still one of my favorite spots."

"It is beautiful."

"That's not it. The world has plenty of beautiful places. What made this so great is that I was happy here."

"In Eternity Springs?"

"No. Here at Lover's Leap. With you."

He sounded so sincere. Sarah's heart hitched. Was he trying to seduce her all over again? *Is that what this is about? What that kiss was about this afternoon?*

She was vulnerable to him. Well, vulnerable to the old, or make that the young Cam. "I expect everyone is a little nostalgic about their teenage days to some extent."

"I'm not talking about nostalgia. I've never been nostalgic about those days; I have nightmares about those days. I'm talking about happiness, which for me means Lover's Leap. I never bought into the whole thrill of the forbidden thing. I hated sneaking around with you. This was the only place we were honest."

He gave his head a shake, then said, "I'm sorry. I sound like a whiny kid. I don't know what's wrong with me. I'm in the weirdest mood tonight."

He's talking about his feelings and emotions. He's a guy. Of course he thinks it's weird.

"You know what I think? I think that you and I both recognize the need to put a period to that part of our lives and that's what brought us up here tonight. It's baggage for both of us, Cam. I know I've been toting it around since the day you left. I hate to use a buzzword, but I think we both need closure."

"Closure?" He stalked back and forth in front of the picnic table. "How can we close anything? We have a daughter together. I'm not going to walk away from that."

"No, of course not. But the Lori you may have a relationship with is Lori the college student. You can't go back and have a relationship with the infant Lori or the toddler Lori or the totally unpleasant middle school Lori."

He sighed and raked his fingers through his hair, but he didn't interrupt her.

Sarah continued, "We can't go back and fix the mistakes we made when we were teens or create a family from the people we used to be. You know that. I know it. I think tonight is all about finally letting go of that baggage. Finally saying goodbye to that time of our lives. That's why I'm here, and I believe that's why you made the rounds tonight."

He took a moment to think it over, then said, "I don't know, Sarah. If that's the case, then what was that kiss this afternoon about? Did that feel like a goodbye to you?"

No.

"Yes." Apparently, this was something she could lie to him about. "I think the teenaged Sarah and Cam deserved to have one last kiss."

One. Last. Kiss. The words seemed to hang there in the night air between them, and Sarah suddenly grew nervous.

She made a show of glancing at her watch, then climbed

down from the picnic table, saying, "I need to get home. My day starts very early. Good night, Cam."

He returned a subdued "Good night."

As she walked, Sarah told herself that this exchange between them had been healthy and productive. She'd almost reached her car when he said, "Sarah, wait."

His long legs ate up the distance between them, and before she quite knew what was happening, he'd taken her in his arms and captured her lips in a long and thorough kiss. When he finally released her, Sarah stood staring at him, her mouth gaped open in a somewhat dazed shock. Cam placed his index finger below her chin and closed her mouth.

"I'll give you the first kiss as a goodbye," he told her. "Consider that one my way of saying hello."

NINE

Two weeks after he returned to Eternity Springs, Cam sat alone at a window-front table in the Blue Spruce Sandwich Shop. It was lunchtime, and he was halfway through a club sandwich. Across the table from him, Devin's plate held only crumbs, and his chair sat empty. Cam's son had gulped down his burger and dashed off after receiving an invitation from two of his teammates to check out the new shipment of fishing tackle at the Eternity Springs Auto and Sports Center before baseball pregame activities began at two o'clock. The kids had a big fishing trip to the Rio Grande planned for tomorrow. Devin had settled into town like a tick, and Cam told himself he was glad about it. Honestly, he was a little concerned.

Dev loved mountain life. He showed no sign of missing home or missing the ocean or even missing the felons-in-training he hung with at home. Surely the new would wear off at some point and the boy would itch to return to the *Bliss* and the *Freedom,* though that probably wouldn't happen until after summer baseball ended. Dev had always liked playing baseball. This year, he loved playing baseball.

In order for Devin to join the team full-time, Cam had committed to staying in Eternity Springs through the end of baseball league play in mid-July. His teammates were a big part of the change in Dev's behavior. The kids' personalities clicked. The coach was a big factor, too. Dev was a little in awe of Colt Rafferty, who, in addition to instructing Dev on his batting stance, talked to his team about winning athletic scholarships to college. Cam noticed that Dev now said the word *university* without a sneer in his tone. Quite a change from a month ago.

"Speak of the devil," Cam murmured softly when Rafferty walked in front of the Blue Spruce's window. Colt spied him, then said something to his companion, Mac Timberlake, and the two men entered the sandwich shop.

"Care if we join you?" Mac asked, resting his hand on the back of the chair Dev had vacated.

"Be my guest."

Colt called out an order for a burger to the waitress behind the counter as he took the third seat. "I appreciate the help at practice, Murphy. I didn't know how badly I needed an assistant coach until you showed up."

"I've enjoyed it."

Mac requested iced tea, then turned a serious expression toward Cam. "We're glad we ran across you. We need to talk to you about Dev."

Cam's stomach sank. Mac Timberlake was a lawyer and a former federal judge. "What sort of trouble is he in now?"

"No trouble," Colt assured him. "This is good news. I hope." He glanced at Mac. "You want to explain, or shall I?"

Mac said, "I'll do the honors, since I'm the responsible party."

Responsible party? "You guys are worrying me."

Mac grinned, then said, "Ali and I have friends visiting from Denver. While the girls indulged in a spa appointment this morning, my friend Bob and I caught Colt's team practice. Devin's arm caught Bob's eye. He's a MLB scout, Cam. He said Devin shows real promise."

"As in Major League Baseball?" Cam repeated, more to buy himself time than because he didn't know what MLB stood for.

"Yep," Colt said, leaning forward, an excited gleam in his eyes. "He said Devin has all the right raw material, and that everything being equal, a full-ride Division One scholarship wasn't out of the question."

"Everything being equal?"

"There's the little detail about your living in Australia." Mac thanked the waitress who delivered his iced tea to the table. "Anyway, Bob also is excited about our pitcher."

"Mike Hamilton?" Cam asked. "The kid can throw heat."

"His slider is coming along, too. Bob has offered to hold a clinic for the kids while he's in town."

"They'll love that."

Colt nodded. "I thought it was important to give you a heads-up before he talked to the kids. Once I explained to Bob that Devin doesn't live and go to high school here . . . well, sometimes if the status quo can't change, then it's easier all around if we don't dangle impossible options in front of the kids."

"You're asking whether or not I want Bob to keep his opinions about my son's athletic ability to himself?"

"Yeah." Colt nodded. "That's pretty much it. My goal as a teacher and coach is to help kids, not complicate their lives. Not knowing what your situation is, well, something like this could be a huge complication."

Mac said, "International students can compete for college scholarships in the USA, but it's difficult enough sending your son off to college in another state. Didn't know how you'd feel about the prospect of sending him off to another continent."

Cam frowned as he devoured another bite of his sandwich and considered the question. "Well, we do have professional baseball in Australia now. I imagine if he were good enough to get a slot on an American collegiate team, he could play baseball at home."

"So you're okay with Bob being straight with him?"

"Sure. I've had little success so far getting him interested in college. Maybe baseball is the answer. Besides, when you get right down to it, it's his life to live, not mine. Although . . ." Cam slashed a grin. "I do plan on using every trick in the book to get him to complete his education."

Next the conversation turned to more general subjects. When Colt complimented the meal he and Sage had had at the Yellow Kitchen earlier that week, Mac said, "Ali is toying with the idea of going Greek with her cuisine at her restaurant."

"So that's where the talk of a cruise of the Greek islands came from," Colt said. "You guys have certainly caught the travel bug."

Mac slashed a grin. "What can I say? There's something special about vacation sex."

"There's something special about sex, period," Colt returned sagely.

"Is there?" Cam asked, his expression glum. "It's been so long that I've forgotten."

Just then Celeste Blessing opened the door and swept inside. She greeted or waved to all the customers and staff before zooming in on Cam's table. "Well, hello, you three. Care if I join you for a few moments? It'll help my reputation to be surrounded by such handsome men."

"Please," Cam said.

Celeste took the seat Colt offered her and said, "It's fortunate that I found you. I had intended to track all of you down today. I have new assignments for each of you in regards to our Redemption Plan."

As she reached into her handbag and pulled out a notebook, Cam asked, "You're actually calling it that?"

Colt shrugged. "Just go with it. She's done wonders with her Angel Plan."

"Yes, I am all about planning." Celeste flipped through her notebook. "Let's see, we can check off the interview. I got a sneak peek at it, dear, and you did an excellent job."

Cam had spoken to the reporter two days ago, and the article was scheduled to run next week. He'd talked primarily about living in Australia and the tour company, though when Devin chimed in about diving, the reporter's follow-up question managed to elicit the facts surrounding the adoption. Publicizing that private family business rubbed Cam wrong, but once Dev opened his mouth, the damage was done.

Celeste continued, "I happen to know that two of our more mature citizens commented in a positive manner after seeing you do all the toting and lifting for Sage for Vistas's sidewalk sale last week. It always reflects well upon a gentleman to assist an expectant mother."

"My man." Grinning, Colt slapped him on the back.

Mac snorted and asked Colt, "Where were you while Murphy played step-and-fetch-it for your wife?"

"I was sitting around, drinking a beer. Just doing my part for the Redemption Plan."

Cam rolled his eyes and explained to Mac, "He's doing an online safety seminar for a bunch of chemical engineers meeting in Miami, so I stepped in to help. It was no big deal."

Celeste tore off a sheet of paper and handed it to Colt, saying, "You can return the favor. Item number four."

"Yes, ma'am." Colt glanced over Celeste's notes, then arched his brows. "A double date with Cam and Sarah?"

Celeste nodded. "Yes. And you should go to the Yellow Kitchen so that Mac and Ali can join you for a time. Just because you're married doesn't mean you shouldn't take Sage on a date."

"Hey, I'm not complaining. I love Ali's cooking." He flashed Cam a smile and said, "You can pick up the check."

"Anytime at Ali's place," Cam replied, accepting his own list from Celeste. "If it were the Bristlecone Café, that would be another story. The food is half as good and twice as expensive."

"Only thing keeping it open is the tourist trade. I doubt it lasts through the winter," Mac observed.

While the residents discussed the restaurant, Cam glanced over his list. He didn't mind showing up for the stuff Celeste had planned for him. None of it was onerous, and he enjoyed spending time with Sarah. The qualities about her that had appealed to him as a teen remained part of her today. She was friendly, feisty, and fearless, with a quick wit and a practical sense. Beautiful, both inside and out.

The conversation they'd shared up at Lover's Leap had marked a change in their relationship. When they'd met again the following day during a prearranged "public" meeting at the Angel's Rest hot springs, they'd done so sans the baggage that had weighted their interchanges prior to that. They met as acquaintances, not lovers, which allowed them both to relax and get to know each other as they were today. Cam wasn't surprised to discover that he liked the grown-up Sarah. The fact that the grown-up Cam was attracted to her didn't surprise him in the least. Hadn't he been looking for a woman like Sarah almost since he left her?

No, the activities on Celeste's list didn't bother him, but the reason for them was beginning to chafe. He was just about done with this whole begging for Eternity Springs acceptance BS.

His trip down memory lane to the Bear Cave and Lover's Leap might have been the first step on the road to making peace with his past, but he still had miles to travel. The snubs and slings and arrows aimed his way pretty much bounced off his tough hide, but seeing Devin caught in the undertow was wearing on him. He got closer by the minute to telling people like Pauline Roosevelt and other friends of the Cook family to yank the sticks out of their asses and get over themselves. His concern for Lori held him back.

Dev claimed not to be bothered by what anyone thought of him, and Cam didn't doubt him. Devin didn't care about much other than baseball these days. Cam recognized the lucky break there. What would he do if Lori's best interests collided with Devin's? He didn't want to even think about that.

He set his list on the table and said, "I appreciate your efforts, all of you. Everyone has been kind to pitch in and help. But I wonder if this is really the right approach. Maybe—"

"It's the perfect approach," Celeste interrupted. "Believe me when I say so. I have excellent instincts, Cameron, and my Redemption Plan is important for the happiness of your family—your entire family. Now, I understand you're frustrated with Lori's stubbornness, but remember that patience is a virtue. Besides, never forget that you know not what the Big Guy"—she hooked a thumb toward the sky—"has planned for you."

Celeste's words floated through Cam's mind an hour later as he walked toward the baseball diamond to meet the team for their pregame warm-ups. She certainly spoke with authority. He wished he could be as certain as she—especially when it came to the top item on the to-do list she'd given him.

Celeste had instructed him to show up with Devin at the church of his choice in Eternity Springs. Cam's gaze sought and found the tall white steeple of St. Stephen's, and he sighed.

It made sense. This was a Redemption Plan, after all.

Cam didn't have a real objection to going to church. He was a religious man. A man couldn't sail the ocean or dive the deep or climb mountains like the Colorado Rockies and not believe in a higher power. He and Devin attended a nondenominational congregation at home, one Dev had chosen due to the pancake breakfasts they served every Sunday after the service.

They hadn't been to church since arriving in Eternity Springs. There was history there, though Cam doubted Celeste knew it. His mother had taken him to St. Stephen's every Sunday. His father never went, but he and his mother never missed. Cassie Murphy's faith had been a comfort to Cam, and he had continued to go to church for months after she died. That changed after a particularly bad beating from his dad when he'd finally worked up the nerve to ask for help from the pastor.

Turned out the old codger had been a drinking buddy of Brian Murphy's. He'd refused to interfere, and Cam had quit going to church. Rather loudly, as he recalled. He'd caused quite a stir with some of his pronouncements.

He suspected he'd cause quite a stir walking back into St. Stephen's after all these years next Sunday. "I hope you know what you're doing, Celeste."

He turned the corner onto Spruce Street, and as he caught a glimpse of the baseball diamond backstop half a block away, his thoughts turned to Devin and baseball.

Baseball. Well, what do you know. Cam had recognized that the kid had an arm, but he never would have guessed that his son could catch the eye of a major-league scout. The boy was a water rat, not a ballplayer. Baseball had never been a focus of his. Oh, he'd played casual games in the neighborhood when he was younger, but he didn't play for his high school team. Baseball wasn't popular at his school, or at least, not with his running buddies—those sorry little ratbags.

Cam hoped the extended time away would create an irreparable break in the relationship between Dev and his friends. That was part of the reason for the open-ended tickets for their return trip, too. He had hoped that he and Dev—and, with any luck, Lori—could spend some time traveling the USA.

Well, that hadn't exactly worked out, had it? So far their sightseeing had been confined to the bounties of nature here in Colorado, but at least the separation-from-troublemakers part of the plan appeared to be working. From what Cam had observed, Dev spent less time communicating with them via the Internet each day.

How might today's unexpected news change things? What if this trip opened new and exciting doors for the boy? Baseball. Could that be Devin's ticket to higher education? Could sports be the motivating factor that Dev needed?

And if it was and he had the opportunity to attend school over here, then what? As badly as Cam wanted his son to get an education, Mac Timberlake had a point. Was Cam ready to have Dev make his future in America?

Why not? No reason you couldn't come back to the States, too.

Cam stopped in his tracks. Where had that thought come from, and why had the voice sounded suspiciously like Celeste Blessing's?

Once he got past the shock of the idea, he considered it. *Repatriate? Well, again, why not?*

"Maybe the fact that you own a business in Australia?" he muttered to the troublemaker in his head. "A good business? One you built from the ground up?"

A business that appears to be running just fine without you. One that has lost its fun for you since the challenge of building it is gone. One that has taken a sport you loved and turned it into a job. A business you could probably sell for a pretty penny in a matter of weeks.

"Stop it," Cam fired back to the annoying voice. It was too early to think along those lines. The MLB scout could be blowing smoke. Lori hadn't so much as deigned to speak to him yet. And Sarah . . .

Sarah.

Possibilities tantalized, but Cam refused to give them further thought. It was way too soon to hike that particular mountain trail.

He made a conscious decision to change the direction of his thoughts as he headed for the bleachers. He should figure out something to do tomorrow while Dev was off fishing with his new friends. He could go fishing himself. Maybe rent a boat and go out on Hummingbird Lake. It'd be nice to be back on the water again.

It'd be even nicer to get into the water again. He'd finally had an answer from Jack to his email. Davenport did store scuba equipment at his mountain home, Eagle's Way, and Cam was welcome to use it and the pool. Tomorrow might be a good day to start those lessons he'd promised Sarah.

So much for changing the direction of his thoughts. Cam sighed aloud as he arrived at the baseball diamond and looked around for a distraction. The ball field was part of Davenport Park, a nice three-block section of land donated to the city by one of Eternity Springs's founding fathers, Lucien Davenport, a century ago. The park of Cam's youth had been spruced up with a new design courtesy of Gabe Callahan. New playground equipment saw plenty of use by both residents and tourists. The ballpark was empty—Cam was a full half-hour early for practice—and while the sound of laughter coming from the playground attracted him, he knew better than to wander over to watch the kids. Sure as shooting, someone would call the sheriff and turn him in as a perv casing the park.

He chose to wait on the bleachers. Taking a seat behind home plate, he stretched out his legs, crossed them at the ankles, then propped his elbows on the bleacher row behind him. Lifting his face toward the warm summer sunshine, he shut his eyes and made a valiant attempt to clear his mind of Sarah Reese and concentrate on the upcoming ball game. Colt had said the visiting team would be a real challenge for their kids.

"Hey, Murphy!" a familiar voice called. "If you're gonna sunbathe, take your shirt off and give the playground moms a thrill."

He grinned before he ever opened his eyes and sat up. Nic Callahan pushed a double stroller along the sidewalk. Her goofy, crooked-tailed boxer trailed alongside at the end of a dog leash modified to have two small handle loops so that both of the twins could walk the dog. They presented a postcard-worthy picture—a tall blond beauty out walking her identical twins and the family dog, framed against a background of red-and-yellow flower beds with a snowcapped mountain rising into an azure sky behind them. Cam's heart twisted at the sight. He wished he'd been around when Lori was pretty in pigtails like the Callahan girls.

Brushing the heartache aside, he called back, "I wouldn't want to start a riot."

Nic made a show of giving him a slow once-over. "You could do it."

"Careful, there, Mrs. Callahan. Your husband may get jealous."

She steered the stroller off the paved path and onto the grass, moving toward him as she said, "That's okay. You should have heard him flirting with Sarah today at

Fresh. The man has no shame when he goes begging for cookies."

"Sarah's cookies are worthy of supplication."

"I guess you would know, wouldn't you, Mr. Murphy?" Nic drawled, her tone dripping with innuendo as she sat down beside him.

He almost pretended not to follow her but decided directness was most likely better for both him and Sarah. "Not recently, no."

"Oh." Nic's face fell. "I was hoping . . ."

When her voice trailed off, he pressed, "Hoping what? I've been here two weeks. Besides, I live in Australia, Nicole."

"I know, but do you have to?"

That she would ask him that question not long after he'd asked it of himself made him itchy. He went for what he thought would be a sure distraction. "Uh, Nic? I think maybe one of your girls just ate a bug."

She spared the stroller only a quick glance, then gave an unconcerned wave. "A little extra protein won't hurt them. So talk to me. I've watched you and Sarah. You appear to be getting along very well."

He tried again. "Could I hold one of the girls?"

She looked at him and sighed. "You are pitiful, Cam Murphy. Just pitiful." Then she leaned over and gave him a kiss on the cheek. "Nevertheless, I think you're a good man. I think you deserve to be happy, and you won't find a better woman than Sarah."

Cam's suspicions roused. "Did she put you up to this?"

Nic burst out in laughter. "Heavens, no. She's in bigger denial than you are."

"She is? In what way?"

Grinning, Nic made a zipping motion over her mouth.

"Celeste, then? She strikes me as a woman with an agenda."

"Nope. I'm speaking for myself, from my heart. Now,

my group has a date with a jungle gym, so we'd best be going. Girls, say goodbye to Mr. Murphy."

Cam tickled the Callahan twins under their chins until they giggled their goodbyes. Nic stood and prepared to leave, then Cam shot to his feet. "Nic?"

"Yes?"

His emotions were a jumble. He respected Nic. He always had. To have her call him a good man, to say in so many words that he was good enough for her best friend, well, it meant a lot to him. He grabbed her hand and squeezed it. "Thanks."

She smiled like a cat with a saucer full of cream, then innocently asked, "For what?"

He laughed, then bent down and gave her a quick kiss. "You're a good friend."

"I know." She finger-waved goodbye, then said, "C'mon, girls. C'mon, Clarence. It's playtime."

Cam watched them go and again thought of Sarah and Lori. He knew in his bones that until his dying day, he would regret never having seen Sarah push their toddler-aged daughter in a stroller around Davenport Park.

That's when he heard Celeste Blessing's voice in his head, clear as a church bell. *It could still happen. It's not too late. All you have to do is make the leap. Close your eyes and jump, Cameron. You might just find a soft place to fall.*

Crack. The ball hit the bat square on the sweet spot and sailed high over the head of the center fielder and beyond the fence. Home-team fans leapt to their feet and cheered Devin as he dropped the bat and loped toward first base for the walk-off home run.

In her signature style, Sarah put her two little fingers in her mouth and whistled loud and long. On the field, the Grizzlies lined up behind home plate to greet Devin with hand slaps, Coach Murphy exchanged a handshake and grin with Coach Rafferty, and then the kids lined up to do their "good game" exchange with the opposing team's players.

Sarah watched Cam greet the opposing coaches, then turn to speak to the father of one of the Grizzlies. The father said something that made Cam laugh, then he shook Cam's hand and slapped his back. Sarah couldn't help but smile. Celeste's plan appeared to be working like a charm.

Or maybe the charm was Cam himself.

He'd certainly charmed Sarah over the past couple of weeks. How could she not develop a soft spot in her heart for a man who made a special trip to her bakery to buy sugar cookies every day? More than once she'd found herself thinking about his "hello" that night at Lover's Leap and wondering what she'd do if he returned to that particular conversation.

She suspected she might welcome him with open arms, literally.

She had loved Cam Murphy and she had hated Cam Murphy. In the past two weeks, she'd discovered that she liked Cam Murphy, too. He was interesting and witty and smart—just the sort of guy she might have set her sights on, had they not already shared a history. A part of her would have liked to forget that history completely. But then, that would require forgetting her daughter, wouldn't it?

She looked at Cam now, saw him ruffle the hair of one of the Grizzlies and grin. Why did the man have to be so darned appealing? Why was it that this man, more than any other, lit her wick?

The spectators began filing out of the bleachers and folding up their lawn chairs. Glad to have the distraction from her troublesome thoughts, Sarah turned to her mother. "Mom, you ready to head home?"

"Is that what I'm supposed to do?" Ellen Reese asked.

"I think it would be good, yes. You've probably had enough sun for today."

"All right."

Sarah waved to Sage Rafferty, who waited for her husband, and called, "So are we still on for dinner on Tuesday?"

"Sure," Sage replied. "It's girls' night out at Hummingbird Lake."

"Will you promise me that it's not another intervention-type thing? I'm really not in the mood."

Sage laughed. "That I absolutely will promise. This is a fun-only evening. No drama allowed."

"In that case, I'll be there with bells on."

Sarah gathered the lawn chairs and looped her arm through her mother's. She veered toward the dugout and called her congratulations to the team, then waited to make eye contact with Devin. "Awesome game, Devin."

"Thanks." The boy's grin stretched from ear to ear. "That's the first three-run homer I've ever hit."

"It was a thing of beauty."

She waved a goodbye toward Cam, who was on the field with Colt, talking to the other coaches. He took two steps toward her, then stopped when one of his players called out his name. Sarah's mother turned the wrong way on the sidewalk, asking, "Where's your daddy?"

As always, Sarah's heart hitched a bit when she lied, "He's at the store, Mama."

This was a result of Alzheimer's that Sarah found particularly cruel. Sometimes her mom remembered that her husband was dead. Other times, she hadn't a clue. Those times when someone informed her of her widowhood, she relived the moment of loss all over again, her grief as harsh and as fresh as it had been the moment she found her husband dying of a heart attack in their backyard.

At the advice of her mother's doctor, Sarah had recently begun lying to her mother when Ellen asked about Frank. It was kinder, true, but Sarah didn't think she'd ever get comfortable with it. Each time she offered an excuse for her father's absence, she experienced a little hitch in her heart.

Sarah had parked along the street, and upon reaching her car, she helped her mom into the passenger seat. As she stacked the lawn chairs into the trunk, she heard a woman call her name. Pauline Roosevelt hurried down her front porch steps, saying, "I've been watching for you. I need a few moments of your time."

Oh, great. What piece of gossip has her all in a dither now? "Mom is tired. I need to be getting her home."

"It'll just take a moment. It's very important."

Sarah swallowed a sigh. "What can I help you with, Pauline?"

"Oh, it's the other way around, dear. I want to help you." She clucked her tongue and added, "It's just such a delicate matter. When I saw that you had come to Davenport Park to watch the baseball game, I almost crossed to talk with you there. But, really, I thought it better to do this privately."

Oh, boy. What sort of nonsense was she going to report about Cam this time?

"I'm very concerned about our Nic."

Sarah blinked. *Okay, that one came out of left field.* "Nic Callahan?"

"Yes. I'm very worried about her, and I think that as her friend, you should step in and do something about it."

"About what?" Sarah asked, despite knowing she'd regret it.

"She's flirting with danger, that's what." Pointing toward the baseball diamond, she declared, "I saw her kissing that horrible Cam Murphy not three hours ago. And here she is, married to such a nice young man. What is wrong with her? Why, she even cheated on her husband in front of her poor, innocent children!"

"Wait one minute, Pauline."

Unfortunately, it was difficult to stop the woman once she got rolling. "It's that man. He hasn't changed. Time doesn't change the wicked. It's so wrong that he's here walking around town after what he did to poor Andrew. And now he's luring Nic into his web of wickedness. It's that bad blood of his. That bad Murphy blood. Blood will tell, you know."

"Stop it!" Sarah slammed the trunk lid hard. "That's enough, Pauline. You need to get your mind out of the gutter and keep your tongue in your mouth. Talk about wicked—I cannot believe you would be so disrespectful of Nicole."

Pauline gasped and slapped her hand against her chest. "Why, Sarah Reese! That's just mean."

"So are your insinuations."

"No insinuating about it. I saw it with my very own eyes. She kissed him, and he kissed her back."

"They're friends. I kiss Gabe Callahan all the time, and there is nothing shady about it."

"Well, that's because he's Gabe, and Gabe is a good person. Cam Murphy is another kettle of fish entirely. He's trouble, Sarah. You more than anyone should know that."

Sarah put her hands on her hips and clenched her teeth. She was so angry. If she were a cartoon she would have had steam coming from her ears and fire shooting from her eyes. That poison-tongued busybody. She'd always been a gossip queen, but had she always been this malicious?

Sarah drew in a deep, calming breath. She wouldn't say what she wanted to say. She wouldn't.

Then Pauline had to go and say one more thing. "I feel so sorry for Lori, having that man's blood running through her veins. Now I understand why you had so much trouble with her during those tween years."

A thin, shrill squeal of fury escaped Sarah's throat. *I'm going to hit her. I swear, I'm going to slap her so hard her head will spin on her shoulders.* She took two steps toward the old battle-ax and drew back her arm, her hand flexing for a slap. Whether she would have actually gone through with it was difficult to tell, because during her backswing, a hand reached out and grabbed her arm in an iron grip. "Mrs. Roosevelt," Cam said with a winter's chill in his voice. "Say what you want about me. I don't care. But I suggest you refrain from speaking of Lori. I'm not at all opposed to suing someone for slander."

Pauline sniffed. "Well, I never."

Probably not in a very long time, anyway. Sarah relaxed her arm, but Cam retained his grip. "Sarah, I think your mom is ready to head home now."

"Yes," Sarah agreed. "I'm sure she's had enough . . . sun."

Sarah turned away from Pauline Roosevelt, dismissing her without a word. The gossip queen gave another loud sniff, lifted her nose into the air, and marched back up her sidewalk toward her house. She did not, however, resist slinging one last insult from her front porch, referring to Cam's maternal grandfather when she said, "Carlton Cavanaugh must be spinning in his grave."

Her door banged shut behind her.

"Why, that battle-ax." Sarah reached for the handle on the driver's-side door. "The nerve of her. I swear, since she moved into the top gossip spot after Glenda Hawkins moved to Florida, she's become ten times worse. I think Glenda slapped her down a time or two, and that kept her in check."

"Don't let her get to you," Cam said. "That only feeds her power."

"I know. I just—" She broke off upon hearing Celeste calling her name. Turning to the sound, she saw her friend hurrying toward the car.

Celeste wore cute capri pants in a warm gold with white angel's wings embroidery around the cuffs, a matching blouse, and canvas espadrilles. Just looking at Celeste soothed Sarah's temper.

"I just heard the news about Devin's home run," Celeste said as she walked up. "Tell him I said congratulations."

"Thanks, I'll do that."

She bent down to peer inside the car and finger-waved. "Hello, Ellen."

"Hello."

Celeste reached out and patted Sarah's hand. "I'm so glad I ran into you. There is something I think Ellen needs to see at Angel's Rest. The rose garden is filled with butterflies. Since I'm on foot, why don't you let me drive, and you can walk home? Cam, you'll see her home, won't you?"

She didn't wait for an answer. As smooth as a state-fair pickpocket, she took possession of Sarah's keys, slipped by her, and slid into the driver's seat. "Ellen, shall we go look at the butterflies?"

"All right."

Celeste started the car, and Sarah took a step back. Cam's green eyes gleamed with amusement as he said, "I'll be happy to see Sarah home."

Celeste actually spun the tires as she pulled away from the curb. Sarah called out, "Fasten your seat belt!"

Cam said. "That was subtle."

"Celeste can be impossible," Sarah replied, flustered. "Cam, I've lived here all my life. I think I can find my way home by myself."

"Ah, don't spoil Celeste's fun. Besides, I wanted to talk to you about something."

"Oh?"

"I heard back from Jack Davenport. He's been out of the country and out of touch, but he has cleared us to use his swimming pool and scuba gear. How does tomorrow afternoon sound?"

Tomorrow? Sarah's pulse leapt with excitement, followed immediately by nervousness. Taking a scuba lesson meant getting in the pool. Getting in a pool meant putting on a swimsuit. Was she really ready to wear a swimsuit in front of Cam? *Oh, holy cow.* She was two sizes larger than she'd been in high school. Of course, she'd been stick-skinny in high school, but still.

Oh, stop it. I don't have anything to be ashamed about. I look darn good in a swimsuit.

Maybe if she repeated that to herself long enough, she'd come to believe it.

Bracing herself, she forged ahead. "Sure. That sounds great."

"What time should I pick you up?"

She considered her workload for tomorrow. "How about two-thirty?"

"Two-thirty sounds perfect." He gestured toward the Aspen Street intersection. "Shall we?"

As they began to walk, Sarah's thoughts returned to her exchange with Pauline Roosevelt. "I think I'm going to bake up a recipe of prune brownies especially for Pauline."

Cam's mouth twisted in a wry smile. "Some things never change."

That statement triggered a memory of Pauline at the Trading Post, accusing Cam of shoplifting. Cam had denied it, but her father had made him empty his pockets. Sarah remembered how his face had flushed red with anger and how her father had failed to apologize when those pockets proved empty. "You didn't deserve all the grief you got around this town."

He shrugged. "I deserved a lot of it. Face it, I worked hard to live up to people's expectations around here. I'm glad Lori was able to grow up free of the burden of me. You did the right thing, Sarah."

She wrinkled her nose. "I thought so at the time, but I don't any longer. Living a lie is no way to live, Cam. Neither is letting fear make your decisions for you. I'm glad the truth is out. The fallout hasn't been nearly as bad as I anticipated, and being free of the lie is exhilarating."

"Will Lori feel the same way?"

Sarah hesitated. "Maybe not at first, but I think that by the time she comes home, the worst of the gossip storm will be over. For the most part, Celeste's plan is working. People take their cues from me and from you and from the prominent citizens in town. Loud voices like Pauline's just aren't as plentiful around town anymore. Not like they used to be, anyway. The population loss the town suffered wasn't all bad."

Cam let a moment pass, then took the conversation in a new direction. "Have there been any developments where Lori's concerned? Is she any closer to talking to me?"

Sarah delayed her answer by returning the wave of Ali and Mac Timberlake, who were walking their dog. When that excuse turned the corner, she decided to keep it simple. "I'm sorry, Cam. No."

He let out sigh, then shrugged. "I have time." Then he grinned and added, "Devin's not about to leave before baseball season is over."

The most direct route from the park to Sarah's house took them along Aspen Street and past the post office, the Baptist church, and the lumberyard. They made small talk while they walked, and Sarah relaxed and enjoyed herself. If a time or two she said something that might be labeled flirtatious, well, it never hurt a girl to stay in practice.

As they approached the Taste of Texas Creamery, Cam paused. "So, as the owner of the best bakery in Colorado, would you be insulted if I asked if I could buy you an ice-cream cone?"

She considered the swimsuit question again, then thought, *What the heck.* "One dip, lemon chiffon. And sprinkles."

"Sprinkles." He repeated the request, obviously amused.

He held the door open for her, and they stepped inside and got in line. The crowd was an even split between tourists and townspeople. When one of the tourists asked a question about the local art scene, Sarah told them about Sage's gallery, Vistas. As the tourists departed the ice-cream shop, a teary-eyed elementary school girl slumped in.

"Penny, are you all right?"

She looked up at Sarah, her little bottom lip trembling. "I'm supposed to buy an ice-cream cone."

"Has something bad happened?"

She nodded. "Mortimer got out again this morning."

"Oh, dear."

"He ate the water hose at the Franklins' house and a bicycle tire at the rental shop, and he got into the trash behind Miss Ali's restaurant."

Sarah repeated, "Oh, dear."

"Who is Mortimer?" Cam asked.

Sarah lowered her voice so little Penny couldn't hear her. "He's a one-eyed Boston terrorist."

Cam's quizzical expression faded when he got it. "A dog?"

"Or the devil. I'm not sure I'd bet against that being the case. He's at least possessed."

Penny continued, "Then Mr. Roberts came to our house at lunchtime and said that Mortimer bit Jeremy. My daddy said enough is enough. Once Mortimer comes home or somebody catches him, Daddy is going to take him to Dr. Nic's to be put to sleep."

"That's very sad, honey," Sarah told her.

"I don't think it was Mortimer's fault. You know that Jeremy Roberts had to be teasing him. That's what Jeremy Roberts does."

Sarah couldn't deny that charge. Jeremy Roberts was a menace himself.

Someone else in line said, "Putting that dog down is long overdue, if you ask me. It is a public menace."

Sarah frowned at the insensitivity of the comment, but unfortunately, other local people in line felt like they had to chime in, too. "I'm their neighbor," grumbled Mayor Hank Townsend. "Can't say I agree with putting him down for no good reason, but the dog is a problem. He sounds like a mortally wounded pterodactyl when they put him outside."

Alton Davis nodded. "He digs out every other day. Eats everything in sight even while he's leaving what he ate the day before in nasty piles all over town."

"He bares his teeth if you go near him," Hank added. "I always knew he'd bite someone someday."

"He's a terrible dog."

"He's creepy-looking, too. That milky blind eye of his scares the kids."

"But I love him!" Penny declared. "I don't want him to die!"

From behind the counter, Jared Kelley spoke up. "Here, Penny. Let me get you your ice cream. Today's not a good day for you to be standing in line. You like strawberry, right?"

"Yes, sir."

"Cone or cup today?"

Tears swelled in her eyes. "Thank you, Mr. Kelley, but

I don't think I want ice cream after all. I'm just too sad for ice cream."

Cam jerked his gaze around to meet Sarah's. He was obviously appalled. "Isn't putting the dog down rather drastic?"

"No," grumpy old Dale Parker declared.

"I don't have a better solution to offer," Hank added.

"Maybe Penny's father here could reinforce the fence," Cam suggested.

"Dog is a digger," Hank said, shaking his head. "You'd have to pour cement six feet deep to keep that dog in the yard."

"He's a terrible dog," Dale Parker groused. "Harry Leland owned the sire, and that dog was no better. Harry should have neutered that dog rather than bred him. It's bad bloodlines."

Beside her, Cam went stiff. Inwardly, Sarah groaned. *Not this again.* She opened her mouth to comment, but Cam spoke first.

He shot his words like bullets. "I'll take him."

For a long few seconds, the ice-cream shop went dead quiet. The sound of Jared Kelley's ice-cream scoop hitting the floor happened at the same time three Eternity Springs residents let out groans and Penny gasped. "Really, mister?"

Sarah put a cautioning hand on Cam's arm. "Cam . . ."

He hunkered down to eye level with Penny and promised, "Really."

"Oh, for crying out loud," Alton Davis whined.

Penny launched herself at Cam, throwing her arms around his neck in a fierce hug. "Thank you, mister. Thank you so much."

Dale Parker gave a disgusted sigh. "Why would you want to go and do a fool thing like that? That dog is trouble with a capital *T*."

Cam stood and stared around the ice-cream shop,

meeting the gazes of each of the complainants. "I believe in second chances, and I do not believe that any creature is born with bad blood."

With that, the last of the ice that had encased Sarah's heart for more than two decades melted, and a breath of new hope stirred embers of a love that had never completely died.

TEN

“S’truth, Dad. That’s the ugliest dog I’ve ever seen. What are you doing with him?”

Cam held Mortimer secured in his arms. Black with white markings, the dog had an undershot bite that made his muzzle look square, small cropped ears, and a short, compact body. One of his eyes appeared to be damaged, covered with a milky film, and most likely blind. The dog rested quietly and peacefully, but that was all a sham.

Cam narrowed his eyes at his son and glared. “Don’t even start. I need you to go over to the Callahans’. Take the car. Nic has a stack of supplies for you to pick up.”

Dev said a cautious, “O-kay.”

“Don’t speed, but hurry. The keys are by the door.”

“Yes, sir.”

Cam glanced at the wall clock and marked the time. Probably take the kid fifteen minutes. He could manage fifteen more minutes. Shoot, the beast was behaving just fine now. Maybe he’d gotten the destruction all out of his system.

Cam’s legs were tired. He wanted to sit down. Maybe he could try. He took a careful step toward the recliner, then two. Holding his breath, he lowered himself into the chair.

The minute his butt hit the imitation leather, the dog let out the squeal. It was a shrill, thin-throated sound that could peel paint off the walls. Cam had laughed earlier when that guy used the description of mortally wounded pterodactyl, but he didn't consider it funny any longer. He shot back to his feet and resumed walking the dog like a colicky baby. Anything to get it to shut up.

I should have asked Nic for a sedative when I called her. If she wouldn't prescribe one for the dog, maybe he could have talked her into giving him something for himself.

The rest of the evening passed in a blur. The dog simply never stopped. If he wasn't screaming, he was licking something. If he wasn't licking something, he was eating something. Anything. Everything. By ten o'clock, Cam found himself fantasizing about getting in the car, taking him up into the national forest, and tying him to a tree with a pork chop tied around his neck.

Only he wouldn't bet on a bear to win. He seriously could see this ten-pound concentration of wicked coming out on top of that struggle.

At one o'clock, Dev stumbled out of his room and knocked on Cam's door. "You gotta do something, Dad. Anything. Please. I'm meeting the guys at five o'clock. I have to get some sleep!"

The dog was in a crate in the mudroom. The mudroom door was shut, the bedroom doors had been shut, and the sound still pierced the walls like a buzz saw. Cam groaned and pulled his pillow over his head.

"Dad!" Dev repeated.

"Oh, all right." Cam threw off the pillow and rolled from his bed. As Devin retreated to his bedroom, Cam stalked toward the mudroom and the cacophony of ear-blasting noise. He glared down at the dog. "You are evil incarnate."

Arf, arf, arf, arf, arf.

Cam opened the crate, and the dog burst out like a

bullet. He ran through the house, straight for Cam's room. He leapt up onto the bed, curled up on Cam's pillow, and immediately went to sleep.

Cam studied the scene in shocked consternation. *Now what?* Every dog trainer in the world would undoubtedly tell him the proper thing to do would be to use this as a teachable moment.

Yeah, well, in a match between a dog trainer and Mortimer, he'd take the Boston terrorist every time. He could make even that dog-whisperer dude turn in his leash.

Cam braced as the dog's leg lifted and began to scratch behind his ear. *Fleas? Sure. Of course. Why not? Okay, then.* First thing tomorrow, come hell or high water, the dog was getting a bath. In the meantime . . . Cam grabbed the other bed pillow, yanked the top sheet free of the mattress, and carried them into the living area. The couch was a full foot shorter than he, but he didn't care. It was quiet. Blessedly, peacefully quiet.

He fell onto the couch and into sleep. He woke up briefly when Devin tiptoed through the room carrying his tackle box and fishing pole, before drifting right back to sleep. The peace lasted until seven, when he awoke to the sound of retching.

The devil dog had eaten half of one leg of the khaki trousers he'd left draped over the back of the chair in his bedroom.

By the time he left the house to pick Sarah up for their visit to Eagle's Way, he was exhausted. Scratched. Bitten. But the terrorist was in his crate in an empty house where he could dying-bird screech to his heart's content. Cam had half a mind to rent a room at the Creekside Cabins in order to sleep tonight.

He knocked on Sarah's front door, and when she answered, all thoughts of the one-eyed beast faded away. She looked gorgeous, her eyes bright with excitement, her lips glossy pink and smiling, wearing a swimsuit cover-up that was modest but oh, so appealing. She wore silly little flip-flops with sunflowers on them, and hot-pink polish on her toes. "You look great."

"Thank you, sir. I'm excited. I didn't realize just how jealous I was that Lori can dive and I can't until I woke up this morning." She gave him a once-over, then said, "You, on the other hand, look . . . tired."

"My ego would be crushed, except Beelzebub ate it, like he's eaten everything else."

She fought a smile. The light in her eyes said *I told you so*. "Bad night?"

"I don't want to talk about it. I'll start to cry."

At that, she laughed, and Cam's spirits began to lift.

The drive up to Eagle's Way showed nature in all her glory, from snowcapped mountains to wildflower-filled meadows to bubbling creeks and soaring hawks on a gentle wind. Nevertheless, Cam had a difficult time keeping his eyes on the winding road. Mother Nature didn't hold a candle to his daughter's mother sitting beside him.

He couldn't quite put his finger on it, but something was different about Sarah today. She seemed more open. Less worried. More approachable. Sexy, too, but that wasn't new. She was always sexy.

"Is Jack in town?" she asked. "Will he be here this afternoon?"

"No." Which was perfectly fine with him. He still chafed over the idea of the dates between his cousin and Sarah. "We have the place to ourselves."

"Oh. Darn it, I was hoping to go inside. He invited me up once in April, but I couldn't make it. Nic says it's gorgeous. She came up here to see Gabe a time or two. He lived at Eagle's Way when he first came to Eternity Springs."

"We're welcome to use the house," Cam explained. "Jack told me where to find the keys."

"Now I'm beyond thrilled."

Sarah fished in her tote bag and pulled out a pack of Life Savers. She tore back the paper and offered it to him. "Want one?"

"You and your Life Savers. It's nice to know that some things never change." He glanced down at the end of the roll. "Green, hmm? Whatcha got beneath it, Sugar Cookie?"

The old line came out of nowhere, and they both froze. Cam was catapulted back into the past.

They sat facing each other atop a patchwork quilt spread across spring-green grass at the edge of a stand of aspen. A picnic basket weighted one corner of the quilt, its lid flipped up, its contents consumed. The cellophane wrapper containing one last sugar cookie lay forgotten as Sarah giggled and fished for the cookie she'd just accidentally dropped down her shirt because Cam had startled her when he spied a bald eagle in the sky.

Cam forgot all about the eagle as one kind of excitement morphed into another when his gaze followed her fingers and locked on her chest. "Whatcha got under there, Sugar Cookie?" he drawled. "Gonna let me see?"

Sarah went still. Cam heard the wind whispering through the aspens as he waited for her to say something, do something. She moistened her lips with her tongue, and Cam held his breath. Then her fingers went to the top button on her blouse, and Cam's heart pounded. His mouth went dry. His dick stayed hard.

He'd touched her before, but she had never let him see her.

Today, she did.

Years later, with a little bit of rasp to her voice that suggested she might have remembered, too, she said, "Yellow."

Cam cleared his throat. "Green is fine. My mouth is dry."

He popped the candy in his mouth and sucked on it for a moment while he gathered his thoughts. He needed a distraction. "We should go over a few things before you even think about getting into the water, Sarah. Did you check out that website I told you about last night?"

"I did. There's a lot of information there."

"If you decide you want to get certified, you'll need to know it. For today, I want to make sure you know the most important hand signs."

After they went over the signals, he shared some of his favorite tourist stories until they arrived at the gate to Eagle's Way. He thumbed down the driver's-side window and punched in the security code. When the gate swung open, Cam drove onto the estate, then watched the rearview mirror to make sure the gate shut behind them. "Jack has given us free rein with the place. He's just asked that we be sure we lock up and the security system's on when we leave."

"Has he had trouble with break-ins?" Sarah asked, sounding surprised.

"He didn't say that." Cam took a minute and chose his words carefully. He wasn't exactly sure what Jack Davenport did for a living, but he knew it had something to do with the government. Jack didn't talk about it. "Jack is careful of his privacy up here."

"He's careful of it everywhere. Before Gabe came to Eternity Springs, we rarely saw him around town. You wouldn't know he was here unless you saw his helicopter fly over. That hasn't much changed, to be honest."

The house came into view, and Sarah breathed out a near-silent "Wow."

A green metal roof topped the log house that nestled against the base of a hill. Its wall of windows overlooked an alpine meadow blanketed with wildflowers in brilliant hues of yellows and oranges and blues. The swimming pool and a pool house stood off to one side.

"Oh, man. Look at that pool. It's like what you'd see at a resort. Gabe designed it, so I knew it would be awesome, but wow."

"It is impressive. Bet the view from the house is spectacular." Cam slowed the car as the lane before them forked. "Shall we go straight to the pool and tour the house after your lesson? Or would you rather see the house first?"

"Whichever you prefer. You're the teacher."

Sarah's cellphone rang as Cam pulled into a parking spot next to the pool house. She checked the number and said, "It's Lori. I could wait . . ."

"No, go ahead and answer it," he replied. "Take your time. We're in no rush, and it'll take me a few minutes to check the equipment, anyway."

"Okay." Sarah connected the call and said, "Hello?"

Cam shut the car door quietly and headed for the pool house. Another time he might have hung around to eavesdrop on the conversation, but he needed a little space from Sarah right now.

He found the keys where Jack's email had indicated they would be. He unlocked first the pool house and then the walk-in equipment closet. Flipping on a light, he whistled soft and low and murmured, "He could outfit a team of Navy SEALs with what's in here."

He chose items for himself first—a shorty skin suit, mask, snorkel, fins, weight belt, and a BC—a buoyancy compensator device. Next, he went back through the gear, looking for suitable sizes for Sarah and discovered a slight problem—no ladies' sizes, no youth sizes. The men's gear would swallow her. He thought for a moment, then murmured, "Okay, change of plans."

He traded the shorty for a rash-guard top; grabbed a snorkel, mask, fins, and a weight belt for her; then exited the closet and carried the gear to poolside. A glance toward the car showed that Sarah was still on the phone, so he returned to the gear closet for a tank.

Always safety-conscious, he carefully inspected each item he intended to use, judged them good to go, then pulled off his T-shirt and shucked down his pants to his Jammers, the Lycra shorts he'd tossed into his suitcase before leaving Australia.

The hair on the back of his neck rose, and he turned to see Sarah watching him, her gaze warm and admiring. He'd seen that same look from other women many times aboard his boats as he readied to dive. He'd never wanted to preen in response—before today.

You're pathetic, Murphy. He pulled on the rash-guard top and said, "I ran into a minor hiccup, and we're going to do this a little differently than I'd planned. Jack doesn't have any suits small enough for you, so this won't be a typical first lesson."

"No wet suit?" Sarah clarified. "I'll freeze."

"The pool is heated. You'll be fine."

Her brow dipped in a doubtful frown. "So what do I do? Strap the stuff right against my back?"

"No. For today, we will give buddy breathing a try."

"Buddy breathing is what?"

"We'll share the regulator."

"Like in the movies when the bad guy slices the hero's air hose, but the heroine defeats the villain and saves the hero by sharing her air hose with him?"

Cam grinned. "Her regulator. And what movie was it where the heroine saved the hero?"

She waved off his question. "I want to point out that agreeing to this is an act of trust."

"You think I'd want to drown you?"

She ignored that question, too. "Okay, professor. What do I do first?"

"We're going to start in the shallow end and work our way toward deeper water. You ready to get wet?"

She hesitated, cut a suspicious look his way, then blew out a long sigh. "Yes."

Cam told himself not to stare as she began to unbutton her cover-up and revealed a modestly cut fire-engine-red one-piece swimsuit. *Whatcha got under there, Sugar Cookie?*

"All you need to do is to remember to breathe," he said.

"Pardon me?"

Cam gave his head a shake and covered, "Scuba diving isn't difficult to learn. The main thing is to remember to breathe."

She kicked off one flip-flop and then the other. Cam handed her a mask and fins. "These were the smallest I could find. See if you can keep them on."

The mask worked all right, but she couldn't keep the fins on her feet. "That's okay. You don't need them today. We'll get you gear that fits before our next lesson. Why don't you go ahead and get into the pool while I finish suiting up?"

Sarah's eyes gleamed with excitement, but years of experience helped Cam to identify the nervousness, too. He attempted to reassure her. "You're going to enjoy this, Sarah. You've always had an adventurous soul."

"Oh, I know I'll enjoy the scuba part of it. It's the cold-water part I'm not so certain about."

She turned and walked away from him as she carried her cover-up to drape it across the back of one of the deck chairs. Cam's gaze dropped to her ass, and he sucked in air across his teeth. She had some curve back there she didn't used to have. It looked fine on her. Really fine.

He was beginning to think that giving her a scuba lesson had been a very bad idea.

He wanted her. Not the high school Sarah, whom he had kissed when he first came to town, but the grown-up Sarah with the delicious full curves of womanhood and the hint of laugh lines at the corners of her glorious violet eyes. He wanted to see her naked again, to trail his fingers across her silken skin, to taste her and take her in ways they'd never gotten around to trying.

Cam wanted sex with her, but just as much, he wanted to sleep with her, to spoon against her in a bed atop a thick, comfortable mattress. To stay with her all night long. That was something else they'd never done.

She turned toward the pool, and he drank in the vision of her silhouette. Okay, maybe he wanted sex more than he wanted sleep. They could have sex before sleep. *Yeah.*

You're losing it, Murphy. He forced himself to turn his attention to his gear. Moments later, he slipped into the pool. The water temperature was perfect, cool and refreshing. He tried not to gawk at the pointed tips of her water-chilled breasts clearly visible beneath the surface. "All right, let's get started. Show me the underwater sign that you're okay."

She did, and he nodded. "Now show me stop."

Once he'd run through what he wanted her to know for today, he asked, "Okay, then. Let's run down the cautions."

Sarah ticked them off on her fingers, beginning with "Never, ever, ever hold my breath" and ending with "If I do panic, and I'm swimming for the surface, I have to let air out of my lungs as I go up." She frowned and asked, "Even when I'm just diving in the swimming pool?"

"Even then." He stood in front of Sarah and removed the weight belt he'd slung over his shoulder. Cinching it up as small as he could make it, he said, "Let's see if this is small enough so that it won't fall off."

She stood in water that was shoulder-high to her. Standing close, he reached around behind her with both arms, clasped the belt, and fitted it against her back. She lifted her arms as he fastened the plastic clasp. The weight belt slipped from her waist, then settled low on her hips.

He had to put his hands on her then, testing to make certain the belt wouldn't slip off. Maybe they lingered, maybe they copped a caress, but she didn't call him on it.

As Cam's stare lingered on her chest, he tried to remember what he was supposed to do next. Finally, Sarah lowered her arms. "I think that's good."

"Really good," he murmured. His lifted his gaze to her mouth. It would be so easy to lean down and kiss her.

Sarah picked that moment to hold up her mask and ask, "So do I spit in this?"

The question broke the spell. "No. I've rubbed baby shampoo over the lens. It's a great defogger, and cheap, too."

"Tricks of the trade? Cool." She pulled on the mask, then said, "Now what?"

"We're going under. You are going to signal to your buddy that you are out of air and want to buddy-breathe. Then, when I'm ready, I'll hand you the regulator. I won't let go of it. I'm in control of it at all times."

"Why?"

"It's a safety precaution. Now, you'll put the mouthpiece inside your mouth and exhale to clear it. You're going to do that every time."

"Exhale first," she repeated.

"Yes. You'll take two or three normal breaths, then you'll push the regulator out of your mouth. I'll take it away and breathe for a few breaths, then we'll do it all over again. The idea is to establish a rhythm. Any questions?"

"Yes. Lori showed me her equipment, and the octopus thingy had a second mouthpiece. Why wouldn't I use that?"

"Because that's not today's lesson. Ready?" When

she nodded, he put his mouthpiece into his mouth, then took her hand, lifted his feet, and sank to his knees at the bottom of the pool. Sarah knelt beside him. Behind her mask, Sarah's eyes glowed with nervous excitement, and Cam was reminded of how they had haunted him through the years. And throughout nature. Violet coral, fields of lavender, dusky sunsets on a becalmed sea—he had gazed upon them and thought of the girl he had left behind.

She gave him the signal, and he offered her the regulator, watching closely as she remembered to exhale before breathing in. *Good girl.*

Her eyes smiled back at him. Cam thought the sight before him rivaled any beauty he'd ever seen on any dive he'd made anywhere in the world.

Sarah proved to be an apt student, and they quickly found the rhythm he wanted. He had participated in this process countless times over the years, but never before had it seemed so intimate. They stared into each other's eyes, the same way they had when making love, and time hung suspended.

Cam's blood ran hot. He had to taste her. He had to touch her. He'd waited forever, and he could wait no more.

He made the signal to surface and began to unbuckle his gear before his feet found the bottom of the pool.

He allowed the gear to sink as he tore off his diving mask, toed off his fins, and grasped Sarah around the waist as she surfaced and pushed up her mask. "Did I do something wrong?"

"You let me leave you!"

Then he pulled her against him and kissed her.

And kissed her.

And kissed her.

At some point he realized she'd begun kissing him back.

She clasped her arms around his neck and wrapped her legs around his waist. She held on tight as he twirled her around in waist-deep water.

Cam groaned against her lips. She moaned against his. His hands drifted down from her waist to intimately cup her ass and pull her tighter against him. He wanted more. He wanted her naked and beneath him and screaming his name like she had the last time they'd made love.

The time they'd made Lori.

Lori. Cam wrenched his mouth away from Sarah's. "What are we doing?"

"It's been so long I almost forgot," she murmured against his shoulder.

Cam released his hold on her, and Sarah dropped her arms and let her legs drop away from his hips. "Sarah . . . I . . . uh . . ."

"Don't you dare apologize."

He blinked. His pulse raced, his heart pounded. "I wasn't going to apologize."

"Oh. Okay. Well, good." She finger-combed her hair and added, "So what were you going to say?"

He hadn't a clue. Maybe he *had* been about to apologize. Maybe he'd have told her that having a hard-on while wearing Jammers bordered on physical torture. Maybe, just maybe, he'd been working up the nerve to ask if he could take her to bed. When he opened his mouth, he was shocked to hear himself say, "A part of me never stopped loving you, Sarah."

Her response shocked him even more. "I tried to stop loving you, Cam, but I never completely succeeded."

Now he knew what he wanted to say, to ask, to do. Why had he ever been confused about it? Hadn't he dreamed about it for half of his life? He took a step toward her and gently caught her hand in his. "Would you like to go inside with me?"

She licked her lips. "Define *inside.*"

The warm light in her eyes told him she knew very well what he meant. He tugged her hand, bringing her a step closer. "I want to make love with you again, Sarah."

She blew out a shaky little breath. "It is entirely possible that taking that road would lead to more heartache."

He couldn't deny that. He wouldn't try. "I'm willing to take that risk."

"Of course you are. You're a guy." She rubbed her thumb across his knuckle. "I gave up risk-taking years ago. Teenage pregnancy pretty much took care of that. I've spent my time being a worrier. I worried about what people think of me—my parents, my friends, the whole town, even Lori. I think . . ."

Her voice trailed off, and Cam waited for a moment before urging, "You think what, sweetheart?"

"I think that it's silly to worry about the past because I can't change it, and as far as the future goes, why waste the effort fretting over what-ifs? I'll deal with it when it gets here."

She drew in a long breath, then released it slowly. "I think that right now, for this stretch of time that lasts however long it's going to last, I'll try not to care what people think. That's no great sin, is it?"

"No, it's not," he responded. "You deserve to put yourself first for a change, Sarah. You should do what you want to do because you want to do it. It's time that you put your needs before everyone else's."

"Even yours?"

"Why do I think I'm arguing against my own self-interests?" Cam smiled crookedly, then nodded. "Yes, even mine."

She looked down at their clasped hands, and Cam held his breath. When she finally looked up at him again, her eyes were violet pools of emotion. "Take me inside, Cam. Take me to bed."

Thank God. Cam didn't give her a chance to change her mind. He swept her into his arms and carried her toward the house.

The doubts assailed her when he set her down to unlock the door to Eagle's Way. What was she doing? This was Cam Murphy, the number-one target of her fury and frustration since she was in high school.

He's the only man you've ever truly loved.

His hand at her waist, he ushered her inside. Sarah's nerves sizzled. She only vaguely noted the interior of the house that she'd been dying to see, because she couldn't look away from his mesmerizing green-eyed gaze. He shut the door behind them, cupped the back of her head, and pulled her close.

His mouth brushed across hers, a whisper of a touch. His hand drifted down to her neck, where his fingers gently stroked her sensitive skin. Sarah shivered and melted against him.

This wasn't the ogre she'd resented for so long. This was Cam. Her Cam. *I've missed him so much.*

His gentleness seduced her. His touch so soft, his caress so sweet. He held her as if she were the most delicate of treasures, as if she were something to savor, and Sarah's heartstrings quivered in response.

"I've dreamed of having you in my arms again for so long," he murmured.

I've waited for you since the day you left. The truth of that thought hit her like a brick. Startled, she retreated by saying, "We're dripping on Jack's floor."

That reminded her of something else, and she jerked her head up in alarm. "This is Jack Davenport's floor. His entry hall floor!"

Cam's lips twitched. "He wouldn't care about a little water."

"I'm not worried about water. I don't want twins!"

"Excuse me?"

"This is where Gabe got Nic pregnant with the girls." Sarah backed away from him and held up her hand, palm out. "I mean it, Murphy. We've been down this road before. I don't know about you, but I learned my lesson. Unless you're packing protection under that skin-tight suit you're wearing, this conversation is over."

"Oh."

"Yeah, oh." She folded her arms. Her pulse raced.

He frowned. "I wasn't planning on . . ."

"Yeah, well, neither was I."

"Okay, well, this might not be a problem at all. Jack probably keeps his cabinets stocked with all the necessities. Wait here, I'll go look."

"Hold on, Murphy." She held up both of her hands, palms out. "This has totally spoiled the mood, don't you think?"

"That's okay. We can get it back." He sounded a little desperate. "Why don't you look around the place while I do a recon mission?"

Sarah glanced around the spectacular living space, then slowly shook her head. This wasn't what she wanted. Where was the romance? The passion? Just because she intended to be a responsible grown-up when it came to sex with Cam this time around didn't mean she should settle for less. She *wanted* romance. She *wanted* to be swept off her feet. "No."

"No?" he repeated, a hint of a whine in his voice.

"No." Her chin came up. She squared her shoulders. "I am worth more than a borrowed rubber in a millionaire's guest bedroom. I deserve better than that."

Cam drew back and studied her. She couldn't read him

well enough to know what he was thinking, and his intense regard made her just the slightest bit nervous and on edge.

Then he nodded and said, "You're right. I apologize, Sarah."

Okay. Well, good. He'd listened to her.

"You deserve to be wooed. You deserve flowers and candy and candlelight over a five-star meal. You deserve sweet words and sunsets and little surprises that make you smile."

"Thank you," she replied, telling herself it wasn't disappointment making her heart sink.

"I'll go out to the pool and get your tote bag and my stuff. We can get dry and change clothes. Do you want to shower off the chlorine first?"

"Yes." This was the only swimsuit she owned, and she tried to take care of it. "The pool house has showers. I can go—"

"No, I still want to take a tour of the house. If I recall correctly, Eagle's Way has five bedrooms with connecting full baths. Why don't you pick one out? I'll drop off your bag there."

He turned and quit the house before she could do much more than stammer an okay.

Sighing, Sarah turned her attention to the house. It was chock-full of awesomeness, but the idea of exploring it had lost its luster. Instead of heading toward the kitchen—always her favorite part of a house—she took the stairs up to the second floor and peeked into the first bedroom she encountered. Queen-size bed, overstuffed reading chair and floor lamp, basket of essentials on a chest of drawers—definitely a guest room, she decided.

She crossed to the connecting bathroom and saw a whirlpool tub and separate shower and another basketful of soaps, shampoos, and lotions. Big, fluffy white towels hung on racks across from the shower, and a thick terry-cloth robe hung on a padded hanger from a hook on the back of the bathroom door.

Sarah glanced at her reflection in the mirror and frowned at the disgruntled look she wore. *Don't be grumpy. He did what you wanted him to do.*

She heard a sound in the bedroom and turned. Cam set her tote bag on the bed. "Here's your stuff, Sarah. See you in a few."

"Thanks."

He shut the door behind himself when he left. Sarah took her bag into the bathroom and switched on the hot water, stripped off her swimsuit, and rinsed it in cold water in the sink before choosing a lavender-scented soap, shampoo, and conditioner, and stepping into the shower.

She didn't hurry. The hot water felt good, and the scent of the soaps indulged her senses. She consciously turned her thoughts away from Cam and onto the experience of breathing underwater. That had been pretty darn cool. She'd battled a little apprehension when she'd felt that tightening in her chest that signaled she'd needed air and Cam had offered her the regulator. Taking that first breath of air had been scary, then amazing once she fully comprehended that she didn't have to go up in order to breathe. Now that she had a general sense of what scuba diving would be like, she absolutely wanted to get certified.

She turned around and lifted her face, placing her head beneath the shower spray to rinse the conditioner from her hair. With her eyes closed, she sensed the change. Something was different.

She opened her eyes and spied Cam Murphy standing in the doorway.

He was naked, tanned and taut and gloriously aroused.

He watched her with narrowed green eyes that gleamed like those of a cat who stalked his prey in the forest.

Sarah's mouth went dry. Her heart began to hammer. He took two steps toward her and pulled open the shower door.

"You do deserve romance, Sarah," he said, his voice a low, pantherlike purr as he resumed their earlier conversation. "You deserve flowers and candy and candlelight and those other things I mentioned, and I'll give them to you. I promise. However, there is another item on the list that I didn't mention, but I know you desire."

"There is?" she squeaked.

"Yes, there is." His mouth spread in a slow, sensuous smile, and his voice dropped low. "At heart you haven't changed, Sarah Reese. You still want excitement and adventure, and you want it even more than a dozen red roses and a gift of something sparkly."

He stepped into the shower and set a stack of foil-wrapped condoms on the soap ledge. "I think we'll save the flowers for another time and tackle the adventure now. Okay?"

He waited, giving her the chance to say no, the challenge in his eyes demanding she not.

She cleared her throat and squeaked out, "Adventure?"

"Diving a sunken Spanish galleon. Free-falling from a plane. Surfing Oahu's north shore. Making love with me here, now."

Her pulse leapt. "That's pretty egotistical of you, Murphy."

He shrugged. "Try me."

Her heart pounded as he placed his hands against the shower wall on either side of her, leaned forward, and said, "Let me have you, Sarah. I have fantasies. Such fantasies."

"Adventures."

"Oh, yeah."

"Show me."

He leaned forward and licked water off her neck. "I thought you'd never ask."

ELEVEN

Sarah had a bounce in her step and a smile on her face as she walked from her car to Sage Rafferty's front door for girls' night out at Hummingbird Lake. She was gratifyingly tired, deliciously sore, and thoroughly satisfied. She'd had more sex in the past forty-eight hours than she'd had in the past decade. Hot, sweaty, earthy sex. Adult sex, not the angsty, emotional lovemaking of star-crossed teenagers. It was wonderful. He'd been wonderful, delivering the adventure he'd promised while keeping it light and fun between them, just the way she needed it. Risky, perhaps, to indulge this way, since she knew her heart was vulnerable to the man, but she was determined to stick with her decision to live in the moment when it came to Cam.

Sage answered her knock, then squealed when she spied the stack of sweets Sarah had brought as her contribution to the evening's munch-fest. "Tell me you brought brownies."

"I brought brownies, shortbread cookies, lemon bars, and chocolate-chip cookies."

Sage beamed and stole the top tin off Sarah's stack. Peeking inside, she said, "It's times like this I'm glad I'm wearing elastic-waist maternity pants."

"And how is little Parsley Lamb?" Sarah asked, using the silly pet name she'd adopted for Sage and Colt's unborn son.

Sage patted her tummy. "I'm beginning to think Colton Alexander is destined to be a soccer player. The kid can kick."

Sarah remembered how it had been, recalled the first time she'd felt Lori kick. She'd been so excited and at the same time so afraid. Missing Cam. Wishing he was there to share the moment with her. Remembered loss stabbed through her. *Don't. Don't go there. Live for the moment, Reese.* She smiled at Sage and said, "I can't wait to hold him."

"Me, either. Now come into the kitchen and unload, then we'll join the others outside."

"Who beat me here?"

"Nic, Ali, and my sister are out back. Celeste had a motorcycle club meeting in Creede, so she won't be here until later. It's such a pretty evening that we thought we'd sit outside and watch the sunset."

"Sounds like a plan. I think . . . oh, for crying out loud, Sage. Your poor dog. What is she wearing today?" Sarah clicked her tongue in disgust as she knelt to pet Sage's Bichon Frise, Snowdrop, who toddled into the room followed by Colt's Lab, Shadow.

"It's her new bathing suit. Every girl should have a yellow polka-dot bikini."

"I'm so sorry, Snowdrop. This constant humiliation is obviously your cross to bear." Sarah gave the bigger dog some attention, too, then asked, "What is Colt doing tonight?"

"He's actually on his way to Denver to catch an early-morning flight to Saint Louis. He has a safety presentation at a conference there tomorrow afternoon."

"That's the first consulting-related trip he's taken in a while, isn't it?"

"Yes. The man has become such a homebody. It's the last one he's making until after the baby is born, too."

"She says smugly," Sarah drawled.

Sage laughed and set about adding a selection of Sarah's sweets to a tray with veggies and dips, which she then carried to the back door. "Grab the paper plates and napkins for me, would you, please?"

The dogs preceded the women outdoors, where Ali, Nic, and Sage's sister, Rose Anderson, sat looking at the latest portraits of Nic's twins. Sarah said hello, then wiggled her fingers toward the photos. "Ooh, let me see. Let me see."

"Since these are gifts for their granddad's birthday, we dressed them in cowgirl outfits and . . ." Nic's voice trailed off after she looked up at Sarah. "Okay, what's going on?"

"Excuse me?"

"You. I know you, Sarah Reese. Let the rest of the class in on the secret."

While Sarah thought about her response, Nic continued to study her. Abruptly, she shut the photo album and set it aside. She stared at Sarah, and her mouth dropped open. "You got laid."

The other women went silent. They looked at Sarah, their expressions eager and curious.

Sarah blinked. "Now, why in the world would you say that?"

"Because I've known you forever," Nic said. "It's true, isn't it? You slept with Cam."

"Well, well, well," Sage said, folding her arms. "Isn't that interesting? Rose, I'll have my five dollars now, thank you very much."

"He moved faster than I expected," Rose observed glumly. "Dang it, I hate losing bets to my sister."

Ali beamed. "I knew you guys would get together. You set off sparks whenever you're together."

"Now, wait just a minute," Sarah protested. "I haven't admitted to anything."

"You haven't denied it, either," Sage pointed out.

"Dish, sister," Nic demanded.

Sarah pursed her lips. While she wasn't one to roll her personal business out in front of anybody and everybody, these were her closest friends, and this was girls' night out. "Okay, fine. Yes, I slept with Cam."

"I knew it." Nic slapped her leg. "What happened? When? Where?"

"Was it wonderful?" Sage asked.

"It must have been wonderful," Rose said. "Look at her, she's sparkling."

"Well, I don't believe in kissing and telling—"

Nic let out an unladylike snort. "Since when?"

"—so all I'm going to say is that it was . . . an adventure."

"Define *adventure*," Sage demanded.

"No. You guys don't share the details of your love lives with me."

Sarah knew the minute she used the word *love* that she'd made a mistake, and sure enough, Nic pounced. "Love life? Not sex life?"

Then out of nowhere, tears stung Sarah's eyes. She blinked rapidly, trying to chase them away. Ali noticed and leaned forward, patting her knees. "Sarah? What's wrong?"

She shut her eyes and shook her head. "Nothing. I'm okay. Really. I don't know where that came from."

"Is it Lori? Does she know . . . ?" Sage asked.

"No."

Rose asked, "Is she still anti-Cam?"

"Yes, but . . ." Sarah shrugged. "That's not the issue. Lori isn't part of this. That's the deal. For just this little while, it's our time. It's not about the past and not about the future. It's not about anybody other than Cam and me."

Nic asked, "Then why the tears?"

"I don't know." She blew out a heavy breath. "Well, I do know. It's just that I . . . well . . ."

"You never quit loving him," Nic said.

"No, I never did. Not completely, anyway. Not that I ever admitted it to myself before he returned."

"It's been pretty clear to those of us around you. Otherwise, you'd have fallen for one of the guys who wandered through your life."

"Like Zach Turner," Ali said.

Sarah shook her head. "We were never more than friends."

"Exactly." Sage took half of a brownie. "You made sure it never went any further than that."

Sarah looked out at Hummingbird Lake, where sunlight danced on the surface like diamonds. In a voice just above a murmur, she said, "I've been waiting for Cam. All these years, I've been waiting for Cam."

Celeste Blessing's voice came from behind them. "That's because you and Cam were meant to be together."

The women looked around to see Celeste setting the kickstand of her Honda Gold Wing next to Sage and Colt's bicycles. Sage called, "Celeste, you are earlier than we expected."

Celeste approached, saying, "Our speaker didn't show up, so we cut the meeting short."

Rose waved hello. "We didn't hear you ride up."

"I walked the bike in from the road. Snowdrop isn't fond of the sound of my motor, and I don't like to disturb her. So, ladies, what have I missed? Discussion about Sarah and Cameron, obviously."

"Were we talking that loud?" Sarah asked, sending an uncomfortable glance toward the other house on the point, which was occupied by a vacationing family from Texas.

Celeste waved a dismissive hand as she sat in an empty lawn chair beside Sarah. "No, dear. I have exceptional hearing. Now, have you finally relieved yourself of the burden of the grudge you held against Cam? You have forgiven him for the hurt and harm he did you?"

Sarah opened her mouth to say yes, but the words wouldn't come. "It's complicated."

"I see." Celeste shook her head sadly, then asked, "Has he forgiven you?"

Sarah bristled a bit at that. Sage defended her, asking the question so that she didn't have to. "What has Sarah done that Cam Murphy needs to forgive?"

"She failed to defend him here in Eternity Springs. She allowed the myth of his wickedness to simmer unchecked for more than two decades."

"Now, wait a minute." Nic chose a carrot stick from the platter. "Cam the teenager was wicked. He was into trouble all the time. He did put Andrew Cook into a coma, and he did tell Sarah to take a hike when she needed him." She crunched a bite of her carrot stick for emphasis.

Sarah chose a celery stick. "No, Celeste is right. He made mistakes, but he wasn't wicked. He was an abused boy, and no one in town helped him. Remember, Nic? We knew his father was a beast. Everybody knew, but nobody helped him. I loved him, but I didn't help him, either. Then I allowed him to be my dirty little secret . . . for twenty years."

Shame flickered through her at the admission. She sighed heavily. "We both need to do some forgiving. I wouldn't say that we're there yet."

Celeste reached over and patted Sarah's knee. "It's not an easy task, but it is a necessary one for you both. Cam, especially, has much work to do in that area. Primarily, he needs to forgive himself. How do you think he is coming along in that respect?"

Sarah took a bite of celery and considered the question. "I think that hinges on Lori. I think that unless she forgives him, he'll never be able to forgive himself."

"You're probably right," Ali said. "I know that whenever Mac did something that hurt the kids, it tore him up inside. Even if it was something simple, like failing to make it to a Little League game like he'd promised."

Celeste accepted Sage's offer of a glass of tea, then chose a shortbread cookie from the plate of Sarah's offerings. "You know what must be done now, don't you, Sarah?"

"Lori," she replied with a sigh. "Lori needs to listen to him. I need to talk her into it."

"That's not going to be very easy, is it?" Rose asked.

Nic shook her head. "I love Lori dearly, but to quote Gabe's father, 'The girl is as stubborn as a two-headed mule.'"

"Truer words have never been spoken," Sarah agreed with a sigh. "I don't know what to do. I can't make her listen to Cam."

"Balderdash," Celeste said.

The younger women shared a look. Ali repeated, "Balderdash?"

"Lori is an adult," Sarah said.

"True, but she's not yet independent, is she? You still control the purse strings, Sarah. Use your power. Make her come home and sit down and listen to what her father has to say. She owes him the chance to explain himself, if nothing else."

Sarah winced. "Oh, I don't know, Celeste. That's awfully manipulative. It's something my parents would have done to me. I've never had that sort of relationship with Lori, and besides, she does have a right to her anger."

"That doesn't trump the fifth commandment."

Honor your father and your mother. Sarah brooded about it as she finished off her celery stick. Ali swatted at a mosquito, then said, "As one mother of young adults to another, I don't know that I'd call Celeste's suggestion manipulative. I'd consider it more of a reminder to Lori of all that you are doing for her."

"What do you mean?" Sarah asked.

"When you give birth to a child, you are obligated to feed her and shelter her and love her. You are not obligated to provide a college education. Mac and I have good kids, but the sense of entitlement we sometimes see in them and in their friends makes us wonder where we went wrong. I love Lori—you know I do, considering the fact that I'm still holding out hope that she and my Chase find their way back to each other one day—but if you ask her to give Cam a chance, she should at least listen."

Nic nodded. "I agree. Call her home, Sarah. It's time. You can't leave Cam hanging indefinitely. Or yourself, either. You need to put it all behind you and move forward. This limbo isn't good."

But it is good. It's great. I don't have to share him, and I want more time. She'd had roses and candlelight, but he hadn't given her the sparkly thing he'd promised, and they'd only begun to work their way through the list of private adventures he proposed in the bedroom. "I'll think about it. I promise. Now, can we change the subject, please? Surely one of you has something we can talk about. Rose, tell us how your latest book is coming along."

When Rose Anderson first came to Eternity Springs to reconcile with her sister, she'd rented the Angel's Rest garret and attempted another dream—she'd written a book, a medical mystery. The manuscript had not sold, but Rose wasn't deterred. She'd enjoyed the process of writing and found it provided a soothing balance to her life as a medical professional. "It's good. I'm trying to have it finished by the time Sage's baby is born. The whole giving-birth metaphor works for me."

While the conversation turned to details about Rose's

plot, Sarah's thoughts drifted back to Cam. Forgiveness. Did she have it in her? Maybe. Probably. She was already halfway there. But forgiveness wasn't the alpha and omega in their relationship. She could imagine herself forgiving Cam, but would she ever trust him again? Trust him in the all-in, no-doubts, complete-and-total-faith-in-him way that a real relationship needed?

She couldn't see it. Not with her own heart.

So what about her daughter's heart? Could she trust Cam where Lori was concerned?

The answer to that came readily: Yes, she could. He'd convinced her of that. So she would do as Celeste suggested and summon Lori home.

Sarah pictured Cam as he'd been this morning when he and Devin stopped by Fresh. He'd purchased sugar cookies to snack on during their day-tour drive up to Silverton. When he had paused in the doorway as he was leaving and given her a knowing smile and a borderline-salacious wink, she'd melted like a sugar glaze on hot cinnamon rolls right there behind the bakery case.

Yes, she would call Lori and bring her home. Soon.

Just not too soon.

Eight days after Sarah's first scuba lesson, she invited Cam and Devin to dinner. It was, he decided, a surreal experience.

He sat at a table in a house where he'd never been welcome, sharing a meal with a woman who'd done him grievous harm, and dealing with the reality that the anger he nursed toward Ellen Reese and her late husband was a bitter, wasted emotion. Frank was dead, and his wife was ill. Cam would never get any explanations or apologies or even skewed parental justifications for the damage they had done not just to Cam but to Sarah and Lori, too.

Cam never used the word *impotent* in regard to himself, but it damn sure fit his feelings now as he answered

Ellen's repetitive questions with a smile on his face. He could do nothing else. He had to let his grudges go.

Doing so wasn't easy. He was glad that Devin was there to break the ice, because even if Ellen didn't realize the significance of the moment, Sarah did. It had been a little awkward at first.

Devin entertained them with a story about a tourist family and a cutthroat game of miniature golf, and slowly Cam relaxed. Ellen even contributed to the conversation by asking Devin if he'd caught any fish in Hummingbird Lake.

Once angling talk had been exhausted, Sarah schooled her expression into a picture of innocence, passed Devin the mashed potatoes again, and asked, "So how is Mortimer doing?"

Cam dropped his chin to his chest as Dev let out a groan and replied, "You mean the devil dog?"

As Devin gleefully told the story of how the dog had somehow managed to knock Cam's wallet off his dresser and proceeded to eat $135 in cash and Cam's debit card, Cam watched Sarah's eyes sparkle and listened to her joyous laughter and decided the cost was well worth it.

Finally, Devin set down his fork, wiped his mouth with his napkin, and said, "That was the best roast I've ever had, Ms. Reese."

"Call me Sarah, please, Dev, and thank you. I'm glad you enjoyed it."

"Enjoyed it?" Cam looked at his son and shook his head. "He ate enough to feed the entire baseball team."

"Hey, I'm just a growing boy. Besides, having to eat your cooking makes me appreciate good food like this. Of course I'm going to stuff myself."

"Why don't you work off some of the calorie load by clearing the table for Sarah."

"Happy to." Devin rose and began to carry the plates to Sarah's kitchen.

"He's a good kid," Sarah said as the boy left the room. "You've done well with him, Cam."

"Thanks. Sometimes I have my doubts, I'll admit. We've had our share of scrapes."

"All parents do," Ellen said, surprising both Cam and Sarah with the insightful comment.

Alzheimer's is a peculiar disease, Cam thought. He looked at Sarah and asked, "What can I do to help?"

"The Rockies are playing tonight, if you'd like to sit with Mom in the living room." Sarah gently asked her mother, "You still enjoy your baseball, don't you, Mom?"

"I like baseball," Ellen said.

"Well, why don't we go root for the home team, then?" Cam said to Ellen. He rose from his seat and offered her his arm. He saw Sarah in the smile she offered him in return, and the lingering resentment inside him faded away. He would be kind to Ellen Reese. She was Sarah's mother and Lori's grandmother, and besides, it was the right thing to do.

"Dishes won't take long," Sarah told him.

"Dev will help, won't you, son?"

"Hey, I'll do them all myself if it'll earn me a double helping of dessert. Dad, wait till you see the pie that's in the oven."

"I don't need to see it. I can smell it."

"That pie is destined for the shop tomorrow," Sarah said, then laughed at Devin's distraught expression. "Just kidding."

Cam helped Ellen Reese into her recliner, then picked up the TV remote and tuned in to the game. It was the bottom of the eighth inning, and the Rockies led by seven, so he wasn't drawn in by the game. Instead, the photographs on the bookshelves behind the television caught his attention. He walked over to the shelf and picked up a photograph of a preteen Sarah and her parents. "She was beautiful even then."

Ellen Reese said, "That picture was taken at Spirit Cave. We picnic there. It's my favorite place. It's our place. Frank and me."

"Is it?" This was the most engaged that he'd seen Ellen Reese all evening. "I've been there. The view of Murphy Mountain from there is spectacular."

Ellen blinked and asked, "Is Frank dead?"

Cam shot a panicked look toward the kitchen. "Um . . ."

"He's dead, isn't he?"

Oh, hell. What should he say? She seemed to know already, so he answered, "Yes, ma'am."

"Did I go to his funeral?"

"Yes, ma'am, you did." Cam couldn't imagine otherwise.

"And I held his hand when he died?"

Again, instinct told him what to say. "Yes, ma'am."

She turned her gaze back to the television, and soon closed her eyes and appeared to fall asleep. Cam let out a relieved breath. Pity stirred inside him. He felt sorry for Ellen Reese. He felt terrible for Sarah and Lori. How hard it must be to lose someone you love in little bits and pieces this way. Alzheimer's was a terrible disease, and in a way he'd not comprehended before, a family disease.

He admired Sarah for her patience, tenderness, and caring where her mother was concerned. It must be emotionally draining to be a caretaker of someone with this illness. He wouldn't wish it on his own worst enemy.

When Ellen didn't stir and the ball game remained a rout, Cam decided to join Sarah and his son in her kitchen. But as he drew close, he heard Sarah ask Dev if he missed Australia, so Cam paused to eavesdrop on the answer.

"I miss parts of home," Devin said. "I miss the boat and the water and the dives."

"I'll bet it's neat to go diving with your dad."

"Yeah, except that we didn't get to do it very often.

Honestly, we spend more time together now. He worked too much."

"I asked him how he can manage so much time away. He said he prepared."

"He did. It also helps that he's not there to butt into everyone else's business, so people get their work done on time."

In the hallway, Cam scowled.

Devin continued, "Mainly, though, it's because when he's around, people depend on him more than they probably need to. He's a great boss and a good businessman, but he has a hard time saying no when someone asks him for a favor."

"I'll have to remember that."

Dishes rattled, and Cam heard the dishwasher door thump shut. He started to enter the kitchen, then once again stopped when he heard Sarah ask, "So what do you like best about Eternity Springs?"

Dev's reply came swiftly: "The guys. The Grizzlies, I mean. They're good guys. They know how to have fun without doing crazy things."

Hallelujah, Cam thought. He entered the kitchen and asked, "So did I hear the oven go off a few minutes ago?"

"Hot apple pie, Dad." The boy glanced at the kitchen clock and frowned. "Uh . . . any chance I could have mine to go?"

Cam cuffed him on the head. "Dev. That's rude."

"I was supposed to meet the guys at Drew's house ten minutes ago. I thought we'd be done with dinner earlier. We're having a pool tournament, and they'll be waiting on me."

"Then you shouldn't have eaten half a cow," Cam scolded.

Sarah laughed, then removed a pie cutter from a drawer. "Cut him some slack, Dad."

It was the first time she'd used the term in reference to

him, and Cam's heart gave a little twist. He wanted to hear her say it in reference to Lori.

Sarah cut a generous slice of pie and put it on a plate. Then she wrapped the rest of the pie in foil and handed it to Dev, saying, "Share with your friends. Just make sure I get my pie plate back."

"Awesome!" Devin said.

Cam protested, "Wait a minute . . . What if I want seconds?"

"Snooze you lose, Dad." Dev leaned over and kissed Sarah's cheek, saying, "Thanks, Sarah. You're the best."

Sarah softly beamed as with pie in hand, Devin disappeared out the door. Cam found himself crossing the kitchen to kiss her without making a conscious decision to do so. He took her in his arms and took his time about it, tasting her, savoring her, loving her. When she fell bonelessly against him, he wanted to swoop her up into his arms and carry her to bed, but respect of her mother's presence in the other room dampened the urge. He could no more have slept with Sarah in this house now than he could have sneaked into her bedroom at sixteen.

Cam ended the kiss, rested his forehead against hers, and said, "Hello, beautiful."

"Hey, handsome."

"Thanks for dinner."

"You're very welcome." She reached up and touched his cheek. "It was nice to have company for a change."

"Your mom fell asleep in her chair."

"That's normal for her. She sleeps a lot. Or at least that's the old normal."

A shadow passed over her eyes, and seeing it, Cam asked, "There's a new normal?"

"A new worry. Lately I'm noticing more confusion, anxiety, and agitation in the evening. They call it sundowning, and it's a concern. If Mom develops the tendency to wander, it's a game changer. I don't know that I could safely care for her here at home." She glanced toward the living room and sighed. "I'm not ready to do anything else."

He pulled her against him and comforted her with a hug. "If I can help you at all, I will. Just ask."

"Thanks, Cam. I appreciate that. I appreciate this. How is it that a good hug can make you feel stronger?"

"Hugs are a magic medicine."

"That they are." She surprised him when she pulled away from him and said, "I need to make a phone call, and I'd better do it now. Would you like to take your pie out to the back patio, and I'll join you when I'm done?"

"Sure. Is everything all right?"

"Yes. I needed that hug more than I realized. Now, go outside and enjoy your pie."

She sent him off with a brave smile that had him frowning as he took a seat on the porch swing. The pie tasted delicious, but he wondered what was up with this phone call. Unpleasant business, from the looks of it.

The light switched on in a second-story room, and soon he heard the muffled sound of her voice as it floated from the partially opened window. He didn't attempt to eavesdrop, he figured he'd done enough of that already tonight. Instead, he indulged in the peacefulness of the evening.

A gentle breeze whispered through leaves of the old cottonwood tree that graced the Reeses' backyard and carried the scent of steaks cooking on a grill. Eternity Springs in the summertime was a downright pleasant place. Even more pleasant was spending the evening with Sarah because they wanted to spend time together, not because it furthered Celeste Blessing's Redemption Plan.

He took another bite of pie and decided he'd better add some distance onto his daily run tomorrow morning. He'd sampled way too many of Sarah's sweets today, in the literal sense of the word, unfortunately. As he set down his empty plate, a new and disturbingly familiar sound caught his attention. "Surely not," he murmured to himself as he rose and walked around to the side of Sarah's house in the direction of the noise.

Aarf, arf, arf, arf.

Cam muttered a curse as he spied the Boston terrorist go sprinting down Aspen Street with what appeared to be the remnants of a garden hose trailing from his mouth. He reached for the gate, then paused and glanced up toward the lamp-lit window. He couldn't chase after the pup of darkness without telling Sarah where he'd gone.

He turned around and reentered the house, then made his way upstairs and followed the sound of Sarah's voice to a bedroom converted to an office. As he lifted his hand to knock, he heard Sarah say, "Lori, let's not fight about this."

"I don't want to fight, either, Mom." His daughter's voice came clear as church bells through the computer speakers and plunged a knife into his heart as she continued, "But I don't want to see Cam Murphy. I don't want to talk to Cam Murphy. I don't want to hear what Cam Murphy thinks he wants to say to me."

TWELVE

Sarah heard a noise and looked up from her computer screen. Cam stood in the doorway, his expression stricken. *Oh, no.* Frustration rolled through her—at her daughter for being so hardheaded and at Cam for not staying downstairs where he belonged. She refocused on Lori's image, and her voice sharpened. "Here's the deal, Lori. Right now what you want isn't the issue. For once, what matters is what I want, and I want you home. ASAP."

"But, Mom—"

"No buts. I don't play the mom card very often, but I'm doing that now. I still pay your bills, Lori Elizabeth. You may be an adult, but you are not independent. Until you reach that point, you sometimes have to do what I say. This is one of those times. You will come home, and you will listen to the man. That's what I've been asking you to do. Now I'm telling you. Do you understand me?"

Lori's expression grew mulish. "Fine. I'll come home for the Fourth of July weekend. How am I supposed to get there?"

"I'll book a plane ticket for you." The Fourth this year fell on a Friday. "Can you make the Thursday-evening flight, or shall I book Friday morning?"

"I can leave Thursday morning, but Mom, a last-minute ticket for a holiday weekend is going to cost a fortune."

Standing in the doorway, Cam waved to catch her attention, then pointed to himself, mouthing, "I'll pay."

"Thursday or Friday?"

Lori released an exaggerated sigh. "I'll come Thursday."

"Good. I'll email the details once I book the ticket." Sarah knew her daughter was in no mood to listen to her now, but she never liked to end a conversation on an unhappy note, so she tried to smooth the waters by asking, "What would you like me to make for the Fourth of July picnic?"

"I doubt I'll have an appetite."

"Ali gave me her fried chicken recipe."

"The secret spices?"

"Yes."

Lori frowned, but Sarah spotted a softening in her face. "That's not playing fair."

"I love you."

"I love you, too. I just don't want to have anything to do with him."

Had he not been standing there listening, Sarah might have taken another shot at convincing Lori to give Cam a chance. Instead, she decided to end the conversation as quickly as possible. "I'll see you on Thursday, sweetheart. I'll book you into Crested Butte and pick you up at the airport."

"Why not Colorado Springs? I can taxi to the storage lot and drive myself."

"I'll have more time with you this way, and besides, I want to save the wear and tear on your car. It's on its last legs."

"All right." Lori hesitated for a moment, then asked, "You'll come by yourself, won't you? He won't be there."

One step at a time, Sarah told herself. Besides, an airport was no place for this meeting, although she wasn't sure where that right place was. Somewhere private.

Somewhere neutral. Somewhere that Lori couldn't run away. "I'll be by myself, Lori."

They said their goodbyes and ended the call. Sarah's gaze lifted from the computer screen to settle on the vase filled with two dozen red roses that the florist had delivered yesterday. She hated being in the middle.

Cam's voice sounded raw as he said, "She still wants nothing to do with me. Guess I'm not surprised. Why make her come home?"

"Because it's time. Avoiding problems doesn't solve them."

"And that's what I am," he replied. "A problem."

"For Lori, yes."

"And for you?"

Sarah carefully chose her words. She'd called Lori home because she had the power to do so and it was the right thing to do. But that's where her power ended. She hoped Lori would accept her father, but she couldn't make it happen. If Lori rejected Cam, well, Sarah didn't want to think about that. They'd deal with that when and if it happened, but in the meantime, this was still her time. She needed time to be Sarah the woman before she had to put on her mom hat and pick up the pieces.

She turned around and studied him. "Oh, you're a problem, all right. In the past week you've sent me flowers and perfume. You arranged an hour-long massage at the spa at Angel's Rest. And just today I received a special-delivery box from Victoria's Secret."

At the mention of the box, his look brightened. "This is the romance part I promised. I'll admit that today's little gift was as much for me as for you. Did you like it?"

"The negligé is lovely, Cam, but I'm reserving opinion about the underwear. I don't know if I'm ready for thong panties. Lori swears they're comfortable, but—"

"Whoa! Stop right there. Too much information, Sarah."

Oh, yes. What had she been thinking?

You were thinking about flashing him a look at what you're wearing beneath your sundress. Face it. She'd been humming along in a low state of arousal ever since she opened that gift box.

"Sorry," she said. "I'm flustered. Why did you come upstairs, Cam?"

"Oh, I forgot." He scowled and glanced toward her office window. "It's that damn dog. He got out, and I came to tell you I was leaving to chase him down. He's probably started a riot by now."

"Oh." Sarah's heart sank. She didn't want this evening to end on this note. She'd hoped to sit outside on the swing with him. Neck a little bit. Let him get a look at the bra he'd bought her. She started to stand, thinking she would help with the search, but he reached for his wallet and said, "Buy Lori's plane ticket. The way my luck is going, they will have sold the last available seat ten minutes ago."

Sarah didn't argue about using his credit card to book the seat. No sense being stupid about this. Once the task was completed, the information emailed to Lori, she handed him back his card and said, "Let me check in on Mom, and I'll help you look for Mortimer."

"You're going to leave her alone?"

"If she's settled. I won't be gone long."

"What about the wandering thing?"

"She's not actually doing it. I'm just worried that it's in our future."

Downstairs, she found her mother awake and staring at the television. "Hey, Mom. How are you doing?"

"I'm okay. Is it time to go to bed?"

"Sure, Mom." Sarah glanced at Cam. "Why don't you go on and I'll catch up with you after I get Mom in bed?"

"You don't have to—"

"I want to," she interrupted. "Grab a flashlight before you go. There's one in the mudroom cabinet."

"Will do." His rueful tone made her want to laugh as he added, "Just follow the barking and squealing, and I'm sure you'll find us."

Twenty minutes later, her mom was in bed, and she'd grabbed a jacket, a flashlight, and a dog leash and headed out. She didn't hear barking or squealing, but the small crowd gathered in front of the Elkhorn Lodge begged investigation. She caught up with Cam at the pool area of the Elkhorn Lodge.

He stood staring in a shocked stupor at Mortimer, who sat happily beside the pool, chewing on the pool vacuum. A dozen or so people surrounded him, half Eternity Springs citizens, half tourists. The crowd buzzed. The owner of the Elkhorn was giving Cam an earful. One tourist took pictures with his phone, another with a camera sporting a lens worthy of an FBI surveillance team. Sarah threaded her way through the crowd until she stood beside Cam. "I see you found him."

"You won't believe this. That demon animal jumped into the pool and snagged the pool vac."

"You're kidding."

"No. He jumped in, grabbed hold of the machine, swam it to the steps at the shallow end, pulled it from the water, and proceeded to eat it."

"Oh, dear."

"Yeah. Oh, dear. Now the owner wants me to pay for damages. Not just for the vacuum, but for pain and suffering. He says Lucifer there scared a year off his life."

"Oh, for heaven's sake. Just ignore him."

"What's that?" Richard Perry said. "Ignore me? Why, Sarah Reese, what would your father say?"

"He'd say you should quit attempting to extort money from innocent bystanders."

"Innocent? Innocent!" Blustering, Perry shifted his

weight from one foot to the other. "He adopted that dog. That means he's financially responsible for the destruction it causes."

"I said I'd pay for the vacuum," Cam said. "I said I'd pay for the pool vacuum and the hose and whatever that rubber thing was. But you're not going to milk me for pain and suffering." Aside to Sarah, he added, "I'm the one who is suffering and in pain because I'm the one who has to deal with the dog."

That's when Mortimer picked up a hunk of plastic he'd torn from his treasure and darted off again.

"Stop him!" Cam said.

"And risk a finger or a hand?" a tourist said. "Yeah, right."

Cam turned to chase after the dog, but Richard Perry grabbed his arm. "I'll expect my money by tomorrow."

"Fine." Cam turned away.

"I mean it, Murphy," Perry called after him, spitting the name as if it were a curse. "You better not be like your no-good old man and try to run out on my bill. If you don't show up with my money, I'll send the sheriff after you. I'll—"

"Oh, just stop it," Sarah said. "You are one to talk, Richard. You never did pay my father for the window you broke at the Trading Post."

While Perry sputtered with excuses, Sarah headed after Cam, running to catch up with his long-legged strides. She spied Mortimer trotting up the middle of the street before veering sharply into the alley between Vistas and Gabe Callahan's office building. "I swear when I catch that dog I'm going to use him for bear bait," Cam declared.

"How did he get out?"

"The dog is possessed, and the devil is powerful."

Sarah couldn't help it. She burst out laughing, and she

laughed so hard that she grabbed hold of his arm and hung on for support.

"Well, I'm glad you think this is funny."

"Not just funny. Hilarious." She brought it down to giggles and added, "I'm sorry. But the look on your face . . . Oh, Cam. You do realize that rescuing Mortimer is probably the single most important thing you could have done to help propel yourself into Lori's good graces?"

"What?" He jerked his gaze away from the alley and focused on Sarah.

"You know she wants to go to vet school. She loves animals. All animals. When she hears what you did for Mortimer, that's going to knock a big chink in her armor against you."

"Really?"

"Yes, really."

He looked from her to the alley, then back to her. "I guess that means using him for bear bait is out?"

"It'd be a shame to lose the goodwill you've already bought for yourself." Sarah took the lead and started down the alley.

Cam followed her, not speaking until they emerged from the alley and she paused, looking up and down the street in search of the black-and-white dog. "How will she find out about it? Will you tell her? I don't want her to think I was trying to manipulate her or something."

"I think that this bit of news might be better coming from Celeste. She has a gift for knowing just what to say and how to say it." Catching sight of Mortimer, she pointed and said, "There. He just turned the corner."

"I don't suppose I'd still get points with Lori if we never found him tonight and he ended up lost?"

"I doubt it."

Cam gave an aggravated sigh, then linked her fingers with his and deliberately slowed their pace, turning the chase into an evening stroll. Sarah wasn't about to complain. There was something quite lovely about walking hand in hand with a lover on a beautiful summer evening.

"Three days," he murmured. "How do you think we should orchestrate this meeting?"

Lori. He was thinking about their daughter. Was that really a twinge of jealousy she felt? *Don't be ridiculous, Sarah.*

"I do have an idea about that. Do you think Jack would mind if we used Eagle's Way again? It's private and comfortable, and I know she'd like the opportunity to see it."

"That's a good idea. I'm sure Jack wouldn't mind." He brought her hand up to his mouth and pressed a kiss against her fingers. "If we're at Eagle's Way, she'll have a harder time running off if she gets the urge."

Yes, that thought had occurred to Sarah, too.

"What if that's what happens, Sarah? What if she flat out tells me to get lost?"

She gave his fingers a comforting squeeze. "Don't borrow trouble, Cam. You have enough of it as it is with Mortimer."

He groaned. "Don't remind me."

They lost sight of the Boston terrier twice but were able to pick up his trail by asking bystanders if they'd spotted the dog. Soon Sarah realized they were almost to the house that Cam had rented. "I'll bet he's gone home."

"No." Cam glanced toward the house "You think?"

"Better check."

Sure enough, when Cam unlocked the front door and escorted Sarah inside, they discovered Mortimer curled up on a pillow inside his crate. "I don't get it," Cam said. "Was the dog we chased not this one, after all? Could he have a doppelgänger?"

"The evidence suggests otherwise," Sarah replied, motioning toward the chewed remnants of a black plastic hose tucked into one corner. "How did he get out and back in?"

Cam took a closer look at the crate. "The latch isn't fixed. It's bent. And look." He pointed toward some telltale paw prints on the floor, then followed them toward the kitchen, where the door to the basement stood open. The prints led straight to an open basement window and the answer to how Mortimer had achieved the evening's mischief.

"Well, there's the end of the mystery. Dev and I need to be more careful going forward. I wonder where I can buy a straitjacket for a dog? Lori wouldn't have to know about that, would she?"

"I won't tell." Sarah followed him back upstairs, saying, "Now that the big mystery is solved, I should be getting home. My morning starts very early."

"I'll walk you back."

"That's not necessary."

"I want to. How else am I gonna get my good-night kiss?"

That gave her a little buzz, and as they walked the short distance to her home, she reflected on the evening and thought how nice, how normal, the evening had been.

She was a strong, independent woman. A businesswoman. The sole supporter of herself and her child. Caretaker of her mother. A good friend, an excellent neighbor. She didn't need a man to make herself complete, but that didn't mean she didn't enjoy having one around. She had enjoyed cooking for Cam and his son. It had been a pleasure to share her supper table with those who showed such appreciation for her efforts. Sarah was a homebody at heart, a homemaker in her soul.

Had things been different, maybe she would have chosen to be a stay-at-home mom who sent her family off with a hot breakfast beneath their belts and who welcomed them home at night to something savory simmering on the stove. She'd have enjoyed that. At least for a little while. Maybe she would have tired of it in time and wanted something else, but without having had the opportunity to try it, she couldn't know for sure.

As they approached her house, she dampened her lips in anticipation of the good-night kiss he'd promised, her nerves humming pleasantly with expectation. She liked that he'd walked her home. They'd never been able to share this particular rite of dating when they were teenagers, and she'd regretted it. If he made her feel like a teen tonight when she was too close to forty for comfort, then good for her.

Then, hidden by the shadows on her front porch, he drew her into his arms and took her mouth with his. Sarah forgot all about her teenage years. The hum of arousal burst into full song. In this moment, drowning in his kiss, she was all woman. A hot, hungry woman.

So when he finally released her, she asked, "Would you like to come in?"

"More than I want to breathe, but I thought . . . It's your mother's home. I don't want to be disrespectful."

Sarah smiled up at him. "You are really a very nice man, Cameron Murphy, but I am inviting you into *my* home. Come inside, Cam. Take me to bed."

"I love it when you say that. Hell, Sarah, I love—"

"No," she interrupted, placing a finger against his mouth. "No more talk." She had a notion of what he'd been about to say, but she wasn't ready for it. He wasn't ready, either, whether he recognized it or not.

First, they had to deal with Lori.

By Thursday afternoon, as he paced the living room waiting for Devin to return from baseball practice, Cam's nerves were just about shot. He'd done everything he could think of to prepare for meeting Lori. He'd bought flowers to give her to welcome her home. He'd planned the menu for the meal they'd share up at Eagle's Way down to the tiniest detail. He had the earrings to give her, along with another small present and a more extravagant gift.

The little present he'd brought with him from Australia—a soft little stuffed koala bear he'd bought in the airport the day they'd departed. Sarah knew about the earrings and the koala bear. He hadn't mentioned the car he'd bought for Lori.

He'd noted Sarah's comment about saving wear and tear on Lori's car during their online phone call. The next day, he'd flat out asked Gabe Callahan what Lori drove and decided he didn't need the worry about her safety on the road. The car he purchased wasn't extravagant but a mid-size foreign crossover that ranked high on safety, came equipped for mountain driving, and was stylish enough to appeal to women in their twenties. Sure, he'd bought it fully loaded, but he'd had to take what was on the lot at a dealership willing to deliver the car.

He'd halfway expected to catch some grief from Devin over the purchase, but his son was showing an amazing amount of maturity at the moment. Maturity, or inattention. Baseball consumed Devin these days, and Cam didn't have a problem with that. The team apparently filled a hole in Devin's life. Cam believed that hole was related to family, or, more precisely, Dev's lack of family. In a relatively short period of time, the boys on the team had bonded like brothers with Dev. Today, with any luck, he'd form a bond with a sister, too. One that would last a lifetime.

Devin needed Lori. Cam understood it and recognized why. Losing a parent rocked a child's world like nothing else. Losing both parents destroyed it. Cam had made sure from the beginning that Dev would be financially secure should something happen to him, but emotional security had proved to be more elusive.

Personal experience had taught Cam that the missing ingredient in Devin's life had been family. Still, he'd drawn the line at marrying someone he didn't love in order to provide more of it for Devin, and thank goodness for that. He didn't know how this second chance with Sarah would end, but he was certain that he had needed to take it. Sarah had needed it, too. Now a future that he'd never dreamed possible dangled before them like a big old brass ring if they chose to reach for it.

And if they could get past the obstacle that was Lori.

"That's not gonna happen if Dev doesn't get his butt home," Cam said to Mortimer, who was snoozing peacefully in his crate. The devil dog had been shockingly angelic since his pool-vacuum destructo derby. Cam credited the extra-heavy-duty latch he'd installed on the crate. Sarah claimed Celeste had orchestrated the change with the lecture she'd delivered to the dog during a visit.

Finally, he heard the sound of a truck pulling into the driveway. He grabbed his keys, snapped the leash onto Beelzebub's collar, and headed out, locking the door behind him. He met Dev on the front lawn, saying, "Get in the car. We're late."

Devin glanced up at him, a distracted look on his face. "Huh?"

"I said get in the car."

"But I need to change clothes." He held up his duffel bag. "I need to put my stuff away."

"I put clean clothes in the car already. You can shower up at Eagle's Way. Just throw your duffel on the porch."

"Dad, no," he protested. "It's got my, uh, ball glove inside. Someone might steal it."

"No one's going to steal it. This is Eternity Springs.

Bring it with you if you want. I don't care. But get in the car."

Devin looked at his bag, then at Cam's car. "But, Dad—"

"*Now,* son."

Devin's eyes rounded at Cam's tone, then his lips thinned. While Cam muscled Mortimer into the carrier he used to cart the dog around, Devin tossed the duffel onto one corner of the porch, where it lay hidden from the street behind the boxwood hedge.

Cam had the car started and ready to roll by the time the boy got inside. "What kept you?" he asked. "When I left the ballpark, you said you were right behind me. That was half an hour ago."

"Sorry," Dev replied, his tone sullen.

"Sorry" wasn't an explanation, but Cam decided not to rag on the kid anymore. Devin could go from sullen to surly fast, and that wasn't the tone he wanted or needed today. "Look, sorry if I barked at you. I'm nervous, you know?"

"Sure. Okay. Not a problem."

Cam spared a quick glance at Devin. He seemed distracted. Was he worried about meeting Lori, too? Had Cam's preoccupation with Lori hurt Devin in some way? "Listen, buddy, if you're upset about the car . . ."

"Huh?"

"Is something wrong, Dev?"

Devin opened his mouth, and Cam thought he was going to open up. Instead, he shrugged and said, "No. Everything's cool. Sorry I was late. So have you talked to Sarah? Did Lori's plane arrive on time?"

"Yes. They're coming straight to Eagle's Way. They'll be about forty minutes behind us, I think. I think I've decided to wait for them out beside the pool. I've got chips and Cokes—snack sort of stuff to set out. If you want to swim, that's okay by me. I threw your suit into the bag."

"Nah, I'll probably play videogames. Jack's home theater is totally awesome. Besides, you'll probably want some time alone with Lori and Sarah."

Cam took his gaze off the road long enough to frown at Devin. "No, I won't. We're in this together, son. You are my family. Nothing is going to change that."

"I know, Dad. Don't worry about me. It's all cool."

No, it wasn't all cool, but Cam figured he'd get to the bottom of it later.

When they arrived at Eagle's Way, Devin grabbed his clean clothes and took a quick shower before disappearing into Jack's home theater. Cam set up the soft tent crate he'd purchased from Nic and said a prayer that Mortimer had left his pterodactyl scream back in town as he secured the dog inside it with the biggest bone Cam had been able to buy. He carried inside the house the cooler filled with food he'd prepared for dinner, placing the steaks and salad into the kitchen refrigerator, and leaving the foil-wrapped potatoes on the counter. He wasn't much in the kitchen, but he could grill a steak. He'd brought rib eyes, since Sarah had told him that was Lori's favorite cut of meat.

Once that was done, he carried the snacks and soft drinks out to the pool. Next he unloaded the scuba gear he'd ordered for Sarah from his trunk and stowed it in the pool house's supply closet for their next lesson.

The memory of sharing his regulator with her flashed through his mind and momentarily distracted him. He'd been so hot for her. It's a wonder the water in the pool hadn't begun to boil.

What if this goes badly with Lori? What will happen to me and Sarah then?

"It won't go badly," he murmured. "I won't let it."

With all his preparations made, he checked his watch, then sat down to wait. Two minutes later, he was up, pacing. After five minutes of that, he told himself to sit down again. That lasted three minutes this time around, then he was back up, pacing again. He even tried to coax the dog to play fetch. Mortimer didn't cooperate.

He needed a distraction, so he called Devin's cell. "I'm dying here, bud. Would you please pause your game and come out to the pool and wait with me?"

Dev said, "That's just sad, Dad."

"Tell me about it."

"I'll be right there."

"Thanks, son."

Moments later, Devin exited the house and strolled casually toward the pool. When he drew near, he took one look at Cam and slowly shook his head. "You're pitiful. I swear you weren't this scared-looking the day that great white almost took a hunk out of your leg. Calm down, Dad. It'll be okay."

It'll be okay. Cam held on to Devin's assurance a moment later when he first heard the sound of the car coming up the drive. He drew a deep breath, then exhaled in a rush. Darned if the voice in his head didn't sound like Celeste Blessing's when he heard one more time, *It'll be okay.*

He turned to face the drive. As Sarah pulled her car to a stop, an unexpected and most welcome sense of peace descended on him. His hungry gaze locked on Lori. Emotion bombarded him like bullets. Pain. Sorrow. Regret. Mourning.

It'll be okay.

On the heels of the first emotions came the balm to the wounds. Yearning. Joy. Pride. Hope. Lori looked like her mother. Love swelled inside him, an ocean full of love. Pressure built behind his eyes, and he swallowed hard.

She wore sunglasses. He wished she'd take them off. The saying about eyes being a window to the soul was spot-on. Eyes revealed so much about what a person thought, what she felt. Cam wanted to see his daughter's eyes. Choosing to greet them here beside the pool had been a mistake for that reason alone.

Well, it was too late to change it now. On the plus side, he hoped his own sunglasses hid the insecurity he was feeling—not to mention the wash of wetness in his own eyes.

Sarah climbed out of the car first, giving him an encouraging look. Devin wandered nearer, not so close to Cam to make it appear as if he were staking a claim but close enough to offer support. Finally, the passenger door opened, and Lori—his daughter—exited the car.

Cam drank in the sight of her. Something about her—the tilt of her chin, perhaps?—reminded him of his mother. He forced words past the sudden tightening in his throat. "Hello, Lori. Thank you for coming."

Her shrug wordlessly conveyed that she'd been given no choice. Cam had known to expect resistance, so he cautioned himself to remain patient. "I thought we'd sit beside the pool for a little while, but if you'd rather go on inside . . ."

When Lori didn't respond, Sarah rolled her eyes and said, "The pool is fine. It's a beautiful afternoon."

"Great." Cam attempted a smile. He'd never felt so awkward in his life. "Can I get you something to drink? I have bottled water, soft drinks, or iced tea."

"Tea would be nice," Sarah replied. "We're both iced tea fiends. Thanks."

"Okay. Great. Dev?"

"No, thanks."

Cam gestured for the women to take seats at the wooden umbrella table where he'd set out snacks, then turned toward the poolside bar. He'd just opened the ice maker to fill plastic glasses when he heard the crunch of tires on gravel. Looking up, he saw an SUV painted black and white, sporting lights on the top and a gold sheriff's shield on the door, headed toward the house. "That's Zach," Sarah said. "Does he do regular patrols out this way?"

"I guess so," Cam responded. "He must know the security code." Inside, he cursed the sheriff's timing.

"Maybe he came to see me," Lori said.

Her voice. That was the first time he'd heard her voice. It was huskier than he'd expected, and was that the tiniest hint of a drawl—the influence of attending college in Texas, perhaps?

"Zach is a dear friend of Mom and me," Lori added.

"Cam knows that," Sarah said, her tone chiding.

Sheriff Zach Turner parked his truck next to Sarah's car. As the driver's-side door opened, something—a sound or a movement or maybe just instinct—made Cam glance at Devin.

His son had gone pale. His wide-eyed stare was locked on the sheriff. When Cam saw the boy's reaction, his gut clenched. *No. Aw, Devin, no.*

"Hey, Zach!" Lori walked toward the sheriff and gave him a warm hug.

The sheriff greeted her briefly, then said, "Sorry, honey, but I'm here on business."

Lori took a step backward, her brows arching in curious surprise as Zach's expression went grim. He looked from Devin to Cam, then back to Devin. "Sorry to interrupt. I know the timing isn't the best, but I have a job to do."

Cam stepped toward the sheriff. "What is this about?"

"I have to ask your son a question." He opened the back door of his SUV, then held up Devin's duffel bag. "Is this your bag, Devin?"

Devin closed his eyes. Cam started to walk toward him. "Son?"

Devin didn't look at Cam. He shrugged and spoke in

a sullen tone that Cam hadn't heard since they arrived in Eternity Springs. "Lots of guys have bags that color."

Zach set the bag on the hood of his vehicle. "The ball glove inside it has your name written on it."

The boy shrugged.

Cam tried to remain calm. No need to worry. This wasn't Cairns. Dev had a new group of friends here in Eternity Springs, a good group. He set a reassuring hand on Devin's shoulder. "Hold on a minute. Maybe Devin—"

"I picked the duffel up off of your front porch." Zach stared hard at Devin.

"Did you have a search warrant?" Devin demanded.

Cam muttered a curse beneath his breath as Zach replied, "I didn't need one, son. The bag was outside the house."

As Devin once again closed his eyes, Cam asked, "What's this all about, Sheriff Turner?"

"I'd like to take the boy in for questioning."

Sarah stepped forward. "Zach, wait a minute. I'm sure this is all a mistake. Devin is—"

"Real lucky I'm not here to arrest him, since he has a bag of weed in his duffel and an eyewitness has him dealing," the sheriff snapped. "At a playground."

"What?" Shocked, Cam gripped his son's shoulder and turned him around to face him. His son wouldn't look at him. "Devin?"

Nothing.

"Devin!" Cam gave his shoulder a little shake. "Talk to me, son."

Now the boy shook his head, still refusing to meet Cam's eyes, his mouth still stubbornly shut. Cam didn't miss the tremble of the teenager's hands, which he held clenched into fists at his side. *What the hell is going on?* Cam gazed from Devin to the stony-jawed sheriff, then back to his son again. As he tried to make sense of the lawman's charge, he came to one unshakeable conclusion.

Cam looked Zach Turner in the eyes and said, "Devin is not a drug dealer."

"Then answering my questions will clear the matter up. Come on, son. Why don't you get in the car?"

Briefly, Devin met Cam's gaze. "Sorry, Dad."

Sorry? He was sorry? Sorry for what? What was this all about? Cam stood frozen in stunned disbelief as his son climbed into the backseat of the sheriff's SUV, behind the metal partition and doors with automatic locks. He couldn't believe this. How could this be happening?

The slam of the door startled Cam from his shock. "I'll go with you."

"No," Zach said. "You'll want to follow in your own car."

"But he's a minor. You can't talk to him if I'm not there."

"Actually, I can. You should consider calling a lawyer, Mr. Murphy."

As Zach Turner climbed behind the wheel of his vehicle, Cam called to Devin, "I'll be right behind you, Dev. Don't worry. We'll get this straightened out."

The sheriff started his car and drove away. For a long moment, Cam stood and watched them go. He was having trouble processing his thoughts. Drugs? He couldn't believe it. He wouldn't believe it. Dev was not that stupid.

Cam dragged a hand down his face. He closed his eyes. He needed to think. Who could he call? *Timberlake. Mac Timberlake. He's a lawyer.* Probably a pretty good one, too, since he used to be a federal judge. With any luck, Timberlake could be at the jail before Devin arrived. *Good. That's good. That's a plan.*

The memory of another meeting in that same jailhouse rolled over him. Cam's knees went weak.

Cam took a step toward the house and his cellphone when the sight of Sarah and Lori drew him up short. *Oh, hell.* Sarah stood with her hands steepled in front of her mouth, worry shining in her eyes. Lori had her arms folded, her chin up, her mouth set.

Oh, hell. He'd forgotten all about them. "I'm sorry. Obviously, this is not how I wanted this afternoon to go. It's not what I . . . uh . . . had planned." He dragged a hand down his face. "I can't believe his. I cannot believe this is happening."

"Call Mac. He'll help," Sarah said.

"Yes, I thought of him. I'd better . . ."

"Go on, Cam." Sarah waved him off toward his car. "Don't worry about Mortimer. We'll take care of him. You go take care of your son."

"That's right," Lori said, speaking to him directly for the first time ever. Her green eyes dripped disdain as she added, "You go take care of your *son. He* needs you, and it's vitally important for a parent to be there for his child when that child needs him."

Cam shut his eyes, accepting the blow. Then he did the only thing he knew to do. "I'm sorry, Lori. I'm so, so sorry. I failed you, and I failed your mother. It's the biggest regret of my life, and if I could wind back the clock and do it over again, I would. I know you probably won't believe this and maybe don't even care, but I want you to know that I love you."

Without waiting to see her reaction to his words—he couldn't take another blow—Cam turned his back on his daughter. This time, to follow his son.

THIRTEEN

Sarah watched Cam leave and tears swell in Lori's eyes. She wanted to sit down and burst into tears herself. Devin dealing drugs? She didn't believe it. She felt certain that Zach would get it all straightened out, though his timing here couldn't have been any worse.

Lori had pretended to be calm, cool, and collected when she deplaned at the Gunnison–Crested Butte Regional Airport, but Sarah knew her daughter better than that. The quiet anger had been real enough. Unwilling to put up with cold-shoulder treatment for the trip back to Eternity Springs, Sarah had refused to start the car in the airport parking lot until they'd talked it out. Sarah hadn't explained how close she and Cam had grown—she wasn't stupid—but she had listened at length while Lori expressed her anger and frustration at having been summoned home. Once her daughter finally wound down, Sarah had sympathized with the turmoil Lori felt and made a simple request. She had asked Lori to meet Cam with as open a mind as she could manage, and to do it as a favor to Sarah.

Having said her piece, Lori agreed. Sarah seldom asked for favors, and besides, from the minute she'd realized who he was that morning in Australia, Lori had known this day would eventually come.

The closer they'd drawn to Eagle's Way, the quieter her daughter had grown. Sarah hadn't missed the nervous way she played with her dangling earrings or the near-constant shifting in her seat. When she'd taken the turn onto the private road leading to Eagle's Way, Sarah had reached over and given Lori's hand an encouraging squeeze. Lori had returned the squeeze as tight as a tourniquet.

And now this.

"Oh, baby," she murmured as the tears overflowed and spilled down Lori's cheeks.

"This is just stupid." Lori swiped at the tears. "I don't know why I am crying."

"Come here." Sarah took her daughter in her arms and held her, rocking her gently. "It's okay, sweetheart. I'd be shocked if you weren't crying. I'm crying. Look."

Lori glanced at her mother's watery eyes and smiled brokenly. "I feel like a five-year-old who had her feelings hurt because Daddy paid more attention to the baby than to me."

"I know." Sarah brushed Lori's hair back from her face. "This wasn't fair to you. Or to Cam, for that matter. I don't know what Devin has gotten himself into, but I'd like to give him a swift kick in the tush right about now."

Lori's mouth twisted. "He must be a real troublemaker. Remember how he'd had that black eye from a fight when he picked us up in Cairns?"

"Yes, but he's been a good kid since he's been here." Sarah's gaze trailed toward the gate to the estate. "He's polite and industrious about his independent-study projects. He wrote an excellent report about the Silver Miracle strike and the founding of Eternity Springs. I just don't believe he's involved with drugs. Especially selling them."

"Don't be naïve, Mom."

Sarah lifted her chin. "Hey, I am not someone who trusts just anyone. You know that. My friends will back me up about Devin. I have good instincts, and I'm telling you that there is more going on here than meets the eye."

"Fine. Whatever. Let's go home. I'm anxious to see Daisy and Duke."

Sarah nodded, then glanced back toward the pool. "Let's put the food away first, and see if the house is locked up. I doubt Jack wants to come home and find bears watching Yogi and Boo-Boo in the theater room."

"Great. First he ditches me, and then I have to pick up after him?"

"And take his dog home, too."

"He left his dog behind, too?"

"Yep, but before you start thinking he's evil for that, I need to tell you about Mortimer. It'll make your heart melt."

Lori snorted and gave an exaggerated roll of her eyes, but she lifted a bowl of tortilla chips and one filled with salsa and nodded toward the house. "On the bright side, I've always wondered what Eagle's Way was like. We'll be able to snoop around to our hearts' content."

"I don't know about that," Sarah warned.

"Oh, come on, Mom. Who is gonna know?"

Eyeing the sky, Sarah watched the dark shadow growing bigger. "I think he might."

"Who?"

"Look up, sunshine. Look east. See that black dot?"

Lori turned around and looked. "I can't see . . . Wait. Is that a helicopter?"

"I think it is. I've seen it a few times before. Hold on to your corn chips, missy. I think Jack Davenport is on his way home."

Soon the *whop-whop-whop* of the whirling blades filled the peaceful meadow. The black helicopter flew over the house, then circled it and hovered for a moment. Sarah lifted her face toward the sky and waved, figuring Jack was trying to identify the squatters on his property before landing. When it moved on toward the concrete helipad some hundred yards or so from the house, Sarah returned the veggie platter to the table and went out to meet the new arrivals.

The noise decreased as the pilot cut the engine and the blades began to slow. Moments later, a door slid open and Jack Davenport climbed down from the pilot's seat. Sarah's curiosity was piqued when she spied a second pair of legs—female legs—descending from the far side of the helicopter.

A smile on his face, Jack strode toward her, his long, confident stride eating up the distance. As always, Sarah was tempted to sigh over the man. Standing beside her, Lori did exactly that. Jack Davenport was as gorgeous as ever. Thick black hair crowned a strong-jawed, angular face with a thin blade of a nose that showed signs of a break sometime in the past. Dark lashes framed winter-ice blue eyes, and a small, faint scar ran along his right eye. But it was the jagged inch-long mark on his left cheek that made him look dangerous.

He was tall and broad-shouldered like Cam, the shared family genetics obvious now that she'd seen them both within a short period of time. No wonder she'd been attracted to Jack, Sarah thought.

"Hey, beautiful," Jack said, taking hold of both of Sarah's hands, then leaning down to place a swift, friendly kiss on her mouth. "I didn't anticipate arriving home to such lovely scenery."

"Please don't arrest us for trespassing," she returned. "Cam brought us."

"More scuba lessons?" Jack asked as he turned to Lori. His expression, already welcoming, warmed. "You're Lori. Lovely Lori. You have your father's eyes and your mother's smile. Welcome to Eagle's Way, cousin." Then he leaned over and kissed her, too. Lori's complexion flushed prettily pink.

Sarah's gaze shifted from Lori to the woman who had arrived with Jack. She wore a khaki pencil skirt, a white blouse, and a murderous expression as she walked past them carrying a dust mop of a dog and speaking not a word. Upon reaching Sarah's car, she stopped and glanced inside. Jack frowned and asked, "You didn't leave your keys in the ignition, did you?"

"No," Sarah replied, fascinated, as the woman turned and started walking . . . down the road, away from the house. In heels. "Where is your friend going?"

Jack's mouth twisted with an amused grin. "Not as far as she thinks. She doesn't realize how isolated we are up here. The exercise will do me good."

"Do *you* good?" Lori repeated.

"We've been cooped up together traveling for a while. She's not very happy with me. I'll let her walk off some of her steam, then I'll go pick her up." Looking toward the house, he added, "So where's Cam?"

Sarah's concern for the Murphy men came rolling back as she relayed the news to Jack. "That's crazy," Jack said once she finished. "I could believe that the kid might be smoking, but dealing? Not in a million years."

Sarah glanced toward her car, anxious to be headed back to town. "I know. Cam was going to call Mac Timberlake. He's a great attorney, and Zach is a levelheaded sheriff, too. I'm sure they'll be able to help straighten the whole thing out."

Jack settled a sympathetic look on Lori as he asked, "Did you and Cam have a chance to get to know each other before this happened?"

When Lori only looked away and shrugged, Sarah explained, "Zach arrived right after we did, so no."

"That's lousy." Jack reached for Lori's hand and squeezed it. "I've known Cam a long time, and I know how much today meant to him, how much you mean to him."

Sarah could tell from Lori's expression that Jack's words were about to make her tear up again. She looped her arm through Lori's and said, "We're going to head back to town now. How long will you be in Colorado this time? Will we see you in Eternity Springs?"

Jack shifted his gaze toward the departing woman. "I'm not quite sure, but I'll ask a favor of you. It's fine if you mention that you were here when I arrived, but please don't tell anyone that I have a guest."

The request piqued Sarah's curiosity, but she had better manners than to ask more. Her daughter, unfortunately, must have left her manners on the horse farm. "Why not?" Lori asked.

Jack rolled his tongue around his mouth, and his eyes gleamed with rueful humor. "It's a long explanation, but technically, I kidnapped her."

"You what?" Sarah exclaimed.

"Don't worry. She's my ex-wife. Besides, her mother asked me to do it."

Cam parked his truck and rushed toward the front door of the sheriff's office. Seeing him coming, Mac Timberlake opened the door. "What's going on?" Cam asked him when he stepped inside.

"Not much of anything," Mac replied. "Devin isn't talking to Zach, but he's not talking to me, either. I decided to leave him alone for a little while to think about some of the things I said."

Seated at his desk, Zach Turner hung up his telephone. He rose and joined Mac and Cam. "I talked to Colt. It's like I figured, he's never picked up a whiff of drug use on the team."

"Where do we stand, Turner?" Cam asked. "How much trouble is Devin in?"

"That depends," the sheriff replied.

Mac spoke up: "Zach has a lot of leeway in a case like this."

"What takes this whole thing up a level is that he had drugs on a playground. Legally, that's much more serious than smoking a joint behind the Bear Cave. I don't want to bring the hammer down on your son, Murphy. He wasn't caught cooking meth or pushing crack, but right now, Eternity Springs doesn't have a drug problem, and I intend to make sure it remains that way. I need to know where he got the stuff and why he had it at the playground."

"He wasn't dealing," Cam insisted. "I'd bet my life on that. You said you had an eyewitness? Who was it? What exactly did he see?"

Zach didn't answer right away. He glanced at Mac, then admitted, "Pauline Roosevelt is the one who called."

"Pauline Roosevelt?" Cam threw out his arms. "Well, of course. I should have known. That woman hates me. She's hated me since I was six years old and accidentally threw a baseball through her kitchen window. Hell, it wouldn't surprise me if she planted the stuff on my kid. Who did she claim he was dealing to?"

"She couldn't tell. Kid had his back to her." The sheriff folded his arms. "Look, I didn't believe her myself, but it's my job to follow up, so that's why I went by your place. The duffel was there. The stuff was inside. I don't think Pauline planted it there, so I want an explanation from your boy."

He looked at Mac and said, "Do you think we've let him sweat long enough? You want to take another run at him?"

Mac glanced at the wall clock. "Yes."

"I'll go with you," Cam said, stepping forward.

Mac shook his head. "I think that would be a mistake. In my experience, kids almost always clam up when a parent is in the room. Let me go in and see where we stand with him. I'll call you in if I think it'll help."

"But—"

"You called me in, Cam," Mac interrupted. "Let me do my job."

Cam knew Mac was right. He nodded once, grimly, then leaned against the hallway wall with his arms folded while Mac went in to speak with his son. Zach watched him and looked as if he was going to speak, but Cam wasn't in the mood to talk to the lawman. Turner had screwed up Cam's world where both of his children were concerned today, and besides, he couldn't forget that this was another man that Sarah had kissed.

His gut churned. His thoughts whirled. He'd always tried to be realistic about Devin. He wasn't one of those parents who believed his kid never did anything wrong. If anything, he tended to believe worse of Dev than he probably deserved. He didn't believe this. Dev damn sure wasn't dealing. He probably wasn't using.

Cam could think of two possible explanations. Either someone planted the weed on him or it somehow figured into a favor Devin was doing for one of his friends.

Friendship had been the boy's downfall in the past. It was easy to believe that it could be so again. But if that were the case, one or more of the Grizzlies had fooled Cam completely.

The minutes ticked by like hours, but finally the door to the interview room opened and Mac exited. He looked at Cam. "That's one stubborn kid you have, Murphy."

"He's still not talking?"

"He's told me most of it." To Zach, Mac said, "I don't foresee the need to make an arrest in this one, Sheriff Turner."

"I hope you're right, Judge Timberlake."

Cam fervently did, too. After Zach cautioned him to keep quiet during the interview, Cam followed the sheriff and attorney into the conference room. He took one look at Devin and wanted to put his fist through the wall. The young man's face was a picture of guilt.

Zach and Cam both took a seat. Zach flipped open the cover of a spiral-bound notebook and took a pen from his pocket. Mac said, "Okay, Devin. Start at the beginning."

Devin's head was down, his chin resting on his chest. He mumbled a bit as he said, "It all started when we went camping last week. We ended up sharing a campsite with these guys from Oklahoma. They were older than we were. They had beer and weed that they kept offering to us. Some of the guys, well . . ." Devin dared a glance up at Cam. "I drank the beer, but that's all. I swear."

"Tell us about these guys from Oklahoma," Zach said.

Devin's stare dropped to the table once again. "They were just guys. Tourists. Three of them. Mark and Steve and Larry."

"Last names?" Zach asked, making a note.

Devin shrugged. "I dunno. I don't think they ever said."

"So then what happened?"

Dev's gaze flashed quickly to Mac, who nodded encouragingly. "Nothing. We went to sleep, got up in the morning and fished, then came home that afternoon. I didn't think any more about it."

Devin took a gulp of water from the clear plastic cup in front of him, then continued, "It's so stupid. I heard about it at practice. One of the guys needs money for something really important. He's pretty desperate. So that night, after everyone in camp went to sleep, he got the bright idea to steal the campers' stash and sell it."

Of all the stupid things to do, Cam thought, frowning with disgust. But he'd been right about one thing—this *was* a case of a friend leading Devin into trouble.

Zach asked, "This was last week, Devin?"

"Yes."

"And you bought that bag from your friend when?"

"I didn't buy it!" Devin insisted, his head whipping up. "I didn't even know about it until today. I found out just before practice. I got pissed because it's such a dumbass idea. If he needed money that bad, he should have told us. We'd have all pitched in and given him the money. I told him that, too, but he just clammed up."

"Why is that?" Zach asked.

"He's proud. He said he doesn't need charity. I told him he needed a brain. He's too proud to let us help him out, so he's willing to do something criminal? Stealing and selling pot? He might be book smart, but where's his common sense?"

Book smart? Cam stiffened subtly as Zach continued to question: "How did you end up with the pot?"

"I made him give it to me. I was going to take it home and flush it." He shot an accusing glare toward Cam, then added, "I just didn't have the chance."

"Who, Devin?" Zach asked. "Which of your friends are we talking about?"

Devin flicked a troubled look toward Cam, and Cam knew what his son was about to say. "I'm not going to be a snitch."

Zach set down his pen. "I have to know, son."

"Why?" Turmoil swam in Devin's eyes. "He hasn't actually sold anything yet. Nobody was harmed. So he swiped something. Now that I think about it, maybe I misunderstood. Maybe he didn't swipe it after all. Maybe they gave it to him, instead. Who is to say?"

"Devin," Zach said, giving the boy a chiding look.

"He realized he made a mistake, and he tried to correct it," Devin said. "No harm, no foul."

Zach leaned forward. "Devin, I understand your reticence, but I need to know—"

"No, you don't!" Devin shoved to his feet. "These are my friends, and they'll hate me if I snitch. Besides, it'll ruin everything. This would screw up his life and ruin his future, and I'm not going to be responsible for that. He screwed up, but I screwed up, too. Don't you see? He'd have been better off selling the stuff than giving it to me to get rid of. I know I said I made him give it to me, but I didn't beat him up or anything to get it! He didn't really want to go through with selling it. That's why he told me to begin with. He was looking for someone to tell him not to be such an idiot."

Devin turned a teary-eyed, apologetic gaze toward Cam, then squared his shoulders. "Throw me in jail. I don't care. I'm not gonna lag on my mate."

Mac drawled, "Like I said, stubborn."

It didn't matter. Devin's outburst had provided Cam the information he'd needed. He knew who'd had the pot that ended up in Devin's bag, and he knew why the kid had taken it.

Speaking for the first time since he'd entered the conference room, Cam said, "Sit down, Devin."

"Dad, I—"

"Sit down." Addressing Zach and Mac, he said, "Could I speak with you two outside?"

The two men followed Cam out into the hall. After Zach shut the interview door behind them, Cam faced them and said, "I figured it out. I know who it is, and Devin is right. If this got out, it could prove very harmful to the kid."

"Who is it?"

"Our pitcher. Mike Hamilton." Cam watched both men think it through. "The 'book smart' remark gave it away. The kid knocked his SAT out of the ballpark."

"His mother's medical bills," Zach said, referring to the breast cancer treatment Lisa Hamilton had undergone the previous year. "I know the Hamiltons are strapped for cash."

"And my friend wangled him an invitation to a select player baseball camp in Saint Louis," Mac agreed.

"That's why he needed money. He'd get plenty of exposure there."

"But he can't afford to go, and he's too proud to ask for help." Zach sighed, shaking his head. "The town had a fund-raiser for Lisa earlier this year, and it was painful to watch Mike Senior's reaction to receiving 'charity.' I swear he's the proudest man I've ever met."

Mac asked the sheriff, "What do you want to do?"

"I don't want to arrest anybody over this, but the situation isn't contained, and I'm going to have to do something. Pauline won't keep her mouth shut. I can't have a sixteen-year-old holding out on me." Zach looked at Cam. "He's going to have to name Mike."

"Not if Mike turns himself in," Cam suggested. "Look, could you give a little time? Mike is a good kid, and I think if I explain what's going on, he'll solve this problem for us. I suspect Devin called it when he said Mike was looking for someone to stop him."

Mac nodded his agreement. "He'll turn himself in. Knowing Mike, the guilt is already eating him alive. I know people like to think that kids don't have moral values anymore, but that's simply not true. I have a suggestion that might work well for everyone. Zach, you could put the fear of God into the boys with a lecture. You're good at that. They can offer to do some community service. We can present that to Pauline and ask for her discretion. It might placate her, and besides, she is friendly with Lisa Hamilton. She won't cause that family unnecessary grief."

"I don't know," Cam said bitterly. "There is a Murphy involved. If discretion means letting Devin off the hook . . ."

"She's not totally unreasonable, Cam," Zach said. "And I like your idea, Mac." To Cam, he said, "How long do you think you'll need?"

"I'm not exactly sure where he is. Give me an hour?"

"Sounds like a plan."

Cam used his cellphone to call Colt Rafferty as he left the sheriff's office. He gave his new friend and Grizzlies head coach a brief summary of the afternoon's events and asked if Colt knew where to look for Mike Hamilton. Ten minutes later, both men walked into the Blue Spruce Sandwich Shop, where the teen was in the back washing dishes, finishing up his shift.

Mike Hamilton took one look at the solemn expressions on his baseball coaches' faces and color washed from his complexion.

Cam spied movement in the periphery of his vision, turned to look, and groaned. *Could this day get any better?*

The Boston terrorist was on the loose again.

FOURTEEN

Sarah had trouble keeping up in the chase after Mortimer, because she couldn't stop laughing long enough to catch her breath.

It had started when Celeste arrived at the house to visit with Lori in the wake of the planned meeting with Cam. The older woman had made the mistake of hugging Lori with the door open, and the rest was history or, in Sarah's viewpoint, hysterical.

Mortimer dashed out of the house. Lori let out a squeal and darted after him. Once outside, Mortimer stopped and waited for Lori to come almost within reaching distance. Then he took off again, Lori chased him again, squealed again. That's when Mortimer began squealing back. His pterodactyl squeal.

The horrified look on Lori's face upon hearing it was priceless, and that's what started Sarah laughing. She and Celeste followed the girl and dog, enjoying the show, as her hardheaded daughter met her match.

Their path took them up and down Aspen, weaving around bushes, cutting through yards, ducking into alleyways. Celeste walked alongside Sarah, pushing the bicycle that was her most frequent summertime mode of transportation. Between bouts of giggles, Sarah told Celeste what had happened at Eagle's Way.

Celeste clicked her tongue. "That foolish boy. What was he thinking?"

"Who knows."

"Well, Devin has a good heart. I'm sure they'll get everything worked out."

"I hope so." For all of their sakes, Sarah added silently.

She spied Cam up ahead, walking toward them. She lifted her arm to wave at him just as Mortimer took a sharp left turn on Cemetery Road and darted up the hill, Lori hard on his trail. Cam returned her wave and reached the intersection moments before Celeste and Sarah arrived. He waited, a harried look on his face. Harried but not devastated, she realized. Dev's situation must not be too horrible.

"Tell me you have a tranquilizer gun in your bike bag," he said to Celeste.

"Now, Cam," Celeste said. "You can't shoot the dog."

"I want it for myself."

Sarah asked, "How is Devin?"

"Stupid and stubborn, and lucky that he pulled his stunt here, where the sheriff has a brain and a heart."

"Is he home?"

Cam shook his head. "No. I suspect Zach has him cooling his heels in a jail cell right now. I almost hope he keeps him overnight. Knuckleheaded kid."

"He's in jail?" Sarah asked, touching Cam's sleeve.

"Hey, that's fine by me if it scares some sense into him." He looked up the hill toward where Lori and his dog had disappeared from sight. "I was in the sandwich shop and saw the dog run by with Lori on his heels. I thought I'd better deal with it. So how bad did I screw things up with Lori when I left Eagle's Way this afternoon?"

Sarah debated her response for a moment, then finally said, "It was never going to be easy."

His mouth twisted. "That bad, huh?"

Celeste climbed onto her bicycle. Reaching for her helmet, she said, "Perhaps you should consider the interruption a blessing. I know you both thought the neutral grounds of Eagle's Way would be an appropriate place for Cam and Lori to meet, but I suggest this hillside might be better."

"It's not a hillside, Celeste. It's a cemetery."

"I know that."

"You're telling me to meet my daughter in a graveyard? You think our relationship is dead right out of the gate?"

"I think Pearl Buck said it best. 'If you want to understand today, you have to search yesterday.' Both of you, your yesterday is up that hill. Lori's yesterday is up that hill."

"In graves," Sarah said.

"History," Celeste insisted. "Both of you have blood ties to the town's founding fathers. According to my research, Lori is the first descendent of all three men."

"I didn't realize that," Cam said.

"It's true. You may live half a world away, Cameron, but your roots are here. The boulder you tote around on your shoulders came from Murphy Mountain, and it has made you strong. You should draw from that as you open your heart to your daughter, because that's what it will take, and doing so is never easy. This town formed you, it shaped you. Explain that to your daughter. Help her understand. Understanding leads to healing—for all of you, and for all of us."

Celeste turned her attention to Sarah. "You have perhaps the hardest job in all of this, with two halves of your heart at odds. You, too, can find strength in your history. Strength in the place. It's a beautiful spot, peaceful and serene. Now go. Find your daughter. Find your family. I must be getting back to Angel's Rest. I want to take a soak in the hot springs and watch the sun go down."

She pulled on her bicycle helmet, fastened the chin strap, and rode off. Cam watched her go, then shook his head. "That woman is an eerie combination of brilliant and daffy."

"Not daffy," Sarah corrected. "She just sometimes drifts off onto her own little philosophical, metaphysical cloud that's a little too misty to grab hold of."

"Well, I don't want to bare my soul to Lori in a graveyard with Beelzebub on the loose," Cam said as he started up the hill.

"That's your choice." Sarah held up her hands. "It's our fault that Mortimer got loose, and we'll worry about rounding him up. If you need to get back to Devin, I understand."

"Devin can wait. I want to talk to her. I want to do it somewhere else. Anywhere else. Celeste and I have different visions of peaceful and serene. I don't like the symbolism of having my first father-daughter talk at a cemetery. On top of everything else, it's on a dead-end road."

Sarah couldn't help but laugh. "You're superstitious. I didn't know that about you."

"I carry enough ghosts around with me as it is, thank you." He eyed the climb with resignation in his eyes and added, "I don't need any others hitching a ride while I'm walking around their living room."

The road up to the hilltop meadow curved in a series of three switchbacks, which moderated the steepness of the climb. Nevertheless, Sarah felt the burn in her leg muscles by the time they walked beneath the arched iron sign that read simply *Cemetery.*

"See any sign of them?" Cam asked. "I don't hear the dog."

"If we walk down the center aisle, we should see Lori, if not the dog. It's not that big." Sarah visited the cemetery regularly to put flowers on her father's grave. Like Celeste, she found it to be a relaxing, peaceful place.

Cam followed a couple of steps behind her, his hands shoved into his pockets, his shoulders slightly hunched.

Sarah was surprised by his obvious discomfort. According to Devin, this man regularly swam among sharks. Strolling through a graveyard should be a piece of cake for him.

A minute later, she spied both Lori and the dog. Mortimer lay sprawled on his belly in front of a gravestone opposite one of the oldest and largest trees on the hill. Lori sat on an ornate stone bench placed beneath the tree's spreading branches decades ago by a Cavanaugh family member across from the Cavanaugh family plots. Lori sat with her back toward the Cavanaughs, however, looking toward the Murphy family gravestones. *Well, shoot.*

Sarah halfway expected Cam to bolt. Instead, he released a heavy breath, then walked past her, approaching Lori and one particular grave—his mother's. Cam stood staring down at the marker for a long moment and though she didn't understand quite why, Sarah held her breath.

Lori surprised her by speaking first: "What was she like?"

Cam twisted his head and looked at his daughter. "The thing I remember most about her is her voice. Mom had a beautiful voice, and when she was happy, she sang. She loved Beatles tunes."

Sarah didn't remember Cassie Murphy singing Beatles songs, but she did recall her singing hymns in church. Lori had a beautiful voice, too. Had Sarah mentioned that to Cam? She wasn't certain. She should. He'd like to know.

He removed his hands from his pockets, turned, and took a seat beside Lori. Leaning forward, he rested his elbows on his knees and said, "I was only eight when she died. My memories of her are limited. She made her bed every morning, then knelt beside it to say her morning prayers. She unloaded her dishwasher early in the morning—loudly. More times than not, that's what woke me up. She loved tending to her flowerpots and reading paperback books."

"What kind of stories?"

A faint smile hovered on his lips. "*Star Trek* books."

Sarah crossed to the tree and leaned against its wide trunk, close enough to offer her silent support to both her daughter and her daughter's father without intruding on their conversation.

"What about your dad?" Lori asked.

Cam's smile disappeared. "He died after I left Eternity Springs."

"I know." Lori pointed toward the dates on Brian Murphy's headstone. "I was four years old. What was he like?"

Now Cam sat up straight, his spine stiff, his expression harsh. "He was a mean SOB. He was not a good husband to my mother. He yelled at her, said horrible, ugly things. He was a drunk. The first time he beat me was the day of my mother's funeral. The last time was the day I finally hit him back."

Lori gave him a sidelong look. "Did he hit your mother?"

"No. Not that I ever saw. That doesn't mean he didn't wound her. Words can wound as much as fists, in some cases."

"I always heard that she married him as a way to rebel against her parents. Like Mom and you."

Sarah saw his protest form, but he bit it back and kept the conversation on his parents. Lori's grandparents. "My mother loved him. In the beginning, she loved him, and I think he loved her, too, or else he was a liar in addition to his other sterling qualities. She had letters tucked away in her Bible, and I found them my sophomore year in high school."

As soon as he said it, Sarah remembered. He'd told

her about the letters. Finding them had left him shaken. It had bothered him to think that his father had loved his mother, then treated her so poorly.

"Maybe rebellion was part of it, but I do know my mother loved Brian Murphy when she eloped with him."

"What changed?" Lori asked.

"I don't know. I think it's safe to assume that the booze didn't help, but was that the cause? Who knows? As mean as he was to her, he grieved for her when she died." Cam's gaze focused on his father's gravestone, and he slowly shook his head.

Lori stretched out her legs, crossed them at the ankles, then abruptly changed the subject. "What do you want from me?"

"Anything you are willing to give me. I'd like to get to know you, Lori. I want you in my life."

"Why? You already have a kid. The drug dealer."

Cam lifted his gaze skyward, then briefly explained why Devin had pot in his duffel. "He's a good kid, and while I hate that he lost both his birth parents, I'm happy that he's with me. But, Lori, Devin hasn't taken your place. I have a hole in my heart where you belong. You are a piece of me that's been missing."

"And whose fault is that?" she snapped.

"Mine," he fired back. "I made a huge mistake. I'm asking for the chance to rectify it."

Now she pushed off the bench and began to pace. "Look, I'm trying to be a grown-up about this situation, but I'm not having much luck. I'm not a mistake for you to rectify."

"That's not what I said. The mistake was turning away from your mother when she needed me the most. I loved her, and I let her down. I let you down. I'd like the opportunity to attempt to explain why."

"Look, it doesn't really matter. Water under the bridge and all that."

"Nevertheless, I'd like to tell you what I was thinking."

"You're not listening to me. It really doesn't matter. See, whenever I start thinking about you, I get squishy inside. It's an unpleasant squishy. I'll admit that it surprises the heck out of me, because all my life, I wanted a dad. But once I saw you in Australia, I've figured out that the dad I want isn't you. You're not my dad, you're the sperm donor."

Oh, Lori. Sarah's heart went out to Cam as she watched the blow land.

"Being home in Eternity Springs, being *here*"—she pointed toward the ground with both hands—"it brings home the importance of family history. Having no history is too much history to overcome."

At that, Cam shot Sarah a look that said *I knew it was a mistake to come up here.*

"You're wrong, Lori. We do have history." He pointed toward his father's grave. "It's right there. It's eight years of fists to the head and boots to the ribs. Eight years of a belt. I thought I had him in me. I had just put another human being into a wheelchair, proving it. I was afraid of what I might do to your mom and to you. I was a kid. I didn't trust myself. I honestly believed you two would be better off without me than with me."

Lori *had* heard him. Sarah could tell by the way she momentarily went still. Sarah could also tell that while she'd heard, her daughter wasn't yet ready to listen, so she wasn't surprised by what Lori said next.

"Okay. Fine. Family didn't work for you then. It doesn't work for me now. You made a choice, now let me make mine. Just because we ran into each other halfway around the world doesn't mean that you are now my family. I'm not trying to be mean. I'm trying to be honest. That ship has sailed—all the way to Australia."

Watching them, Sarah was pulled between heartache

and frustration. Celeste had been right on the money when she referred to these two as two halves of her heart.

"Okay, fair enough," Cam replied. "What if I don't ask to be your dad? What if I say simply that I want us to get to know each other. What if we gave friendship a try?"

Lori folded her arms, stubborn as ever. "Why? I have friends. Plenty of them."

Clearly frustrated, Cam tried again. "Okay, then. Don't you at least want my medical history?"

That got Lori's attention. "Why? Do I need it?"

"You have your grandmother's eyes. Maybe you have her high blood pressure?"

"Did she have high blood pressure?"

Cam simply shrugged.

"Now, that's low," Lori snapped.

His grin came slow and sad. "I'll do whatever it takes, Lori Elizabeth. Please give me a chance. Would you spend some time this holiday weekend with me? No demands, no conditions, no attempts to be a father or your family. Let me talk to you about diving. I'd love to hear about your course work at A and M. Biomedical science major, right? I'd love to hear about your internship. I'd love to get your insight into animals and listen to any and all suggestions you might have where that demon dog is concerned. He's about to drive me crazy. He'll only sleep if I let him sleep at the foot of my bed."

"You let that dog sleep with you?"

"It's either that or listen to him scream all night. You heard his scream, right?"

"It's the most horrible thing I've ever heard."

"Do you have any suggestions for me?"

"Well, of course. You cannot allow your pet to be the leader of the pack. You must assert your authority."

"I don't know about that. He's been independent for a very long time. I don't want to break him. I'd like him to stop running away from me. I want us to get along together."

Lori eyed him warily. "Tell me you are not trying to equate me and Mortimer."

"Absolutely not." Cam drew back, but Sarah spied the glimmer of amusement in his eyes. "Mort is half blind, four-legged, ugly as sin, and he squeals like a bird. You are a beautiful young woman who has a way of holding your chin that reminds me of my mother."

Lori glanced at Cassie Cavanaugh Murphy's grave. "Back before Mom told me the truth about you—when I thought the Y-chromosome part of my genetics was unknown—I used to study myself and try to figure out what I got from Mom and what was wild card."

Wild card, Sarah silently repeated. That described Cam Murphy at sixteen very well.

Lori crossed over to the Cavanaugh family graves. She slipped her hands into her jeans pockets and rocked on her heels. "I haven't been up here since my senior year in high school when I came with you, Mom, to put flowers on Granddad's grave on his birthday. It does help put life into perspective, doesn't it? No matter where I go or how long I stay away, this hilltop is part of me, isn't it?"

Cam's gaze rested briefly on his father's small, plain marker. "Your friend Celeste owns the house I'm renting here in town. She has sayings and quotations all over the place. A wall plaque has a quote that made an impression on me. It says, 'There are only two lasting bequests we can give our children—one is roots, and the other, wings.' "

"Celeste is all about wings," Lori said. "Mom has done an excellent job giving me both wings and roots."

"Your mom is a special woman."

That earned him a frown from Lori and an exasperated

scowl from Sarah. It would do Cam's campaign no good at all to have Lori figure out that her mother and father were . . . friendly again.

Lori drifted back toward the Murphy plots, where she stared down at Cam's mother's grave for a full minute before she said, "You grew up with only one parent, too."

"Lucky for you that you got to be with the good parent."

Lori glanced at Sarah and nodded. "Lucky me."

Cam cleared his throat. "I understand there's a big picnic at Hummingbird Lake tomorrow before the fireworks show. Would you and your mother like to go with Devin and me?"

Lori shook her head. "No. Tomorrow is Nana's birthday. Mom and I and Nana always spend the day together. It's a family tradition."

With that, Sarah had enough.

"And there is no reason you and Devin can't join us," she said, stepping forward. "Lori, I told you about Celeste's Redemption Plan. She and our other friends have gone to quite some effort to make it easier for us around town with the old-timers who still hold being a Murphy against Cam . . . and now against you."

"Well, people who want to believe that are stupid, and I don't care."

"I agree that it's nonsense. Nevertheless, I do care. My friends have gone out of their way for me, and now it's time for us to do our share. This is my home. These are my neighbors. We will attend the picnic together tomorrow."

"What?" Lori said, petulance in her tone. "Like a *family*? Mom, that's not fair. You said that I had to talk to him. Now I've done that."

"You can do it some more."

Her daughter's eyes flashed as she rolled them in that exaggerated way that only teens and young adults can do. "Fine. In the meantime, I have things to do. I told the Timberlakes I'd stop by and show them the pictures I took of Chase when he came to visit."

Sarah didn't know if she'd ever seen anyone flounce out of a graveyard before. She saw it now. When she and Cam were alone—well, alone with Mortimer—he exhaled a heavy breath. "That went well—or not."

"I think it did go well." When the dog lifted his head, Sarah took the precaution of fastening the expandable leash to his collar before taking a seat beside Cam. "It was a start."

He rubbed the back of his neck. "I'm beat. Between Devin's nonsense and this . . . I'm toast."

"You should go over to Angel's Rest and soak in the hot springs."

"I can't." He linked his hand with hers. "I have to go back to the sheriff's office and see where that whole thing stands. I have to tell you, sugar, this is not how I hoped today would go."

"Some days are bigger challenges than others, that's for sure."

"What do you expect from tomorrow? Will she cooperate?"

"Yes. Lori talks tough in private, but in public . . ." Sarah shrugged. "She's proud. This is her first trip home since everyone found out that you are her father. She won't pretend that we're all a happy family, but she won't snub you, either. Honestly, Cam, this went better than I expected, especially after this afternoon."

"I guess you're right. I could have ended the day at the local cemetery under different circumstances."

"Different circumstances?"

"She was angry . . ." Cam pointed toward the dirt. "But not that angry."

Sarah's laugh settled over him like a song, and for the first time in hours, Cam looked toward the following day with hope.

* * *

Cam had been told that the Fourth of July in Eternity Springs signaled the start of the busy, busy season, as tourists arrived in droves, fleeing the summertime heat for the cool, unspoiled beauty of the Colorado Rockies. As a rule, merchants chose to forgo the holiday and open for business in order to score the holiday sales, but at four o'clock, the shops shut down for the traditional town picnic now being held in the public park on the shores of Hummingbird Lake. Sarah had instructed Cam to meet her at the parking lot where Angel Creek flowed into the lake at four-thirty. She was providing the food. He was in charge of bringing a cooler filled with drinks.

Anxious, he arrived ten minutes early—driving the car he'd bought for Lori. He cooled his heels by striking up a conversation with a tourist who watched his preschool-aged children having a glorious time throwing rocks into the lake. Turned out the man was one of Gabe Callahan's brothers—Matt—and the boys he watched were his nephews. "The whole clan came up for the Fourth this year," he explained. "Ordinarily, we spend the holiday together at our lake place in Texas, but we've already had ten days above one hundred degrees this summer, and the Colorado climate called us."

"Gabe told me y'all are putting together a regular family compound along the western shore of Hummingbird."

Matt Callahan nodded. "We started out with one place, but the kids like being here with their cousins, and we had the land, so we figured we'd spread out."

Just then one of the boys picked up a rock that was almost bigger than he was and dropped it on his cousin's toes. Callahan sputtered a curse, excused himself, then hurried to deal with the children as Cam spied Sarah's car pulling into the lot. Lori drove, and Ellen Reese occupied the passenger seat. Sarah sat in back. He saw the moment Lori spied him. Rather than pull toward the empty parking spot beside him, she turned down another row.

"Hard head," he murmured. He hadn't necessarily planned to give his daughter the new car right off the bat, but it had been a possibility. After Lori parked, Sarah opened the trunk and removed folding lawn chairs, a quilt, a picnic basket, and a canvas tote bag.

"Showtime," Cam said beneath his breath. He hefted his cooler and walked toward the three women who had altered the course of his life. "Hey there. Can I help carry something?"

Sarah's carefree grin relaxed him just a little. "Happy Fourth of July, Cam. We've got everything. It looks like you already have your hands full."

Shifting his gaze to Ellen Reese, he said, "Happy birthday, Mrs. Reese."

"Thank you." Ellen Reese gave him an absent look.

"Hello, Lori." He nodded toward his daughter. She nodded back.

"Where's Devin?" Sarah asked, a note of concern in her eyes.

"He and Mike have been helping the mayor since seven o'clock this morning. Apparently, most of Eternity Springs's maintenance workers are down with a virus, and Mayor Townsend is shorthanded. The boys, uh, volunteered their services, and Zach suggested Hank put them to work. He sent them out here to set up extra Porta Pottis to accommodate the holiday crowd. After that, they were going to empty trash cans in all the parks. He's going to meet us as soon as Hank cuts him loose."

Last night, after leaving the cemetery, Cam had dropped off Mortimer at his house, then hurried to the sheriff's office, where he found Colt, Zach, and Mike Hamilton's grim-faced father finishing up their discussion. The relief on Devin's face had been easy to read. Mike looked miserable but not devastated.

The boys were lucky. Zach had sent them home with a warning: "I'm a believer in second chances. Not so much thirds. Consider yourselves on notice."

Cam relayed the details to Sarah as she led the way to a shady spot with a great view of the lake. There, they discovered Celeste spreading a red, white, and blue quilt on the ground.

"Doesn't that look festive," Sarah said as Celeste added a red plastic pail with mums and mini American flags to its center. Lori helped her mother spread a quilt done in shades of yellow and green close to Celeste's.

Lori spoke to her grandmother: "Nana, here's our happy home quilt. We used the old curtains from the kitchen. See?"

Ellen Reese studied the quilt. "I remember."

Cam suspected she didn't remember at all, but then she added, "Butterflies. We had butterflies in our kitchen."

"We sure did, Mom." Sarah turned to Cam. "Would you set up a lawn chair for the birthday girl?"

"Sure will."

Once Ellen was settled, two other women joined their group. Sarah introduced them as Cora Jenkins and Linda Moore, members of the women's group at her church and contemporaries of Ellen's. Cam didn't miss the subtle tension in both Lori's and Sarah's expressions. He braced himself. He didn't recognize the ladies or their names, but he surmised they must be part of his Eternity Springs fan club.

Sure enough, after they'd shared birthday best wishes with Ellen, Cora Jenkins said, "Pauline Roosevelt is in our book club."

Of course she is.

"Pauline talks about you fairly often, Cam," Linda Moore added.

Of course she does.

To his utter shock and surprise, Lori spoke up. "It's a holiday weekend and my grandmother's birthday. Could we please save the Murphy bashing until another time?"

"Oh, we don't mean to bash, Lori," Cora Jenkins said. "That's just it. We wanted to apologize. Cam, I went to school with your mother. I knew your father before he lost his way. I have always felt badly about the way this town treated you after your mother's death. I'm sorry for my part in it."

"As am I," added Linda Moore. "I was a friend of Maribeth Cook's. My son Dennis was Andrew's best friend. I'm afraid I let the Cooks' . . . intensity . . . drown out the fact that Andrew's own actions brought most of his trouble to his door."

Now it was time for Cam to go tense. He remembered Dennis Moore. He'd been at the Bear Cave that night. Cam darted a quick glance toward Sarah. Had word gotten out about the reason behind the punch he'd thrown? "Look, that was a long time ago. It's all water under the bridge."

"Not exactly." Linda's expression turned rueful. "More like the water ran into Hummingbird Lake and settled on the bottom until you returned to town and stirred up the silt."

Silt wasn't the particular S-word he would have used.

"I didn't know the truth until I mentioned to my Dennis that you'd returned to Eternity Springs," Linda continued. "He lives in Boston now. He's an attorney. Doing so well, he made partner last year. He has a lovely wife, and his two sons are the apples of my eyes—but I digress. Dennis never shared details about that night before now. He told me he's always felt bad about keeping quiet. What Andrew did was wrong, and you did right by Sarah and Nicole by stepping in."

She knew about the picture.

Cam felt Sarah's curious gaze, but before she asked a question, Linda reached over and patted her hand. "You were smarter than the rest of us all those years ago, weren't you? You saw a hero in Cam Murphy when the rest of us saw a James Dean wannabe rebel, didn't you?"

Ellen Reese spoke as if by rote. "That Cam Murphy is trouble."

Cora Jenkins placed a hand on Ellen's shoulder and gave it a reassuring pat. "No, Ellen. He's not. That Cam Murphy is a treasure."

Lori's and Sarah's jaws both fell open, then, after the two older women departed for their own picnic quilt, Lori observed, "I guess Celeste's Redemption Plan really is working."

Sarah studied him with a measuring look. Sensing that she was about to ask how he'd done her and Nic right, Cam debated his response. When a chorus of hellos interrupted the moment, he sighed inwardly with relief. Now was not the time or the place to tell her about the locker room snapshot.

Nic and Gabe Callahan arrived with a whole gaggle of kids and adults, obviously Gabe's brothers and their wives, which meant the old man arriving in a golf cart with a Chihuahua on his lap must be the Callahan family patriarch, Branch.

A few minutes later, the Timberlakes arrived with their three adult children. Behind them, Cam spied the Raffertys making their way through the growing crowd. Colt carried folding lawn chairs and a picnic basket. Devin was with them, toting a cooler. Lori spotted them, too, and said, "Wow. Sage has always been pretty, but now she looks gorgeous. Like an earth-mother fairy queen. When is her baby due?"

"Next month," Sarah replied.

Some of the Callahan children called for Lori to join them throwing a Frisbee. She seemed happy for the escape, especially, Cam deduced, since Devin was about to join them.

Devin's mouth twisted in a wry smirk as Lori fled, but then he shrugged and greeted Ellen and Sarah politely before plopping down onto the quilt. "I'm exhausted."

"Are you done for the day?" Cam asked.

"Yes, sir."

"Would you like a soft drink or some peach iced tea?" Sarah offered. "I have cookies, too."

Devin's expression lit. "What kind?"

"Ginger and"—Sarah gave Cam a sidelong glance—"sugar cookies."

They shared a private smile as an oblivious Devin said, "Ginger cookies and peach tea, please."

Cam glanced toward the Frisbee players and saw Lori frowning in their direction. Stifling a sigh, he said, "Lots of people in town today."

"I had a great day at Fresh. I sold out forty-five minutes before closing time, and that's after increasing my usual daily production by a third."

"Awesome," Devin said. "I'll bet you are as tired as I am."

"I'm happy to sit and rest a bit."

"I hope you're not tired, Dad."

"Why is that?"

"I signed us up for the kayak race."

"You what?"

"It's a two-man race. Actually, it's a couples race—one guy and one girl. It starts in an hour." He polished off a cookie, then looked over at Lori as he added, "I put us down for two boats. I thought it would be a good opportunity to show the whole town that we are okay together. We can cancel if you guys don't like the idea."

"I think it's a great idea," Sarah said.

"What will she think?" Cam asked, nodding toward Lori.

"Honestly, I think this is right up her alley. Lori loves to compete."

"She'll partner with me?"

"Honestly, I don't know." As Devin helped himself to another cookie, Sarah added, "It depends on which of you two she's feeling more resentful toward at the moment, which of you she wants to defeat most."

Cam and Devin shared a look, then Devin grinned. "Two bucks says she wants to be in your boat."

"I'll take that bet."

"Well, let's have a chin-wag with the Sheila, eh? See what she has to say." Devin rolled to his feet, picking up his canned drink and yet another cookie, and sauntered toward the Frisbee free-for-all.

FIFTEEN

Lori watched him come. Whereas dealing with Cam left her numb, the very idea of Devin scraped against her brain like shards of broken glass. She understood that her reaction was emotional rather than logical, but she couldn't help it. He prodded at things deep within her—things like envy and jealousy and resentment. Her feelings toward Cam were justifiable. These things she felt toward Devin were not. It wasn't his fault that his mother had died and Cam had decided to adopt him. He wasn't to blame for the fact that he'd had a father around when he was growing up. Just because his last name was Murphy and hers wasn't didn't give her a legitimate reason to despise the guy.

But she did. Deep down inside herself, she did. She didn't like it that she felt this way. She wasn't happy to be so childish, but she couldn't seem to help herself.

Cam had adopted this boy, but she'd never rated so much as a phone call. Okay, so he'd tried to send money, but he hadn't tried too hard, had he? He'd given up. He hadn't wanted her bad enough to keep trying—and now she had a full-blown case of sibling rivalry going on. *How stupid is that?*

Devin walked up to her and shot her a cocky grin. "Hello again, Lori. I'm here to challenge you to a race."

"A race?" She frowned. "What kind of race?"

He pulled a folded sheet of paper from his back pocket

and handed it over without comment. Lori scanned the page. The kayak race. "You're kidding."

"Nope. I've already entered us." He put his hands on his hips, rocked back on his heels, and lifted his chin. "Whose ass do you want to whip more, Sis? Me or Dad?"

She narrowed her eyes and literally bit her tongue to keep from saying *Don't call me Sis.* She needed to talk to him, but she did not want to do it within the line of sight of her mother and Cam. "I need to get something out of Mom's car. Want to walk with me?"

"It's not a baseball bat, is it?" He scratched a nonexistent beard. "You know, to beat me over the head with?"

"Very funny." The Frisbee came her way once more, and she tossed it to a Callahan kid, then called, "I'm out!"

Lori felt her mother's questioning gaze on her as she led Devin away from the picnic area, but she refused to look. At this particular moment, she acted on instinct alone. She sensed she needed to deal with Devin on her own.

When they arrived at the parking lot, he abruptly stopped. "Did you really leave something in the car?"

"No. I didn't want to talk in front of everybody."

"That's what I figured." The teenager leaned against the back hatch of a shiny new car and folded his arms. "I'm glad, because I feel the same way. I want to talk about something, and I'd just as soon not do it in front of the world."

Warily, she asked, "You're not going to try to sell me drugs, are you?"

Hurt flashed across Devin's face, then settled into a scowl. He spoke with an edge in his voice. "I'm trying to apologize, okay? I wasn't selling drugs. I was trying to help a friend."

"Oh, so you were buying?" she asked, knowing she was being a snot but not able to stop herself.

"No!" He gave her a brief summary of what had transpired, ending with, "I screwed up, and so I messed up the big meet between you and Dad. He went to a lot of work to make it nice and everything. He wanted you both to have the perfect opportunity to say everything that you needed to say, and I went and screwed it up so that instead of having your talk at our friend Jack's mountain mansion, you had it in a cemetery."

"You know Jack Davenport?"

"Yeah. He's kind of a cousin of my dad's. He's visited us a bunch."

"I see." A wave of jealousy rolled through her. She set her teeth and fought it back.

"The whole cemetery thing sucks, and it's my fault, and I'm sorry. I told Dad, but I wanted to tell you, too."

He told Dad. Dad. Bitterness bubbled up and spilled out before she could stop it. "I am jealous of you, and that makes me crazy. It's stupid for me to feel that way. I don't care that he adopted you. I don't care about him."

"In that case, you're stupid, too," Devin shot back, his eyes flashing with righteous anger. "People make mistakes, you know. Nobody is perfect. You don't have to look any further than your gramma to prove that."

"Hey, don't you talk about my grandmother."

"She interfered. She stole ten years—"

"Stop it!" she demanded, even as, deep down, she acknowledged the truth and it hurt. Yet family loyalty made her defend her grandmother. "Don't you talk about her."

Devin drew a deep breath and tried again. "Fine. I'll talk about Dad. He's a great dad. I'm so lucky to have him, and you are, too, even if you're too pigheaded to admit it. He tried to do the right thing, you know. What if he *had* turned out to be like his father? You should see the scars Brian Murphy left on his back. If Dad turned out like his father, you'd have been glad he cut your mother loose."

Scars? Lori's chest felt tight. He'd said his father hit him, but he'd never mentioned scars. Angry tears stung her eyes. "The capacity for cruelty isn't genetic."

"Maybe not, but people repeat what they're taught. Cam is a good man, Lori. He's been a great father to me, and he wants to be that for you, too."

"Too bad. You're wasting time trying to pull my heart-strings."

"Cause you don't have a heart?"

No, because Cam bailed. He left. He chose to live elsewhere. He chose you! She gave her head a toss. "I don't need him."

Devin sneered with disgust. "Then you're an idiot. Do you know what I'd give to be in your shoes? My parents are dead, Lori. Dead! My mom can't bake me ginger cookies and blueberry pies. I love Cam. I really do. But do you know what I would give if my real dad could show up out of the blue and buy me a freaking car? You're throwing away a chance I'll never have."

Shame washed through Lori. He'd been an orphan. That had always been one of her greatest fears. She used to imagine what would happen to her if her mother died. Who would care for her? Who would . . . buy her a car? "What? What did you say? A car?"

Devin winced, then started babbling. "He's sacrificed a lot to come to the States to meet you. He'll say that the tour operation gets along fine without him, but that's not mentioning all the hours he puts in on the phone in the middle of the night. He's been working his ass off and missing sleep in order to hang around Eternity Springs until you decide to stop being a twit and talk to him."

Lori waved her hand. "Wait. Stop. Did you say . . . Did you mean . . . Devin, did Cam Murphy buy me a car?"

The man himself responded: "I did."

Lori turned to see Cam striding toward her from the

trees. Her mother was with him, but she'd stopped walking. Her mouth gaped open, and her eyes were round with shock. Guess she hadn't known about the car, either.

"Oh, great," Devin muttered. "Another day, another screw up."

Cam's steady, hopeful gaze never left Lori's face. He offered a hesitant smile. "Your mother mentioned that she worried about the high mileage on the car you drove. Nobody wants to see you breaking down on the highway in the Texas panhandle on your way back to school."

"You bought her a car!" Sarah exclaimed. "Without bothering to mention it to me?"

At that, he finally tugged his stare from Lori and gave Sarah a sheepish look. "There hasn't been a good time."

"Oh, for heaven's sake," Sarah said, starting forward.

Soon the four of them stood together behind the car where Devin originally had stopped, the car where Cam had been standing when they arrived for the picnic, Lori realized. "Oh, wow."

It wasn't just a car. It was a *new* car. A too-cute crossover with dealer tags on the back. A hot-off-the-dealer's-lot car. With a sunroof!

Cam folded his arms. "I hope you like it. Choices were limited, since I wanted to have it here for you this weekend. This model ranks high on safety and is equipped for mountain driving. The salesman told me that this kind of crossover between a car and an SUV is popular with young women your age."

"Wait just a minute," Sarah warned. She braced her hands on her hips. "I think I'm angry about this. You should have discussed it with me, Cam."

"You're right." He shrugged boyishly. "It was a spur-of-the-moment decision."

Sarah arched her brows. "And you figured it was easier to ask for forgiveness than to ask for permission?"

"Something like that, yeah."

Lori watched the exchange between Cam and her mother and frowned. Something was weird. Mom acted way too . . . comfortable with the man. It was almost as if she . . . liked him.

Excuse me? Whoa. No. Emotion rolled through Lori. *Uh-uh.* She had to be misreading the looks. Her mother wouldn't do that. She'd been angry at Cam Murphy for two decades. He couldn't change all that in two weeks.

Could he?

She's probably just shocked about the car. No one's ever tried to make things easier for us this way. Surely she's just stunned.

"What is this going to do to my insurance?" Sarah groaned. "We only carry liability on Lori's car."

"I'll pick up the insurance, too," Cam assured her. "I want to do more for my daughter. I should do more for her."

"You can't buy me." Lori tore her gaze away from the car and met Cam's stare. "I won't like you any more or any less if you give me things."

"I never expected that you would," Cam replied, his tone matter-of-fact. "I will admit that I did hope that the car might soften you up toward me a bit, but I never anticipated I'd be able to buy your affection. From what everyone has told me, you have too much integrity for that."

Okay, well, good. Lori stood a little straighter.

Cam continued, "To be perfectly honest, I bought the car as much for myself as for you."

"How's that?"

"I want you to be as safe as possible at all times, but especially when you're on the road. Knowing you are driving a reliable car will help me sleep at night."

Wow, Lori thought. That sounded just like something her mother would say. Like something a parent would say.

Like something a father would say.

Her heart cracked, just a little, but Lori recognized it and resisted, attempting to shore up her defenses. As an adult she knew she should accept his gesture and open her heart to the possibility of someday allowing him inside. But Lori the child still existed, and Lori the child nursed a fierce anger toward Cameron Daniel Murphy.

"Any other surprises I should know about, Cam?" her mother asked.

Sheepishly, he asked, "You mean gifts?"

"Yes."

"I brought a couple of things for her from Australia."

Sarah frowned the Mom frown. "Expensive gifts?"

"No." Sarah obviously didn't believe him, and he added, "Not when you consider that I have lots of birthdays and Christmases to make up for."

"I don't want any gifts," Lori declared even as she stole one more look at the car and wondered what the other gifts were. *How could he top a car?*

Sadness dimmed his eyes, and once again, Lori felt ashamed. "All right, Lori. I won't try to force gifts on you. The car shouldn't be counted in that category. The car is basic support." He looked at Sarah as he added, "I'll bet your mother will agree."

Sarah slowly nodded. "Cam is right, Lori. I worry myself sick when you're on the road. Knowing you're in a safe, reliable car will make my life easier."

"So you want us to keep it?"

"I do."

Cam pulled a set of keys out of his pocket. "Want to take it for a spin?"

Excitement sizzled through her. *A car.* Her own brand-new, totally awesome automobile. Heck yeah, she wanted to take it for a spin. She opened the door and caught a whiff of that awesome new-car smell. From the side of her eyes, she saw Devin glance at the race flyer that she continued to hold in her hand.

Lori opened her mouth and surprised herself by saying, "I do want to take it for a spin, thank you. I'll go right after the kayak races. Right after . . ." She waited until she caught Devin's attention, then offered a sisterly gesture by sticking her tongue out at him and finished, "Right after we whip baby brother's butt at the boat race."

Cam went still. "You're in my boat? With me?"

"Well, you do run a dive operation, right? So theoretically, you're good with a boat. I like to win." Lori gave a little shrug. "It's a start."

Cam Murphy beamed as if he'd just won the America's Cup.

"C'mon, Sarah," Devin urged. "Dig. They're pulling away."

"I'm digging, I'm digging." Sarah frowned as Cam's back shot over her shoulder, then got momentarily distracted by the sight of his muscles working to propel the kayak across Hummingbird Lake. *Yum.*

"Dig harder."

"My arms are too short."

"My mistake for letting Lori choose," the teen grumbled. "I should have guessed she'd stick me with the runt."

"Hey, I have muscles. Baking bread for a living does that for a girl." Sarah attempted to toss a glare over her shoulder, but the good-natured glimmer she spied in his eyes made her smile instead.

Of course, everything made her smile today. Sarah dipped her paddle into Hummingbird Lake filled with a sense of peace and a little hum of happiness.

The day was going well. Cam and Lori were getting along together about as well as Sarah could have hoped. While a part of her continued to be a bit resentful over his high-handedness with the car, she couldn't deny that it had been a brilliant move. Presenting a gift couched in the terms he'd used—legitimate parental concern over a child's safety—took wind out of any protest she might have tried to make. Lori valiantly had tried to hold on to her snit but failed. She'd totally loved the car, and as a result, her resistance toward him softened. Sarah had seen it even if Cam couldn't.

He'd been so cute as he showed off the car's features to Lori in the few minutes they'd had before making their way to the lake. He'd reminded her of Duke when the dog brought a dead rodent to drop at her feet, then waited expectantly to be petted and praised.

He didn't know Lori well enough to recognize her cues, her reaction to Devin being the biggest. From the moment she'd accepted the teen's kayak challenge, she'd treated him like a younger brother. That was a huge step for Lori, the beginning of acceptance. Sarah could tell that Cam didn't realize it, and she intended to help him see that the first chance she got.

"This is pitiful," Devin observed as Cam and Lori's kayak glided past the finish line. "We're a good thirty seconds behind. I hate to lose."

"Then you shouldn't have given Lori the chance to choose your dad as her partner."

"Yeah, but that's the reason we're out here, isn't it? So that Lori will choose Dad?"

"You are a good kid, Devin Murphy. Smug but good." Sarah lifted her paddle from the water and propped it across the bow of her boat. "Now paddle me home."

"Hey, no deadweight allowed."

"Are you calling me fat?"

She heard him fumble his paddle. "Uh, no, ma'am! I would never do that, even if you were fat. But you're not, of course. You're tiny."

She laughed, delighted with his panicked-man reaction, until Cam maneuvered his kayak around and—for the first time—she saw Lori share an open, unguarded, triumphant laugh with Cam.

It was a picture-perfect moment. Beautiful daughter laughing with her handsome father, sitting in a boat on sapphire Hummingbird Lake, surrounded by snowcapped mountains. Sarah's heart melted, and tears stung her eyes. What a joyous instant in time.

So why did it make her want to cry?

As the crowd on shore cheered, a dozen different thoughts bombarded her like bullets. They should have had a lifetime of moments like this. Or at least a decade of them. Why had her mother and father stolen that from Lori and Cam, from the three of them? Why hadn't Cam tried harder? Why had he let them do it? Why had he gone and hit Andrew Cook to begin with?

And at the core of all of those . . . *You can't have her. She's mine.*

"Oh, I'm messed up," Sarah murmured as Devin took them across the finish line.

"Winner winner chicken dinner," Lori called, her accompanying laugh just short of maniacal. "That would be me, not you. Too bad so sad, Devin."

Then, as Sarah's kayak glided close, Lori caught sight of her mother. "Mom? What's wrong?"

Sarah attempted a stoic smile, then realized she failed miserably when even Cam started to frown. "Sarah?"

"I'm fine," she called out. Then when both her lover's and her daughter's expressions grew doubtful, she lied, "I had a cramp."

"Gee, Sarah," Devin said as he paddled toward the pier. "I told you to stretch."

"I'm fine." Sarah waved away the comments as Devin guided the kayak toward the fishing pier behind Cam and Lori. After Lori climbed from the boat, Cam motioned for Devin to draw close.

"Ladies first," he said.

Sarah hauled herself onto the pier, as Cam pulled alongside it. Just as Lori plopped down onto the pier, Sarah felt a bump at the back of her legs. Gabe Callahan's boxer, Clarence, rushed to greet his old friend, Lori, and knocked Sarah off balance. She teetered, windmilling her arms, then tumbled forward.

On top of Cam's boat.

Tipping Cam's boat.

Both she and he spilled into the icy-cold waters of Hummingbird Lake.

"I'm so tempted to drop-kick that kid off the end of the boat dock," Cam grumbled, glaring toward his son, who continued to chortle with laughter as he described the spill to his baseball friends.

"I'll be right beside you, shoving Lori overboard," Sarah added, scowling at her daughter, who giggled like a child while she explained the incident to Ali and Mac Timberlake. Clarence stood beside her, his crooked tail waving.

"I'm so sorry," Nic said as she hurried onto the dock and handed Cam and Sarah towels. "I don't know what got into Clarence. He pulled the leash right out of Meggie's hand and raced toward the water. He never does that sort of thing."

"It was great entertainment, though," her husband added, wrapping a quilt around Sarah's sopping shoulders. "I didn't know you could reach those high notes with your squeal."

"Oh, bite me, Callahan." Sarah hunched her shoulders and shivered. "Your dog is officially in my doghouse. Has he been hanging around Mortimer, by any chance?"

"Hey, now," Cam protested. "The devil dog had nothing to do with this." Then he called to his son, "Hey, Chuckles. Where did you park?"

His laughter finally subsiding, Devin responded, "I'm all the way on the other side of the lake."

"I'll drop you off, Cam," Sarah said as she waved to get Lori's attention, then called, "I think the concert is about to start. Are you going to sit with your grandmother?"

"Sure, Mom." Lori scratched Clarence behind the ears and said, "I'll be right there."

Cam waited while Sarah spoke with Ellen, who sat between Celeste and Pauline Roosevelt in the front row of a section of folding chairs while the Eternity Springs Combined School Choir lined up on risers for their concert featuring patriotic songs.

"We'll keep Ellen company," Celeste told Sarah. "Don't fret, and don't feel as if you have to rush back. Take your time."

Five minutes later, inside her car, Sarah twisted the dial to turn on the heater. "Wearing wet blue jeans is bad enough. The fact that they're cold adds insult to injury."

The offer to help her take them off hovered on the tip of Cam's tongue, but he surpressed it. No sense starting something they couldn't finish, so he turned his thoughts in a different direction. "How do you think it's going with Lori?"

"Honestly, better than I expected. Your bribe was brilliant."

Brilliant? He hadn't expected that. "So you're not mad about it?"

"Mildly annoyed but smart enough not to do the bite-off-the-nose-to-spite-the-face thing. That car of hers has been a real concern." She paused for a moment, then asked, "Did you enjoy the race?"

A warm smile stole across his face as he recalled the event. "It was great. Once we were on the water, she wasn't guarded at all. Maybe because she didn't have to look at me to talk to me. It was a great icebreaker. She actually asked me some questions about home."

"Oh, really?"

"Yep."

"That's a good sign from Lori."

He reached across the seat and rested his hand on her thigh. "It's a beginning. I'm hopeful. I feel as if I have a chance with her now. Thank you, Sarah."

She dropped her hand from the steering wheel and gave his hand a squeeze. "I'm glad I asked her to come home. It was time. She'd had time to adjust to the fact that you've come to meet her, but putting it off any longer would have made it a higher hill to climb."

Cam abandoned his valiant effort not to stare at the way her wet, transparent shirt clung to the fullness of her breasts. Her shirt was white, her bra a delicate peach. He could see the dusky circles of her nipples outlined against the fabric.

She said something about Devin, but he didn't catch just what. He'd gone as hard as the granite on Murphy Mountain, and all thought of the kids in his life had evaporated. She was so beautiful. So beautiful, so good-hearted. So courageous.

He loved her. He'd never stopped loving her. He always would love her.

Marry me.

The words flashed into his mind and floated to his tongue, but he had sense enough to bite them back. It would be downright stupid to broach that subject without serious consideration ahead of time. This involved more than just the two of them. They had Lori and Devin to think about, not to mention the minor little detail that the female half of the family lived half a world away from the male half.

Of the family.

A family. With Sarah. Maybe they could even have another baby.

"What?" she asked.

"Hmm?"

She braked her car to a stop in front of his house. "What's with the weird look?"

He couldn't begin to explain the thoughts flittering through his brain, so he cut to the heart of the matter: "Come inside with me, Sarah. I need to take you to bed."

Her eyes widened. Her tongue peeked out of her mouth to make a slow, deliberative circle around her lips. "I'm all nasty. I fell in the lake."

"Sometimes nasty can be fun."

A wary light entered her eyes at that, so he added, "Or we can shower first."

"I think I would enjoy another shower."

He climbed out of the car, walked around to the driver's door, opened it, and held out his hand. "Come inside with me."

She placed her hand in his, and he led her inside 354 Seventh Street. Today, old ghosts didn't meet him at the door. Right now he had room in his mind, his heart, his soul, for one thought only.

Sarah.

He shut the door behind her and took her into his arms. Accompanied by phantom music in his mind, he whirled her to AC/DC, the music of their youth. He twirled her to the calypso tunes of those long, lonely years as he'd bounced his way across the world from one boat deck to another. Then he lowered his mouth to hers and kissed her to the sound of every love song he'd ever heard.

And he kissed her.

And he kissed her.

His hand slipped under her shirt, moved slowly up her slender back, then down the tantalizing curve of her spine as she melted into him, pliant and open to his desire. Her hands were wrapped around his neck, her fingers idly playing with the damp strands of his hair. Touching her, tasting her, was as vital to Cam as air and water.

He had crossed the globe trying to escape her, but she had always traveled with him. She had come to him in his sleep, and in his dreams he would touch her and love her and be with her. He would awaken warm and happy and content. Then reality invariably returned, and with it, loneliness.

He'd been lonely for Sarah for so long.

He skimmed his hand across the silk of her bra to capture the full, soft weight of her breast. Her own hand slipped beneath his shirt, splayed across his chest, and her thumb brushed across his nipple.

Heat ignited, shot through his entire body, and stark, demanding hunger clawed at his control. He wanted bare skin and a yielding body. He wanted to throw her down onto the floor and strip away her jeans and take her, hard and fast. He wanted to claim her once and for always as his own.

He knew the delight that awaited him. Knew how she would whimper with need, how her moist, hot flesh would clench around him. How she would meet and match his deep strokes with a fierce surge of her hips, driving them higher and higher and higher until their own intimate version of Fourth of July fireworks would burst in hot, pulsing splendor across their personal sky and they'd drift back to earth aglow with glittering pleasure.

With effort, Cam fought the instinct back. This time was different. This time was more than heat and physical satisfaction.

This time was love.

How did I ever survive without her?

Cam broke the kiss and took a necessary step back. "Why don't you take that shower."

She took the suggestion like a douse of cold water. A pinch of petulance spicing her tone, she said, "What, do I stink?"

He brought her hand up to his mouth and kissed it. "Not at all. I need to slow down."

"Why?"

Cam drew a deep breath and held it. This was the moment. He should do it now. *Say it now.* Here in this house, within these walls filled with such bitter, painful memories. Here, where he'd been vulnerable. Where he still felt vulnerable.

Do it. Tell her.

Here in this house? he silently questioned.

Yes. Here. Now. Tell her.

"Because I don't want to have sex with you, Sarah. I want to make love with you. I'm in love with you. I love you."

SIXTEEN

I love you.

Sarah blinked. He'd said that? He'd really said that?

She didn't know how to respond. She hadn't a clue about what to say to him. Loving this man would take a leap of faith that she didn't know if she could take. "Cam . . . I . . . Oh. I thought we were keeping it simple."

One side of his mouth lifted in a crooked smile. "I know. I did, too. I guess my mind and heart weren't on the same page."

She shut her eyes for a long moment, then met his gaze and spoke from the heart: "It's too fast for me, Cam. It's barely been a month since you came back."

His wince was so fleeting that she would have missed it, had she not been watching so closely. Then he cupped her face in the palm of his big hand. "I'm not trying to rush you, sugar. I just needed to say it, needed you to know. I don't want things unsaid between us. I'm not going to let my pride or ego get in the way."

He sent her off to his shower, which was way too small to fit two, but he managed to make it yet another supercharged erotic experience by standing in the doorway and watching her until steam coated the glass and hid her from his sight. The hot water felt wonderful, chasing away the lingering chill from the spill into the lake, and Sarah dawdled with Cam's declaration echoing through her mind.

I want to make love with you. I'm in love with you. I love you.

Wow.

It made her heart sing but at the same time left her quavering with—what?—trepidation? Distrust? Fear? She couldn't quite wrap her mind around how she felt about it. What if she went for broke and gave him her heart once again? Could she trust him to keep it and care for it this time around? She'd been down that road before, and look at how that turned out: Sarah Reese, roadkill on the highway of love.

Not that she was immune to him now, because she wasn't. All he had to do was look at her in that heavy-lidded, hungry way and she melted. But ever since that day at Eagle's Way, she'd been telling herself it was just sex. How could it possibly be anything more? Logistics alone were enough to stop a relationship before it started. Her romance with her last lover hadn't been able to survive a distance of a few hundred miles. How could she and Cam possibly make anything work long-term? The man couldn't take tours out to the Great Barrier Reef from the fishing pier on Hummingbird Lake.

That wasn't the only obstacle in their path, either. There was Lori. Her mother. Not to mention Sarah's own doubts and insecurities. Could she ever trust him to stick? Could she ever have faith in his love? Could she ever drop the shields around her heart and love him back? And if she couldn't, then what? Would he resent her? Would love turn to hate? Where would that leave Lori?

It's too much. There were simply too many obstacles, too much history between them. The risks were too big.

She shut off the water. He was probably mistaken about his feelings, anyway. It had been an emotional twenty-four hours for him, first with Devin's trouble and then meeting Lori. It's understandable that he'd be mixed up. This wasn't love. He couldn't love her. He hadn't had time to fall in love with her.

I'll tell him. I'll explain that.

They probably should forgo the sex. Darn the bad luck. It was obviously confusing things.

She opened the shower door to find Cam gone and a fluffy white towel and a black terry-cloth robe waiting for her. A single red rose likely cut from the bushes outside lay atop the robe. Soft, romantic music played in the background. "Oh, Cam."

He wasn't going to make this easy. She took time to blow-dry her hair, bracing herself for the conversation to come. She stepped out of the bathroom and turned toward his bedroom, expecting to find him there. The sight that met her eyes shocked her speechless.

Cam wasn't in the room, but he'd been there. The bedcovers were turned back in welcome. Dozens of red rose petals lay scattered across the white sheets. *He must have stripped the bushes outside bare.*

A black velvet jeweler's box lay on one of the pillows. Her breath caught even as it registered that it wasn't a ring box.

Behind her, the bathroom door snicked shut. She heard the shower switch on. Sarah knew she should move and look for something to wear. Devin wouldn't mind if she borrowed a pair of his shorts and a T-shirt, would he?

But she couldn't tear her gaze away from the bed, the rose petals, and the box, and before she knew it, Cam stood behind her, a towel draped around his hips. "Hey, there."

"This is . . . romantic."

"It's a little fantasy I've had. Care to indulge me?" He stroked his hands up and down her arms, and when she leaned back against him in silent surrender, she felt a tug on her belt. The robe floated to her feet.

Cam scooped her up into his arms and carried her to his bed, where he sat her gently atop the rose petals. Reaching for the jewelry box, he said, "I've had the big stone for years, won it off a miner in a game of dice. When I went to buy earrings for Lori, I showed it to the jeweler and asked him how to best display it. I wouldn't admit it to myself at the time, but I had the necklace made for you, Sarah. I knew all along that this stone was meant for you."

He flipped open the box, and Sarah gasped. The gold necklace held a free-form pendant that took her breath away. Set against gold and accented with diamonds, the dark stone at the center provided a surface for brilliant colors to dance upon. Scarlets and oranges and yellows blazed around a splash of purple at the center of the stone. "Oh, my gosh, it's beautiful. I've never seen anything like that. What is it?"

"Australian black opal."

"The colors are . . . gorgeous. Like bright coral surrounded by a deep blue sea."

Cam shook his head. "No. It's you. Violet eyes at Lover's Leap in autumn when the aspens are changing." He took the necklace from the box and said, "Will you wear it for me, Sarah? Here? Now?"

She drew in a deep breath of rose-scented air and nodded. When he moved around behind her, she sat staring into a mirror. Her mouth went dry as he draped the necklace around her. The pendant nestled against her skin at the swell of her bare breasts, its cool weight a contrast to the vision of heat in the colors on its surface. Cam cupped her breasts with his large hands and met her gaze in the mirror. "Magnificent."

Then he dipped his head and kissed her neck, and Sarah gave herself up to the moment and the man.

She lost track of time as he took her on a slow, sensual journey unlike any she'd ever known before. Sometimes hot and fierce and fast. Other times so sweet and slow that she wanted to weep. Cam Murphy told her he loved her wordlessly and with words. He told her he loved her without touching her anywhere and by touching her everywhere.

When finally she lay boneless and spent and deliciously sated, he placed one last tender kiss upon her lips and spooned against her, holding her as if she were the most precious thing on earth.

Sarah wanted to weep and wasn't sure why. The other times she'd been with Cam, she'd felt delicious and upbeat in the aftermath. Today she felt . . . reflective. Uncertain. Even confused. Was it because the experience had been so romantic and bittersweet? Or was it because she recognized that Cam had made love to her, but she'd held something back with him?

The mood remained with her as she rose from his bed and dressed in Devin's gym shorts and a T-shirt that Cam provided. Glancing into the mirror above the dresser, she touched the necklace that looked so gorgeous—even against a Colorado Rockies tee. Cam might see Colorado in the gemstone, but Sarah saw the Great Barrier Reef. Emphasis on the words *great* and *barrier.* He said he wanted a relationship, but had he considered the changes that a relationship would entail? Surely he didn't expect her to yank out her roots here in Eternity Springs. Even if she wanted to, she couldn't. Even if they could find a way to make it work living half a world away from Lori, whose education plans tied her to Texas for the next few years at least, Sarah couldn't leave her mother, and neither could she uproot her. Sarah was as bound to Eternity Springs today as she'd been when she was a teenaged mother dependent on her parents for support.

But what if Cam was ready to repatriate? The idea whispered through her mind like a song.

Maybe . . . just maybe . . .

The back door opened, and she heard the clatter of paws on the kitchen floor as Cam brought Mortimer in after a backyard potty break. She walked into the small living room, where she noticed the clock and registered the time. "Oh, no. Cam, we've been here well over an hour!"

"You don't rush perfection, sugar."

She couldn't help but smile. Perfection was an apt description. "Nevertheless, I need to get back to Mom, and I still need to run by home and change. I don't think I should show back up at the picnic wearing Devin's clothes."

The drive to Sarah's home took less than five minutes. Since they'd be only a couple of minutes, she parked in front of Fresh so they'd have the straight shot up Aspen toward the lake. They walked around the corner to enter the house from the front door, and with her thoughts divided between the past hour and the rest of the day to come, Sarah didn't notice the car in her drive or the person waiting on the front porch until Cam murmured a soft, "Oh, hell."

Lori stood on the front porch, her arms folded and a thundercloud on her face. "Really, Mom? You leave your car parked in front of his house for more than an hour? In the middle of the day? For all the town to see? Really? And you leave wearing different clothes than you wore when you arrived? Not to mention that the freaking windows were open! For all the town to hear!" She mimicked in a whorish, falsetto tone, "Cam. Cam. Oh, Cam!"

Oh, crap.

Cam watched the color drain from Sarah's face, then almost immediately return in a flush of embarrassment.

Lori took a step toward her mother, her face tight, her eyes emerald flames. "How could you, Mom? How could you!"

Calmly, Cam said, "Why don't we go inside to discuss this."

"What does it matter?" Lori fired back. "She already told the whole town. And you weren't exactly silent yourself!"

Cam felt his face flush with embarrassment.

Lori's charge wasn't true, of course. With the picnic and other holiday events taking place out at Hummingbird Lake, the town proper looked like a ghost town. Cam didn't bother to argue the point. He'd rather the whole town had heard instead of his daughter. What mattered right now was damage control.

Sarah appeared rooted where she stood, shaken and tense. He placed his hand at the small of her back and applied gentle pressure, pushing her forward as he quietly said, "Sarah, let's go inside. We don't need to do this in your front yard."

"Why not?" Lori said. "You've already let Eternity Springs see you soiling the linen. Why not air it out in public, too?"

Oh, for heaven's sake. Save me from young drama queens. Shifting from embarrassed to slightly annoyed, Cam didn't respond to his daughter as he escorted her mother up the front steps and inside her home. Ellen Reese sat in her customary chair, sleeping, and he put the clues together. When Lori's grandmother got tired, Lori had brought her home. When she didn't find Sarah, she must have gone looking for her.

Cam ushered Sarah through the front room to the kitchen, where Sarah was most comfortable. He pulled a chair out from beneath the table and gestured for her to sit down. Then he turned to face his daughter, who had followed them inside. "Why don't we all sit and discuss this like adults?"

When Lori marched over to the table and sat, he

recognized that he'd chosen the right approach to take with her. He joined them, but neither woman appeared to notice. Their attention was focused on each other. Lori's eyes shot daggers. Sarah looked stricken. Cam glanced from one woman to the other, helpless about what to do or say until he was distracted by the dripping faucet at the kitchen sink. He'd thought he'd gotten that fixed the last time he was here. It was easier to think about the faucet than the disaster in front of him.

Lori placed her hands on the table and leaned forward. "It was never about me, was it? All this time you've been pushing me to have a relationship with him, it was never about me. All that talk about why I needed to try with him, why I needed a father, that was just an excuse. You didn't summon me home for me. You did it for you."

Sarah's voice trembled as she replied, "That's not true. Lori, it's not like that."

Cam literally bit his tongue, sensing that now wasn't the time to interrupt. Lori was obviously feeling angry and hurt. Let her vent, and then maybe she'd listen.

"What's the deal, Mom?" Scorn filled Lori's voice. "You never outgrew being the town good girl who just can't resist the bad boy who wears leather and rides a Harley?"

"Stop it." Now Sarah shoved to her feet. Tears swam in her eyes. "What happened between me and Cam is our business. It's not your place to judge me or to question my morals. I don't need your permission or your approval."

"You should have told me, Mom," Lori said, blinking back tears of her own. "You shouldn't have left it for me to find out this way."

"I know." Sarah closed her eyes and rubbed them with the tips of her fingers. "For that I'm sorry."

"But you're not sorry that you've been sleeping with him? You're not sorry that you've made a spectacle of yourself in front of the entire town? What in the world are you thinking? I swear, I feel like we have this role-reversal thing going on. I'm an adult, and you never made it past your teenaged years. Mom, why? Why, after all these years, after some of the really nice guys you wouldn't give the time of day, do you let Cam Murphy worm his way back into your bed? Cam Murphy!"

She said his name like it was interchangeable with the words *dog crap.* Cam ground his teeth. The Eternity Springs attitude was sure coming out in his daughter this afternoon.

Sarah wrapped her arms around herself. "Lori, honey, you don't understand."

"I'll never understand. You could have married a great guy like Zach, and instead you hook up with him." She jerked her head toward Cam. She hadn't looked at him or so much as acknowledged his presence since he walked into the house.

He needed to do something with his hands. Something to keep him from punching the wall in frustration. Cam strode toward the sink. He pulled a wrench from the junk drawer and went to work tightening the fitting. Why wouldn't she just shut up and give her mother a chance to talk? He wanted to say that aloud, but he knew he couldn't. He hadn't been her parent for twenty years. Now was not the moment to start.

Sarah began, "Your father and I—"

"Don't call him that. I've told you how I feel about that. Surely you don't think we can be one big happy family." She gave Cam a cutting glance.

Great. She'd give a nicer look to someone who poisoned Daisy and Duke.

"No." Sarah shook her head. "That's not what this was about. I . . . we . . . Oh." Sarah buried her face in her hands. "This was a mistake. The entire thing. I knew it."

A mistake. Cam drew up straight. She might as well have plunged a knife into him.

Frustration churned in his gut. He had to be careful here. He sensed that his future relationship with Lori—and, hell, maybe even with Sarah—hung in the balance right now. He needed to keep his temper and choose his words carefully.

What could he say that could reach past her anger? What would she hear? *Keep it simple, stupid.* Cam turned around and faced his daughter. "Lori, I'm in love with your mother."

Damned if she didn't roll her eyes and sneer. "Oh, really. And that's supposed to make this all okay? Seems like she's been down this road before. Tell me you at least used protection this time."

Why, the little witch, Cam thought as Sarah gasped a breath, then said, "That crosses the line, Lori Elizabeth."

"You can't trust him, Mother!" Lori warned, facing Sarah. "You know that. He'll run out on you again. He'll break your heart again."

"He's not going to break my heart."

Because you haven't given it to me, have you? Anger simmered inside of Cam, and he clenched the wrench in his hand hard.

He closed his eyes. Summoned his patience. Told himself to cut Lori some slack. She obviously felt threatened and probably betrayed. In her shoes, he'd probably think the same thing.

"Lori, I know this is confusing, but—"

She snorted, her eyes filled with derision. "It's not confusing at all. It's pretty clear to me that none of it was real. You never wanted me in your life. That was just a way to get into Mom's"—she paused significantly, and when she dropped her gaze to Sarah's hips, Cam glared right back at her—"good graces. I'll bet she threw a wrench in your works when she asked me to come home. You probably thought you could show up here, get you some, and get out without ever having to lay eyes on your little mistake."

"Lori!" Sarah said. "That's so wrong. It was my idea to bring you home this weekend, my decision. It was time. He's your father."

"No, he isn't!" The fury in her tone brooked no argument. "He can take his new car, his new son, and his DNA, and go back down under. It can't be far enough away."

Lori shook with anger as she rose to her feet, focused on Cam, her gaze hard and hot, her fists clenched at her sides. "You didn't want me then. You don't want me now. You know and I know it. The problem is that Mom is gullible where you are concerned. She's obviously fallen for your line of father-of-the-year wannabe BS. That crap about sending her money all those years ago . . . You really had her fooled. What did you really come back here for, Cam? Did you think she had money, and that was why we could afford a trip to Australia?"

"That's enough," he told her. He'd allowed her just about all the slack he was going to.

"No, it's not nearly enough. But I've had enough of you." She looked at Sarah. "You don't have to explain, Mom. It's all pretty clear now. How long did it take him to get back into your pants? A day and a half? Once an easy girl, always an easy girl."

As Sarah gasped, Cam saw red. He advanced on Lori, saying, "I said that's enough. You are not going to speak to your mother that way."

Lori shot him a killing look. "You don't get to tell me what I can and cannot do."

"In this instance, yes, I do."

"What are you going to do? Hit me with that wrench? You are a Murphy, after all. Go ahead. This time when they send you off to jail it won't be juvie!"

You little brat. Cam closed his eyes and silently counted to ten. Once he could speak in a level tone, he said, "You will show your mother more respect."

Lori's chin came up. "I will when she deserves it."

Sarah let out a little mewl. She'd been annoyed up until now and at her wit's end. Lori's last verbal arrow had wounded her.

Cam was as angry as he could ever remember being. "Stop! You will apologize to you mother right this instant, young lady."

"Again, you don't get to tell me what to do. You are not my father, Cam Murphy. You're just my mother's sleaze of a hook-up."

"Dammit!" Cam roared. He threw the wrench at the open junk drawer and missed, hitting a ceramic canister of flour instead. The jar shattered, and a small cloud of flour billowed up.

For half a minute, the room was silent but for the sound of their breathing. Cam stood, frozen in place. Sarah had her hands over her mouth. Then Lori iced her cake of insults by saying, "Wow, guess you are like your old man, after all."

Bile rose in Cam's throat. He felt sick to his stomach. He reached toward the canister, intending to clean it up.

"No. Don't." Tears spilled down Sarah's face as she looked at him and said, "Go. Just go, Cam. Just go away."

He drew a deep breath, nodded stiffly, then strode toward the door. As he stepped out onto the porch, he heard Ellen Reese speak from her chair in the living room: "That Murphy boy is no good."

Devin was a little worried. His dad had never returned to the picnic, and neither had Sarah. At first he hadn't thought twice about it, but when Cam didn't show up for the father-son horseshoe tournament, Devin had started to search for him. Then Sheriff Turner had asked for his help and he'd gotten distracted. When darkness fell and neither Dad nor the Reeses showed for the fireworks display, his worry returned. Maybe something had happened to Sarah's mother.

He decided to check the rental first before showing up at the Reeses'. The house was dark, and he almost drove past it, then decided he should stop and let Mortimer out to do his thing.

When he stepped inside, he noted the open back door right away. *Uh-oh*. Sure enough, Mortimer's crate was empty. "What is it about that dog? He's a Houdini hound."

But when Devin stepped into the backyard, he saw that he was wrong, and he went from worried to downright afraid.

Moonlight cast a faint, silvered glow over Cam, who lay sprawled in a lawn chair, Mortimer lying on the ground beside him. Cam's left hand idly scratched the dog behind the ears. His right held—*holy hell*—something Devin had never seen in his father's hand before. Cam held a whiskey bottle by the neck.

"What the hell? Dad?"

"Hey, Dev." Cam took a long swill from the bottle.

"Dad, what happened? What's wrong? You're full as a boot. Why? You never drink!"

"I'm a Murphy, son," Cam replied, a slight slur to his words. "Of course I drink. It's in my genes, you know."

"That's bull." Devin's heart pounded. Something had happened. Something big. He took a seat in the other lawn chair, rested his elbows on his knees, and leaned forward. "What's wrong?"

"I found my old man's last stash." Cam's leg slipped off the lounge chair and flopped over the side. "Isn't that something? After all this time, a remodel and everything, nobody ever found the cache in the basement. The old bastard even had a mid-grade grog tucked away. He must have come into some change before he croaked."

"Dad. You're scaring me!"

He dropped his head back against the lounge chair, shut his eyes, and said, "Sorry, Dev. It's been a hell of an afternoon."

"What happened?"

"Had a bit of an open slather at the Reeses'."

A free-for-all? He had a fight at the Reeses'?

"I think maybe it's time for us to go home, Devin."

"Home? To Oz?"

"Yeah."

Because he was, after all, a teenager, Devin's first thought was *What about baseball?* But after that first bit of selfishness, his attention focused on his dad. "What exactly happened, Dad? I talked to Lori. Everything was fine after the kayak race."

Cam pried open one eye and looked at Devin. "Ordinarily, I wouldn't discuss the details with you, but since you have a vested interest in it . . ."

Without going into much detail, Cam explained that Lori had caught him and Sarah going at it. She'd freaked.

"Well, that's just cockeyed. It's none of her business. Of course you and Sarah wanted to be together. It's obvious that you two are in love."

"You're half right." He paused and took another sip of his whiskey. "I think the best thing I can do for them is to leave, Devin."

Give up? His dad never gave up. "Why do you say that?"

"They do just fine without me. They're happy without me. They formed a family years ago, and they don't need us. I'm complicating their lives instead of making them better. That's not what I want for them. I've never done anything for Lori. I can do this for her."

"Leave? Rack off?" Devin couldn't believe his dad would quit and run away.

"It's time."

"That's bull, Dad. They're a whole lot better off with you in their lives. I should know. I'm an expert on the subject."

That coaxed a grin from him. "You're a good kid, Devin Murphy."

"And you're a great dad, and if Lori is too hardheaded to see it, then she's a mug." Silently, Devin decided he needed to have a talk with his sorta sister. Set her straight. No way was she getting off the hook. And then, if she still didn't want their father, then she didn't deserve him. "I'm happy to do anything you want to do, Dad, but don't you think you might be pulling the plug on this whole thing a little fast? Maybe if you gave Lori time to get over herself, things would all work out."

Cam shook his head. "If it were just Lori, I might do that."

Well, hell. Sarah must have done a number on him.

"So you don't mind going back?" Cam asked, staring at Devin with one eye cocked open.

"When are you thinking of leaving?" Bracing himself, he added, "The championship tournament starts Monday."

"We're not leaving before the tourney's done." Cam struggled to sit up. He set the bottle down, and Devin was glad to see it. "We're not running out on our team. We'll go when it's over, okay?"

"Aye. Sounds like a plan. You want me to put that bottle away for you, Dad?"

At that moment, the first of the fireworks lit up the sky. Cam handed his son the whiskey, lifted Mortimer into his lap, and lay back down on the lounger. He scratched the terrier behind the ears, and as the sky above Eternity Springs lit up in bursts of red, white, and blue, he murmured, "There's no place for us here. I should have known. There never has been a home for me in Eternity Springs."

Devin watched his father and ached. The man was true blue. Why didn't that stupid girl see it?

SEVENTEEN

Sarah watched the door to Fresh the entire morning, but Cam never came by for his daily dozen sugar cookies. As the hands on the clock worked their way toward closing time, Sarah tried to decide what to do. Thinking wasn't coming too terribly easily to her today.

She'd barely slept at all last night. After Cam left she'd wanted to sit down with Lori and talk it through, just the two of them. It had been a horribly ugly scene, and everyone's emotions had been a mess. But her mother had been agitated—probably from all the tension in the air—and by the time she'd managed to calm Ellen down, Lori had left the house, using the excuse of a walk with Daisy and Duke to get away from Sarah.

This had been the most upset, angry, and betrayed that Lori had been in her life. Sarah worried about her relationship with her daughter in the aftermath. She'd wanted desperately to talk to her, but Lori had taken the longest dog walk in history, and Sarah fell asleep waiting for her. When she'd awakened during the night, Lori was home with her bedroom door shut and the lights out. Sarah turned in, then tossed and turned the rest of the night until she crawled out of bed for the start of her workday.

Work was a blessing and helped her keep her mind off the turmoil. Lori showed up to help earlier than Sarah had expected. Things were stiff between them, but there wasn't time for a personal discussion. The shop bustled with customers, and Sarah was thankful for her daughter's help, recognizing it as the olive branch it was.

Nevertheless, she did have time to think about the situation the entire morning, so when she locked Fresh's front door and flipped the "Open" sign to "Closed," she knew exactly what she wanted to say to her daughter.

Lori stopped her cold by speaking first. "Mom, I'm so sorry about yesterday."

The heaviness around Sarah's heart suddenly lightened. "It certainly wasn't how I hoped the day would go."

Lori wrapped her arms around Sarah and gave her a hug. "I said some horrible things, and I hurt you, and that's the last thing in the world I ever want to do. I apologize, Mom."

"Thank you. I accept your apology, and I want to say that I'm sorry that my actions hurt you."

Lori sighed. "I acted like I was ten instead of in my twenties. I felt like I was ten."

"It wasn't the best of circumstances."

Lori answered with a rueful look, then said, "I regret what I said, Mom, but I haven't changed my mind. Cam Murphy isn't the right guy for you."

"How do you know?" Sarah fired back.

"I don't trust him."

"You don't know him."

"Do you? Really? He's been here a month, Mom."

He's been in my heart for years.

"Look, your sex life is none of my business—"

"True."

"—but I think you are vulnerable where he's concerned, and he's taking advantage of that."

"He's not like that. He says he loves me, Lori. I believe him."

Lori didn't roll her eyes, but she came close before Sarah asked, "Will you see him again before you go?"

A pugnacious chin jutted. "I don't want to."

Sarah studied her daughter and felt torn in two. No matter what happened between herself and Cam, there had to be a way for father and daughter to find their way to an understanding. "This whole thing makes my stomach hurt."

"I'm sorry you're in the middle."

Sarah wondered what Lori would say if she told her she reminded her so much of Cam. A chip off the old granite head. "I'm going to go talk to him. Sure you don't want to come with me? You said some pretty awful things to him."

"I'm sure. You can tell him I'm sorry for any words that he took as cruel, but the emotions behind them were honest."

"I wouldn't say that is much of an apology."

"I don't have an apology in me where he is concerned, Mom. I'll just keep my distance until I leave tomorrow. I'm going to see if Nana would like to go sit by the creek with me for a little while. Remember how she always used to say that she found the sound of running water relaxing? I thought she might like that."

"That would be great," Sarah said. "The sunshine will do her good. I told you how she's been anxious and agitated lately? That's part of something called sundowning that sometimes affects Alzheimer's patients. Her doctor suggested we make sure she gets outside for a little while each day that the weather allows."

Also, if Ellen was with Lori, that would give Sarah the chance to pay a call on Cam Murphy—if she could track him down. Ball practice was scheduled to end at Fresh's closing time, so she stood a decent chance of finding him at home if she hurried. Once he'd had time to shower and change, no telling where he might get off to.

She detoured into the house, brushed her hair, touched up her makeup, then spoke with her mom as she and Lori left the house for the banks of Angel Creek. Ten minutes later, Sarah knocked on Cam's front door.

Devin was drying his hair with a towel when he answered the door. Seeing her, his eyes widened, then immediately narrowed to just shy of a glare. No longer the friendly teen she'd known for the past month—this was an angry young man.

Okay, well, at least I know which way the wind blows.

"Is your dad home, Devin?"

"Yeah." He flipped the towel over his shoulder.

"I'd like to speak to him. May I come in?"

The teenager shrugged and stepped back, wordlessly inviting her inside. Once he shut the door behind her, he gestured toward the sofa and asked stiffly, "You want to sit down? Dad's on the phone. He'll be out when he's done."

"Thank you."

Devin disappeared into the kitchen, then appeared a moment later with a leash and Mortimer. The dog, at least, seemed happy to see Sarah. "Tell Dad I took the mutt for a walk, would you?"

He was gone almost before she got the word *sure* out of her mouth. She'd never before realized what a handy excuse dogs made for practicing avoidance.

With Devin gone, she was able to hear the murmur of Cam's voice coming from his bedroom. Devin hadn't told Cam she was waiting, but no way in heaven would she walk into his bedroom and let him know. Not his bedroom. Not today. Not after yesterday.

He walked out of his bedroom wearing only gym shorts that hung low on his hips. His head was turned away from her, his cellphone up to his ear. He didn't see her.

"I'm not familiar with that airport," he said as he opened a drawer in the kitchen and rummaged for a pen.

"I understand the connecting flight departs from a different terminal. Forty minutes seems like a close call . . . Yes . . . Yes. Good . . . I think that's better . . . Yes. Two seats."

Sarah went still.

He made notes on a pad that lay atop the kitchen counter. "Okay. Great. You said Flight 642? And it arrives in Sydney at what time? . . . Got it."

Sydney. As in Australia. Her heart began to pound.

"Same credit card information. Excellent. I appreciate your help, Andrea. Last-minute arrangements like this are always a challenge, and you did great. Thanks. Goodbye."

He disconnected the call, set the phone down on the counter, turned around, and saw her. He stopped dead in his tracks. "Sarah."

"Australia?"

"I didn't know you were here."

"You're leaving." She said it flatly.

He hesitated. His eyes met hers briefly before sliding away. "What reason do I have to stay?"

She heard the question through a fog in her brain. One crystal-clear realization consumed her. He was doing it again. He was leaving her again. *He loves me one day, then leaves me the next?*

Welcome to yesterday, sugar cookie.

Hurt rolled over her like a tidal wave. *He's quitting. On Lori. On me. Without even fighting for us.*

She widened her eyes and willed away tears. She refused to let him see her cry. "When are you going?"

He watched her with flat, emotionless eyes. "Wednesday. After the tournament in Durango."

"Oh, yes. The Grizzlies. It's the championship."

"Yeah."

Of course he'd stay long enough for that. Can't quit

on baseball. He'd stay for Devin but not for them. Never for them. Lori might not even rate a goodbye from him.

Now anger rode in on the wave of pain. Cam Murphy was a quitter. He'd quit on her years ago, and he was quitting on her today. *Life is an obstacle course, and he gives up at the first wall.*

Well, she didn't work that way. She never gave up. She didn't have the luxury of doing so. She had a daughter to nurture and support and a mother who depended on her and a business to run. She'd had to fight to keep her head above water all these years, and be damned if she'd let herself drown now.

Cam Murphy didn't know the first thing about love. Be damned if she wouldn't call him on it.

Her chin came up, and she managed to keep most of the bitterness out of her tone as she said, "Seems like a quick decision for a man in love to make."

His jaw hardened. "I don't dawdle over important things. I know how I feel, and I act on it."

Her temper blazed. "That's not fair. What happened to taking things one day at a time and not worrying about the future? You're leaving because I didn't say 'I love you' back to you yesterday? Because Lori said things that you didn't like? It's love on demand? On your timetable? That's the way it's always been with you, hasn't it? Life on your timetable."

"This isn't just about Lori. I laid my heart bare to you!"

"I can't trust you!" Sarah fisted her hands at her sides. "You weren't there for me when I needed you most, Cam. You weren't there when I was sixteen and the doctor told me I was pregnant. You weren't there when I labored to bring our child into the world. You weren't there when I cheered to get two hours of sleep in a row or when I struggled to buy diapers and pay for braces. You've never been there for me."

"Oh, yeah?" Bitterly, he added, "Actually, I was there for you one time. I was there the night Andrew Cook flashed a picture of you and Nic naked that he'd taken in the locker room at school. Look where that got me."

Sarah gasped. "That's why . . . The fight?"

He shrugged.

"You never told me. Why didn't you tell me?"

"What good would it have done? I know you. You'd have felt guilty, and it wouldn't have changed anything."

The reminder made her bitter. "Right. You were going to sail away anyway, free as the wind, to all those places we dreamed about as kids."

"I didn't sail away free. I fled this godless town."

"You left me behind to run the obstacle course alone! Now Lori is grown and my finish line is in sight and you sail back in on the wind and expect me to forget the walls I've spent twenty years climbing because you are great in the sack?"

He lifted his chin, just like Lori did, and seeing it only made Sarah's hurt worse. "I don't expect anything," he told her, his voice rich with fury. "I hoped you would forget and forgive because you loved me, too. Dammit, Sarah! I'm sorry I wasn't there for you. I'm sorry you ran the course alone. I did what I thought was best for you and Lori." He pointed toward an old scar on his chest and added, "I was Brian Murphy's son!"

"And God knows I feel for the little boy who didn't do a thing to earn those scars. But I've got my own set of scars, Cam. Your initials are on a couple of them."

He shut his eyes at that. Sarah continued, "I can forgive. I can possibly even forget. But trust? You didn't trust yourself, Cam. How can you expect me to trust you?"

"Because I know myself now. I'm not full of 'bad blood.' I'm not an abuser, and I'm not a liar. I am worthy of trust. I would never hurt you or Lori."

"You are hurting us now!"

It took the wind out of those sails of his. Quietly, he said, "There's hurting, and then there's hurting. I don't want to do either one, Sarah. And that's why I'm leaving."

Sarah couldn't stop the tears now. Feeling raw and wounded, she closed her eyes.

His footsteps approached, and she held her breath, wanting desperately for him to take her into his arms and tell her he'd wait, tell her he'd give her time. Instead, he passed her. She heard the door open. "Goodbye, Sarah."

She wanted to drop to her knees and bawl. Something was dying here, and she wanted . . . She needed . . . to mourn. Sarah didn't do that. She did what she always did. She drew in a breath, squared her shoulders, and continued to fight her way along life's obstacle course.

She turned, walked to the door, then paused and went up on her toes. His jaw was set, as unmovable as Murphy Mountain, as she kissed his cheek. "I'm sorry we didn't have more time. Goodbye, Cam."

She walked away, listening hard, hoping he'd call her back. Hoping . . . just like she'd hoped when she was sixteen and pregnant and walking away from juvie jail.

"Sarah?"

Her heart in her throat, she turned. He stood in the threshold of his childhood home, his hand clenched around the door handle in a white-knuckled grip. "Love without trust never works in the end. It hurts me, too."

He took a step back and closed the door.

As Lori helped her grandmother into the passenger seat of her new car, she heard someone call her name. She glanced around to see the new owner of the Trading Post, Logan McClure, crossing the street, headed her way, carrying a brown accordion file. "I found something of your mother's. Could you give it to her for me?"

"Sure."

He handed over the file. "We're doing some work on

the store and tore out some flooring in the basement. Uncovered a hidey-hole, and this was inside."

"What is it?" she asked, eyeing the elastic string that wrapped around a button to keep the file closed.

"Some letters addressed to your mom. A couple addressed to your grandfather. Other papers, but I didn't snoop any further once I figured out who the file belonged to. It was dusty. Obviously been down there awhile. I figure your mother just forgot about the file."

Letters to Mom? Lori's stomach sank. Could these be *those* letters? She eyed the file envelope with a sense of curious trepidation. "Thanks, Logan. I'll make sure she gets it."

Lori set the file in the backseat of her new car and drove toward Angel's Rest. She parked in the lot nearest the creek and assisted her grandmother from the car. From her backseat, she grabbed a canvas tote filled with water bottles and a tin of ginger cookies. At the last minute, she stuck the file into the bag, too.

"What am I supposed to do?" Ellen asked.

"You are going to come with me. We are going to sit beside the creek and enjoy the sunshine."

"Okay."

Lori linked her arm with her grandmother's, and they strolled along the stone path to the pair of white wicker chairs that sat beneath the shade of a big cottonwood tree. She drew a deep breath of rose-perfumed air and listened to the music of the bubble and rush of the mountain creek and willed herself to relax. In all honesty, Lori had proposed this outing as much for herself as for her grandmother. She shared her grandmother's love of mountain streams. She, too, found them soothing.

She couldn't remember the last time she'd needed soothing as much as she needed it today.

At creekside, she guided Ellen to a seat in the wicker chair, then took her own seat beside her grandmother.

Inhaling a deep breath, she sent up a short, silent prayer for peace. She took her grandmother's hand in hers and gently squeezed it. "See that little pool across the creek, Nana? I remember one time when you and me and Granddad stretched out on our bellies and hung our heads over the pool and watched a trout. He was so still, but every so often he'd flick his tail. I wanted to try to catch it with my hands, but Granddad convinced me just to watch it."

Ellen's brow furrowed. "Where is Frank?"

"He's gone, Nana," Lori softly responded, her heart twisting.

"He's dead?"

"Yes."

"I knew that." She lifted her hand and placed two fingers against her temple. "I'm not so good here anymore, but"—she put her fist over her heart—"this still works. I miss him. I miss him so much."

"I know, Nana. Me, too."

"Love hides, but it's always here." Sunlight glinted off the diamond anniversary ring Ellen Reese wore every day in addition to her wedding ring, as she thumped her chest. "Always. Remember that."

"I will, Nana. I will."

Lori closely studied her grandmother's face. She sometimes experienced a flare of clarity during which the old Nana surfaced. Back in May she'd had an entire afternoon when she came out of her fog almost entirely. Mom had called Lori, and the three generations of Reeses had enjoyed a wonderful hour-long conversation. It would be awesome if she'd come back while Lori was home. She'd sounded a little bit with it just then. Could it be? No, her eyes didn't have it.

She squeezed her grandmother's hand once again and repeated, "Love is always there."

Lori's gaze drifted to the tote bag. "Would you like a cookie, Nana?"

"No, thank you."

Temptation rose within Lori, and it had nothing to do with the tin filled with delicious-tasting calories. She shouldn't. She knew she shouldn't. That brown file could be a real Pandora's box. She chewed on her lip, then chomped on a cookie and chugged her water.

Before ten minutes passed, she surrendered. While her grandmother dozed in the sun, Lori opened the file and reached inside. She found a stack of papers, two letters from a bank addressed to her grandfather, and six envelopes addressed to Sarah Reese in a masculine scrawl, postmarked Australia. The envelopes had been opened.

With trembling fingers, she pulled a letter from one of the envelopes—three sheets of paper, folded twice.

Dear Sarah,

First let me say I screwed up. Royally.

The letter went on for pages and detailed Cam Murphy's life from the time of his release from juvenile detention to when he settled in Cairns, Australia. It was both an explanation of the events of his life and, Lori realized, a plea for understanding. A couple of paragraphs toward the end caused her heart to catch.

I think about our little girl often. I picture her with your lovely eyes and dark curls. I have many regrets in my life, Sarah, but leaving you and our daughter is at the top of the list. I wish I could have believed in myself, trusted myself, more than ten years ago, but I can't rewrite history.

The future, though, is different. Say the word and I'm there, Sarah. I missed the terrible twos, but I'll help with the teens. The enclosed check is a small start. No *matter what you decide about my coming home, you can plan on my sending checks.*

He finished by listing contact addresses and numbers, and closed with his hope to hear from her soon.

Lori slowly lowered the letter. She was breathing as if she'd just run five miles. She reached for the second letter, devoured it, then ran quickly through letters three, four, and five. With each letter, the length shortened and the tone sharpened.

The sixth letter wasn't really much of a letter at all.

Sarah:

If receiving my letters is as painful for you as the eternally empty mailbox is for me, then I apologize for having hurt you yet again. Your continued silence sends a crystal-clear message. I won't write you again. I will, however, continue to contribute to our daughter's support through an account I set up through my local bank.

He provided information on who to contact to access the funds, then added:

I admit to the fear that I may be failing my daughter once again by taking this path. However, I have confidence in the fact that the Sarah Reese I knew and loved would always, always, put her child first. You must believe it is in our child's best interest to have no contact with me, so I'll accept that. If that ever changes, please let me know. If you ever choose to tell her anything about me, I hope it will be this: Right or wrong, I tried to do what I thought was best for her. Someday she should know that I love her. I always have, and I always will.

Cam

Lori didn't realize that she had tears streaming down her face until her grandmother patted her knee and said, "What's wrong, sweetheart?"

The question came from her heart, though she knew better than to expect an answer. "Why did you keep Cam Murphy away from us, Nana?"

"Cam Murphy broke my Sarah's heart. She doesn't think we know, but we do. We have to protect her. We love you both."

"Oh, Nana." Lori swiped at the tears on her cheeks. "Why does love have to cause so much heartache and grief?"

"Now, Lori," chided a voice from upstream. "Love isn't the problem. Love is the solution."

Lori looked around to see Celeste Blessing standing in the middle of Angel Creek, wearing waders and holding a fly rod. Embarrassed, flustered, and feeling way too vulnerable at the moment, Lori tried to pretend that she had not been overheard. "Hi, Celeste. I'm sorry, I didn't see you when we sat down. Are we disturbing your fishing?"

Celeste dismissed the question with a wave. "Not at all. Here, I fish for relaxation more than with the thought of catching anything. I'm glad to see you. Now, what's this about love causing heartache and grief? Is the weekend with your father not going well?"

"No, not really."

"What's the problem?"

Lori didn't know how to respond. Contrary to Lori's expectations, her mother's slutty behavior yesterday afternoon appeared to have gone unnoticed by the gossips in town. But had Mom shared her sex-life secrets with her friends? Uncertain, she attempted to be discreet and replied with a shrug. "It's complicated."

Celeste clicked her tongue. She splashed toward the bank, set down her fly rod, complimented Ellen on her outfit, then addressed Lori. "Lori Elizabeth, you are dear to me. I have a request to make of you."

"I love you, too, Celeste," Lori interrupted, "but if

your request has anything to do with Cam Murphy, I'm going to say no."

Celeste frowned over the top of her sunglasses. "I didn't plan to mention your father."

"Oh. Sorry." Lori gave a sheepish smile.

Celeste removed her waders, then folded her hands over her bosom. "My request is that you look deep inside yourself and find your inner angel."

"My what?"

"Your inner angel. You see, Lori, your inner angel will show you how to drop the anchor of emotional burdens and fly. Your inner angel knows where to find light to chase away the darkness. Your inner angel helps you balance when the world pushes and pulls. And, most important of all, your inner angel has a wingspan that is broad enough to lift the hearts of those in pain."

"I don't think I have an angel inside me, Celeste."

"Sure you do." She patted Lori's shoulder. "You actually have a powerful angel inside of you."

Lori thought Celeste was so cute when she went off on one of her angel tangents. "I do?"

"You do. Your inner angel possesses angel thoughts that have the power to heal. Don't be afraid of them, Lori. All you need to do is send them out into the world and you can effect great and glorious change, true and lasting healing." Celeste leaned down, squeezed Lori's shoulder, and spoke softly into her ear. "Seek your angel with an open heart, an open mind, Lori Elizabeth, and you will find her. You will find unwavering inner strength and an abundance of joy. Your angel will lead you to your dreams."

Cam dreamed of angels on Saturday night.

Surrounded by darkness, the *Freedom* floated on a flat, glassy sea, its sails hanging limp. Cam stood at the wheel, alone, possessed of the certain knowledge that *Freedom*'s voyage had lasted aeons.

Before him, far away in the distance, the sun dipped toward the snow-whitened crest of a mountain range. Cam focused on the crimson and gold of sunset, and a deep, profound yearning filled his soul.

Red sky at night, sailor's delight.

But the *Freedom* stood becalmed. Cam's heart began to pound. The light of day was dying, and he couldn't get there. He remained stranded, trapped, lost on the cold, lonely sea.

The dulcet voice as soothing as harp strings whispered in his ears. *Call up the wind, sailor. You have the ability. You have the power. All you need do is forgive. Resentment is an anchor holding you back from that which you desire most. Find the angel within you; cut the anchor line and beat your wings. The winds of forgiveness will stir a hurricane of healing and call up a tide of love that can carry you home.*

On deck of the *Freedom*, Cam shook a fist at heaven. *I tried. I tried, but I failed!*

So what? asked the voice. *Isn't the privilege of flying worth falling on your face a time or two?*

The privilege of flying.

Flying. A coveted dream. Wasn't that what called him to the water? Wasn't sailing the next best thing to having wings of his own?

Why settle for second best, sailor? Why remain earthbound? Reach for your wings, Cam Murphy. They'll carry you to heaven.

Cam awoke to a sunny Sunday morning.

Covered in feathers.

He blinked. "What the hell?"

A quick inspection of his bed solved the puzzle. His pillow was ripped at the seam. Mortimer must have started to eat the pillow at some point. No wonder he'd dreamed about the angel again.

A dream. Just a dream. He stood, yawned, and scratched his chest. A silly, stupid dream. He didn't have an inner angel. The only way he'd fly anywhere was in a 747.

In the bathroom, he started the shower and waited for the water to get hot. When steam began to rise on the cool morning air, he stepped into the shower. Darned if he didn't hear the chime of angelic laughter in his head.

If you believe that, Cam Murphy, then why did you just check out your back in the mirror?

Sunday was Sarah's day off, but she usually awoke early out of habit, and today was no different, despite a sorry night's sleep. Her mother had awakened her three times as she wandered about the house. Each time Sarah had trouble getting back to sleep, plagued as she was by thoughts of Cam.

A naked picture of her had led to the fight that night, not beer, and not his father. Cam had hurt Andrew while trying to be a hero—trying to be *her* hero—and *now* he tells her about it? All these years later? Stupid male pride. And yet how wonderful that he'd tried to protect her and Nic that way. At their age, they'd have been devastated by the violation of their privacy. Beneath that pride, Cam had a good heart. He'd told her he was worthy of her trust . . . Was he? Was she making a terrible mistake?

Now, with dawn a rosy glow outside her bedroom window, she abandoned the effort and rolled wearily from her bed. Plans for the day included the late church service, then brunch at Ali's restaurant before driving Lori to the airport to catch her flight back to Virginia. She'd be busy, which was good, but she'd drag all day if she didn't do something to boost her energy level.

She decided to go for a run. A quick mile might be just what she needed to chase away the weary and the blues.

She dressed in gym shorts, a T-shirt—her own, this time—and running shoes, and headed out. Her route took her up Aspen, and when she reached Cemetery Road, she challenged herself to take the hill. She huffed and puffed her way to the top, and once she arrived at the arched iron sign that marked the entry, she paused to catch her breath.

That's when she noticed Celeste Blessing on her knees, weeding a flower bed, in the oldest section of the cemetery. Now why in the world would she be here, tending the cemetery, this morning? That was a task the garden club tackled on regularly scheduled dates.

Even as she asked herself the question, she dismissed it. Celeste had her own peculiar way of interacting with the world. It was part of her charm. Lori had mentioned she'd had one of those strange conversations with Celeste just yesterday. She'd worried that dementia might be hitting their friend, too.

Of course, every time Sarah misplaced something, Lori was certain it indicated a sign of early-onset Alzheimer's.

"Hello, Celeste," she called. "You're out early."

Celeste rolled back on her heels. "Hello, dear."

She stood and dusted off the knees of her jeans. Sarah noted she'd been working in the Murphy family section of graves. *Ah, she must have seen something here that bothered her the other night.*

"I'm so glad to see you. I wanted to talk to you."

"Oh? What about?"

Celeste waved her over, then folded her arms and leaned casually against Daniel Murphy's grave marker. Okay, that weirded Sarah out a little bit. Once Sarah approached, Celeste knotted her brow and said, "Of our little group of friends, you've always struck me as the most plainspoken. You call a garden spade a garden spade, and you demand accountability in yourself and in others."

"Um . . . yes." Where was this going?

"That's why I have decided to speak plainly with you in return. You wear your heart on your sleeve, Sarah. Today, the heart I see has a big old crack down the middle."

Sarah grimaced. "I don't really want to talk about it."

"Fine. Don't talk, just listen. Listen and hear me."

Celeste stood up straight, then reached out and thumped Sarah on the nose. "Leap like a lunatic."

"Excuse me?"

"You have been courageous all of your life. Don't let that courage fail you now. Life has taken you to the edge. It's time for you to find the faith to leap, and the trust to know that love is the net that will catch you if you need it."

"Who have you been talking to?"

"I know Cam is planning to leave for Australia when they return from the tournament in Durango. I know that it will be the biggest mistake of your life if you let him go."

"Celeste . . ." Sarah protested.

The older woman folded her arms and arched a brow.

Disgruntled, Sarah said, "Aren't you going to tell me to find my inner angel or something like that?"

"Oh, heavens, no. Your angel is right out there for everyone to see. What I'm telling you is to pay attention. You see, angels notice when their dreams are about to come true."

At that moment, the bells of St. Stephen's chimed the half-hour. Celeste said, "Oh, dear. I spent more time with Daniel than I had intended. I must hurry. I'll see you in church."

With that, she gave the gravestone a pat, then hurried to her Gold Wing and fired up the engine.

"Tell me that wasn't a wheelie?" Sarah muttered aloud as she started down the hill.

Celeste's words plagued her through her run, and later as she showered and dressed.

Leap like a lunatic.

They bothered her during the late church service.

Leap like a lunatic.

They even continued to whisper through her mind as she indulged in a most delicious order of veal parmigiana at Ali's.

Leap like a lunatic!

"Oh, all right!" she exclaimed as she tossed her napkin onto the table and shoved to her feet. Feeling a little wild, she looked at Lori. "Tell Ali to put this on my tab. There is something I need to do."

She left the Yellow Kitchen and, on foot, headed for the park. She wasn't exactly sure what she intended to say or do. She just knew she had to see him, speak to him, before the Grizzlies left town. At the corner of Spruce and Fourth, a sense of urgency gripped her. Sarah started to run.

She arrived at Davenport Park just as the yellow school bus pulled into the parking lot. Cam was there, standing beside Colt. He wore jeans and a T-shirt sporting the Adventures in Paradise logo and a Grizzlies ball cap. He looked like a different man from the one she'd spoken with yesterday, wearing a smile instead of a frown, his stance relaxed. When he threw back his head and laughed, it made her heart hurt.

And doubt crept in. *She* couldn't laugh today if her life depended on it. How could he laugh? Didn't he feel like his heart was torn in two? Maybe his talk of love was just that—talk. Maybe she should forget all about leaping and keep both feet firmly on the ground.

She hesitated, and that hesitation made the choice for her. Cam was one of the first people on the bus. Sarah stayed and watched as it pulled out of the parking lot, her heart heavy, tears a constant threat. The bus turned her way.

Her gaze met Cam's through the open bus window as it passed. Upon seeing her, his smile died. Yet he didn't appear angry like he had the day before. He looked sad and resigned.

Then the bus was past her, and Cam Murphy was on his way out of Eternity Springs. "But he'll be back," she murmured. "He'll be back one more time."

She had another chance. Would she find the courage to act? Would she leap or hang back again? What was holding her back? Well, she had until Tuesday to get her mind straight. Then she'd have to decide once and for all if she was going to look or if she had faith enough to leap.

Sarah returned home to find Lori packed and ready to leave. Ellen indicated she had a headache and wished to lie down, so Sarah called a teenager to stay with her mother until Sarah returned from the airport.

Mother and daughter spoke very little as they left Eternity Springs in Lori's new car with Lori at the wheel. The weekend had been an eventful one for both of them, and Sarah suspected they both nursed regrets. She knew she did. An hour and twenty minutes into the drive, Lori finally brought up her father, albeit indirectly.

"Did you know that Nic agreed to board Mortimer?"

Sarah blinked. "During the baseball tournament?"

"Longer. Until he can be sent to Australia. I guess there is quite a bit of red tape where importing a pet is concerned."

"Oh."

"Cam should have started the process as soon as he decided to keep the dog. He shouldn't have waited until the last minute."

Sarah could think of a number of arguments she could have used in Cam's defense, but she wasn't in the mood to defend the man to his daughter right now.

"Are you glad they're leaving, Mom?" Lori asked, her expression troubled.

Sarah took a long moment before she responded. "Honestly? I'm afraid."

"Afraid! Why?"

"I'm afraid I'll learn that letting him go was the biggest mistake of my life."

After that, they drove another five miles in silence before Lori spoke again: "Because you're lonely?"

"Because, despite everything, I never stopped loving him, Lori."

This time only two miles passed by before Lori asked, "Am I the reason he's leaving?"

Sarah thought it over. Had Lori asked, he might have stayed. But would she have wanted him on those terms? "I suspect if you had asked him to stay, then he would have stayed."

"What about you? Would he have stayed if you'd asked him to?"

Love. Trust. Faith. Inwardly, Sarah sighed. "I don't know. I think maybe he would have, but we never had that conversation."

Lori's hands clenched the steering wheel. "Mom, there is something I need to tell you. Logan McClure gave me a file he found in the Trading Post's basement. It had a bunch of papers in it, including letters from Australia."

Sarah drew in a breath. "Cam's letters?"

Lori nodded. "The envelopes were already open, so, well, I read them, Mom."

Sarah absorbed the news, torn between the desire to scold Lori for overstepping and the need to demand to know what the letters had said. Before she'd decided what to say, Lori continued, summarizing the contents and finishing with "I wish I hadn't been so nosy."

"Why is that?"

"Because it just confuses me. He thought he was doing

the best thing by staying away. Your parents thought they were doing the best thing for us by keeping him away. It's not so black-and-white as I thought."

"Life seldom is, baby."

"This has all just happened too fast for me. I wish we had more time to . . ."

"To what?" Sarah asked just as her cellphone rang. Lori waited while Sarah dug it from her purse and checked the number. *Home. Oh, dear. What could this be about?*

"Hello?"

"Sarah? It's Jennifer."

Hearing panic in the girl's voice, Sarah tensed. "What's wrong?"

"Oh, Sarah. I don't know how this happened, but your mom . . . Oh, Sarah. She's gone."

The bottom fell out of Sarah's stomach, and her hands began to tremble. As Lori steered the car over to the road's shoulder, Sarah forced the words from her throat. "She . . . passed?"

Beside her, Lori gasped. She braked the car to a stop.

"No . . . no . . . I'm sorry. That's not what I meant."

Sarah breathed a sigh of relief and smiled reassuringly to Lori until her sitter's next words wiped the smile away.

"She's gone, as in missing. I don't know how she got out of the house without me seeing her. It had to be one of the times I went to the bathroom. I went twice. I thought she was taking a long nap, and her door was always closed, but then I decided I should check on her, and that's when I discovered she wasn't in her room at all! And, Sarah? I think she took your car."

"The car!"

"It's not in the garage. I called the sheriff's office before I called you, and he's going to put out a bulletin and start looking for her."

Sarah closed her eyes and rubbed her forehead. "Okay, call Nic for me, too, would you, please? Tell her what's happened and ask her to phone everyone. I'll be home as soon as I can."

She ended the call and relayed the information to Lori. "So what do we do? Go on to the airport or—?"

"No! Of course not."

"But your job—"

"Is just an internship. She's my grandmother. I'm turning this car around, Mom. We're going home."

EIGHTEEN

The Grizzles trailed 8–2 in the bottom of the eighth during the second game of the day. They'd won the first game 6–1 with Mike Hamilton pitching, but their pitcher for this game had struggled. Cam coached third base. Colt was at first. As the next batter stepped up to the plate, Cam saw Colt answer his cellphone and his eyes widen in alarm.

Oh, no. Cam didn't like the looks of that. Colt carried his phone onto the playing field because his wife Sage was only a few weeks away from her due date. He wouldn't be taking anyone else's call. *Hope there's nothing wrong with Sage.*

When Colt glanced his way as he continued his conversation, Cam felt a stirring of unease. At that point the batter hit a line drive into the outfield. Colt motioned the runner to second and ended his call, and Cam's focus returned to the game. That hit sparked a rally that scored five runs before the end of the inning. At the door to the dugout, he remembered the call and asked, "Is everything all right with Sage?"

"She's fine." Colt hesitated for a fraction of a second before adding, "I'll explain after the game."

Since their pitcher put away the batters in order and the Grizzlies' bats remained hot in the bottom of the ninth, the game ended sooner than Cam might have expected. After Colt instructed the boys to pick up the dugout, he motioned Cam aside. "The call from Sage was about Sarah."

Cam went still. "What's wrong?"

"Apparently Ellen wandered off yesterday while Sarah was taking Lori to the airport. She took the car. The whole town is searching for her now, Zach has bulletins out, but so far, nothing."

"Oh, no." Cam's thoughts raced. An older woman with Alzheimer's driving a car and missing overnight? Sarah must be out of her mind.

"Sage said Sarah held it together at first, but now she's just a basket case. She blames herself and won't listen to anyone. Sage thought you should know, but she asked me to wait until the end of the game to tell you."

"I need to go back," he said. "What about Lori? Did she leave?"

"No. She's with Sarah."

Cam nodded, glad for that, and pondered his options. "I need a car. Is there a rental place here, do you know?"

"I don't know about that, but the Hamiltons arrived midway through the last game. He could take you back or loan you his car, and they could ride back on the bus. After the incident last week, he owes you."

Cam looked toward the bleachers and spied Mike Hamilton's parents. "I'll ask them."

"What about Devin?"

"He'll want to come with me, but let's ask him. Would you do that while I talk to the Hamiltons?"

"Sure."

Fifteen minutes later and with three and a half hours' travel ahead of them, Cam and Devin were on the road, headed back to Eternity Springs. Devin hadn't thought twice about bailing on the tournament. Like he'd said, whether she liked it or not, Lori was his sister, and family should be there for family.

Once they were on the road, Cam called Nic Callahan

for an update. After speaking with her, his concern escalated. A thorough search of Eternity Springs proper had been completed with no sight at all of Ellen Reese or Sarah's car. After Cam caught Devin up on the details, the teenager asked, "You're not holding a grudge in the least, are you?"

"Against Ellen?"

"Yeah."

Cam thought about it. "Maybe just a little bit. Someone told me not long ago that resentment was an anchor, and I'm doing my best to cut the line. Besides, my beef against Ellen Reese is with the woman she was ten years ago, not the Ellen of today."

"I wonder why she'd take off like that," Devin mused.

Cam explained about Alzheimer's disease and sundowning.

"That's wicked cruel," Devin observed. "I feel bad for Sarah and Lori."

"Me, too, son. Me, too."

Cam managed to cut fifteen minutes off the trip without killing them, and as they hit the Eternity Springs city limits, he debated where to go first. According to Nic, the staging area for the expanded search was Davenport Park. Would he find Sarah there, or would she be at home?

He decided to swing by her house first, and as he arrived, he saw Lori open the door to admit Nic, Sage, Celeste, and Ali. "Sarah must be here."

He stopped the car and got out. Lori was still at the front door. Her reaction upon identifying him would be forever etched into Cam's mind.

Lori's eyes widened and filled with emotion. Relief. Hope. Anguish. She clasped her hands to her chest, and Cam held his breath.

Lori took off running. Toward him. Toward him! She called, "Cam!"

The look on her face turned Cam's knees to water.

"Help us. Please, help us."

His daughter threw herself into his arms. Cam's heart grew three sizes. Her hair smelled like baby shampoo, and tears filled his eyes.

"You have to help us find Nana."

Lori burst into tears, and Cam held her while she cried. He swore to himself that he would do just that, or die trying.

"I'll sure try, honey." He stroked her hair and shushed her. "Now calm down and talk to me. Okay? How is your mother?"

"Terrible. She's scaring me. She's over the top with guilt. When we finished searching the town without finding Nana, Mom came back to the house and sat down on the sofa, and she hasn't said a word since. I'm afraid for her, and I'm afraid for Nana. Please, we need help. I need help. I don't know how to get through to Mom. All my life I've dreamed of having a father to fix things. Fix this, Cam. Please, make it better."

"Ah, baby." Cam drank in the sensation of holding his daughter in his arms. "I don't know that I'll be able to fix this, but I'll try. I promise you that I'll do my best. I give you my word."

"What if we don't find her?"

"Then we'll keep looking."

Sarah stepped out onto the porch, and upon seeing them, she covered her mouth with her hand. Their gazes met and held. Tears spilled from her eyes, and she reached for a post to steady herself.

Just as Cam extended one arm to invite Sarah to join their embrace, an angry voice sounded from behind him and doused icy-cold water on his heartwarming moment. "It's your fault that this has happened, Cam Murphy!"

Pauline Roosevelt. Cam swallowed a sigh.

"Ellen has been all het up since you came back to town.

You stirred her up. Things were just fine around here until you returned to Eternity Springs. Now poor Ellen has driven off in a fog of confusion, and there's no telling what has happened to her. She could have picked up a hitch-hiker. She could have driven off the side of a mountain. She could be lost in a national forest. She could be dead! It's all your fault!"

Throughout Pauline's diatribe, Lori had stiffened in his arms. Now she pulled away from him—to Cam's regret—and whirled on the older woman. "That's ridiculous! For one thing, we don't know where my grandmother is, and for another thing, Mrs. Roosevelt, you need to stop saying such wicked things about my dad! That's just wrong."

My dad. Dad! She defended me. Lori just defended me and claimed me publicly.

If the circumstances weren't so serious, he'd feel like shouting "Hurrah!"

Pauline stood sputtering in indignation. She was, Cam realized, the personification of all the wrongs done to him by the people of Eternity Springs. He thought of sailboats and anchors and angels and—the winds of forgiveness.

"He's a Murphy!" Pauline exclaimed.

He's a Murphy. That says everything, doesn't it?

This time, for the first time, Cam had the perfect response. He unsheathed his mental knife, cut the anchor line, and allowed the winds to blow. He gave Lori one more squeeze, then released her and stepped toward Pauline Roosevelt. "Mrs. Roosevelt, I need to say something to you, and I truly believe you need to hear it. I know that my father was a difficult neighbor. I know you must have been frightened of him and wanted nothing to do with us. I forgive you for not answering the door when I came to you for help the night my mother died."

She gasped. "Why, how dare you . . . I didn't . . ."

He said no more, just looked at her.

"I didn't . . ." she tried again. "It wasn't . . . Oh . . .

oh . . . oh, dear." She wilted right before his eyes and burst into tears.

"It's all right, Mrs. Roosevelt. Really."

"I'm sorry, Cameron. I'm so sorry. I did you a terrible, terrible wrong."

Cam wasn't ready to hug her, but he did place a comforting hand on her shoulder. "It's all right. The truth is, you couldn't have saved her. Neither one of us could have saved her."

"I've felt so guilty all this time. I knew he was hitting you, and I didn't do anything about it. I didn't help you. I am ashamed."

"It was a long time ago, and I'm not concerned about it one bit." He glanced toward Sarah and said, "Right now, I'm concerned about finding Ellen."

This time Sarah was the one who wilted. She sank down onto the porch and wept. Cam was beside her in seconds, and he took her into his arms and rocked her, murmuring, "Ah, sweetheart, I'm so sorry."

"I shouldn't have tried to keep her at home this long," she said, her voice breaking. "This is my fault."

"Don't say that."

"It's true. It was selfish of me, stupid of me. I thought I could do a better job than anyone else, and what do I do? I leave the car keys hanging right out in the open." She looked up at him with her soulful red-rimmed and watery violet eyes. "If she's hurt . . . If we don't find her and bring her home safely, I'll never forgive myself."

"We'll find her." Cam gently wiped her tears away with his thumb. "We will find her, Sarah, and you know how I know? Because for the first time in my life, I believe that miracles can happen."

He held her while she cried for a few more minutes. Then, when she finally appeared to be out of tears, he asked, "Now, what can Devin and I do to help?"

"Honestly, I don't know what any of us can do. We searched every inch of town, we searched out at the lake. Zach says now it's up to law enforcement. Since she's driving and we only have two main roads out of town, he says that narrows the search grid. He told me Jack Davenport called and offered to sweep the area from his helicopter. Jack told him you called."

"I knew he was at Eagle's Way. I spoke with him yesterday." Cam had called his cousin to let him know that he and Dev were headed back to Australia.

Nic Callahan said, "Sandwich stuff is out in the kitchen. Why don't you come get something to eat, Sarah? You haven't eaten all day."

"I'm not hungry."

"Doesn't matter." Cam rose and tugged her to her feet. "You need to stay on top of your game and ready to give Ellen all the TLC she needs when we find her."

Cam coaxed her into eating a sandwich, and while she ate, Sage managed to distract her briefly with tales from maternity world. Sarah actually had a faint smile on her face when Lori approached the kitchen table. "Mom, the youth group at church is holding a prayer vigil. Dev and I thought we'd go over there for a little while, if that's okay with you."

Sarah blinked away sudden tears. "I think that's a great idea."

Once the kids had left the house, she rose from the table and tugged a tissue from the box. "I didn't cry once until mid-morning. Now I can't seem to stop."

Celeste reached out, gave her a hug, and quoted, " 'There is a sacredness in tears. They are not the mark of weakness, but of power. They speak more eloquently than ten thousand tongues. They are messengers of overwhelming grief . . . and unspeakable love.' "

"That's lovely," Sarah said.

Ali Timberlake snapped her fingers. "I know that quote. I've seen it somewhere."

"Washington Irving," Cam said. When everyone in the room except for Celeste gaped at him, he explained, "It's the quote hanging over the john at the house."

Sarah laughed, and then everyone joined in, happy to hear the sound. The moment was cut short, however, when Zach's cruiser pulled into the driveway. Sarah reached for Cam's hand and squeezed it like a vise. She tugged him out onto the front porch, where they waited as Zach approached.

He wore sunglasses, so Cam couldn't read his eyes, but his body language was clear. He didn't bring good news. Cam moved to stand behind Sarah. He wrapped both arms around her, holding her as the sheriff said, "We found the car. We didn't find your mother."

In a little voice, Sarah said, "Okay. Where did you find it?"

Zach reached up and removed his sunglasses. "Sarah, the car went off the road going down Sinner's Prayer Pass."

Oh, hell. Sarah shuddered, and Cam tightened his hold on her.

Zach continued, "There were two people in the car. Two men."

"Two men!" Nic Callahan exclaimed.

"You are sure Ellen isn't at the scene?" Cam asked.

"We're sure she's not in the car, but they're just starting to search beyond it. I'm on my way there now. I wanted to update you first."

Sarah didn't respond, so Cam said, "Thanks, Zach."

Once the sheriff returned to his SUV, she finally spoke in a thready voice: "I have to go, too."

Sage said, "Oh, honey, are you sure you want to do that?"

"No, I don't want to go, but I need to be there."

"I'll take you," Cam said. *This could be bad. Really bad.* She'd need him, and he'd be there for her this time, by God.

"Thank you." She turned in his arms and rested her head against his chest. "Thank you. I don't know what I'd do without you, Cam."

This wasn't the time to go into their own situation. Nevertheless, he thought it important for her to know one thing. He pressed a gentle kiss against her hair and said, "You don't have to worry about that. I'm not going anywhere."

Sarah sat in the passenger seat of Lori's new car and tried to hold her imagination at bay as Cam drove toward Sinner's Prayer Pass. She did not want to picture an image of her mother lying bent and broken at the bottom of a mountain. "I can't believe this is happening. Mom hasn't driven anywhere in three years. How did two men end up with her car?"

"No sense speculating, sugar. We'll find out soon enough, and there's no sense in you fretting about the possibilities. You'll make yourself crazy. Try to think about something else."

Mom had been wearing her green polo shirt and khaki slacks. Were there bloodstains soaking into—"Yes. You have a point. I do need to think about something different, so I'll ask . . . what did you mean earlier when you said you weren't going anywhere?"

He took his focus off the road long enough to spare her a questioning glance. "Are you sure you want to talk about this now?"

"Yes. I think I am."

"Okay, then. I'm not going back to Australia. Well, not permanently. I'll have to make a trip there from time to time to deal with the business. But Devin and I are going to stay in Eternity Springs. He's going to go to school here, and I'm going to figure out some way to make money. I have a couple of ideas."

Okay, he'd managed to catch her attention. Her full, complete, total attention. "Why?"

"Because I'm going to wait for you, Sarah. I love you. I am going to believe that someday you will find it in your heart to forgive me. I think we were meant to be together. I think we are meant to make a family together."

Sarah's pulse began to pound. Her chest tightened, and the darned tears threatened to spill all over again. "Cam, I . . ."

"No, sugar." He reached over and took her hand. "Don't worry about it now. The last thing I want to do is put more pressure on you about anything."

"But that's not—" She broke off when her cellphone rang. "It's Zach." She blew out a breath, then answered. "Hello?"

"Still no sign of her," he said, showing the sensitivity to let her know the most important news first. "Did you follow me?"

"Yes."

"I figured you would. I wanted to let you know that there's a trooper waving cars around the site. Just tell him who you are and he'll let you park."

"Thanks, Zach."

Sarah relayed the information to Cam, and he said, "I see the flashing lights up ahead."

"Okay. Look, about the other conversation . . . We will finish it later, okay?"

"Absolutely, sugar." Tenderly, he added, "Like I said, I'm not going anywhere."

The next few hours were a nightmare. Had Cam not been there, Sarah would have fallen apart. The two male passengers in the car had died on impact. The car had not burned. That had delayed its discovery, but it had also preserved the identification of the bodies, driver's licenses issued in New York state that matched the features of the deceased.

Each man had a record. One of them had done prison time. Upon learning that, Sarah had moaned aloud, and her knees went weak. What had they done to her mother?

Zach and fellow law enforcement officers from the surrounding area conducted a thorough search of the crash scene. Zach relayed the information that tire tracks indicated the car had been headed toward Eternity Springs rather than away when it crashed. That expanded the search area, so it wasn't considered especially good news.

Cam and Sarah remained out at the site until Zach, the last on the scene, was ready to leave. Sunset was half an hour away.

"So what's next?" she asked him.

"We will verify their identities and trace their movements. We will find out where they were before they came here. I expect we'll turn up something about your mother then."

When Sarah lifted her hand to wipe a tear from her eyes, Zach placed a hand on her shoulder and spoke friend to friend: "This isn't terrible news. I'm encouraged. It's entirely possible that she's at a mall or some other public place, and she hasn't asked for help so no one has reported it. She may have wandered off and left the keys in the car, giving those guys an easy opportunity. Keep the faith, Sarah."

Keep the faith. The phrase ran through her mind like a litany as they drove away from the scene of the accident. She stared at the road without seeing it, and it was only after Cam turned off pavement onto a dirt road that she realized he had taken her somewhere other than home.

He'd brought her to Lover's Leap.

Sarah smiled. Despite everything, he'd known exactly what she needed.

"Nothing brings me peace like watching the sunset,"

he said. "I thought we both could use a little sunset tonight."

"Yes. Absolutely."

The warmth of the summer day was dying with the sun, and a cool evening breeze carried the breath of pine, fir, and cedar as they took seats atop the gently rounded boulder that offered the best western view. They sat in comfortable silence, holding hands and watching the fiery red ball dip toward the shadowed mountains on the other side of the valley. Thin fingers of pink-and-purple clouds stretched across the muted blue sky. Then the sunset magic began as soft colors disappeared and brilliant ones took their place. Bright crimsons, oranges, and golds flashed above and behind black mountain summits. Sarah broke the quiet by saying, "Mom used to say that sunsets like this give us a peek beyond the gates of heaven."

"I wouldn't argue the point."

When the sun finally slipped behind the mountains, Sarah drew a deep breath and released it slowly. She felt calm for the first time since the call had come during the drive to the airport. "Thank you for this."

"My pleasure."

They watched until darkness swallowed the palette of colors, allowing stars their time to shine. As her gaze locked on the brightest star in the western sky, Sarah said, "Cam, earlier, when you said we were meant to be together, I didn't get the chance to tell you what I think. I'd like to do that now."

He waited for a long moment before saying "Okay."

Suddenly she needed to move, so she slid off the rock and began to pace. Cam followed her lead and stood as if braced for bad news. She searched for the perfect words. She wanted to do this right. But she also wanted to do it before twilight faded to night, so she'd better get her rear in gear.

She abandoned the effort toward perfection and spoke

simply and from her heart: "I love you, too, Cam. I gave you my heart when I was sixteen, and apparently it was for keeps. I was angry for so long, and I tried really hard to take it back and give it to someone else, but first love turned out to be only love for me. I think I've always known it, deep down inside."

She paused, and after a moment he spoke into the silence. "I sense there is a *but* coming my way? What is it? You can't forgive me?"

"No. That's not it at all. Forgiveness is easy. It's trust that is hard."

"You don't trust me?" He couldn't hide the hurt.

"I didn't trust you not to leave me again. That wounded me so deeply, so grievously, that I never got over it. I knew you loved me when we were teens, Cam. You loved me, but you left me."

"And you haven't forgiven me for it."

"That's not true. Listen to what I am saying. I understand why you did it. I probably would have done the same thing if I'd been in your shoes. I *do* forgive you. Forgiveness and trust are two different things, and it was my lack of trust that was holding me back."

"Is that a past verb tense I'm hearing? *Was,* not *is?*"

"Someone told me recently to leap like a lunatic. I can't think of a better place to do that than here. Yes, it's past tense, Cam. I'm making a leap of faith. I trust you not to leave me again."

"Okay, um . . ." He cleared his throat and spoke in an uncertain tone. "Where does that leave us?"

Sarah wanted to laugh and cry at the same time. "This is the point where you sweep me into your arms and kiss me. You don't have to wait for me any longer, Cam. I'm yours. I always have been, and I always will be."

"Thank God." He was there in two strides, wrapping his arms around her, lifting her off her feet and twirling her around and around as he kissed her. And kissed her. And kissed her.

Sarah allowed herself this little moment of happiness, knowing it would serve as strength to her in the challenging hours to come.

When he finally lifted his mouth from hers, he allowed her feet to slide back to the ground. In a gruff tone, he said, "I love you, Sarah Reese. Under other circumstances, I'd carry you back into the trees to our spot and make wild, passionate love to you and ask you one very important question. But with your mom missing, it doesn't feel like the time is right."

"I know. I agree." She cupped his face in the palm of her hand and blinked away tears. "I'll take a rain check on both."

"I'll bring a picnic basket. You can bring a quilt. And sugar cookies. Gotta have those sugar cookies. We'll christen our spot all over again."

"That sounds perfect. It's a date."

He kissed her once again, then turned her so that her back rested against his front, his arms around her, and together, they watched the sprinkle of stars burst across the heavens. Sarah stood awash in emotion as love and contentment battled worry and concern. She sent up a silent prayer of thanks for the man who held her, and one pleading for her mother's safe return.

"You know, life has recently proved to me that miracles do happen. You returned home to me. Maybe my mother will, too."

"Gotta keep those positive thoughts flowing," he murmured into her ear. "Whatever else happens, I'm here. I'm here to stay. I know what you mean about miracles. I've been to a lot of places in this big world. Seen a lot of beautiful sights. But no place on earth called to me like this one. Long after I left Colorado, left the United States, I dreamed of this place, our place. I dreamed of being with you here, at Lover's Leap. I never thought it could happen. I never thought . . . Hmm . . ." His voice trailed off. He suddenly went still. "Huh."

"Cam?"

"It just occurred to me . . . Did your parents have a Lover's Leap? A special place? Didn't your mother tell me that her favorite spot in the world was—"

"Spirit Cave," Sarah breathed, following the path of his thoughts.

"That's it. She mentioned it to me that night I had supper at your house."

Hope rekindled and began to burn. "Do you think she might have gone there?"

"If it called to her as much as this place called to me, I wouldn't be surprised." He grabbed her hand and began to pull her toward the car.

"Those men could have been there," she said, excitement in her voice. "They could have stolen her car. Maybe they didn't hurt her at all! Maybe she did leave the keys in the ignition."

"Let's go check it out."

The drive took twenty-three minutes that felt like twenty-three hours. Sarah had a lump the size of Murphy Mountain in her throat as Cam turned off the highway at the brown-and-white sign that read *Spirit Cave.* "I'm not sure where to go now," he told her.

"Go to the end of the road, then park. There's a trail to the spot where we always fished. The cave is a little beyond that." Sarah leaned forward in her seat, willing them there faster.

When they made the final turn on the rutted dirt road, the headlights flashed on a pickup truck parked at the end of the road. Sarah caught her breath. The truck's hood was up.

"Looks like someone is inside the cab," Cam said. "On the passenger's side."

"Please, God," Sarah prayed.

Their headlights helped to illuminate the truck as Cam pulled up behind it. Sarah was out of the car before he'd shifted into park. She ran forward, calling, "Mom? Mom? Is that you?"

A familiar voice replied, "Frank?"

"Mom! Oh, Mom." Sarah's hands trembled as she wrenched open the door. "Mom, are you okay?"

Ellen Reese frowned and pointed toward the trees. "Sarah, go find your father. He's fished enough. It's time for us to go home."

Tears spilled from Sarah's eyes as she wrapped her mother in her arms. "It sure is, Mom. It sure is."

She looked around for Cam. He stood a few feet away, watching them with a relieved grin on his face. Love lifted her heart. He'd been here for her. This time, he'd been here.

And I know he always will be.

NINETEEN

One week after Ellen Reese's rescue, Cam and Sarah arrived together for the monthly town hall meeting in the Eternity Springs school auditorium. Cam hadn't wanted to attend, but Sarah insisted that if he was serious about running a fishing guide service out of Eternity Springs during the summertime, then that made him an official business owner, which meant he needed to be at the meeting.

They entered the auditorium, and Cam spied what he privately termed Sarah's posse seated together toward the front. Ali Timberlake saw them first and waved them forward to the two saved seats beside the Timberlakes and behind the Callahans and Raffertys and Celeste Blessing. Sarah took a seat next to Ali, while Cam sat at the end of the row behind Celeste.

Nic twisted around in her seat and asked, "So how's the sunburn? Must be better if you're sitting down."

"Nic!" Sarah protested, her cheeks going rosy. The cheeks on her face, that is. The ones on her butt were already rosy from exposure to the afternoon sun on Sunday.

He and Sarah had stopped by Lover's Leap after seeing Lori off at the airport for her trip back to Virginia. They spent a long, luscious afternoon hidden away in the private bower well off the trail at Lover's Leap, lying in the sun on the quilt Sarah had brought and sharing the contents of her picnic basket—complete with sugar cookies.

He'd asked her to marry him at sunset and offered her the amethyst-and-diamond ring Celeste said she'd found tucked away in the basement at Angel's Rest. The ring matched the description of the one Eternity Springs's founder Daniel Murphy had offered for sale to his fellow town founder, Lucien Davenport. It was the ring he'd intended to give to his lost angel, Winifred Smith, on the day they wed.

At first Cam hadn't wanted to take the ring when Celeste offered it. For one thing, Daniel Murphy had been a wealthy miner at the time. Worth a fortune in the 1880s, it had to be worth five fortunes today. Celeste had been able to convince him to take it by making two points: One, it should have been a Murphy family heirloom, and for Cam to give it to the woman he loved completed the circle his great-something-grandfather couldn't when his bride-to-be disappeared. Second, the amethyst matched Sarah's eyes. The ring was meant for her. At Celeste's suggestion, Cam donated the money he'd intended to spend on an engagement ring to the Alzheimer's Association. Sarah had all but swooned when he gave her the ring. They'd made love a second time that afternoon, then she'd collapsed on top of him and they'd dozed together in the sun. Hence her rosy cheeks.

He wouldn't say he understood why she'd felt she had to share those details with her girlfriends, but oh, well.

Nic laughed, then turned to him and said, "Lori called me today. She asked about you."

Cam leaned forward in his seat. "She did?"

"She asked me if I had any photographs of you when we were kids. She's putting together a surprise for the wedding."

"Really." Cam sat back, pleased. Before she left, Lori and he had spent time cautiously getting to know each other. Things weren't perfect between them—real life isn't that easy, she'd told him—but they both tried, and they both wanted a good relationship. He had every confidence that they would get there in time.

With her hands resting on the basketball in her belly, Sage asked how the wedding plans were coming, and Sarah launched into her favorite subject. Honestly, why anybody would care so much about table centerpieces was beyond him. Cam's focus was on the honeymoon.

They had chosen the third Saturday in August as their wedding date. Lori would be done with her internship, and Sage's baby would be born—an event Sarah didn't want to miss. Following a ceremony at St. Stephen's and a reception at Angel's Rest, they'd leave for an extended South Seas honeymoon aboard the *Freedom.*

Cam couldn't wait to dive the Great Barrier Reef with his wife.

"Where's Devin tonight?" Colt asked him when the women's talk turned from centerpieces to napkin colors.

"He's working. Loves the new job."

Mac Timberlake said, "Good. I figured he would. Our son Chase enjoyed his stint at the Double R. With Devin's experience with tourists, helping with the trail rides was a natural fit. I'm looking forward to having him stay with us while you and Sarah are away. Ali and I miss having kids around the house."

"I can't tell you how much we appreciate the offer, Mac."

"We're glad to have him."

Sage finally turned Sarah's attention away from the wedding by asking, "How is your Mom settling into her new home?"

"So far, so good," Sarah replied. "Keller Oaks is a first-class memory-care facility. I know I had to take that step, but I can't quite shake the guilt."

Celeste reached for Sarah's hand and gave it a squeeze.

"Ellen is safe and well cared for, and you have nothing to feel guilty about. You are a kind and loving daughter and a blessing to her. Remember, Sarah. 'To every thing there is a season, and a time to every purpose under the heaven.' This is your time. Yours and Cameron's. Enjoy it."

Sarah sent him a tender look. "We will, Celeste. We will."

At that point, Hank Townsend, the mayor of Eternity Springs, took the stage and called the meeting to order. They talked about interesting things like garbage pickup and a change in the due date for water bills. Cam's attention drifted off, so when Celeste rose from her seat to join the mayor on the stage, he didn't have a clue why. He arched a brow at Sarah. She shrugged. Guess she didn't know, either.

Celeste stepped up to the lectern, adjusted the microphone downward, and said, "Good evening, dear friends. I'm so pleased to see you all here tonight for this very special occasion.

"It seems like almost yesterday that we met here to discuss the terrible economic trials facing our town. I stood before you that night and spoke of my belief in this town and in the people who live here. If you recall, I said that Eternity Springs didn't need the state of Colorado to build a prison here in order to save the town. What Eternity Springs needed to do was to free itself from the prison of its past and utilize the gifts a generous and loving God had bestowed upon it. I held that then, and only then, would our wonderful little town heal and thrive and fulfill the promise of its name.

"Now I am proud to say Eternity Springs has done just that. Mayor Townsend, will you please read the proclamation?"

Sarah leaned forward and spoke to Nic: "What's this all about?"

Nic shrugged, but she had a sly little light in her eyes.

As the mayor turned his head and coughed, Cam checked his watch. He needed to get home and feed Mortimer before too long.

"Pauline Roosevelt brought a special proposal to the table at last night's city council meeting. It passed unanimously. Here it is." He cleared his throat and read: "The mayor and city council of Eternity Springs, Colorado, hereby declare the third Friday in July to be Cam Murphy Day. We wish to formally recognize his assistance in the search for our beloved fellow citizen Ellen Reese, and to officially welcome him home. Cam, would you come up here, please?"

Cam froze in his seat as the auditorium erupted into cheers and applause. What the . . . *Cam Murphy Day!*

"You, too, Sarah," Celeste called.

Cam sat in stunned silence until Sarah tugged him to his feet. "C'mon, Cam."

"Cam Murphy Day? What the heck?"

Beaming, Sarah dragged him down the aisle and up onto the stage. The mayor waved a hand, requesting the crowd to quiet. Once they did, he removed a trophy from the lectern's shelf, handed it to Cam, and offered his free hand for a handshake.

"A bowling trophy, Hank?" Sarah asked, focused on the gold figure atop the marble-and-wood trophy.

"Yeah, I know. Supposed to have been a sphere. I didn't have my bifocals, and I read the catalog numbers wrong. I called the company and they said they'd fix it, but we have to send that one back first."

Cam felt the laugh bubble up from deep inside him. "No. This is perfect. Just perfect. Thank you, mayor."

In the front row, Pauline Roosevelt stood and shouted, "Bravo. Bravo!"

Celeste stepped up to the lectern, then motioned for Sarah and Cam to come closer. "I have something for

Cameron and Sarah, too, and I think this is the perfect time and place to give it to you."

Sarah gasped and clasped her hands. "Is it my turn, Celeste? Finally?"

"I told you at New Year's that your time was coming, didn't I?" She pulled two boxes from her pocket and handed one to Sarah and one to Cam.

"What's this?" he asked upon seeing the silver medal dangling from a silver chain.

"It's our Angel's Rest wings," Sarah said. "Sage designed them for Celeste."

"It is the official healing-center blazon awarded to those who have embraced healing's grace. I have one for Lori and Devin, too, because you have healed not just as yourselves but as a family."

"A family," Sarah said. "Our family. Oh, Celeste, you're going to make me cry."

"Don't do that, dear. There have been enough waterworks of late." Celeste smiled up at Cam. "Wear the blazon next to your heart, Cameron. Carry the grace you have discovered here in Eternity Springs along whatever life path you travel."

"Thank you, Celeste." He leaned down and kissed her cheek. "I'll do that."

"Here, let me help." Sarah slipped the chain over his head, then he repeated the favor for her.

"Speech! Speech!" someone in the crowd called.

Cam winced, then gave a sheepish shrug. "I'm not much of a public speaker."

"We're not much of a public," Pauline called, a big smile on her face.

Cam stood at the lectern and couldn't come up with anything more to say than "Thank you. I'm glad to be home."

As applause swelled once again, he gazed out at the

crowd. He saw his elementary school teacher and the barber who used to cut his hair when he was a kid. They were smiling. Clapping. For him. *Unbelievable.*

Celeste slipped her arm through his and murmured, "The past is finally in the past. Congratulations, Cam. You've helped this town to heal."

She leaned toward the mike and raised her voice. "Now, my friends, it appears that my plan A is accomplished. Eternity Springs is thriving. A goodness of spirit once again occupies this valley. Eternity Springs is truly a place where broken hearts can come to heal, and you, my dear, dear friends, will spread wings of compassion and love around wounded souls. My work here is done. I'll use this opportunity to announce that I'll be moving on to another town, another place, where people have need of my assistance."

Beside him, Sarah gasped. In front of him, Nic Callahan, Sage Rafferty, and Ali Timberlake did, too.

Just as Sarah opened her mouth to protest, a voice rang out from the back of the auditorium: "No, Ms. Blessing, I'm sorry, but you can't go anywhere."

Cam recognized the gorgeous redhead who rose from a seat at the back of the auditorium. Cat Blackburn had arrived at Eagle's Way with Jack Davenport the day Lori had come home. She exited her row and hurried up the aisle, saying, "Your work here is far from over. If you know the secret to healing broken hearts, then it's time you did something about Jack Davenport. The man is impossible."

Cam folded his arms and grinned at his bride-to-be. "Well, well, well. Looks like my ol' kissin' cousin has trouble on his hands. Something tells me this is gonna be fun to watch."

EPILOGUE

"It's not that cold, Sarah," Cam said. "Really."

"That's a bald-faced lie," Sarah fired back, eyeing the sapphire surface of the lake with trepidation. "I fell in at the Fourth of July picnic, remember? And that was near shore, where the water was shallow and warmer."

She lifted a pleading look toward Cam. "Can't this wait until we're in Tahiti, where the water is warm?"

"Nope." The blasted man's grin was amused and merciless. "We're doing this certification by the book. If you want to dive the Great Barrier Reef with me, sugar, then you need to hit the water."

Sarah scowled at him. "You're just making me do this because I've cut you off until after the wedding."

"I'll admit I find the cold water helpful, under the circumstances."

She stared at the water, aware like never before of just how deep eighty-five feet actually was. She filled her cheeks with air, then blew out a puff of breath and admitted, "I'm a little scared."

He gently cupped her cheek and turned her face toward him. He studied her intently for a long moment, then spoke with quiet sincerity: "No, you're not scared, Sarah. Nervous, maybe, but not afraid."

"How do you know?"

"Because, Ms. Reese, you are fearless. You have more heart than any person I have ever met. I am in awe of your strength and courage and determination. I am so proud of the woman you've become. I love you. I can't wait to leap into the future with you at my side."

Then he smiled at her, his green mountain eyes warm with love, and held out his hand. "Ready?"

A warm wave of love rolled through Sarah, chasing away the lingering chill of two decades of loneliness. When he looked at her like that, she'd follow him anywhere. "More than ready."

"Me, too."

After positioning their masks and mouthpieces, Sarah and Cam leapt like lunatics into icy Hummingbird Lake and a future filled with boundless love and spine-tingling adventure—both in bed and out.

Dear Readers,

I hope you've enjoyed your visit to Eternity Springs with Sarah and Cam, and that their story touched your heart!

Writers are told to write what they know, and since family and friends are so important to me, they are invariably central to the themes in my books. In *Lover's Leap,* Sarah's struggle with her mother's Alzheimer's disease is especially personal to me due to my own mother's illness. While the story is fictional, I want readers to know that the nonprofit showcased at Eternity Springs's summer quilt festival is quite real.

The Alzheimer's Art Quilt Initiative (AAQI) is a national charity devoted to raising awareness and funding research through art. It turns small-format art quilts donated by its supporters into research dollars through online auctions and sales. The AAQI also sponsors a nationally touring exhibition of quilts, *Alzheimer's Illustrated: From Heartbreak to Hope*. The all-volunteer effort has raised more than $550,000 for Alzheimer's research since it was founded in 2006, and all profits fund Alzheimer's research. Visit their website at www.AlzQuilts.org.

Next up is Jack Davenport's story, *Nightingale's Way,* coming this fall. I invite you to sign up for my email newsletter at www.emilymarch.com for news, contests, and other fun stuff. You can also find me on Facebook at www.facebook.com/emilymarchbooks and follow me on Twitter @emilymarchbooks.

Finally, I want to thank you, readers, for your enthusiastic response to my Eternity Springs series. It's truly been rewarding. Knowing that you love Eternity Springs as much as I do makes sitting down to write each day a joy.

Happy reading,
Emily

ACKNOWLEDGMENTS

My most sincere thanks to the entire team at Ballantine for the tremendous job they've done in support of the Eternity Springs series. Libby McGuire, Gina Wachtel, Scott Shannon, Linda Marrow, Lynn Andreozzi and the art department, Janet Wygal and the production department, and my fabulous editor, Kate Collins, and her assistant, Junessa Viloria—you guys rock.

Thanks also to my creative team—my friends and fellow writers Mary Dickerson, Christina Dodd, Lisa Kleypas, Nic Burnham, Susan Sizemore, Connie Brockway, Teresa Medeiros—for their help with brainstorming, plotting, editing, hand-holding, cheering, and support. I am forever in your debt.

Finally, thanks and love to my family—my sister, Mary Lou, for stepping up and doing her share and mine at the Wellington when I have to work; my niece, Molly, my talented marketing assistant; Steven, Amanda, John, and Caitlin for their love and support. And, as always, my love and thanks to Steve, for giving me the gift of love and family that gives me the ability to "write what I know."

Read on for a preview of
Emily March's next novel
in her Eternity Springs series:

Nightingale Way

"She calls that security?" Jack Davenport muttered with disgust, watching as the idiot wearing a shoulder holster flashed Cat Blackburn a smarmy grin.

Jack sat in a car three houses down from Cat's in a quiet suburban neighborhood where a stranger sitting in an unfamiliar vehicle should send up all kinds of alarms. The pretty-boy bodyguard hadn't noticed him. He wasn't watching the street or surveying the surroundings. Jack had followed Cat and her escort from her home to the grocery store, then to the dog groomer, and back home again. The fool never looked at him twice. He was too busy checking out Cat's chest and ogling her ass.

Jack wanted to shoot him on principle. He seriously considered breaking bones—a leg would be good—in order to demonstrate to the incompetent imbecile that a career move was in order. Doing so would be a public service.

The sound of Cat's laughter drifted to Jack's ears and he set his teeth. She wore a flirty yellow sundress, strappy heeled sandals, and sunglasses with rhinestones on the frame. She carried a designer dog tote filled with a puffball of four-legged fur. Cat's wavy red hair was pulled up in a ponytail, and she looked more like a co-ed than a woman in her mid-thirties who paid no more attention to her surroundings than did her sorry excuse for security.

He had thought the woman had more sense than this, but maybe not, since she'd managed to stir up a hornets' nest of trouble with her exposé about dog fighters. Some jack-wagon had left a pipe bomb on her porch the day before yesterday. Her response was to hire protection who was more bodybuilder than bodyguard.

As much as he wanted to teach the guy a lesson, Jack knew he had to restrain the urge. The operation needed to be slick and quick. Better he stick to his original plan.

When the security guy reached up and playfully tugged Cat's ponytail, Jack reconsidered. Maybe one well-placed kick wouldn't hurt anything.

He checked the rearview mirror, then the side views. Clear. He started his car and pulled away from the curb. He realized with a touch of chagrin that his pulse pounded in a way that it rarely had on missions. Honesty made him admit that he worried more about dealing with Cat than he ever did about dying on a job.

He was less than two car lengths away before Bodyguard Ken pulled his gaze away from Ponytail Barbie and spared him half a glance. No, make that a quarter glance. The little Cooper Jack was driving didn't threaten the man at all. "Idiot," he muttered as he braked and steered the car toward the curb.

It took only seconds. In a smooth, practiced, lightning-quick motion, he put down the pretty boy and pulled Cat and her pet carrier into his car. He had the dog stored safely in the backseat and Cat secured and silenced with duct tape in the front before she emerged enough from shock to resist.

"Don't be afraid," he told her as he pulled away from the curb. "I'm here to help you, not hurt you."

At the sound of his voice, she froze.

Though he concentrated on driving, Jack remained intensely aware of the woman seated next to him. She no longer looked like Co-ed Barbie. This Cat was mature, a sleek, wary mountain cat on alert and assessing danger. Damn, she was beautiful.

He took a corner a bit too sharply and she fell against him. Jack felt the heat of her like a brand. The car was too small, his memories too big. She lurched away from him and Jack didn't try to hide the bite in his voice as he said, "We'll change cars in the mall parking garage. We want the cameras to see us. I'll take off the duct tape after that."

Thankfully, the garage in question was less than a mile from the spot of the snatch. He felt like he was driving with his knees up around his ears in the cramped car. But the Cooper had been necessary, part of the on-the-fly disguise he'd developed. This particular grab was all about misdirection, hence the bright orange Baltimore Orioles jersey and ball cap, the wraparound sunglasses, and the ridiculous hoop earring designed to catch any observer's attention and keep them from looking closely at his face.

He sensed Cat's attention on the earring now. He glanced her way. She'd gone white as a sheet, and Jack felt a twinge of guilt. He'd told her she need not be afraid. Why wouldn't she ever listen to him? "Believe it or not, I'm still one of the good guys, Catherine."

This time, anyway.

In response, she shut her eyes and slumped back into her seat. He said nothing more until he'd parked the Cooper in the garage next to a sedate black sedan. "Someone will check the security tapes, so I'll be playing for the cameras. Hang in there. This part will be over shortly."

He moved her dog from one car to the other. Walking to the passenger side of the Cooper, he opened the door and said, "Feel free to struggle."

Had this been a true abduction, he'd have carried her to the sedan. In fact, that had been his original intention today. But now that the time had come to hold her close, he found he didn't want to do it. He wasn't ready for the intimacy, and that particular fact annoyed him. He yanked his knife from his pocket, then slashed the duct tape binding her ankles.

He dragged her from the car a little more roughly than was probably necessary, then excused himself because, after all, this needed to look real.

She made it look real, all right. As he tugged her around the back of the Cooper toward the sedan, the woman twisted in his grip, as slippery as an eel. Her eyes flashed. She made a growling noise in her throat.

Then she kneed him in the junk. Hard. Pain radiated through him and only the force of will kept him from dropping to his knees.

His grip on her arm loosened, and she yanked herself away and took off running. Once he could breathe again, Jack cursed. Once he could move again, he hobbled off after her.

With her long, lovely legs, Cat was fast. Were she not wearing those heeled sandals, she might have gotten away from him. Those shoes were something else Security Guard Ken should have cautioned her against.

He'd almost reached her when he heard an echoing clang at the far end of this level of the parking garage. *Great. Just great.* They had company. This half-minute delay she'd caused could turn costly. It needed to end now.

He gritted his teeth and caught up with her. He scooped her up, threw her over his shoulder, and toted her back in a fireman's carry to the sedan, where he tossed her inside with a curt, "Stay!"

The duct tape muffled her screech, but the furious glare in her eyes spoke loud and clear.

Jack slammed the passenger door and stalked around to the driver's side just as a pair of men walked into view. They were both dressed in suits. One toted a briefcase. They carried on a conversation and paid little attention to their surroundings. Jack doubted they'd seen anything, but for safety's sake when he took his seat, he pulled Cat down out of sight. Her head rested in his lap. Good thing her mouth was still taped because she might have bitten him otherwise. The very thought made his nuts draw up.

He started the car and drove out of the garage slowly and safely. After turning onto the street, he released his hold on her. She yanked herself up and shot him an angry glare.

He glared right back. "Hey, don't give me that. I said feel free to struggle, not attack. I couldn't treat you nice after you went ninja on me."

She narrowed her eyes, her look disdainful and condemning, until she lifted her chin and jerked her head around. She stared out the window and he altered his plan slightly. He'd leave her arms bound and her mouth taped for the time being. Conversation could wait until after they were in the air. He had his plane standing by.

Twenty minutes later, he escorted her and her dog aboard his Citation. Once the door was shut, he braced himself for the explosion promised by the look in her eyes, drew his knife, and sliced the tape that bound her hands. He'd let her remove the tape from her mouth herself. "I sit up front during takeoff. After that, we'll talk. There's water there"—he pointed toward a cabinet—"and the head is in back if you'd like to use it before takeoff. Be in your seat, buckled in, in five."

He was halfway to the cockpit door when her voice stopped him cold. "Who *are* you?"

Jack's spine snapped straight and he stiffened. Of all the things he'd thought she might say to him, this wasn't one of them. *Who am I? Who am I! I think about her every damned day of my life and she doesn't damn well remember me?*

Coldly furious, he tossed over his shoulder, "You know, Cat, I don't recall your being such a bitch when we were married."

He slammed the cockpit door behind him with a bang.

Jack Davenport was back.

Cat sat buckled into her seat, a bottle of water clenched tightly in her fist as the plane climbed. She couldn't believe this was happening. And to think that she'd thought the day before yesterday had been crazy. Having a bomb explode on her front porch should have been the insane moment of the month, but oh no. That was just the beginning.

Now Jack Davenport was back.

She didn't want to believe it. She never thought she'd see him again. She'd never wanted to see him again.

A little voice whispered in her head, *Liar.*

Okay. Well. Maybe this man wasn't Jack Davenport. Maybe she hadn't recognized his voice, recognized the scent of him. Maybe this was all part of a nefarious plot against her and this guy was an imposter, an employee of the powerful senator she'd ruined with her story. After all, this man was bigger than Jack. He outweighed Jack by ten or fifteen pounds. Ten or fifteen pounds of muscle. Jack's shoulders weren't that broad. He'd never been fat, but he hadn't had a six-pack like this guy did, something she couldn't help but notice when he changed out of that baseball jersey and into a T-shirt on the airport tarmac. Jack certainly hadn't had scars like she'd seen on this fellow's chest, either.

Yeah, right. Since when did you start writing fiction? This man is Jack.

"He can't be Jack." She chugged a gulp of water as if it were whiskey. Jack had walked out on her four years ago and she hadn't heard a word from him since. For all she knew, the real Jack Davenport could be dead. This could be his doppelgänger. Hey, stranger things had happened.

Yeah, like a pipe bomb exploding on your porch two days before your ex kidnaps you off a public street.

Which only supported her argument. Jack could be living in Timbuktu for all she knew. She'd never tried to find him. She might be an investigator by profession, but Jack Davenport was one individual she had left alone. Been there, done that, got the broken heart.

He's Jack.

But this man had hidden his eyes from her, Cat argued with herself. He had replaced the wraparounds with Oakleys and worn them even after they'd boarded the plane. Maybe he did that because he'd known she would recognize the real Jack's striking blue eyes.

Just like you know Jack's walk. Just like you know his scent. Just like you know his voice and his thick black hair and his strong jaw and tiny little crook in his blade of a nose where he got hit with an elbow during a basketball game at your parents' house.

Stubborn, she gave it one last try. *Jack doesn't have a jagged inch-long scar on his left cheek.*

How do you know? You haven't seen him in four years. This man is Jack. Jack Davenport is back.

"No," she said, and it came out in a little moan. As the cockpit door opened, she softly murmured, "Oh, heaven help me."

"Sure, Celeste, put me down for a thousand," her ex-husband said into a cellphone as he stepped into the main cabin. "It is a good cause."

No matter how much she'd like to pretend otherwise, he *was* Jack Davenport. No one else on earth had eyes like his, the crisp blue like a gas flame that, once upon a time, had burned with passion for her. Now when they settled on her, they were cold as ice.

"Sure," he said into the phone. "I will. Absolutely. All right. Good-bye, Celeste."

When he ended the call, Cat decided that going on offense was her best defense. "What is this all about, Jack? I don't hear a word from you in more than four years, and then you show up out of the blue one day and abduct me? Why in the world would you do this?"

He looked hard. He looked formidable. He looked dangerous. She wasn't afraid of him physically, but emotionally, he scared her to death.

One side of his mouth lifted in a sneer. "Your mother asked me to."

Had she not been sitting down already, she would have fallen down. "My mother! You've talked to my mother?"

He nodded sharply.

"When?"

Now he shrugged. "I call her from time to time."

What? "Since when?"

"You were with a guy named Alan the first time."

Cat sucked in a sharp breath. She'd dated Alan three years ago. Jack had been talking to Mom for three years? And she'd never bothered to mention that little detail to Cat? "You took my cellphone out of Fifi's carrier. I need it back, please."

"Why?"

"I need to call my mother."

"Why?"

"She never said a word to me about your calls!"

"I asked her not to."

"So? She's *my* mother. She should have told me!"

"I'm not giving you your phone."

"Why not?"

For the first time in forever, she saw a smile flash across

his face. "You've been kidnapped. Kidnap victims don't get to call their mommies."

Oh, how I've missed that smile. Dismissing that disturbing thought, Cat lifted her chin. "Sure they do. I watch TV. It's proof of life for the ransom."

"But I'm not asking for ransom. Besides, your mother already has proof of life—me. I'm your proof of life, Catherine. I'm going to keep you alive—in spite of yourself."

She winced with chagrin. "I didn't—"

"Sure you did," he interrupted. "You ruined the career of two politicians, three sports stars, and a freaking *American Idol* winner with your little exposé."

It wasn't little, she wanted to point out. It had been a twenty-thousand-word series.

"As if that wasn't enough," Jack continued, "the scumbags running the dog-fighting ring were connected to the mob. I'm surprised they started with a pipe bomb. You're lucky you weren't taken out in a drive-by shooting the day the story came out."

He put her on the defensive and she didn't like it. "I took precautions."

"I took out your 'precaution' with one little kick. Where did you get that sorry excuse for a security guard anyway? Who recommended him?"

Cat figured he didn't need to know that her hairdresser had recommended the agency, and that she had already decided she needed someone less . . . flirtatious.

She folded her arms and crossed her legs. "Look, I can understand why my mother might have been concerned, but why didn't she just talk to me about it? Why bring you into it? Why the elaborate show? An abduction off the street? Really? It'll make the stink over my story even bigger."

"I'm counting on it." Jack crossed to the bar and poured himself a drink. "I don't want the pipe bomber looking for you. This way he'll think that another one of your enemies got to you first. He'll sit back and wait to see where you turn up. That'll give my people time to find the pipe bomber and to analyze the likelihood of other enemies of yours committing acts of retribution against you."

How many enemies did he think she had? Cat scowled as she asked, "Your people? I thought you left the Agency."

He gave her a sharp look. "You checked up on me?"

"Mother mentioned you a time a two. I asked her to stop."

His smirk suggested he didn't believe her, and Cat told herself she didn't care. "Who do you work for now?"

He remained stubbornly, but not surprisingly, silent.

He's doing some sort of black ops, she surmised. She tried another question. "You said 'where I turn up.' When and where is that going to be?"

"I'll make that decision at the appropriate time."

He'll make that decision? Cat had the urge to go six-year-old on him and stick out her tongue and say, *You're not the boss of me.*

"We're going off the map for a little while, Catherine," he continued. "You might as well sit back and enjoy it."

Enjoy it? With you around? Yeah, right. "Off the map? Where are you taking me, Jack? Mars?"

Again, he showed her that smile. "Not Mars, but it is a little bit out of this world, I'll admit. We're going to the mountains, Cat. A little place in Colorado called Eternity Springs."